SONGS OF VALOR
LIBRI VALORIS II

Edited by
Chris Kennedy and Rob Howell

New Mythology Press
Coinjock, NC

Chris Kennedy/New Mythology Press
1097 Waterlily Rd., Coinjock, NC, 27923
http://chriskennedypublishing.com/

Publisher's Note: This is a work of fiction. Names, characters, places, and incidents are a product of the author's imagination. Locales and public names are sometimes used for atmospheric purposes. Any resemblance to actual people, living or dead, or to businesses, companies, events, institutions, or locales is completely coincidental.

Cover Art and Design by J Caleb Design.

Songs of Valor/Chris Kennedy and Rob Howell -- 1st ed.
ISBN 978-1648551420

The measure of a life is a measure of love and respect
So hard to earn, so easily burned
In the fullness of time
A garden to nurture and protect

- Neil Peart (1952 – 2020)

Preface by Rob Howell

Welcome to Songs of Valor, the second in the Libri Valoris series of fantasy anthologies. Thanks to all of you who are taking the time to read this. I'm proud of what we've done here, and I think you'll love it.

If you read When Valor Must Hold, you know what to expect: swords slashing, dragons roaring, and spells flashing. More importantly, each of these stories has great characters you want to root for.

I've been greatly honored to be a part of this project. I want to thank Chris Kennedy and FantaSci for entrusting it to me. It's been a great thrill to work with some of the greatest authors in the business.

I get to edit something by Larry Correia? Excellent! David Weber sent in one of the first things he ever wrote? Yes! Indrajit and Fix are two of my favorite characters in current fantasy, and this was my second chance working with them and Dave Butler. Oh, and Glen Cook sent me a Black Company story. How cool is that? And that's not even getting to Quincy J. Allen, Sarah Hoyt, Jon Osborne, and Kevin Steverson.

It might be surprising, but getting to judge the short story contest was an even bigger thrill. I've loved Benjamin Tyler Smith's Necrolopolis world for a while. Jamie Ibson had a great hook inspired by Stan Rogers and then fun characters to go with it. Melissa Olthoff gave us a team fighting against something far too powerful. Casey Moores blended history, dragons, and a dash of steampunk to deliver a powerful twist at the end. And I've cried every time I read James Chandler's story.

Truly blessed to be a part of this all.

For that, I have to thank Chris again. He's given a ton of people the opportunity to grow in this business. He's carved a niche in the industry not just by his own hard work but by, as Kacey Ezell would say, #RespectingTheHustle of others. He created an ever-growing pool of talent who help each other out, whether that's promoting each other's stuff, passing on what we've learned, or just encouraging each other. It's fantastic to be a member of this team, especially as my role is expanding in 2021.

The key thing, though, is that we all strive to put out great stories, and this anthology exemplifies that. You'll laugh, cry, and cheer at various moments. There are great heroes here, facing challenges worthy of their skills, and success is guaranteed to no man, woman, gnome, or undead elf. Not even to queens of crime, company chroniclers, or those with royal blood. All they can do is strive against their foes, whoever or whatever they might be.

So I think it's time for me to shut up and let you get to all that action.

—Rob Howell

Contents

* * * * *

The Dragon and the Drunkard by David Weber

.I.

I don't know if anyone will ever read this. Even if someone does, I don't know whether or not they'll believe it. Not that it matters much. Even if you are reading this, unless you're a very…unusual individual, there's not much you can do to help me out. On the other hand, if you're the sort of reader who *could* help me, you won't have any trouble believing me at all.

My name is Richard Osteen. Until very recently, I was a writer of popular history, and I did fairly well at it. I was probably no higher than mid-list, but fortunately my family's always been at least moderately affluent, so I didn't have to rely on book sales for a living. I wasn't one of the esoteric economic or social scientist historians, just a plain old-fashioned military historian. A pragmatic, nuts-and-bolts kind of guy. I certainly never got mixed up with things like "paranormal phenomena" or witchcraft, although a couple of my friends did. Never had time for them, myself. Don't get me wrong—it's not that I went around muttering "Bunk!" or anything like that. It was just that nobody had ever come along with any proof—to my satisfaction, at least—that such things existed.

That's changed now.

It was, appropriately, Halloween. A classic Halloween, actually, complete with thunder, lightning, rain, and a wind wailing out of the east. It was, in fact, an *excellent* Halloween, so far as I was concerned. A Halloween perfectly suited to sitting home with a good book, a good fire, and a better bottle, safe from trick-or-treaters (a breed I am thankful manifests but once a year). Confident my solitude would remain undisturbed, I had just poured my second dram (or perhaps it was my third) of Glenlivet XXV, swirled it with a single ice cube, and raised it to appreciate its aroma properly…when the doorbell rang.

I ignored it, on the assumption that it was merely some hardy soul who had ventured forth with mask and sack on his annual plundering expedition despite the weather. But then the peal was repeated a second time—and a third. The house was set well back from the road, but it was also the only one visible from the highway for several miles, and it was possible some distressed motorist had seen the light from my study window. It was a long slog from the road to the front door—which did not, under normal circumstances, preserve me from trick-or-treaters, alas—and the thought of someone standing out there—wet, cold, and miserable in the pouring rain—got the better of me. The Good Samaritan in me impelled me to the door.

As soon as I opened it, I decided that must have been my *fourth* dram. Instead of the stranded motorist I had anticipated, I found myself face-to-face, in a manner of speaking, with the most improbable figure I had ever seen. He was dressed in a leather jerkin over a green shirt, brown breeches, and mustard-yellow boots. He wore a green, Robin Hood cap, complete with a long white feather, and carried a yellow rucksack over his right shoulder.

He was also approximately eleven inches tall.

Without so much as a thank you, the little man brushed past my ankles and made a beeline down the short hall. My head turned automatically to follow his progress, but disbelief—understandably, I suppose—kept me rooted in place until he'd disappeared into the study. At that point, the rain blustering into my face brought me back to what I had once fondly believed was reality, and I closed the front door and followed him.

I got to the study entrance just in time to watch him wade across the pile carpet—which lapped around his ankles—to the hearth. He kicked off his sodden boots and set them to steam before the flames, then made another beeline, this time for the whiskey bottle I had incautiously left in plain sight on the coffee table. My brain was sufficiently boggled that it seemed completely reasonable for the apparition to scale the table, select one of my Glencairn tulips, half his own height, and pour it two thirds full of *my* whiskey. The purist in my soul was offended when he knocked back half the glass in a single endless gulp, but he only gave a long, happy sigh and seated himself, leaning back against the bottle and dangling his stocking feet over the edge of the low table.

At some point during the sequence, I closed the door behind me and edged my cautious way into the study. I sank back into my chair, groped up my own glass, and took a quick (and large) medicinal swig.

No good.

He was still there.

The peculiar little man removed his cap and examined its white feather carefully. Satisfied it had come to no harm, he hooked the cap over the lip of the bottle to dry and dragged out a pocket watch half the size of his head. As he peered at its hands, my own gaze was riveted to him in an unblinking stare of wonder.

He looked up, noted my glazed eyes, and gave a sour chuckle. Then he slid the pocket back into his watch—I mean, slid the *watch* back into his *pocket*—and frowned at me.

"And would yer name be Richard O'Stane?" he asked in a piping basso.

Look, I can't help it. The voice was basso, and it was also piping. And if it confuses *you* to read it, imagine what it did to me to *hear* it!

"Uhhhhh…"

I looked reproachfully into my glass before I glanced back at him.

Nope. Still there.

"Well, mon, is it?" he asked more brusquely.

"M-More or less." I took another sip of my drink and nodded more firmly with the treacherous courage of its glorious golden fire. "Yep. Only we changed the name to Osteen about four—no, five—generations back."

"But yer the firstborn O'Stane of yer generation?" he prodded.

"So I've heard." I sipped my drink more composedly. "Of course, Dad may not have told me everything."

"Then yer the mon I'm after, laddy." The little man reached into his yellow rucksack and extracted a rolled sheet of vellum tied with a faded red ribbon. He glanced at it, then tossed it to me.

"Read it."

I must admit my fingers trembled as I caught the document. I like to think it was due to the whiskey I'd already tippled, but it was more probably due to the fact that his roll of vellum was un-bent…despite the fact that it was a good six inches longer than his rucksack's longest dimension.

I set that little oddity resolutely aside and unrolled the crackling sheet. The ink on the yellowed surface was faded, but I tilted it to catch the light, then looked back at him.

"Sorry. My Gaelic is a little rusty."

"*Tchah!*" He had a truly eloquent snort. "What the divel do they teach in these schools o' yers?" He seemed truly exasperated, and he snatched the sheet back from me. "Verra weel, then, I'll tell yez what it says here. 'Tis an agreement—signed and sealed in blood by a full moon, mind yez—between me and the first O'Stane, concernin' the prosperity o' his family and meself. By the provisions o' this document—" he rolled the words in an ungodly combination of Irish and Scottish accents, "—the O'Stane commits himself t'aid me in the recovery o' me crock o' gold, should any foul thief deprive me of it, in return for me seein' to the prosperity o' him and his descendants. Weel, laddy buck, I've kept me end o' the bargain, and now that me crock's been stolen by as foul a knave as ever lived, it's up t' you t' help me get it back."

"Excuse me?"

I took another hurried sip of Glenlivet. It was perfectly clear I'd gone insane, I decided calmly. Nothing to get upset over.

"I *said*," he began again, more loudly, as if he thought I must be a little deaf, "that this document binds—"

"I think I got the provisions clear," I said. If my disordered mentality had conjured up this preposterous little rat, I was only interrupting myself. If he was the product of the liberal amount of Glenlivet I'd ingested, then I wasn't interrupting anyone, because he didn't exist.

"What I don't see," I went on, ignoring the offended look in his beady little blue eyes, "is who you are, what a crock is, and why the hell you think *I* owe you anything."

"Yer as rude as ever yer ancestors were, laddy!" His purplish color clashed nicely with his red hair and beard. "But I'll put it t' yer lack o' proper education and overlook it fer the now."

The thought seemed to mollify him somewhat, and he took another sip from his—my—glass, then went on more calmly.

"As t' who I am, me name's Egbert. As t' what a crock is, it's me pot o' gold, which—as any fool should know—all leprechauns must have. And as t' what makes me think yez owe me anything, it's this document, the which bein' signed in blood in the light o' a full moon is bindin' on all who are or become party to it, under penalty o' persecution by ghosties an' ghoulies an' long-legged beasties an' things that go boomp in the night."

I blinked. What if this little jerk was on the up-and-up? Worse, what if he actually *existed*?

"Um," I said. And then, "I see," which I didn't. "Just what *are*, 'ghosties and ghoulies' et cetera?"

"Weel," those blue eyes lit with an unwholesome gleam, "there's witches, an' haunts. Then there's banshees an' werewolves. Maybe a vampire or two. An' trolls, an'—"

"I get the picture," I said faintly. "But why should all of that affect *me*? I never signed your document—not even in ink."

"True enough." He crossed his legs and leaned forward earnestly. I had a professor who lectured just that way, once. "'Twas the O'Stane as signed it, y' see, an' 'tis binding on th' blood o' his blood an' th' bone o' his bone. In other words, bucko—" He stabbed at me with a well-gnawed forefinger. "—it's bindin' on yerself."

"Who says?" I asked faintly.

"The Chief Justice o' Elveron," he said shortly, and I winced. I'd never heard of Elveron, but something told me I never wanted to, either.

"I—uhhh, I see," I said. "This…I take it there's some, uh, precedent for this?"

"Case o' the Divel versus Timothy O'Ryan," Egbert said promptly. "Court found fer th' plaintiff."

"I see."

I groped for the bottle, and he snatched his cap off it and moved to one side so I could slop more whiskey into my empty glass. That's what I did, too. I *slopped* Glenlivet XXV, and the lip of the bottle danced on the rim of the glass like a castanet. I took a sip and settled doggedly back in my chair, silently cursing the soul of my remote ancestor.

"That being the case," I said carefully, "what evidence can you present that you've kept your side of the bargain and guaranteed the prosperity of my family?"

He waved a hand around my (admittedly) graciously appointed study.

"Ye built this house wi' yer father's money, didn't yez?" Again I nodded. "Well, laddie, th' first O'Stane was a successful horse thief, granted, but he had a little help from meself in gatherin' the first installment o' the O'Stane family fortune, as it were. An' 'twas me advised yer great-great-great grandfather t' sell out before the crash o' Twenty-Nine, as well. I've meddled a time or two besides, an yer family's no been the worse fer me interference."

"I see." I was a little tired of that response, but I couldn't see any way to improve on it. In fact, I thought I was doing well to get out any response at all.

"An' that bein' the case, an' me crock bein' stolen, it is up to you t' see I get it back, see?"

"Pardon me." I took a firm grip on my courage. "I may seem a bit obtuse, but if you've been around as long as your answers imply, and if you've done that much for my family, it seems to me you could get your crock back quicker and more easily by yourself. And also—" I leaned forward suddenly, "—my family is *Scottish*, not Irish. Just what the hell are we doing hobnobbing with a leprechaun, anyway?"

"That last is a long story, laddy buck," he said, "but 'tis shortly answered. When Saint Patrick—Oberon rot him!—drove the serpents an' spirits out o' Erin, most o' us wee folk got run out wi' them, d'ye see? Scotland was the best place t' go in a hurry. I ran across yer grandsire durin' me stay abroad an' saw a chance t' do a little safeguardin' o' me own by dealin' wi' a mortal. T' answer the first part o' yer question, there's some things a mortal can do that one o' the little folk can't, an' one o' 'em is t' recover a stolen crock o' gold fer an honest leprechaun. Th' union won't let us get 'em back oursel," he added moodily.

"I see," I said yet again. "So, if you've got me over a barrel, so to speak, with that thing—" I pointed at the rolled contract. "—then I've got *you* over a barrel of my own with the fact that you need me if you're going to get your gold back at all?"

"True enow," he said, suddenly earnest. "Yer the only mortal I can trust t' give th' crock back after ye've got it in yer hands, because I've th' contract t' hold over yer head. Yer kind calls my kind tricksy," he added indignantly, "but everyone knows 'tis mortals as always try t' get somethin' fer nothin' out o' us!"

"Speaking of mortals." I leaned back and crossed my legs, cradling the whiskey glass in my hands. "I thought there was a protocol for this. Something about demanding three wishes?"

"Aye, sae there is," he said grumpily. "But that only works fer mortals. For them as knows how t' use it, a leprechaun's crock's magic is worth more than all the *wishes* in th' world."

"The person who stole your crock isn't...mortal?" I asked very carefully while Arctic centipedes ran up and down my spine.

"O' course not! I'd've had me crock back years ago if he was."

"Um, Egbert, I'm not really very good at dealing with immortal, magical beings that can turn me into, say, a cockroach."

"Oh, buck up, mon!" Egbert shook his head scornfully. "All it needs is a bit o' cold iron. Can't handle the accursed stuff meself, but 'tis ward an' weapon fer such as yerself. That's the only reason yer kind was able t' th' banish us t' th' hills in th' first place."

"Oh."

I filed that bit of information away carefully, casually feeling my right pocket and cherishing the outline of my pocketknife. I'd never thought of its four-inch blade as a sword and buckler before, but tonight seemed to be broadening my conceptual boundaries.

"As may be," I said, suddenly calm, "and even allowing that you've got a point about mortals bargaining with...your kind. I'm not exactly the most altruistic person in the entire universe. But I do have a counteroffer for you."

"An' what might that be?" he asked darkly.

"Admittedly, you've got the contract." I nodded. "But I'm about ready to call a priest and see how a little exorcism works against you and your Chief Justice of Elveron. The way I read it, you and your kind have been losing out in the new order of things. I'm willing to bet I can break that contract if I wanted to take the risks involved."

"Perhaps," he said unwillingly. "But ye'll be takin' th' big chance t' think so, laddy! I've been around, an' let me tell yez, it'll be th' divel's own foot race t' see who gets t' who first—you t' th' priest, or th' Banshee McCrea t' you!"

"Probably." I nodded again. "And that's why I'll make you a counteroffer instead. You agree to tear up that blasted agreement, or to enter into a nullifying agreement—or whatever it takes—to ensure you can't work the same trick twice on me or my family, and I'll help you get your gold back...this time. Otherwise—" I shot out a hand and grabbed him up by the jerkin before he could dodge. "—you and I go see the priest together and find out how you like a bath in holy water!"

"Why, ye doubledealin' knave!" he spluttered, kicking like an angry rabbit as he dangled from my grasp. "I warn ye, ye great bully! 'Tis easy enow t' lay hands on a leprechaun, but 'tis another thing entirely t' keep yer grip!"

"Maybe," I agreed grimly, as I hung onto him. "But I'm about ready to take that chance. I want no more of your help *or* your imposition, Egbert, and if I never believed in you before, I do now. So you'd best believe me when I tell you I'm serious. Either you tear up that damned contract, or I do my damnedest to get you to a priest before dawn!"

"All right!" he said finally. "All right! All right! Ye've me word, sworn upon me crock itsel'!"

I considered that for a moment. I didn't really know how likely any oath was to hold him, but it seemed likely that one would be more binding than most. So, after a few more seconds, I set him back down.

He glared up from the coffee table at me, hands on his hips. But then an unwilling sort of gleam lit his eye.

"Ye've th' right spirit fer the job, I'll gi' ye that," he said ruefully. "Once we get me crock o' gold back, I'll be willin' enough t' be shut of yez! Little enough I've gotten back fer all me time an' effort! Bring us some paper an' we'll get it done."

"Do we need a full moon?" I was suddenly doubtful, aware of my lack of knowledge about how the rules of jurisprudence worked in Egbert's peculiar world. No doubt he could out-finagle me without breaking a sweat if I wasn't careful.

"Not fer this," he said and snapped his fingers.

A red calfskin volume, as tall as Egbert, thumped down on the tabletop. The spine, printed in delicate golden ink, proclaimed it to be *The Legal Code Of Elveron, With Certain Pertinent Observations And Comments Drawn From Many Years' Practice At The Bar, With Index And Appendices, Compiled With A Foreword By His Majesty, King Oberon, And Edited By H. Merlin, Chief Justice Emeritus.* It was, I saw as Egbert opened it, a beautifully illuminated, hand-copied work. He flipped a few pages and prodded a finger at a chapter entitled "The Nullification and Abrogation of Obligatory Compacts Entered into by Ancestors of Mortals and Immortal Beings by the Light of the Full Moon." That certainly seemed to the point, and I skimmed several pages of dry legalistic terminology until I came to the section I wanted.

"Under the terms of the Uniform Code of Magic (UCM), nothing is required for the enactment of nullification or abrogation of an obligatory compact entered into by an ancestor of a mortal and any immortal beings (see sec. vii, para 14-a of UCM regulation 11769-ci) beyond a clear understanding of intent on the parts of both parties as to the contents of the said articles of nullification or abrogation (see test case: *Genie Malog-v-the Estate of Aladdin of Baghdad*), provided the terms are clearly and unambiguously set forth in language intelligible to both parties. Unlike a formal covenant of obligation, such agreements as the said nullification require no extra-normal rites or conditions, but rather rest simply upon a signature by each party, which is binding upon both to enact a full and total revocation of the said original obligatory compact in all its stipulations as to duties, penalties, rewards, etc., etc."

"Well, that certainly seems clear enough," I said a bit dubiously. "Just a minute."

I crossed to my desk and drew a legal pad and fountain pen from the top drawer. I also frowned, aware that I'd sampled quite a bit of very good whiskey that evening, as I considered how best to draw up the bones of a document which, I fervently hoped, would satisfy Chief Justice Emeritus, H. Merlin.

"I, Egbert the Leprechaun," I wrote finally, "herewith set forth my agreement that, in return for the recovery of my crock of gold by Richard Francis Osteen, direct male descendant of The O'Stane, I do hereby acquit the said Richard Francis Osteen and any and all of his descendants, siblings, cousins, or other relatives, male or female, by blood, marriage, or adoption, from any obligation to further aid me in any way.

"And I, Richard Francis Osteen, do hereby acquit the said Egbert the Leprechaun of any and all obligations to aid myself, my descendants, siblings, or other relatives, by blood, marriage, or adoption, in the furtherance of our family fortunes, this acquittance to take effect immediately subsequent to the fulfillment of the preceding paragraph, provided only that no sudden decline in that fortune shall take place specifically due to the withdrawal of the influence of the said Egbert.

"Done this thirty-first day of October, two thousand and twenty (Christian reckoning) by Egbert the Leprechaun and Richard Francis Osteen."

Egbert glanced at it, nodded, and scratched an illegible signature across the bottom. The illegibility probably owed something to the difference in scale between him and the fountain pen. In turn, I signed with a slightly inebriated flourish and tucked it away in my wall safe, where, presumably, it remains to this day.

I wouldn't know; I've never had a chance to check.

.II.

H ave you ever driven all night on a rainbow?
Thought not. Not many have.
I wouldn't have agreed to, either, if Egbert hadn't flourished that contract at me when I hesitated. Still, if you have to travel, it's a great way to do it—no traffic and you don't even have to turn on your headlights at night, because the roadway itself generates more than enough illumination.

I found out later that the five-foot trumpet Egbert produced from that incredible rucksack belongs to a fellow named Heimdall, who is somebody or other in Norse mythology. The rainbow itself is called Bifrost. At the time, all I knew was that the lopsided blast Egbert coaxed out of the trumpet brought a beautiful, shimmering rainbow into existence at the very door of my garage.

Despite lingering misgivings, I was absolutely entranced as I watched Bifrost appear out of the rain and wind and darkness, gleaming in all its light-flowing glory. I had never imagined anything like it, and I found myself wishing I'd paid at least a bit of attention to those "paranormal phenomena" for which I'd never found the time.

The pint-sized tyrant convinced me, not without difficulty, to get my dad's old 1969 Jaguar E out of the garage. Rainbows, in my previous experience, lacked a certain solidity, and while this specimen did seem somewhat brighter and firmer than those I had previously examined, it took a lot of talking to convince me to try actually driving on it. Not only that, it was difficult to coax the front wheels up onto the rainbow's edge, since there was a gap of about two inches between it and the concrete garage apron.

Nevertheless, we managed it. And, once firmly settled onto the rainbow, we waited out its alarming initial tendency to sway under the weight and then drove smoothly off into adventure.

Ha! *Sure* we did.

About six in the morning, the sun came out. By that time, Egbert had emptied all three of the whiskey bottles he'd thoughtfully stowed in his sack when I wasn't looking, which meant he was too busy sleeping it off to answer any questions. Left to my own devices, I estimated that despite the fact that it was October—well, November by now—the brilliant arc of light that blinked over the horizon at me was a summer sun. The light was enough brighter than the rainbow to set our roadway's surface aglitter, as if it had been coated in dew—which it may well have been, for all I know. It was a late June sun, I thought. Not that it matters. Where we were going, the sun is always a late June sun.

Now that we had light, I glanced over the edge of the rainbow and saw that we were nearing the ground again. That was a good thing, as far as I was concerned. Rainbows spend a lot of time up in the air, at heights from which a falling Jaguar (and contents) would make a nasty, noisy splat upon impact.

About half-past ten, we arrived. Don't ask where, because I don't know. There's a difference, I discovered, between going somewhere and arriving. When you're going somewhere, you usually have some notion as to your destination. But when you simply *arrive* somewhere, all you know is that you're there—wherever "there" is. I knew we'd arrived when the rainbow curved gracefully down to the top of a rolling green hill and deposited us with a six-inch thump on a dew-spangled, smoothly emerald sward.

The Jag swayed for a moment on springs and shocks, then came to rest. I breathed deeply of the sparkling air and, for a single moment of weakness, thought more charitably about the eight-pound Jesse James sleeping soddenly beside me.

The moment passed quickly.

I switched off the ignition, then prodded my companion, none too gently, in the ribs.

"Ufff?" he remarked.

"Rise and shine, little buddy," I said briskly. "We're here. Wherever here is."

"Ooooh, me achin' head," he moaned.

He sat up unsteadily, gazed blearily at the glittering hillsides, and muttered something nasty under his breath. Well, when you're a foot tall and you spent the night putting away three bottles of one of the finest single malt whiskeys ever made, I suppose the resultant hangover is bound to be monumental. Not that I was too sympathetic.

After all, the superb (and expensive) single malt in question had been mine.

"Hangover?" I asked sweetly.

"In a manner o' speakin'," he allowed with a groan. I nodded in crocodile-tear commiseration.

"Someone else's whiskey will do that," I said solicitously, which earned me a rather bitter glare all my own.

"I'll be thankin' ye t' keep a civil tongue in yer head, laddy buck," he said with ominous patience. "This here is *my* ground, not yerz, and there'll no be anyone t' interfere if I take a notion t' curse ye now!"

"Maybe," I said with my best Cheshire Cat smile. "But if you curse me now, there'll be no one to get your crock back. And if you curse me after, you'll answer to the Chief Justice of Elveron. So don't come the ugly with me, *laddy buck!*"

"That's as may be," he said with a smile of his own. "But, then, I know somethin' as you don't."

"Which is?"

I tried to sound casual, but his malicious grin suddenly reminded me that this little ragamuffin was undoubtedly more dangerous than I knew.

"I know who 'tis ye have t' get me crock from."

"And who might that be?" I asked, feeling more hollow by the moment.

"A fellow by th' name o' Sylvester," Egbert said cheerfully. "Have ye heard of him?"

"Can't say as I have," I admitted cautiously. "What's he like?"

"Oh, a most cultured gentlemen," Egbert assured me gravely. "A thief, 'tis true, but cultured fer all o' that."

He paused for a moment, eyeing me sideways, then went on with exaggerated casualness.

"O' course, he *is* a matter o' two hundred feet long."

My plunging jaw crushed my right toe.

"Two...*hundred*...feet?" I asked stupidly. Then an even nastier thought occurred to me. "Long?" I repeated. "Not 'tall'?"

"Long." Egbert's reply was firm, and he grinned from ear to ear.

"Just...uhh—Just what *is* this Sylvester?" I asked finally, although a numbness in the vicinity of my stomach suggested I already knew.

The numbness' suggestion was confirmed a moment later.

"Why," the black-hearted little devil said, innocent as the new fallen snow, "he's a dragon. Did it slip me mind t' mention that?"

I fainted, of course.

Egbert wasn't the man—pardon, leprechaun—to let a little unconsciousness get in the way of progress. Before I'd even worked up a good nightmare, he'd brought me back to face the one *he'd* provided.

"Come now, lad!" he said breezily. "'Tis only one wee little dragon, when all's said."

"'Only a dragon'? Like with scales and wings and teeth and claws and all like that?"

"That's him, lad!" Egbert said encouragingly, standing up in the passenger seat to clap me on the shoulder.

"Well, now look, Egbert." I looked at him cautiously. "This...this kleptomaniac lizard of yours doesn't have anything of *mine*! I don't know if I want to go calling on him this early in the morning and all."

My chuckle sounded a little weak, even to me.

"He may not have anythin' o' yerz, laddy," Egbert's eyes glittered nastily, "but *I* do!"

He seized his trumpet and blatted out a note that vanished the rainbow. I stared stupidly at where it had been and groaned inwardly. Without the rainbow, there was no way I knew of to get back to that nice, quiet, safe, and—above all—dragon-free fireside of mine.

"Egbert." I tried to be patient. "Egbert, you didn't *tell* me this...this Sylvester was a *dragon*! That's not fighting fair."

"But I am no fightin' yez." Egbert sounded pained, but his eyes still held that triumphant glitter. "'Tis Sylvester yer fightin', an' I am after helpin' ye t' do it!"

"*Help?!*" I snorted. "If this is 'help,' why don't you go help the other side? Look, if this is a dragon and all, and this is your world and all, couldn't you just sort of sneak up on him or something and get your gold back yourself? I mean, it's *your* crock, after all, and you're bound to know your way around better than I do."

"I've already explained that t' ye. It takes a mortal t' get me crock back. Besides, them as have the crock are safe from them as lost it. 'Tis in the rules, Dickie."

"Don't call me Dickie!" I snapped. "That's a little too much, on top of everything else!"

"Sorry," Egbert said contritely, and I'd swear he really meant it.

"I'll try this one more time, Egbert. In short, easy words. There is no way—no way!—I am going to fight a two-hundred-foot dragon for you. Contract or no contract, agreement or no agreement. If you want somebody to fight an overgrown cigarette lighter for you, you're going to have to look someplace else. I'll take my chances with that foot race to a priest!"

"Now, I don't think ye'll be doin' that, laddy," Egbert said in a musing sort of tone. "Ye see, there's nary a priest in this whole world we're in, so if yer thinkin' o' backin' out, bucko, 'tis me an' you, wi' no one t' interfere. Which would ye prefer to spend eternity as? A frog or a newt? I've old friends I'm sure'll be willin' t' help us out."

"Thanks," I said bitterly.

Now I knew why the little rat had been so willing to nullify the agreement. My father always used to say, "Sober up before you sign something, Richard," and now I saw why. I'd had a feeling then there might be some sort of catch, even if I had written it out myself, and now I knew what it was. It was the part that specified Egbert would let up on us Osteens in return for my regaining his crock for him. Which meant that if this Sylvester ate me up tooth and toenail before I got the crock back to Egbert, my part of the contract would be unfulfilled. Which meant, in turn, that Egbert wouldn't have to fulfill his end, either. So he could just go back and keep on picking up Osteens with that damned contract of his until there weren't any of us left. Worse yet, now that he had me safely sewed up in a world with no priests—somehow I didn't doubt he was right about *that*— my original exorcism threat was useless.

I sighed. It was wormwood and gall time.

"All right, Egbert," I said wearily. "Where does this Sylvester hang out?"

"Why, in his lair, o' course!"

"Oh, of course. Where else?" I chuckled sourly.

"Best be on our way!" he said briskly, hopping out of the Jag. I followed him, not at all happily, but without much choice.

"By the way," I asked, "how do I fight him? Marquis of Queensberry and no stomping in the clinch?"

"Why, in th' traditional manner," Egbert said, as if surprised I should ask. "I brought along yer armor. Do ye want a sword or an ax?"

"A sword or an ax?" I sighed gustily as visions of recoilless rifles and fifty-caliber machine guns dropped regretfully from my mind. Swords and axes!

What next, I asked myself wearily, hiking along behind the dangerous little lunatic. *What next?*

.III.

I've never been one for early morning constitutionals. Not since the four years of my life the Marine Corps had claimed after ROTC, anyway.

Since my unfortunate acquaintance with Egbert, it's occurred to me more than once that if I'd only cultivated the sober, steadfast manner of living that appreciates a brisk turn about the moors, ankle-deep in crystal morning dew, I might never have met him. Or Sylvester. But hindsight is always clearer than foresight, and there was many a splendid all-night pinochle game—and even better bottle of whiskey—I might have missed by cultivating such a reputable lifestyle.

As walks go, this could have been as pleasant a trip as one could wish. Always assuming one could forget its probable end. Looked at in the proper light, of course, it possessed all the charm of a brisk, early morning jog to the gallows. The dew sparkled under a bright sun, the air was brisk and pre-industrially pure, and the sky was that color of blue you see only once in a very, very long time, speckled with fleecy white clouds that curtsied and bobbed to one another. All in all, a perfectly splendid morning to take a picnic lunch out to the hills.

I hated it. But the thought of spending the rest of eternity (which it occurred to me was a *long* time) squatting on a lily pad and tongue-fishing for flies was a little much, too. Only, the closer I got to Sylvester, the more attractive such a future became.

At least it *was* a future.

After a while, I caught a whiff of something besides simple purity in the air—a resinous sort of smell, like you might notice around a bonfire with lots of pine in it. I sniffed thoughtfully.

"That's Sylvester," Egbert confirmed my unspoken guess cheerfully. "Eats a Cedar of Lebanon every morning, does Sylvester. Just t' keep his breath sweet."

For just a moment, I considered squashing Egbert under my heel. But then it occurred to me that if he was immortal, it might not be possible to kill him. And if it wasn't, making the attempt and failing might not be the best idea available. Given the motive for revenge, he might turn nasty—and considering what he'd already gotten me into, an enraged Egbert didn't bear thinking on.

A kindred and disquieting thought intruded on my brain. If it was impossible to kill an immortal creature, I certainly hoped dragons fell into the category of "long-lived but mortal." I considered asking Egbert, but not very hard. If I couldn't really kill one, I didn't want to know.

"Okay, Egbert." I came to a halt. "Pull out the aluminum pants and let's get on with it. I might as well get suited up before we get any closer."

He nodded with appalling cheerfulness, and, as he dropped his rucksack to the turf, I felt a momentary regret for my lapsed Blue

Cross policy. But then, marvelous as modern medicine may be, there's not much even it can do with a well-gnawed shinbone.

Egbert reached into his sack and began tugging on something. It wasn't easy, but after a brief struggle, he dragged a cross-guard hilt out of the bag's mouth. He got a better grip and heaved at the rest of the thing. After a several minute tug-of-war, he produced, in panting triumph, a sheathed two-handed sword which was easily four or five times as long as he was.

I took it as gingerly as you can take something the size and weight of a bridge girder and regarded it with misgiving as I drew the blade and held it awkwardly out in front of me. I heard a faint groan from Egbert as I took up my stance, but he flashed me a smile when I looked at him. It was a rather feeble one, I noticed.

While I experimented with the unwieldy weapon, Egbert continued to produce things. Next out of the bag was a helmet, complete with visor and nodding white plume, followed by a breastplate, arm guards, gauntlets, chain mail hauberk, quilted underwear, pauldrons, a gorget, steel boots…

He must have had an army surplus store in there.

"Ah! That's the lot!" He puffed, dropping a brass-worked baldric atop the triangular shield. I looked at him with grudging respect as he stood next to the mountainous pile of gear he'd evidently been lugging around the whole time.

Not too much respect, though.

"That's pretty good," I admitted. "Now, how about helping me get into this mobile ironworks?"

"Oh, aye—aye!" he muttered quickly. He shook himself and went on more loudly. "'Tis some time since last I passed this way, boyo. Let me have a moment t' see if Sylvester's still about his old haunts."

"If he is, I hope he eats you on sight," I muttered at his back as he dashed off to spy out the land. Not that I really expected it to happen, you understand, but one can always hope...

While he was gone, I started pulling on the armor, with many a muttered curse along the way. I didn't do too badly—I only made five mistakes in four layers—and I was getting the hang of it by the time he came back up the hill. Whichever way was most uncomfortable, was the way it went on, I'd discovered. Better yet, the burnished steel soaked up the sun like a sponge. Before long, I knew why clams open up in an oven, and I wished I could, too.

"I see ye've figured it out fer yerself, more or less," he said, saving me from putting the gorget on backwards. "An' I am happy t' report Sylvester's still in his auld lair, an' sound asleep, as near as I can tell."

"'Happy to report'!" I snarled from inside my helmet. "Hip-hip-hooray! Let's hear it for Sylvester and his lair, folks!"

"Nay, then! Don't be bitter, lad," Egbert said soothingly. "As I've said before, 'tis only a dragon, when all's said an' doon."

"And if you say it one more time, I'll see about making some Egbert purée," I said, raising a heavy iron boot.

"Lad, lad!" Egbert's sorrowful voice carried a malicious edge as he danced back out of range. "It grieves me heart t' hear ye carry on so! Courage, lad. Courage!"

"Courage!" I snorted in an altogether different tone.

"Ah, lad!" he sighed.

"Stop being pained and tell me if I've got this junkheap on right way round," I growled.

"Oh, aye," he said, walking around me with a cocked eyebrow. "Aye, aye. Ye'll do right enough. Just remember t' keep yer shield high, boyo! Well, then—come along. Sylvester's waitin', the sly, slimy worm!"

"So am I," I said unhappily. "And I wish I could go *on* waiting."

I hefted the massive sword and laid the back edge of the blade across my pauldron as I clanked along in Egbert's wake.

"For a long, *long* while," I muttered.

.IV.

Egbert and I made our way across the brow of the hill—he jauntily and I clankingly—then paused as the valley beyond came into view. There, in the stony side of the straight up and down, gentle slope of the hill (see what careful description can get you into when you blunder off on an adventure?) was a craggy opening. Craggy openings were fine with me. What I objected to was the curl of smoke seeping out under the sooty overhang. Well, that and the large heap of well-gnawed bones in front of it.

"You're sure this is the place, Egbert?" I asked hopefully.

Not hopeful that it was; hopeful that it *wasn't*.

"Aye," he said.

"That's what I figured." I swallowed heavily. "You know, Egbert, I hate you."

"That's hard, lad—mortal hard," he said complacently. "Just wait. It'll all come right in the end. Ye'll see!"

"Who's end?" I asked nastily.

"A neat point," he agreed in a thoughtful tone.

I would've sworn at him, but that would've been childish. Instead, I walked past him in an icy, dignified silence, which was only slightly marred by the way my knees clanked together.

The tunnel beyond would have been dark, dank, and damp if not for the hot, smoky wind blowing down it and the glow like that from an open furnace door at its far end. I would've settled for dark, dank, and damp any day. Still, it was rather pleasantly scented smoke. As well as the cedarwood smell, it seemed to carry a trace of cinnamon and maybe a little nutmeg.

I turned a corner, and there he was—Sylvester the Great, in all his glowing glory. He was rather like a firefly in one respect, because his glow grew and lessened as he inhaled. Doubtless the momentary draft fanned the fires in his belly.

I walked (as quietly as I could in that damned, clanking armor) to a point about ten feet in front of his right eye. As I stared nervously at the eyelid—which was about three feet taller than I am—I was suddenly aware that I had a two-handed sword but only one hand with which to swing it. The other was all tangled up in my shield strap. I cursed Egbert silently, sweat trickling down my forehead, and debated how to get rid of the shield without waking this monster up.

No brilliant idea had come to me when something woke him up.

He nearly got me before he even knew I was there. There is nothing—nothing at all—worse than standing in front of a yawning dragon who doesn't know you're there. He singed my plume into stinking, shriveled feathers and nearly did the same for me. I think it was the smell of burning lubrication that put him wise to my presence, because when he stopped yawning, I found it very difficult to move my right ankle, since all the oil was burned out of the joint.

Whatever awoke him, he stopped yawning and showed me close to forty feet of grin.

Goodness but he had large teeth.

"Good morning," he said courteously in a booming bass voice. "Can I help you?"

"Uhhhhhh..."

"Speak up, please," Sylvester said, still courteous, as he shifted languidly on the immense pile of gold and gems he used for a bed.

"Er, Egbert wants his crock of gold back," I quavered finally. "Sir," I added weakly as a hasty afterthought.

"He does, does he?" Sylvester waved the tip of his tail idly in the air, blinking his great, green eyes thoughtfully. He seemed terribly amused by something. "Let me see...Are you the third or the fourth fellow he's sent in this week? Well, no matter. I'm afraid he can't have it, you know."

"W-w-well, he won't let me go home till I help him get it," I said lamely. "So. I guess we'll just have to...do battle?"

"I'd really rather not, you know," Sylvester said in a cultured accent that sounded very "public-school British" to me. "Battles to the death are the very devil for tiring one, you know. Besides." He cocked a reptilian eye ridge playfully at me. "You don't really look to be up to my weight at all, old fellow. Can't very well fight with a two-handed sword with just one hand, eh?"

He blew a purple smoke ring about the size of a Prius.

"That's...what I've always heard," I agreed feebly, trying to find a way to shake the shield off one-handed.

"So, why not just explain the exact situation to me?" Sylvester asked. "Perhaps we can negotiate some sort of settlement. I say, did you know you're the first chap he's sent in that I've had time to talk to? All the rest were just up with the sword and onwards! I rather wondered if he'd recruited them from that Marine Corps of yours. You don't know? Ah, well."

He blew another smoke ring.

I tried to ignore the aspersion upon the Corps—it wasn't as if I'd never heard one before—and nodded.

"I'd certainly *like* to settle it peacefully," I said fervently, my mind busy with images of Osteen cutlets sliding down that huge throat. "But, somehow, I don't think it'll work out."

"Alas," Sylvester sighed, rolling slightly to one side and blowing another ring—this one was violet—as he polished his yard-long claws on the stony cave wall. "So do I, you know. But one must always try, don't you think?"

As he said, one must always try—especially when one seems slated for the main course at the diplomatic luncheon if a solution can't be found. So…

"Well, you see," I said, searching feverishly for an out somewhere, "there was this ancestor of mine who made a deal with this leprechaun named Egbert. Under it, I have to help Egbert get his stolen crock of gold back from you. I thought I had him outfoxed, but I slipped up when I drew up the nullifying agreement. So, after he brought me here on a rainbow and explained you were, well, a dragon, I didn't seem to have any choice. He won't let me use the bridge to go home if I don't get his crock back, and unless I *do* get it, he'll turn me into a newt or a toad and go get the next Osteen on his list. An…and that's about it," I finished lamely.

"Very, ummm…concise," Sylvester said thoughtfully as he inspected his newly honed claws. "But, dear sir, I fear you have been the victim of a monstrous fabrication."

"You mean he *lied* to me?" I demanded.

"That *is* what I said," he replied rather huffily.

I staggered back to my feet in the wake of his statement and bent over to readjust the greave that had somehow wrapped itself around the calf of my left leg.

"That's what I thought you said," I explained mildly as I straightened. "I just wasn't sure. Um. How much of what he told me was a lie?"

"Almost all of it, I should imagine." Sylvester seemed mollified by my explanation. "First of all, he told you he was Irish, hmmm?"

I nodded.

"Well, the nearest he's ever come to the continent of Europe is Long Island. He was born and reared in New Jersey, I believe you call it? Yes? Fine."

He seemed quite proud of his knowledge of geography.

"Now, as to this business of his crock of gold being a portion of my hoard, that's preposterous old boy. Simply preposterous! Every gem and gold piece you see before you was assembled—not always honestly, mind you, but those were the old days—by the efforts of my ancestors over the last few millennia. Why, I don't suppose I've added more than twenty or thirty pounds of diamonds to it, myself.

"Now, as to the reason he needed someone else to steal the gold for him in the first place. The Uniform Code of Magic expressly prohibits the use of one's powers to obtain goods or money to which one is not lawfully entitled. That regulation was passed—oh, two or three centuries ago, I believe. There are still those on the dark side who try to evade it, mind! But the Auditing Department soon catches up with them, which explains Egbert's need for a mortal accomplice. No *immortal* being would be foolish enough—Oh, I say, I do hope you forgive a little plain speaking?"

He cocked his head, gazing at me earnestly, and I nodded.

"Good fellow! As I say, no immortal being would be foolish enough to cooperate in such a scheme, since under the UCM such an act would almost certainly result in revocation of his or her license to practice magic. And there are the *strictest* of penalties for practicing without a license, you know.

"Considering Egbert's need for an unknowing tool, I am most definitely inclined to doubt the authenticity of that supposed agreement with your ancestor, as well. Really, it's quite too convenient for his ends, and I should heartily doubt he ever possessed a crock worth stealing. He's really rather more of a chicken thief, you see. Besides, he's never been in Scotland at all, to the best of my knowledge. Operations there were shut down…oh, at least a century before he was born.

"Finally, I don't really know whether he said or you simply assumed that he could send you home once the deed was done— always assuming you survived the doing of it, of course. But whichever it might have been, the notion is simply ridiculous. Unless I miss my guess, that's Heimdall's horn he's playing with this time, and I very much doubt Odin One-Eye will permit Bifrost to be diverted from its rightful course again under any circumstances. The Aesir are mobilizing for Ragnarok, you know."

"How long will Bifrost be out of order?" I asked, fastening instantly on the part of his speech of most immediate concern to me.

"Umm? Why, forever. That's how long Ragnarok lasts."

"Forever?"

Any merely mortal voice would have seemed small and frail compared to his conversational bellow, but mine sounded even smaller just then.

"Well, it's not precisely *out of order*," Sylvester corrected himself. "It's still there, and I'm sure you can still go from any nexus point to any other, if you wish. But I'm afraid that would require either a guide or the trumpet, and by now, all the Aesir who might have been able to guide you have been drafted, while I'm certain Heimdall has already reclaimed his horn. Well, you can see where that leaves *you*, of course."

"Oh, of course," I said.

I thought about what he'd said so far, exploring it for possible falsehoods. Once burned, twice shy, I seemed to remember having heard, and it was obvious to me that one of these two was being less than honest. On the other hand, it seemed likely to prove unhealthy to ask a two-hundred-foot dragon if he was lying to me.

"I see you seem troubled," Sylvester said thoughtfully. "Perhaps you've heard that the...um, veracity...of dragons is sometimes open to question? Well, no need to be so defensive, old boy!" He chuckled at my uncertain reaction. "We never would have gotten the name if there weren't some truth in it. However, in this case, the truth serves better than any lie I could've thought up, don't you know, and there *are* ways to check."

He buffed his claws noisily on his belly scales.

"Such as?" I asked nervously.

"Well, now." He cocked an eye ridge at me again. "We could always ask Heimdall about his horn, now couldn't we? But, there! I'm sure he's too busy at the moment. Would Merlin do?"

"You mean *the* Merlin?"

"Of course. The old boy's getting on, you know. Rather past it, in some ways. But as fine a character witness as a being could ask."

"Well, that seems likely enough," I agreed.

"Fine, then." He scrabbled through his hoard with a single claw and raked out a small crystal ball. "Take a look in there," he invited me. "Direct line to Elveron."

By now, I was past wonder and simply did as he asked. At first, there was only a confused swirl of light, but, gradually, the colors settled down into the head and shoulders of an incredibly old, bearded man. He looked up at me from under bushy brows as the image cleared.

"Well, what is it?"

He had a testy voice. It reminded me of my third-grade principal.

"Er, excuse me, sir," I said. "But I need to ask a question, please, sir."

"Well, don't stand there gawking," the old man said truculently. "What are you willing to pay for it?"

"Pay for it?"

"Oh, these mortals!" the old man said bitterly. "What? Did you think it would be *free*? Young fool! Why, I—"

"Excuse me, Mage," Sylvester boomed, "but I believe this gentleman is owed an answer under the Distressed Travelers' Code."

"Eh? What's that? Who—Oh, Sylvester!" The old man scowled, playing with his beard with the fingers of his right hand. "*Another* distressed traveler, is he? Zounds! There seem to be a great many of 'em about these days!"

He scowled, then turned his attention back to me.

"Well, young man, just what is this question of yours? Make it quick, if you please!"

"Well, sir…"

I explained what had happened as concisely and clearly as I could, and the oldster listened with a fair show of patience. When I'd finished, he nodded sharply.

"Had our eye on this Egbert of yours for some time, young man," he said less sharply. "Deucedly clever little blighter, though. Haven't been able to prove a thing. As to your problem, I'd say you have a case worth bringing before the Council, but I'm afraid all we could pin on Egbert would be unethical conduct—only a misdemeanor. Couldn't possibly revoke his license for it. Hold him liable for damages though, fine him whatever it costs to right them. *That* much we could do."

"But you mean if I bring a case before your court I might even get sent home?"

"Home? Home? Of course we could send you home! Might be a century or two before we could schedule the case, though. Dreadful backlog just now. Simply dreadful!"

"A *century* or two?"

"Well, possibly, given the immediacy of your need…seventy-five years?" He shrugged. "Perhaps. I couldn't promise, of course."

"I…I see," I said slowly. "Er, just one more question, sir. Sylvester here suggested I might consult you as to his character."

"Oh, he did, did he?" A gleam entered the rheumy old eye. "And just why might you have thought of me, Sir Dragon? Wouldn't have anything to do with that little matter of the goblin infestation, would it?"

"Well, I must confess—" Sylvester seemed amused, "—that it did occur to me that you might still feel somewhat well disposed towards me, Mage."

"Did, did it?" Merlin gave a dry chuckle. "Well, young man," he said sternly, turning back to me, "no dragon can always resist the temptation to lie—bred into 'em, you see—but Sylvester's more honest than most. Settled down quite a bit in the last few hundred years. Mind you, you can't trust even him if there's money to be had. But from the story you've told, I'd say he's been honest enough this time. Anything else I can do for you?"

"Uh, no, sir. Not just now, thank you, sir."

"Welcome," the old man said briskly. "Sorry I couldn't be of more help. Call me back if you think of something else. Ta!"

The crystal went blank again, and I set it down numbly.

"That puts rather a different light on things," I said slowly, turning back to Sylvester. "Since Egbert couldn't send me home again anyway, one reason to help him no longer applies. But as long as he's got that damned fake contract, there's no reason he can't just take himself home and play the same trick on more Osteens—or somebody else entirely, for that matter. And if he can still send more patsies in after you, it seems like you'll still be in the same fix you were in, as well."

"True," Sylvester said sadly, examining his claws again. I wished he'd stop doing that. "Mind you, the warriors he's been sending along so far *have* been tasty, but it gets so wearing, defeating them every few days. And besides, I'm getting rather past it myself, you know. Why, just between us, I've not even wanted to devour a maiden in—oh, ages! And as for *warriors*! Sooner or later, the little blighter's bound to send along someone who can actually defeat me. And then, you know, he'll have it all anyway."

He heaved a great dragon's sigh, but this time, I was ready for it, and it only knocked me to my knees.

"Well," I said, as soon as I got my breath back, "I've been thinking about that. I think I may know how to help us both, Sylvester."

"Indeed?" He rolled onto his back and stretched, extending all his claws in a great, smoky yawn. "That would certainly be nice, old boy."

"Uhhh, yes." I coughed a little on the leftovers of his yawn and opened my visor to mop my streaming eyes. "Well, I was reading this story the other day about Saint G—" I remembered who I was talking to and instantly choked off the name. "Um, about this knight and another dragon, you see. And it seems…"

.V.

"Ready?" I asked.

"Yes." Sylvester settled himself comfortably atop his mountainous horde. "I say, old boy. Do you really suppose this will work?"

"I hope so," I said grimly. "It's the only way I can think of to pin the little rat down long enough. I don't know about you, but I, for one, want him pinned down *permanently!*"

"Oh, I say!" Sylvester was delighted. "That's the spirit, old boy!"

"Right." I stepped over to a convenient boulder and rested the flat of my sword on it. "Ready? A one, and a two, and a *three*—!"

On the three, Sylvester let out a snorting bellow like a steam engine on a steep downgrade. His tail clashed against the cavern walls with gusto, hard enough that bits and pieces of stone pattered down from above on the vibration. The racket sounded as if the downslope engine had met another headed uphill. I beamed encouragement and began to batter the sword blade up and down on the boulder, adding my own terrific clamor to the din of colliding trains and toppling skyscrapers. The sword blows tolled like a drunken bell while the cavern's acoustics picked up and amplified the screams and bellows like a megaphone.

"More smoke!" I shouted, my voice completely lost in that mind-boggling tempest of sound, but Sylvester heard it, and obliged with a gorgeously sulfurous belch of orangey-green fire that set the cave walls themselves to coughing.

"More heat!" I wheezed.

I was well to one side, but the burst of flame nearly welded my helmet to my ears. A tongue of fire ten or fifteen feet long must have blasted out of the mouth of the cave.

I paused and reached into my helmet with a handkerchief Sylvester had provided, wiping sweat from my forehead. Then I turned back to the boulder, clanging away with a will. The heat and smoke were terrible, but I consoled myself with the thought of Egbert, no doubt hopping up and down in anticipation just beyond the cave.

We spent at least an hour pounding out our own version of the anvil chorus. We paused between stanzas to let Sylvester put a few artistic touches of char and soot on the shield propped against the far wall. He scorched my armor artistically, too, although that was less than pleasant, since I hadn't remembered to take it off first. Then back to the boulder with the sword, more screams and bellows, more smoke, more fire—

Finally, I glanced at my watch and gave him the high sign.

Instantly, he let fly with an even more horrendous series of screams, belching more smoke than the London Fire. Then, with a suddenness that left my ears ringing in protest, he shut it all down and lay quietly on the floor. I winked a smoke-smarting eye at him, picked up the scorched, burned, and smoked-up shield, and limped out of the cave. Smoke streamed from every opening in my armor and trailed from the heels of my iron boots.

Egbert waited just outside. I looked him over through the visor's slots and savored the George Washington straightforwardness of our plan.

"Well?" He shivered in anticipation and avarice. "*Well?*"

"Why don't you go get what you came for, Egbert," I said wearily. "I'm bushed."

Then I sat down on a rock as he dashed toward the cave entrance.

Please note the moral superiority of my plan as compared to his own. Unlike Egbert, I told no lies, nor did I make any threats, true or false. I merely suggested that he go and collect what he'd come for and remarked that I, myself, was tired—which I certainly was. I made no remarks, true or false, as to the condition of the rightful owner of the gold in question.

I sat contemplating the beauty of the grass, the clarity of the sky, while I listened to the patter of footsteps fading into the hill. I suppose a nasty little smile *might* have lingered beatifically on my lips, but I can't be certain.

I waited, ears cocked.

There came a sudden roll of basso thunder as Sylvester welcomed Egbert in with gently smiling jaws. The deceitful little leprechaun gave a single dreadful cry—composed, I should say, of almost equal proportions of anger, terror, hatred, and surprise. Then a small puff of smoke curled from the mouth of the cave, followed by silence.

I smiled and reached inside my breastplate for my meerschaum pipe.

Ten minutes later, Sylvester pushed his huge bulk out onto the hillside. Egbert's cap stuck ridiculously between two of his massive canines, and he seemed at peace with the world.

"Well?"

"I really don't think—" Sylvester gave a rather complacent burp, "—that our stringy little imposter will be back."

"I suppose," I said with a straight face, blowing a far more modest smoke ring of my own, "that you might say you finally got your just dessert."

"Frightful, old boy! Simply frightful."

.VI.

Well, that was about three weeks ago, Standard Faerie Sundial Time. But weeks are funny here, because the days seem to be about a month long each, if you understand. Sylvester says there's a time difference between our world and this one, too, just to complicate things a little further. From what he tells me, something like a year of our time must have passed since I left...and that's his minimum estimate.

He and I get along fine, and we've come up with a way to earn a decent living off the locals. I wish I could claim credit for originality, but why futz around with something you're already pretty sure will work?

First, he terrorizes a town for a week or so—making off with sheep, worrying the shepherds, demanding maidens. You know, all the standard dragonish things. After that, he and I stage a battle off in the hills somewhere, where no one can get hurt. And then I collect my fee from the grateful citizenry, and we split the profits.

It's really amazing how just the thought of more gold—even a *little* more gold—rouses Sylvester's enthusiasm, and it's certainly the easiest earnings he's ever come across. As for me, I've discovered there are side benefits to a dragonslayer's status. Like Esmerelda.

She wasn't exactly popular in her hometown, because her father was its wealthiest citizen and she was its most beautiful maiden, a combination which made her the one most likely to be voted off the island when Sylvester and I turned up. I will admit that we modified our standard approach slightly once I'd set eyes on the proposed dragon appetizer. Normally, I turn up and defeat the foul predator before anything more significant than a sheep or two gets handed over to him. In this case, we…delayed that somewhat.

Esmerelda was astounded when she didn't get devoured. She wasn't any too happy with her fellow citizens, either. Turned out she'd been bored as hell trapped in a small town, too. When I explained what was happening, she'd cheerfully told me who—besides her father—was best suited for squeezing and insisted upon becoming a full partner.

She was the one who found the local priestess of Brighid and insisted on "doing things proper" once we found out she was pregnant, too.

There's only one thing that really bothers me. Nice as Sylvester is, and as smart and loving and beautiful as Esmerelda is, I'm homesick.

Not for the traffic or the rat race, mind you! It's just that, now, I understand the way Egbert reacted to my whiskey. There's nothing here but some sort of moonshine—literally—the elves whip up. It makes a nice change, but it's not Glenlivet, and it's not Glendronach, and it's not Balvenie.

In short, I'd like to go home and lay in a supply.

But Sylvester was right about old Heimdall. He's a real nice guy and awfully polite and understanding—I think that may be because we engineered the comeuppance of the horn thief—but those Norse gods just aren't much help at the moment. They're all busy fighting a war somewhere, and they're pretty preoccupied with it all. He told me to feel free to use Bifrost, but they can't spare me a guide just now, and they don't have any maps.

So, like I said at the beginning, even if you find this message, I don't think there's any way you can help me out. But, on the off chance that you can do some good, would you try doing me a favor?

Go online and see if you can find anyone who carries rainbow maps.

* * * * *

David Weber Bio

David Weber was born in Cleveland in 1952 but grew up in rural South Carolina. He was a bookworm from childhood, with an interest in history which perplexed his parents, who nonetheless encouraged and supported him in it. He was also blessed with a father from the south side of Chicago who collected autographed copies of every E. E. Smith hardcover and introduced him to Jack Williamson at the age of 10, and with a mother who taught high school and college English, ran her own advertising agency, and encouraged him to write. (And who went back to graduate school in her sixties to earn her PhD in Literature.) An avid tabletop gamer (who, alas, no longer has room in his schedule for his hobby,) he's wargamed every era from ancient Rome to World War II armored conflict, and began RPG playing with Gary Gygax's *Chainmail* rules in 1972. His younger sister went on to become a hand weaver, and his younger brother was a production potter for thirty years, so it's probably not too surprising that from that start he would find his way into the world of science fiction and fantasy rather than pursue honest work. He sold his first novel to Jim Baen at Baen Books in 1989. Since then, he has published 68 solo and collaborative novels (and another has been delivered but not yet scheduled). He has also edited six anthologies and appeared in several more. He is best known for his Honorverse, with 27 solo and collaborative novels in print centered around his character Honor Harrington and her universe, and the Safehold series, with ten novels in print. He still lives in South Carolina with a wife, Sharon, who he is fortunate loves him enough to put up with him, their three children, one dog, and six cats. And, as Sharon is fond of saying, don't get him started talking if you expect him to ever shut up again.

# # # # #

Smoke and Shadow by
Jon R. Osborne

"Hey sweetheart, how about giving me your number?"

Grace Ramirez affixed her expression before she turned around. She could feel the man's eyes burning into her backside. The overture didn't surprise her—far from it. His gaze had lingered on her all afternoon and, trapped behind the bar, Grace had no escape. At least the waitresses could retreat to the kitchen if one of their clients turned creepy.

"Sorry, I don't date customers." Grace's hint of a smile didn't reach her eyes. She trod the thin line between polite enough that he didn't cause a scene but firm enough that he didn't think she was playing hard to get. She handed him his receipt and credit card, certain her tip was about to be zero. The man had dropped hints regarding his supposed wealth between phone calls. Grace hoped he would show off with a big tip and leave it at that.

"Come on. I closed a big deal, and I'm in a mood to celebrate. We can get to Chicago before the clubs are full." He appraised her again. "I'll get us a nice suite for the night. It's not like you have anything better to do here in Peoria."

"Actually, I have plenty to do," Grace retorted, breaking her own rule against engaging a jerk who thought a tight uniform and customer service smile meant she was on the market.

"What, picking up a shift down at Pole Dancers?" The man's grin morphed into a sneer. He tossed the signed receipt onto the bar. Grace held her tongue as the man stalked off.

She collected the receipt and added it to her drawer. The twenty-dollar tip was a surprise—maybe his fear of looking cheap surpassed his ire at getting turned down. At least he was her last customer.

After cashing out her till, Grace changed from the skimpy khaki shorts and safari shirt uniform to her exercise gear and a warm hoodie. She gauged the sun as she stepped out into the spring evening. She should have time to get a jog in before she went home and cracked the books.

"For twenty bucks, I should at least get a lap dance."

Grace froze. She should have slipped out the back door. The jerk leaned against an upscale SUV—not a true luxury vehicle, but pricey for middle Illinois. "Look, I'm sorry about the stripper crack. It was a bad joke. Why don't I make it up to you?"

He stepped toward Grace. Two more paces and Grace's paralysis turned to panic. She fled back into the restaurant.

* * *

Grace let her thoughts drift with the rhythm of her feet on the dirt path. Though the trail wove through a forest preserve, it was clear of tree roots and other obstacles. It freed her mind as she jogged among the trees; the only sounds were her steady breathing and the rustle of branches in the breeze.

Grace cast off the worries weighing her down. The pushy customer who lurked out front for half an hour before climbing into his SUV and driving off. The jerk ex-boyfriend who made the scene at work last week and nearly got her fired. The middle-aged woman at the drugstore who muttered an ethnic slur when Grace's prescription came up first. She let her troubles evaporate like perspiration in the cool spring air.

Out here, Grace didn't have to worry about any of it, even if the reprieve was only an hour or two. After thirty minutes of cathartic jogging, she slowed to a stop at an intersection of trails. The lengthening shadows made it chilly enough to unwrap the jacket tied around her waist and shrug it on.

As she zipped up her jacket, she spotted movement out of the corner of her eye. She grabbed the pepper spray in her pocket and brandished it.

A small form dashed across the intersection, a blur of brown and red. It was a man, but only three feet tall. The leathery face above a long white beard dispelled her first thought of a child. He stopped stock still against a large oak tree and watched her with ice blue eyes. His rust-colored tunic and brown pants blended with the bark and loam, but the red Cardinals ball cap stood out.

The small man remained frozen against the tree trunk, his chest heaving as he stared at Grace. A breeze ruffled his beard.

"You know I can see you, right?" Grace finally asked, keeping her distance.

"You can?" The man blinked. "I guess I must look pretty silly," he replied with a sing-song Nordic accent. A Swedish puppet leapt to Grace's mind. The man stood up straight and brushed off the back of his tunic. "I must say, this is a bit embarrassing." He scrunched his eyes shut and began tiptoeing to the path, his footfall silent despite the twigs and undergrowth.

Grace put her hands on her hips, clutching the pepper spray. "I can still see you."

The little man froze and opened a single eye. "How about now?"

"Yup."

He opened his other eye and eased his posture. "You should not be able to see me. What are you?"

"That's a bit personal," Grace countered out of reflex. With her skin tone and features, she heard the question too often. "My mother was biracial, and my grandmother was Venezuelan. What does it have to do with why I can see you?"

"You are a dunnie, but if you can see me, you must have some otherfolk in your bloodline, such as a Nephilim or a Seelie," the short fellow said, as though it was obvious.

Grace narrowed her eyes. "What do you mean by dunnie? Is that some sort of Swedish slur? For that matter, what does the rest of what you said mean?"

"I see we got off on the wrong foot. My name is Oddr." He bowed. "A dunnie means you are someone born on the Dunwold, the World of Man."

"I was born in Peoria, not Scotland." Despite her lack of accent, people sometimes assumed she was born in Mexico or South America. The odd little man seemed non-threatening, but she didn't want to take chances in a deserted forest preserve. Grace backed up to a boulder next to the crossed paths and sat on it. The stone chilled her through her leggings, but it was that or sit on the ground. "Wait, World of Man? What other world is there?"

"The Glaswold of course," Oddr replied. "I come from the part of the Glaswold called Midgard. I am a tomte."

"So, you're some sort of fairy or spirit?" Grace asked, fighting the urge to laugh. He must be an insane little person who escaped from a mental facility in Peoria, rather than some sort of gnome out of a fairy tale. She gripped her spray canister. "Bullshit."

"You do not believe me?" Oddr challenged. "Well, I suppose you would not. Magic was effectively banished from the Dunwold for centuries, and you dunnies know naught of it. It is only returning to the Dunwold because the Milesian Accords fell."

"I'll tell you what. I'll finish my jog, and you can go back to pretending you're invisible." Grace stood and brushed herself off. It was later than she intended on being out in the park; she wanted to make it back to her car before night fell.

"I was not pretending," Oddr protested. "You must have a spark of magic in you; it is why you can see through my glamour." He marched over to the stone Grace had been sitting on.

"Right, I have a spark of magic." Grace stepped away in case he sprang at her. "My abuela would be so proud."

"Are all dunnies so cynical?" Oddr squatted before the boulder. The short man rubbed his hands together and then stretched out his arms to hug the stone.

"Don't hurt yourself," Grace admonished, taking another step back. "Look, I believe you're from Dunwall or whatever; don't throw your back out."

"You are from the Dunwold," Oddr grunted as he strained against the weight of the boulder. "I am from the Glaswold." With another groan, he straightened his legs, and the rock tore free of the ground. Plants and dirt crumbled from the underside. Oddr staggered across the trail, carrying the stone in front of him, and dropped it with a thud.

Grace stared at the boulder in disbelief. Oddr leaned against it, panting, his face flushed. "That rock must weigh a ton," she said.

"Thereabouts." Oddr wiped his brow. "It was heavier than I expected."

Grace stepped to the boulder and pushed on it, tentatively at first, and then gave it a good shove. The stone didn't budge. "How could you grip it, let alone pick it up?"

"I told you," Oddr puffed, still catching his breath. "I am a tomte. In the old days, we did farm chores for dunnie families; now, my people farm in the Glaswold. There is a lot of heavy work."

Grace sat on the stone again, gazing at the crater left behind where Oddr had uprooted it. "So, you really are some sort of magical creature."

"Creature?" Oddr protested, arching back and flexing his shoulders. "I told you...I am a tomte. I am one of the Exiled Folk. I never caught your name."

"I'm Grace." She extended her free hand toward the diminutive man. She still held the pepper spray in the other as a precaution. "Nice to meet you."

"Hello, Grace." Oddr stood straight and shook her hand.

"So, if you are from a magical world, what are you doing here?" It was the easiest question she could think of, as everything the tomte said brought up new questions.

"Someone opened a wold-ford, so I slipped through," Oddr explained. "I was hoping to scout out farms, before the other tomte, brownies, and croft-hobs come through, since the Champion of the Exiled Folk won the challenge to the Milesian Accords."

"What are the Milesian Accords?"

Oddr goggled at Grace in disbelief. "You dunnies really have lost touch. Once upon a time, the celestials behind the Avramite clashed with the folk of the old gods. As the war ground on and the otherfolk were losing, they challenged the Avramites to a duel to settle the war. The otherfolk lost, and the resulting treaty was the Milesian Accords.

"The old gods and their supernatural followers were exiled from the Dunwold, and magic dwindled in their absence." Oddr paused for a breath. "The Accords contained a provision for a new challenge, to be fought by a mortal champion from the Dunwold. The Champion won, and the First Druid wrote a new set of accords with new rules for magic. It means the Exiled Folk have an opportunity to come back."

"Some dude beat up another dude, and now magic is real?" Grace frowned. Maybe he was a strong dwarf playing a prank. Her eyes went to the boulder. "Why haven't I seen anything on the internet? If there are magical people like you running around, surely someone would have caught them on camera by now."

"Magic has trickled into the world, and the powers that be have limited how many folk can cross over," Oddr replied. "Right now, we should worry about the dog."

"What dog?" Grace swept her gaze across the woods around them. On one of the paths leading into the intersection, a huge black dog lurked in the gathering gloom. Shadowy mist drifted from its fur. The beast's red eyes fell on Grace, and the hound growled.

"Good dog?" Grace's voice caught in her throat, and the words squeaked out. The dog remained in the shadowed path. Clearing her throat, she whispered, "It's some sort of magical dog, isn't it?"

"An astute guess," Oddr answered, keeping his voice low as well. "I do not know which breed; the Glaswold is rife with monstrous black dogs."

"What is it doing here?" Grace stepped back and peered about for anything useable as a weapon. The creature watched her but did not step forward into the patch of sunlight illuminating the intersection. "Can you throw something heavy at it?"

"My talent is good for lifting hay bales or pushing recalcitrant cows," Oddr replied, creeping back from the beast. "I am afraid it is not of much use for hurling, especially for distance or accuracy. Hence why I fled from it before."

The beast prowled along the edge of the sunlit area. Where dappled light struck it, the dog flinched, and the inky fog evaporated. Grace's heart pounded in her chest as time slowed to a crawl. She spotted a long branch as thick as her wrist and yanked it from the undergrowth.

When Grace hefted the impromptu club, the hound growled, and its muscles tensed under the inky black hide. Paws as big as her hand dug into the earth as the dog lunged forward. Its lips peeled back from obsidian fangs as the maw spread wide, aimed for Grace's throat. On instinct, Grace swung the branch like a baseball bat. The stout wood cracked as it slammed into the side of the dog's head.

Grace staggered back from the force of the impact. The shadowy hound snapped at empty air as the blow spun it off trajectory. It crashed into the brush, tumbling through the undergrowth before it could get its paws under it and arrest its momentum.

The creature shook its head as it turned, one eye squeezed shut as inky blood dripped from the corner of its mouth. Grace backpedaled into the sunlight. How long did she have before the sun moved and covered the path in shadow?

The beast stalked forward a few paces, favoring a foreleg. Grace resisted the temptation to test her club. If the beast realized it was compromised, it might embolden the hound. The dog circled warily back in the direction it came from. Giving a last rumbling growl, it limped into the shadows.

A shiver ran down Grace's spine despite the adrenaline rushing through her veins. A breeze gusted from the sunward path. Grace flexed the thick branch with both hands, and the wood promptly snapped. Could she pick up Oddr and run?

Voices followed the wind as a pair of silhouettes resolved on the path. The woman barely reached Grace's shoulder, and, with her tousled lavender and violet hair, Grace would have taken her for a coed from a local college. Even her attire could have passed for a student's—black and pink athletic wear poorly suited for the chill. As the woman regarded Grace, her eyes glowed purple. Grace squinted—the purple-haired girl had a slight greenish cast to her skin, and her ears ended in points.

The man could have walked out of a local farm supply store. Grace pegged him in his mid-30's, with sandy brown hair and a scruffy beard a week past stubble. He was a couple inches taller than Grace, putting him at six feet or so. His physique was hidden under a heavy flannel shirt. He walked with a tall staff, but it seemed an affectation rather than a crutch.

Grace glanced back down the shadowed path. The beast had vanished in the gloom. Oddr remained frozen in place, peering over the boulder. The man gestured to the rock with his walking stick. "Is he a gnome?" A gust of wind swirled brush around Oddr. "Are gnomes a thing?" he asked his companion.

"No, he's a tomte," the woman replied, her violet eyes falling on Oddr. "He thinks he is invisible."

Oddr snatched his cap off his head, and he hurled the hat to the ground. "Can everyone see me?"

The newcomers chorused in the affirmative. "He's similar to a brownie, but from the Old Norse lands," the purple-haired girl added.

The man turned to Grace, ignoring the fact that she clutched a makeshift club. "So what are you? An Aztec ohuican or some sort of Egyptian demi-goddess?"

"She is descended from Venus Walesland and something else," Oddr offered.

"I'm a bartender," Grace corrected. "Do you really think an Egyptian goddess would be running around the middle of Illinois in leggings and a warm-up?"

The man shrugged and jerked a thumb toward the young woman next to him. "She was dressed like this when I met her, and appearances can be deceiving." The man regarded Grace. She was used to men staring at her, both at work and on the street, but this was different. The man's mismatched eyes, one jade green and the other deep blue, gazed through her. Grace zipped her jacket self-consciously.

"She doesn't have a glamour or charm changing her appearance," the man said.

"You don't need to stare so long," the purple-haired woman chided. She stepped closer to Grace, and her eyes glowed brighter. "Hi, I'm Pixel. Who are you?"

Grace felt a buzzing in the back of her mind, an itch in her brain. Was this girl trying to do something to her? "I'm Grace," she replied, without taking the offered hand. "You can knock off whatever voodoo you're trying to do."

The man sighed and shook his head. "What have I said about glamouring random people?"

"You were fine when I mind-wiped those bikers," Pixel countered.

"Typical fairy, mucking around in people's heads." Oddr brushed the dirt off his hat before replacing it.

"Grace, I apologize for my…friend being overzealous," the man said. "It would be for the best if you went home and tried to forget about meeting us." Wind whirled about him, ruffling his clothes and hair. "It will be safer for you."

"Odin's beard! You are the First Druid," Oddr blurted. "Well, that salves my pride a bit. My name is Oddr."

"How did you get to the Dunwold, Oddr?" the Druid asked. "We haven't heard from the Yggdrasil Lands."

"My clan farms the Glaswold not far from here. The wold-ford was open, so I popped through before other tomte, hobs, and brownies screw up the nerve and poach the best farms and families," Oddr replied. "I had not gone more than a hundred yards before the dog showed up."

"Dog? I bet this is connected to the sightings," the Druid remarked. "People have reported strange dogs that vanish into darkness around this forest preserve."

"Wait, you're looking for dogs?" Grace tamped down her irritation. She didn't need some flannel-wearing hippie with a stick to tell her what to do. "A big black dog came at us. I smacked the piss out of it, and it took off up the north trail."

"Do not sell yourself short. You clobbered that beast with a small tree," Oddr interjected.

"A big black dog? It could be a moddi du or a yeth hound," Pixel suggested. "Moddi dus are creepy, but they don't normally attack people. Yeth hounds are native to the Murkwold though, and they're nasty."

"Can they open wold-fords?" the Druid asked.

Pixel shook her head. "It sounds like someone left the ford open, but it wouldn't explain what drew a yeth hound from the Murkwold."

"If it's open, how do we close it?" The Druid peered along the north path.

"It would be easy if we have the keystone," Pixel remarked. She put a hand on the Druid's forearm and flicked her eyes toward Grace. Grace had worked in the bar long enough to recognize the girl's possessive body language. "Even without the key, you should be able to close it. I can help you."

"Alright, let's go. We're almost out of daylight." The Druid turned to Grace. "Seriously, you don't want to be out here. It's not safe." The pair headed down the north path, where the shadows deepened. The air fell still in the Druid's wake.

"If they had been smart, they would have asked me the way to the wold-ford," Oddr sniffed as they disappeared down the trail.

Grace scowled after the departed pair. "Right, you said you came through this wold-ford. Can you describe it?"

Oddr nodded. "It was on top of a circular hill, likely a fairy mound. There was a ditch ringing it; it was deep enough to collect water, but not quite a proper moat."

"You're talking about Widow Mound," Grace said, turning north. "It's a prehistoric earthwork. I've been there; it's not hard to find."

"They can figure it out. After all, he is the First Druid," Oddr stated.

"It didn't sound like he knew much." Grace tossed aside the splintered remains of her club. "The pixie chick knew more than him. What was she?"

"A handmaiden of Blodeuwedd—a kind of Welsh faery," Oddr replied. "I am surprised you shook off her glamours—both the seeming that masked her and her attempt to meddle with your head. I have heard they can charm you out of your last coin, and you will give them your sock to carry it in."

Grace stared up the north path. The smart thing would be to go home and forget about this weirdness. She stepped onto the north path then paused to look back to Oddr. "Aren't you coming?"

"The Druid said it was dangerous," Oddr protested. "It is also getting darker."

Grace snorted. "I get the impression the Druid saw more than he let on when he read my aura or whatever. I want answers. If I go home, I go back to being ordinary."

"Are you not afraid? You saw the dog. What if there are more than the one?" Oddr asked. "Better ordinary alive than special dog food."

"Of course, I'm afraid, but I've spent my life walking on eggshells and jumping at my own shadow." Grace gestured to the intersection. "If you're scared, the south path will take you to the parking lot, and from there you can find civilization. I'm going to check out this wold-ford."

Oddr gazed south for a long moment before trotting after Grace. "You will need a guide as much as I need protection," the tomte said. "You may know these woods, but you do not know what you might run across. I can help you in that regard."

"I'll go slowly, so you can keep up," Grace said, tempering her pace.

"You need not worry about me," Oddr said from five yards ahead. "We tomte can cover short distances in the blink of an eye. Sadly, we are not good long-distance runners."

"It's only a couple hundred yards to where we go off the trail." Grace was tempted to break into a jog; the sun was nearing the horizon. She settled for a brisk stride. Along the way, she watched for another stout stick in case the black dog returned.

They hiked in silence for five minutes. Grace almost missed the faded sign marking the approach to Widow's Mound. A faint path wove among the trees toward a round hill. Over the centuries, the forest had surrounded the mound, but few trees grew on it.

"This is the place," Grace remarked as they picked their way through the woods. The hair on her arms stood up, and a chill ran down her spine; it had nothing to do with the evening cold. She found a fallen tree limb and clutched it for reassurance. Ahead, she could see the ditch, brackish water concealing the depth.

"I put a log across over this way," Oddr said, circling to the right. It would be easy enough for Grace to pick up the tomte and hop across; she didn't know if he would put up with the indignity.

While Grace had to watch her footing carefully in the fading light, the tomte had no problem weaving among the trees, brush, and roots to a fallen tree spanning the ditch. Oddr crossed the log with surefooted confidence. Grace took a tentative step to make sure it didn't shift or roll under her weight. Satisfied, she followed the tomte.

"Where is it?" Grace asked, peering up the hill. She spotted a shimmering at the summit of the mound, like a heat mirage over asphalt. Movement in her peripheral vision caught Grace's attention. The black dog prowled around the base of the hill, the ember red eyes giving it away. Grace shifted her weight, and a twig snapped under foot. The red motes zeroed in on her.

Grace backed away, though it took her farther from the log bridging the ditch. They were on the east side of the mound; she remembered the beast's reluctance to enter sunlight.

"Oddr, you should run, or do your trick to blink away, while I have its attention," Grace whispered. Every step was cautious; the last thing she needed was to catch her heel on a root and fall. "Maybe take the wold-ford back home."

"Leave you to face it alone?" Oddr's voice quaked.

Grace risked a glance over her shoulder. The last few rays of sunlight piercing the woods cast patches of illumination on the western slope of the hill. She angled her path of retreat. The fading light wouldn't last long.

"Oddr, you see the dead tree behind me to my left?" she asked. The hound continued to stalk toward her, picking up its pace. "When I tell you, knock it over toward me."

"I hope you know what you are doing," Oddr replied from behind the tree. The dog's head turned in Oddr's direction.

Grace brandished her stick at the creature. "No!" she shouted. "Over here, you dumb dog!"

She flicked her eyes west. The disk of the sun touched the horizon. She turned and dashed the last few yards into a patch of sunlight. She spun as the beast bounded over the moat. It charged up the hill, slaver dripping from its obsidian fangs.

"Now!" she screamed. Time ground to a snail's pace. Grace jammed her impromptu club into the oncoming maw. The dog's teeth clamped down around the branch, the wood crunching as the hound shook its head, trying to tear the branch from Grace's grasp.

A sharp crack sounded from her left as the branchless trunk tilted, then snapped. Falling in slow motion, its arc would carry the tree behind her, not in front of her as she had planned. Grace released the branch and threw her arm around the dog's neck. It dropped the tree limb to snap at Grace, but she was too fast. She yelled as she twisted her body and threw all her might into spinning the dog around her.

Despite its bulk, the black canine rolled into the sunlit leaves and scrambled to its feet. As it tensed to spring at Grace, the tree finished its descent, driving the beast to the ground with a sickening crunch. In the orange light of the setting sun, the dog's eyes faded from red to brown. The beast groaned and sank to the earth. As its body fell into shadow, its outline became indistinct, and the creature faded into the gloom.

"It worked!" Oddr trundled down the hill. "Sorry if my aim was off; the tree did not want to cooperate."

Grace picked herself up, her heart thumping. She had fallen to one knee as she had thrown her weight into wrenching the dog into position. As adrenaline faded, she felt stinging pain from her legs. Tears in her leggings showed where the hound's claws had raked at her as it scrabbled for footing. Several scratches on her thighs were bleeding, but they seemed superficial.

"Are you hurt?" Oddr asked.

"Nothing a gallon of disinfectant won't fix," Grace replied, glancing at the empty spot where the dog had laid. "I was hoping we could knock it out and pitch it through the wold-ford."

"I have to say, I am impressed." The hollow voice originated from the summit of the mound, near the shimmering air Grace assumed marked the ford. "That was a clever bit of trickery. Your forefathers would be proud."

"Who's there?" Grace demanded. She took several steps along the slope to see past a large tree near the peak. Oddr followed at her heels. Leaning against the tree, illuminated by the waning dusk, a man watched her with black eyes. He was wearing blue jeans and a buckskin jacket; his weathered face and braided black hair reminded Grace of her Venezuelan great-uncle.

"Who am I?" The man took a hand-rolled cigarette out of his jacket pocket and smiled. He stuck it between his lips and then held open his hand. A small flame flickered in his palm, illuminating the crags on his leathery face as he lit the cigarette. He took a long drag. "You could call me Mr. Smoke," he said, exhaling a cloud.

Beside her, Oddr froze, his eyes wide and bulging. Grace noticed the tomte's distress and peered at Mr. Smoke intently. Behind the façade stood another shadowy form. This countenance had an animal skull for a face, and its gangly limbs ended in skeletal, long-fingered hands. One of the hands clutched a lump of stone the size of a softball. The creature's lean form was wreathed in smoky shadow, similar to the hound.

"So, you can see me as I am? Impressive." The human face of Mr. Smoke smiled, while the skull merely cocked in curiosity. "Fear not. I have no quarrel with a daughter of the Feathered Serpent. I wore this seeming to put you at ease."

Grace focused on the human-looking mirage. It also clutched the stone in its free hand. "What are you?"

"I was old before *yunega*, the white men, came to this land. I dwelled in the minds and shadows of the First People who dwelled here and then the tribes who followed before they, too, were driven away." Mr. Smoke took another draw on the cigarette; his shadowy true form pantomimed the movements. "The *yunega* great-spirits had their war, and magic was snuffed, like a fire in the rain. They beat the war drums again, and magic trickles back into this world. My people are gone, but my anger remains."

Leaves rustled in a sudden breeze. "Is that why you've been letting creatures loose on the Dunwold?" the Druid demanded. He and the faerie stood at the foot of the mound, across the ditch.

"Wrong-Eyes, I was wondering if you would show." Mr. Smoke smiled and exhaled smoke through his nose. "I have to admit, I did not smell your pale medicine. Twice in one day, I have been impressed."

"It seems every ancient power with a mad-on wants to talk to—" The Druid spotted Grace. "Didn't I tell you to go home, or are you part of this?"

"First of all, you don't get to tell me to do anything," Grace snapped. "Second, I'm not part of whatever the hell this is."

Mr. Smoke chuckled. "You want no part of the pale medicine. I can see in your blood that Wrong-Eye's people have wronged yours across history. His ancestors built their world on the backs of yours."

"I want no part of whatever *brujería* you're cooking up either," Grace retorted. "I don't need you to remind me what my ancestors suffered. It follows me every day. People tell me I'm too dark, too light, too *gringo*, or whatever based on how I look, how I dress, or how I talk.

"What I do know is your pet shadow dog was ready to rip my throat out." Grace jabbed an accusatory finger at Mr. Smoke. "I get that you're mad over history, but a monster you turned loose killing some random person is not going to make up for the past."

"I like her," Pixel remarked. "She has fire."

"She's right," the Druid said. Using his staff, he vaulted the ditch. "Whatever atrocities my so-called ancestors may have committed, what we do today doesn't change it. Blood won't balance the scales."

"No, it won't, Wrong-Eyes." Mr. Smoke glowered at the Druid. The eyes of the skull-face glowed red. "Blood alone won't balance the scales. I want you to give my kind all the medicine from the old desert tribes of Avram. You can keep your medicine and take your spirit-folk back over the ocean. We will sweep the *yunega* from the land."

"Even if I could, why would I agree to that?" Leaves swirled around the Druid's feet as he approached the summit of the mound. "Don't get me wrong, your people, or rather their descendants, will get their magic back. They were rooked over the past few centuries. But I won't give anyone the power to do what you described."

"This crossing goes to the Summer World," Mr. Smoke said, hefting the stone. "I can also open it to the Shadow World and release more creatures of the hungry darkness. I can open it to the Winter World and draw forth the frozen spirits."

Grace focused. Both versions of Mr. Smoke held the stone in the same spot. She eased a couple of steps closer to Mr. Smoke.

"You assume I won't slam the wold-ford shut," the Druid challenged. A gust of wind roared over the mound, sending leaves tumbling and trees swaying.

"Save your theatrics, Wrong-Eyes." Mr. Smoke chuckled. "You have strong blood, but you have not mastered your pale medicine. Your champion is away, and the great-spirits remain on the Summer World. You were foolish and arrogant to think you can face me."

"I've faced worse." The Druid stepped closer. Could he see the stone as well?

"A blind bison is strong, but it is still blind, Wrong-Eyes." Mr. Smoke smiled before taking another drag on the faux cigarette. A pair of red eyes appeared in the shadows behind the Druid.

"Behind you!" Grace shouted as another black dog pounced at the Druid.

The Druid spun aside to keep the dog from clamping its jaws on him, but the impact staggered him back. He flicked his hand, and a metal blade appeared at the end of his staff as he caught himself with the other end against the earth. The dog snapped its teeth at the weapon and sidestepped a quick jab.

"Liam!" Pixel called out. "The ford!"

The wavering distortion turned obsidian. Another canine head emerged from the shimmer in the air and clamped its teeth on the Druid's ankle. The Druid awkwardly twisted to face the new threat, but the first hound jumped onto his back, bowling him into the rippling ford. The wind fell still as the Druid vanished.

"Liam!" the purple-haired girl cried, her eyes blazing violet in the gloom.

Mr. Smoke laughed and held up the stone. "Care to join him, flower child? I sent him to the Shadow World. The creatures of hungering darkness would find you most enticing."

Grace lunged forward. In a pair of heartbeats, she seized the stone in Mr. Smoke's hand. As she yanked on it, his long fingers closed around it.

"Child, do not mistake my earlier respect for weakness," Mr. Smoke hissed, the human timbre of his voice gone. "Release the key."

"I heard what you said about releasing monsters into the world," Grace snarled as she clung onto the stone with both hands. "I won't let you hurt people for some ancient pissing match."

Mr. Smoke loomed over her. "Give me the stone!"

Grace snapped a kick into Mr. Smoke's chest. Her foot struck him solidly in the torso. The impact uprooted Mr. Smoke's feet and jarred his hands free of the stone.

Grace dove through the ford, rolling on the ground as she landed. She kipped to her feet, expecting the snarling hounds to pounce on her. The beasts stalked nearby, circling a pool of silver light. The Druid stood in the middle of the illuminated patch, leaning on his staff. A torn sleeve revealed a bite wound, and blood stained one leg of his jeans.

One of the beasts spotted Grace and turned. It licked its chops and growled. Black blood trickled from a wound in its flank, and it dragged a rear leg.

"Hey!" The Druid jabbed at the distracted hound, causing the beast to whirl and snap at the blade. The other dog spotted Grace from the other side of the glowing circle. Grace sprinted into the radiance before the beast could reach her.

The shape of the hill mirrored the regular world, but the vegetation consisted of brittle grass, low weeds, and a smattering of stunted trees. Shadows leeched the color from the terrain. Even under the glow around the Druid, the plants reminded Grace of a black and white photo. She and the Druid were splashes of color in the monochrome landscape. That and the glowing red eyes of the two dogs.

"What are you doing here?" the Druid demanded, pulling his staff out of reach of the snapping jaws. "Not that I don't appreciate help, but now you're stuck here until I figure out how to open the wold-ford. Until two minutes ago, I didn't know people could physically go to the Murkwold."

"Does this help?" Grace held up the stone.

"The keystone? That changes things." The Druid eyed the pacing hounds. "It should only take a couple of seconds for me to synch this side of the ford with the home side, but we need to get past Spot and Fido."

"Can't you move this magic spotlight?" Grace asked.

The Druid shook his head. "I would have to let this one lapse before I could channel a new moon circle. I was lucky to get this one coalesced."

"Smoke is right—you're not so hot at this magic stuff," Grace remarked.

"In my defense, I haven't been at it long. We need to get back— who knows what he's doing to Pixel or your little friend." The Druid held out his staff. "Here, trade me. I can't fight dogs and make sure the ford stays open."

Grace accepted the staff. Black blood stained the dull metal blade on the end. The wood tingled in her hands—Grace half expected an electric shock. "I'll try not to break it. What's the plan?"

"I'll use the keystone to align the ford with the Dunwold and open it. You keep the dogs at bay while we run for it. Make it to the other side and skewer Mr. Smoke with that meteorite blade."

"You want me to fight the big bad? I thought you're the First Druid. This is your magic stick. I'm just a bartender," Grace protested.

"You're more than that. If anyone can harm Smoke's physical form, it will be you," the Druid countered. "Ready?"

"Fine." Grace twirled the staff-spear experimentally, then thrust the point at the closest hound. The meteor-iron blade split open the beast's snout before it could duck back. With a yelp, the creature fled into the darkness. The remaining dog paused, staring at Grace. "Whenever you're ready."

The Druid held out the stone toward the faint shimmer. Grace felt a vibration, and the distortion resolved to show the dusk-shadowed world on the other side. Mr. Smoke's true form whirled to face the ford. He splayed his long, bony fingers. A large, dripping log slammed into Mr. Smoke, batting him out of view.

"Go!" the Druid shouted. The remaining hound charged the hobbling man.

Grace whipped the staff around. The dog flinched away, but the blade still bit into its shoulder. The shadowy brute stumbled, its snapping jaws falling short of the Druid's leg. Before the animal could recover, Grace shoved the Druid through the ford.

The Druid staggered, forcing Grace to sidestep as she followed. The hound's head emerged, and Grace jammed the blade into its neck. The beast vanished back into the wavering opening, trailing black blood.

Mr. Smoke shoved the waterlogged tree trunk off his body with a sodden thud. The human-like semblance was gone, and Smoke's eyes glowed the same baleful red as the hounds'. He rose, his gangly limbs unfolding.

The Druid regained his feet and thrust an outstretched hand toward Mr. Smoke. A gale force wind buffeted the hilltop, whipping tendrils of shadow from Mr. Smoke's form. The Druid scanned the surrounding woods. "Pixel!"

"I'm fine!" the purple-haired faerie yelled from a cage of branches and roots. "Focus on him!"

"You should not have come back, Wrong-Eyes!" Mr. Smoke roared over the howling wind. "The elements mean nothing to me."

Grace took a deep breath and lunged forward with the staff-spear, driving the metal blade into what would be a man's ribcage. Grace expected the weapon to pass through Mr. Smoke like his namesake. Instead the meteor-iron blade sank into Mr. Smoke's form until the wood reached his coal-black skin.

"Stop!" Mr. Smoke howled. He clutched the staff and fought to wrest it free. "You should hate the *yunega* as much as me! Think of what they inflicted on your people! Children of the Feathered Serpent were conquered, and people of the Far Continent were sold as chattel!"

Behind Mr. Smoke, the shimmering distortion of the wold-ford changed from polished obsidian to glowing gold with a ripping sound accompanied by the tinkling of broken glass. His feet dug into the earth, the talons on his feet digging furrows, as he forced the blade halfway free of his chest.

"I can take his medicine and avenge my people's descendants and your ancestors," Mr. Smoke continued. "What are you now? A servant to the *yunega*? You take their abuse for scraps from their hearth."

"It doesn't define who I am! Only I choose that, not history, and sure as hell not you!" Grace leaned forward, digging her feet into the turf. Tar bubbled from Smoke's wound as the blade sank into Smoke's corporeal form.

The earth under Mr. Smoke's feet crumbled to dust, leaving him scrabbling as Grace drove him closer to the ford. The tinkling glass warbled to a crystalline ringing. One of his gangly arms stretched out and grabbed her wrist. Cold seeped through her skin, numbing her arm. Smoke hoarsely whispered, "I can make you strong."

Gold sparks erupted where Mr. Smoke's foot slid into the ford, and shadow boiled away from his flesh. The chiming increased in pitch as Smoke drew her toward the ford. Rage and panic welled up within Grace in equal portions. "Go to hell!"

Grace yanked the blade free with one hand and hacked down on Mr. Smoke's arm. The blade bit into the obsidian flesh. The limb buckled with a crack, and the cold hand lost its grip on Grace's arm. She reversed the staff, planted it in Smoke's abdomen, and shoved him into the ford.

"No!" Mr. Smoke's protest was cut short as the ford imploded, taking him with it.

Grace stumbled backward and sat down hard on the cold earth. Colored stars swam before her eyes.

"Grace!" Oddr rushed to her side. "Are you all right?"

Spots clouded her vision, and she rubbed her numb arm. "I'm...a little...winded," Grace mumbled.

The purple-haired girl appeared next to Oddr. She pressed something into Grace's hand. "Eat these."

Grace felt the small lumps on her palm. "What are these, magic beans?"

"No, they're jellybeans," Pixel replied. "I bet your blood sugar is low. Eat those, and I have an orange."

"What happened?" Grace chewed on the jellybeans.

"You tapped into an aspect of magic. That's why you could hurt Smoke," the Druid replied.

"So, I'm some sort of *bruja*? According to family lore, one of my *abuelas* was descended from pre-Columbian witches, but I never put much stock in it," Grace said.

The Druid popped a handful of jellybeans into his mouth. "Interesting. Your ancestry may have been a factor, but you're not a witch. While magic figured predominantly in ancient tales, something else eclipsed it. Heroes—champions who fight supernatural forces."

"Like the Champion of the Accords?" Oddr asked.

The Druid nodded as he collected his staff off the ground. He inspected the wood and twisted his hands toward each other. The staff vanished. "Exactly. My ex…well, the champion's gift allowed her to battle on behalf the Exiled Gods, but I knew the people of the Dunwold would need heroes to stand up to the less savory elements of the returning folk, not to mention possible monsters."

"Why me?" Grace stood, and when the ground wobbled beneath her feet, she leaned against the tree. She felt as though she'd run a marathon, then grabbed a live wire. "Besides a witchy grandmother, I'm nobody."

"Why not you? The Champion of the Accords was a single mother, working two jobs to get by. The greatest heroes often come from humble backgrounds—it keeps them human." The Druid fished a business card out of his pocket. "This is my contact info. I know you'll have more questions."

"That's an understatement. What about this Champion of the Accords? Could I talk to her?" Grace asked.

The Druid peered off toward the space the ford occupied, his shoulders sagging a moment, before he shook off whatever malaise clouded his expression. "She's on the Glaswold—I don't know when she'll be back. I suggest looking into a martial arts instructor for starters."

"What if I don't want to be one of these champions?" Grace countered. How could she squeeze in the time and money for karate lessons?

"Another common theme for heroes—trouble seems to find them. You're the first champion we've run across, other than Erin, so we're making this up as we go, but I bet you'll find yourself drawn to trouble, or vice versa. It stands to reason you should prepare," the Druid said. "If you're worried about the cost, we can work out some sort of scholarship to cover your instruction. Also, I can hook you up with something more practical than an ad hoc spear."

"Look at tonight. You stood up to those hounds and Mr. Smoke when you could have run," Oddr added. "You said earlier, you didn't want to go back to being nobody."

Grace rubbed her arm where Mr. Smoke had grabbed her. What else lurked out there if magic was real? "Fine. I'm in."

* * *

Feidhlim hummed an ancient tune as he guided the waitress toward the parking lot behind Safari Jack's. After crossing into the Dunwold on Beltaine, Feidhlim spent two months acclimating and learning his way around the mundane world. He was ready for his next move.

He'd spent three days over a week patronizing the bar, sizing up the potential targets among servers clad in the bar's tight khaki uniforms. Melody, a pretty blond with a southern accent, caught his eye the first day. He invested another day in glamouring other servers into divulging information as well as gaining access to the woman's social media. It had been a simple matter for Feidhlim to charm Melody into signing in on her phone while he watched. Now her roommate was out of town, and Melody was off work the next two days—plenty of time before anyone noticed she was missing.

Tonight, Feidhlim arrived two hours before the end of Melody's shift. With each visit to his table, Feidhlim layered on another thread of his glamour. By the end of her shift, Melody believed it was her idea to meet Feidhlim outside.

"Where do you think you're going?" A woman stepped into their path. Feidhlim recognized her—a tall, athletic woman with caramel skin who glared suspiciously at Feidhlim from behind the bar. Feidhlim admired how she filled out her khaki uniform, but Melody was too easy a target to pass up.

Feidhlim beamed a brilliant smile. "I am Melody's friend. Right, my dear?"

Melody nodded groggily. "He's my friend."

"Melody isn't going anywhere with you, asshole," the bartender stated.

"Do I know you?" Feidhlim asked. He hadn't spoken to the bartender while inside, but perhaps they had crossed paths before tonight.

"I know your kind," she replied icily.

"There is no need for hostility." Feidhlim added *lledrith* to his words, weaving magic into the glamour. He resisted the urge to charm the bartender and bring her along. If he had learned anything about the mundane world, it was that fae who acted solely on impulse regretted it. "Return to your bar and pour some drinks."

"I don't think so, you Glaswold piece of shit." The bartender put her hands on her hips. "Melody, you're not going anywhere with him."

"I'm not?" Melody wrinkled her brow in confusion. "What's going on, Grace?"

"This asshole hypnotized you," Grace replied. "Go inside and wait for me in the locker room."

"Melody, stay here," Feidhlim ordered. He channeled more magical energy into his next command. "Grace, go inside and forget you saw me."

The bartender stepped forward, and her fist flashed out, sending Feidhlim staggering back clutching his bleeding nose. "Go back to the Glaswold, dirtbag. Your glamour won't work on me."

"Dunnie witch!" Feidhlim drew his fighting knife from his *alfvassi*, an extra-dimensional pocket. "Get out of my way!"

The bartender's hand slipped behind her back and reappeared, brandishing a curved machete. Only the edge of the dark metal weapon glinted. "Mine's bigger, and it's druid-forged meteor iron. You keep pointing your knife at me, and I'll chop your hand off."

Feidhlim suspected she would make good on the threat. He slowly lowered his blade and sidestepped away from Melody. "Fine, take the dunnie wench."

"I know what happens when one of your kind dies—no body to draw questions." Grace pointed at Feidhlim with her machete. "If I catch you around here again, you won't walk away."

"Who—what are you?" Feidhlim demanded as he backed away.

"I'm a bartender." Grace gestured toward the parking lot with her blade. "Tell your buddies there's more than sheep on the Dunwold, and we know how to deal with wolves."

* * * * *

Jon R. Osborne Bio

Jon R. Osborne is a journalism major and veteran gamemaster turned science fiction and fantasy author. The second book in Jon's The Milesian Accords modern fantasy trilogy, A Tempered Warrior, was a 2018 Dragon Awards finalist for Best Fantasy Novel. Jon is also a core author in the military science fiction Four Horseman Universe, where he was first published in 2017.

Jon resides in Indianapolis, where he plays role-playing games, writes science fiction and fantasy, and lives the nerd life. You can find out more at jonrosborne.com and at https://www.facebook.com/jonrosborne.

# # # # #

On a Wing and a Train by Benjamin Tyler Smith

"**M**r. Landas, it's against city rules to operate an ossuary out of a mausoleum apartment zoned for a single decedent."

"They're relatives of mine, Mr. Adelvell." Landas' eye sockets burned a baleful red as he stared at me. "Can't I have visitors?"

"Sure, but *fifteen?*" I indicated a shelf packed with skulls. "What happened to their bodies?"

"Accident."

"For all of them?"

"It was a big accident." Landas pressed his bony hands together, then spread them wide. "Boom."

"And, miraculously, all their skulls survived, perfectly intact to adorn your shelf." I held up my hands. "Never mind. I'm getting them out of here."

Landas stepped forward, his eye sockets flaring. "On what grounds?"

To save them from decades of boredom? Four stone walls, a slab for a bed, and a shelf full of sun-bleached buddies. Yeah, some undead afterlife. That said, one could do a lot worse for accommodations in this city. It wasn't a pyramid, but it wasn't a columbarium niche, either. Mortus, it might've been bigger than my office-apartment back at Necrolopolis Hall.

That was a depressing thought.

"Director Grimina's warned you several times about illegal subtenants." I removed a leather sack from my black robe and reached for the first skull, but it used its lower jaw to catapult itself at me. Its crooked teeth sank into my fingers, hard enough to break the skin. I opened the sack with my free hand and flung the skull into it.

"Hey, that was uncalled for!" one of the skulls said.

"Yeah!" another shouted. "Just 'cause ya still got yer limbs is no reason—Gak!"

I swept my arm across the shelf, sending a cascade of skulls into the sack in a clatter of tumbling bones. They shouted and whined as I cinched the drawstring tight. I flexed my bruised fingers, then slung the sack over a shoulder. At the door, I paused to glare at Landas, who stood with bony hands on bony hips. "Collect your 'relatives' after their interment paperwork and fees have been processed."

"Lousy necromancer," Landas growled.

I whirled around, black energy crackling along my fingertips. "What was that?"

Landas stumbled back. "N-nothing."

I relinquished the hold on my death magic. Mina wouldn't appreciate me using it as a threat, but *I* didn't appreciate the insult, nor the bitten fingers. I shoved his door open. "Good day, sir."

"Don't exile them!" Landas called after me. "Please! You don't know what it's like out there!"

Sympathy pierced my anger as I stomped down the cramped stairwell. This was one of those days where I hated my job. Mortus, I hoped these skulls could afford to stay in Necrolopolis. The city was unique in that it served as a sanctuary for all manner of undead waiting to make the journey beyond the Veil, but like any city, it required money to manage. Individuals who couldn't afford their interment fee were cast outside the city's walls into a world not predisposed to treating the undead kindly.

I left the mausoleum complex for the cobbled streets of the city's Skeleton Quarter. Green aetherlight illuminated the stone buildings to my left and right, their rooftops lost in a twilight made especially dark by concurrent new moons. Inside the sack, the skulls writhed and chattered. I'd take them to Necrolopolis Hall and let Mina deal with them. As director, she decided the fate of repeat offenders, fee dodgers, and general malcontents. As her assistant, I kept her abreast of all the goings-on within the city.

With nearly four million undead calling Necrolopolis home these days, that made for a lot of goings-on. When was the last time I had shared a pint with Ferryman and Mortus over at Mad Molly's?

Of course, neither the god of death nor I have had much free time of late, what with the influx of arrivals from the plague-ridden lands of Delandar. Mortus hadn't left his courthouse in weeks to make room on the docket, and I couldn't remember the last time I'd slept more than two hours at a stretch. It was surprisingly difficult to find homes for thousands of leaking, stinking ghouls. Even the undead had standards.

"I need to get away for a few days," I muttered.

"Careful what you wish for," a sing-song voice answered.

I jumped and spun around, the sack of skulls slapping my backside. A beautiful lady stood nearby, her red irises shining in the gloom. "Mina? Mortus, you scared me!"

Mina's blonde ringlets danced about her face as she laughed. "Sorry, Addy! That wasn't my intent." She clasped her hands behind her back and leaned forward. "Well, maybe a little. It's rare to see a necromancer who gets spooked so easily."

Of course. I held up the sack. "I was coming to see you."

"Mr. Landas again?"

"Yes, and these 'relatives' of his haven't paid their interment fee, nor do I think they can afford it."

"I see." Mina made a face, but her smile soon returned. "I'll take care of that. *You* need to get to the Hall and gather your things. You're needed for an assignment outside the city."

Did I mention that concurrent new moons often brought ill tidings? My stomach churned. The last time I'd left the city on official business, I had chased down a gang who carved up ghouls and sold their limbs to amputees and wealthy eccentrics. It hadn't been pleasant.

"What's the situation?"

"Oh, nothing as messy as last year." She removed a letter from a blouse pocket and held it up. "An old friend of mine was killed and has returned as undead. She needs our help."

Were it anyone else, this seeming nonchalance at a friend's death and reanimation would be disturbing. But Mina was an immortal being who'd spent centuries managing the affairs of the restless dead. Many of her friends had likely walked this same path.

The skulls' chattering grew louder. I shook the sack to quiet them, but they only squawked more. I raised my voice as I asked, "She can't reach the city on her own?"

"She has to be careful of her movements at the moment." Mina took the sack of skulls from me. The chattering ceased the instant her fingers touched leather. No matter how cheerful her disposition on most days, one did not cross Lady Grimina, the half-human daughter of Mortus, god of death. "It'll be dangerous, so I've asked Lilana to tag along."

"The proprietress of Oblivion's Joy?" I blurted. Heat instantly flooded my cheeks. "Er, not that I've ever been there, mind you."

"Uh-huh." Mina's eyes twinkled. "Normally, I wouldn't believe a man who reacted that way, but you're a special case."

In truth, I had been to the city's succubus brothel on several occasions, but only for drinks. Lilana, the teasing minx, refused to accept my patronage beyond that, and it was the same with any necromancer. That afforded me a lot of frustrated time to witness how much coin she and her kind earned from both the living and the undead still capable of such things. I wasn't sure who was thirstier: the clientele or the shape-shifting demonesses.

I frowned. "Why Lilana?"

"The target is a mutual friend of ours." Mina tapped the letter with a finger. "She'll keep you safe."

"Safe? Can't I use my magic?"

"I wouldn't recommend it, not where you're going."

"That's…ominous."

"Oh, don't worry so much." Mina slipped her free arm through mine and pulled me down the street. "It'll be fine."

* * *

"How is this fine?" I murmured as I stepped onto the wooden platform at the edge of an icy lake. A mix of humans, gnomes, dwarves, and elves milled about, but I kept my distance. "How is this even a good idea?"

Lilana leaned close, her tan face shadowed by a broad-brimmed hat. "What's the matter, Addy?" Her hot breath smelled of jasmine. "Nervous?"

We faced a dark, knotty root twice the height of a man. This was a tendril of A'Ealfarnien, the World Tree, and one of many such entrances into the Root Ways, a magical roadway the elves controlled.

I shivered and drew my traveler's cloak tight. "Of course, I'm nervous. Elves don't hold necromancers in high regard." An understatement. Necromancy carried the death sentence. "If I'd known *this* was the job, I'd have refused."

"So you've said every day for the last week. And yet, here you are." She arched an eyebrow. "Why?"

On the way back to Necrolopolis Hall the evening I dealt with Mr. Landas, Mina had filled me in on the details. Lilana and I were to travel to the Graendelvale Marshlands and board a living carriage train in order to smuggle an undead elf out of the Root Ways. Her interment fee had been paid in full, with a bonus for the danger involved for me. And the danger for her was even worse than for me. If discovered, she would be exorcised immediately. That meant her soul would be obliterated, never to cross the Veil into the afterlife.

My duty in this situation was clear, and the bonus money didn't hurt, either. If all went as planned, we'd be back in the odorous confines of the city within a week, two if our undead charge wasn't ambulatory. Still, I couldn't shake the fear that something awful was about to happen. Damn those new moons. "What if we get caught?"

"Why, Addy, if that were to happen, I'd unfurl the black wings wrapped around my tight little body, scoop you up, and fly us to safety." Her smile stretched enough to reveal a fang. "As to whether you'd survive what happened next...well, we'll have to see."

Before I could entertain the thought, an oblong section of the root slid open, revealing a tunnel filled with blue luminance. A wave of balmy air blew out of the portal, and the sudden warmth against my freezing cheeks sent another shiver down my spine. The blessedly hot air carried a low rumble that steadily grew to a roar. "Here's the root train," Lilana said. "Try not to gape like a fool."

A series of linked cylindrical carriages made of living wood and glass soared past the portal, first as a blur and then with more detail as the train slowed. Each carriage was a work of art unto itself: richly colored wood panels adorned the outer walls; trim so freshly painted it looked wet bordered each window and doorway; leafy canopies adorned the rounded roofs, fed by water misting from the root's ceiling; and ornate scrollwork ran along the carriages' bottoms, the runes glowing with soft white light.

Lilana jabbed my arm. "You're *gaping*."

I snapped my jaw shut, but the sense of awe remained. The whole setup raised many questions. Where had the elves come up with such an idea? How had they grown the train carriages? How did they even fit? The root wasn't physically big enough to hold the train and all that empty space between the ceiling and the carriages' canopies. And what happened when the World Tree's tendrils shrank the further they went from the trunk?

Fae magic was a wondrous thing, indeed.

As the train came to a halt, a single carriage filled the oval portal. Its doors opened, and a forest sprite drifted out on fluttering wings.

"All aboard!"

Lilana and I hung back in the rear as everyone lined up. A group of dwarves huddled nearby, miners if the pickaxes and hammers were any indicator. They laughed and carried on about how much ale they'd pound down between here and their destination.

A drink wouldn't be a bad thing right about now, that was for sure. I licked my lips, and tried to steady my nerves as we boarded the train.

Lilana pressed a hand against my back and gave me a gentle push. "No going back now," she whispered.

Red moss covered the floor of the entrance carriage, soft and rich like the carpets in Necrolopolis's courthouse. A canopy fashioned of green vines adorned the ceiling, the leaves glowing with ambient light. Bright will-o'-the-wisps floated about, drawn to the magic coursing through the luxurious vehicle.

A tall, fair-skinned elf in green and red livery examined my pass and handed me a key, then pointed. "You're in Sleeper Carriage Two, sir. Please enjoy your trip."

We stepped into the next carriage, a long hallway lined with doors on either side. Ahead of us, a young gnome couple in the frills and lace traditional for newlyweds waited as a fairy bellhop floated out of their quarters and motioned for them to enter. The two disappeared into the room, giggling and sighing as the door shut. Given the way they were hanging on each other, they wouldn't be dressed for long. *Must be nice,* I thought as the bellhop fluttered past me toward the entrance carriage.

I checked my key for the room number, then realization struck. Lilana was with me. And succubi needed certain things to survive! I turned toward her, my heart pounding. "So—"

Lilana held up a key and pointed to another door. "Mina paid for separate quarters."

"Ah. I see." *Well, at least the gnomes will enjoy themselves.*

"It's for your own good, you know. Necromancer blood is too intoxicating for succubi." She flashed another fanged grin. "I wouldn't stop until you died of exhaustion."

I looked at her for a long moment. "And that would be bad, because?"

She laughed. "Oh, stop!"

* * *

I had just shut the door to my room when the train lurched forward. The sudden movement threw me onto the narrow bed. All around me, the floor, walls, and ceiling hummed with the magic that kept the large vehicle levitating along the Root Ways. Aside from the bed, the room contained a chest of drawers, a small desk, and a three-legged stool. The three big pieces of furniture had all been bolted to the floor, so I didn't have to worry about my bed suddenly upending if the train rounded a sharp bend. I considered using the chest, but decided to keep my bag on the bed for now.

If something happened, I'd need to make a quick escape, and I really didn't want to leave my clothes behind.

There wasn't much left to do but sit and watch the scenery go by. I didn't think there'd be much to see in an oversized root system, but the Root Ways traversed a subterranean world as vibrant and complex as the surface. And whether through some fae magic or some natural aspect of Λ'Ealfarnien, the further along we went, the more transparent the root's walls became. Blue luminance soon gave way to rocky canyons, underground rivers, and "fields" of glowing mushrooms tended by kobold farmers.

Someone knocked, and I jumped. How long had I been gawking at the scenery? I stumbled over to the door. Lilana stood in the hall, a note in her hand. "Time to meet our client."

"They're already here?" That meant they were on the train before we boarded. "Couldn't we have snuck them off back in Graendelvale?"

"And miss out on a romantic getaway with me?" Lilana hooked an arm through mine. "Perish the thought."

"Says the woman who has separate quarters from me," I reminded her.

She laughed as she led me back through the entrance carriage. The forest sprite from earlier sat in a tiny chair suspended over the exit. The diminutive creature cradled a will-o'-the-wisp in her hands and spoke into it. The other wisps floating around buzzed with energy and her voice seemed to come from all of them as she said, "Now approaching Fyrenia. We will be stopping for a quarter hour!"

I suppressed a shiver. Fyrenia was deep within elven lands.

If that bothered Lilana, she gave no outward sign. *Maybe with so much of her attention on anatomy, she didn't have much interest in geography?*

We entered a lounge filled with plush sofas, game tables, and a bar fully occupied by the dwarves. Lilana pointed. "They're in the next carriage."

"How do you know so much about root trains?"

Lilana removed her hat and used its brim to shield her face from the others. Her features shifted from dark to pale. "My *dear* Addy, this isn't my first time in the Root Ways." She wiggled her now-pointed ears.

"Don't do that!" I hissed.

Lilana laughed, and the sound drew the attention of the dwarves. One eyed the succubus's shapely form and raised his frothy tankard in salute. "Och, now that's what I like to see! Am I right, lads?"

The raucous dwarves roared their approval. Lilana turned to favor them with a smile, her appearance fully human again.

"Can't you take this more seriously?" I snapped as we entered Sleeper Carriage One.

Lilana stuck out her tongue. "You worry too much." She pointed. "That's the room we want."

"You don't worry enough." I rapped on the indicated door. "What if exorcists found us?"

"Enter!" a deep voice called from within.

I slid the door open. "Excuse us—"

A tall elf in chain armor stood between a bed and coffee table, a bandage about his head and one arm in a sling. A bared sword lay on the mattress, its blade sparkling with metallic luster. Silver, rather than the laminated wood preferred by most elves. And silver blades went to only one class of warrior in elf society: exorcists.

A trap!

I started to slam the door, but Lilana stopped it with two fingers. "Not so fast, Addy." She stepped across the threshold. "It's been awhile, hasn't it, Ser Belnor? You look like you've seen better days."

I'd never seen an elf show any emotion, much less blush, but Belnor's fair skin turned several shades of red. "Lilana, you're looking...different."

Lilana's features shifted into the alabaster-skinned elf from the lounge. "Keeps things interesting, wouldn't you agree?" Her long blonde hair suddenly curled up into ringlets, and her green eyes turned red. "Or was it Mina you always favored?"

Belnor's face grew redder still.

Lilana giggled as she shifted back into the tan woman. She pulled me into the room and shut the door. "So, what's new?"

Before Belnor could reply, a disembodied voice asked, "Is this the necromancer?"

I jumped, then cursed. Who ever heard of a necromancer afraid of spirits? I could just imagine Mina's laughter at my expense. "I'm Adelvell, assistant to Director Grimina of Necrolopolis. Who are you?"

Flashes of yellow light shone through the room's window from a mine or grotto the train passed by. That light dimmed and warped as the translucent spirit of an elf appeared in front of the glass. She wore long flowing robes splashed with washed-out colors. "I am Idrefe, Maester of the Eleventh Circle."

My jaw dropped. Our client was an *exorcist*?

"Ids!" Lilana threw her arms around Idrefe. Her skin started to sizzle from the exorcist's holy magic, but she didn't seem to mind.

Idrefe returned the embrace. "I had forgotten your kind can touch spirits, Lilly. It's a welcome sensation." She studied me over Lilana's shoulder. "Thank you for coming, Adelvell. Give Mina my best."

How had an exorcist become friends with a death demigoddess and a succubus? I'd have to hear *that* story later. "You can give her your best when we get to Necrolopolis." I frowned. "That's why we're here, right? To help you escape?"

"Not exactly." Idrefe broke free of Lilana's embrace. "We need you—both of you—for a special mission. Please sit."

Lilana and I shared a look, then we sat on the small couch bolted against one of the cramped room's walls. Belnor poured tea for us both, his movements practiced and graceful despite only having use of one arm. If it embarrassed the warrior to be reduced to serving tea to a necromancer and succubus, he didn't show it.

"What sort of mission?" Lilana's blistered skin had already healed as she put the cup to her lips. She took a sip of the rose-scented liquid and gave a satisfied sigh. "You always make the best tea, Belnor."

Idrefe floated around the room as if she were pacing. "Three months ago, my party set out from Ith'Lingar for the Anatolian Northlands, to hunt the demon R'Nal after he infiltrated the Root Ways." Idrefe spread her arms. "As you can see, things did not go according to plan."

My heart skipped a beat. R'Nal the Mindless? A powerful demon with a taste for pure souls, he made the mistake of consuming a holy man of legend known only as the Paladin, who unleashed all of his magic right before his soul was devoured. The magic shattered R'Nal's mind and filled him with an insatiable hunger. Hell expelled him for this, at great cost to Legion's numbers. Necrolopolis also suffered during that time, as the city lay at the point where the Veil was thinnest. That had been well before my time, but the city's denizens still spoke of it.

"He was invisible." Belnor grimaced. "By the time we sensed his evil aura, it was too late."

"R'Nal struck me down, and wounded Belnor, when he rushed to my aid. My other six companions fell quickly." Idrefe clutched her robes so tightly, I expected the fabric to rip, even though it was only a spectral illusion. Through gritted teeth, she added, "He immolated their flesh and devoured their souls."

"You have my condolences," I murmured. As someone who worked with both the dead and undead, I was keenly aware of the immortal nature of sentient souls. For their lives to be snuffed out permanently was unconscionable, even if they were exorcists who did the same to others. At least, the exorcists could argue there were times they had no choice.

"I used the last of my power to drive R'Nal away, but he still plagues this part of the Root Ways, near the Prismatic Expanse. Worse yet, he targets exorcists and clerics specifically." Idrefe balled her translucent hands into fists. "I can't rest, not until my land is rid of this monster."

My stomach tied itself in knots. "You don't mean—"

"Lilana, as a fellow demon, you can neutralize R'Nal's invisibility. Adelvell, you must lend me your necromantic strength." She shook her fist. "Together, we will stop this monster before it can kill any more innocents."

The door's lock suddenly clicked, and the door slid open with a bang. Elf warriors stood outside, flanking one in robes similar to Idrefe's. "The death energy came from this room!"

I jumped up from the couch and spun to face the door. *Mortus!* They must have detected Idrefe when she manifested. I drew on my magic. I couldn't do much against mortal elves and their silver weapons, but I could at least neutralize the exorcist's magic. I raised my hands—

Cold silver pressed against my neck. "Relinquish your magic," Belnor demanded. "I'd hate to stain my quarters with your foul blood."

What in the Eighteen Hells was Belnor thinking? I glared at him, but he shook his head ever so slightly.

Idrefe had vanished, her apparition had fled back to whatever object she was bound to. And as for Lilana, the succubus had transformed herself into a proper elf exorcist, her silver-inlaid robe marking her as one of much lower rank than either Idrefe or this newcomer. She pressed herself against the back wall, eyes full of fright.

"It seems like you have things well in hand, Ser Belnor," the exorcist in the hall said.

"I hoped reinforcements were on the way, Maester Aelfus." Belnor backed up to make way for a pair of warriors, who entered the room and clapped manacles around my wrists. My magic power drained out of me, and I silently cursed. Mage bindings, a specialty of exorcists and witch hunters. It couldn't completely block my innate abilities, but I'd be capable of very little.

Aelfus studied me. "Who is this human?"

"A necromancer, come to steal the remains of Maester Idrefe and her companions." Belnor nodded toward Lilana. "The maester's remaining apprentice detected the death magic in this one, so we distracted him until help arrived. Your presence is most welcome."

"Necromancy?" Aelfus's expression hardened. "That's a grave crime, if true. Is it, human?"

Yeah, because that's what any sane man would admit to. I pointed with my bound hands. "This elf must've taken one too many blows to the head! I don't know what he's talking about!"

"'This elf' is the honor guard of Maester Idrefe, my mentor and one of the greatest exorcists of the age!" Aelfus jabbed me with a finger. "I trust him implicitly, and if he says you're a necromancer, then so be it. Your presence dishonors Idrefe's glorious memory!"

The warriors tensed, their weapons gleaming in the light of the will-o'-the-wisps. Fear shot through me. *Lilana, that winged rescue is looking pretty good right about now!*

"Stay your hands!" Belnor barked. "I will execute him myself, but not until Maester Idrefe's remains are returned to Ith'Lingar."

"Very well." Aelfus waved a hand at his sword-happy warriors. "Secure the prisoner. We'll question him later."

* * *

A elfus's warriors tossed me in the baggage carriage at the rear of the train. They locked the door, but not before laughing at the fate awaiting me in Ith'Lingar. *Wonderful.* I'd been betrayed by my client, captured by a stuck-up exorcist, and thrown into a glorified closet with mage bindings. Could the day get much worse?

Bad thing to think, I know. It could always get worse.

And where was Lilana? Last I'd seen of her, she was still in Belnor's room. Knowing her insatiable appetites, she and the wounded warrior were probably getting *reacquainted.* Damn her sexy hide. I needed rescuing or I was a dead man!

I brooded about that until the will-o'-the-wisps in the carriage buzzed with energy. *"We will soon be entering the Prismatic Expanse,"* the forest sprite conductor said. *"Please enjoy the view from the lounge and dining carriages. For those with light sensitivities, remain in your rooms with the curtains drawn."*

Well, I wasn't going to escape by sitting here. I clambered onto a crate and reached for a will-o'-the-wisp. Its spectral wings thrummed against my palm, but it made no move to escape. I walked around the carriage, shining the wisp on stacks of bags and satchels. I found random baubles, an endless supply of clothing, and locked chests for merchant or noble passengers. One bag contained a treasure trove of Gnomish prophylactics, sized accordingly. Three guesses as to who *those* were for.

The wisp's light fell on an iron cage bound to the wall with stout ropes. Six wooden boxes lay inside the cage, each lacquered and inlaid with silver runes. A pouch fashioned of green lagola leaves rested atop the boxes.

The pouch's contents hummed with spiritual energy. I tapped into my very limited magic reserves and saw a soft glow emanating from inside, the color of a soul I'd just met. "Maester Idrefe, I presume?"

"Astute." Idrefe appeared next to me, her ghostly form bright in the darkness. "I apologize for Aelfus's behavior. Belnor and I did not anticipate his coming here."

I spread my arms as far as the manacles allowed. "He's doing what exorcists do."

"Most of them, yes." She touched the cage's lock, and it opened. "Take the pouch."

I picked it up, marveling at the silky feel of the lagola leaves. I untied the cord securing the pouch's opening, then reached inside and withdrew a silver ring. It bore the mark of the Eleventh Circle, and glowed with the same energy Idrefe gave off. I nodded at the boxes. "Your companions?"

She caressed the small containers. "Cremation is not our way, but their bodies were so badly burned we had little choice. At least, it made them easier to transport, something Belnor and I needed."

Something they needed? Now that I looked closer, the ring wasn't the only item radiating energy. Shimmering tendrils flowed from the boxes into the silver ring, which in turn sent energy into the surrounding area. "You've tied their spiritual essence to yours, and then tied yours to something else—" My eyes widened. "The root train?"

"Like I said, astute. Mina always knew how to pick talented individuals." She tapped the wall. "So, Adelvell, why do you think I tied my people's essence to the root train?"

R'Nal was attracted to exorcists and other wielders of holy magic. And now the train's energy "smelled" like Idrefe and her men. "You're using all of us as bait!"

"An unfortunate necessity. R'Nal kills through stealth and ambush. We must draw him into a battlefield of our choosing."

"You think a *train* is an ideal battlefield?"

"What choice do we have?" Idrefe snapped. "Every day R'Nal is allowed to roam free, people die."

"You mean exorcists die."

"Yes, exorcists." Idrefe glared. "Are you saying our lives don't matter because we cleanse the world of your *precious* undead?"

Anger flashed through me, but I pushed it down. "I'm saying this isn't about justice, not fully." I pointed at the urns. "You want revenge."

"I don't deny the vindictive desires within me." She pressed a hand to her translucent chest. "That I exist in this state is proof of that!"

I couldn't argue against that.

"Besides," she added with a thin smile, "is it not your duty to alleviate Mina's burdens by tending to the needs of the restless dead?"

Again, I couldn't argue. "All right. I'll help you, but on one condition: you're coming to Necrolopolis with us."

Idrefe recoiled as if slapped. "Once my duty is complete, I will be exorcised, as is fitting."

"No."

She shook her head. "You don't understand."

"No, *you* don't understand! Your interment fee's been accepted, and Mina's sent me to collect you." I pointed at myself with both thumbs. "That makes you my responsibility."

"I never asked for—"

"And I'll be damned if I let one of my charges perish in a Mortus-damned exorcism!" I tried to bite back the anger, but the thought of Mr. Landas pleading with me over the fate of his relatives just added fuel to the fire. "There are many who wish they had someone like me to help them in their hour of need, like you do now. Show some respect for your soul, elf!"

"That's the spirit, Addy!" a voice called from outside the carriage. One of the windows popped open and Lilana slipped inside. She swept dirt and leaves from her shapely bottom as she added, "I love a man with a backbone."

I scowled at her. "Where in the Eighteen Hells have you been?"

"Getting my hands on this." She reached down the front of her blouse and removed a small key. She arched an eyebrow. "Unless bondage is your thing?"

"Do I even want to know how you got that?"

Lilana unlocked the manacles. "Let's just say there's a certain warrior who's going to be very sore when he wakes up."

Lucky bastard. With the bindings off, I could sense my full reserve of magic, thank Mortus.

"Ids, you heard Addy," Lilana said. "We're not helping unless you come with us."

Idrefe looked uncomfortable. "It's not my place to go against the traditions of my people, Lilly. You know that."

"Oh?" Lilana crossed her arms beneath her ample breasts. "And being friends with a succubus and Mortus's demigoddess daughter is in keeping with that tradition?"

When Idrefe didn't respond, I asked, "How did that happen?"

"It's a long story." Lilana favored me with a half-smile. "Idrefe was younger and quite rigid in her thinking. Exorcise everything, no questions asked!"

"And can you blame me?" Idrefe demanded, though there was no heat to her words. This seemed like an old argument. "I completed my apprenticeship during the Fallen War."

I winced. The Fallen War hadn't been necromancy's finest hour.

"Then, a few generations ago, young Maester Idrefe and her lover—"

Idrefe gasped. "Lilly!"

"Maester Idrefe and her *attendant* Belnor were attacked by a demon and an army of imps. Their party fought bravely, but would have been overrun if not for the intervention of the director of Necrolopolis and a company of undead soldiers. Oh, and yours truly." She leaned close to me. "They're totally lovers; don't let her fool you."

"As I recall," Idrefe said, "it was *your* fault we were in that mess. R'Nal wouldn't have come our way if you hadn't been chasing him."

I blinked. "Wait, you met when R'Nal was cast from Hell?"

"And he's brought us back together!" Lilana clapped her hands. "It's fate, Ids. We'll help you defeat R'Nal and then you get to go back to the city with us. Mina will be so excited!"

Idrefe glared at her, then sighed. "Very well. Let's go to the front of the train. Belnor and I prepared a magic circle to trap R'Nal."

"Will Aelfus's goons let us through?" I asked.

"We can take the roof!" Lilana gestured at the window as the blue light of the Root Ways gave way to a wide space filled with multi-colored light. Here, the root was no longer a solid tube. Only the lower half remained, its transparent edge close enough to the window to touch.

The Prismatic Expanse lived up to its name, its outer perimeter and bottom lost somewhere out of sight. The ceiling was hundreds of feet above, and every square inch of it covered in crystals glittering with rainbow hues. "A'Ealfarnien draws strength from the crystals' light," Idrefe explained. "The light enters the exposed root and travels for hundreds of miles in either direction."

Like I said, fae magic was wondrous.

Lilana climbed onto the leafy roof, then reached back through the window. "Come on, Addy!"

I grasped her hand just as the door slid open. "All right, human, time for some questions…" The warrior's voice trailed off, his eyes widening.

With strength at odds with her size, Lilana pulled me free of the carriage and hauled me to the leafy roof all in one go. I scrambled to get a foothold, then crouched next to her in the canopy's branches. Balmy wind rippled through the leaves and tugged at the corners of my cloak, and I had to blink away sudden tears. It took me a moment to notice Idrefe had vanished again, presumably into the ring in my pocket.

"The necromancer's escaped!" the surprised warrior shouted from inside the baggage carriage.

"So much for the quiet way." Lilana bounded to her feet. "Let's go, Addy! Shake a leg!"

I carefully got to my feet, aware of how precarious my footing was. One wrong step and I could trip on a branch jutting up from the tightly woven roof. "Easy for you to say!" I called as I chased after her. "You have wings in case you fall!"

Lilana leaped from the baggage carriage to the kitchen carriage without once looking down. I slowed to test the footing of the canopy in the space between. *Maybe I could walk across the branches?*

A sword thrust through the leaves, the silver gleaming in the multi-colored light. The blade missed my legs and other, more sensitive areas, by mere inches.

I dove across the divide. "Wait for me, Lilana!"

Lilana halted, but not because of my plea. A pair of elf warriors had scrambled up through the canopy ahead of her. I came to a stop next to Lilana and turned around as two more warriors climbed to the roof.

"Front and back at the same time?" Lilana clucked her tongue. "These elves are so *naughty.*"

Aelfus joined his warriors a moment later, along with Belnor. "I see our necromancer has a companion!" He struck the roof with the butt of his staff. "What is she, your apprentice?"

Before I could reply, Lilana held a finger to her lips. "Shhhh."

Aelfus and Belnor looked at each other, then at me. I shrugged.

Lilana cupped her hands to her ears. She sniffed the air, then hissed. "He's here."

An unearthly howl rang out from the depths of the Prismatic Expanse. Belnor winced and drew his sword as the other warriors clapped hands to sensitive ears. "What in Idricaine's name is that?" Aelfus demanded.

Something slammed into the warriors behind us. There was a spray of bright blood, and one elf collapsed to the canopy roof in three pieces. The other disappeared over the side, his gurgling screams soon lost as the train plowed onward.

Idrefe materialized next to me. "Aelfus, listen to—"

"Evil spirit, be exorcised!" Aelfus raised his staff and fired a ball of white light at Idrefe.

I stepped in front of her and raised a spirit shield. White magic struck black, and both spells fizzled. Painful reverberations rippled through my hands and arms. "Damn it, Aelfus, we're not the real threat here!"

"Stay your hand, Maester Aelfus!" Belnor pleaded. "You're attacking Maester Idrefe!"

Aelfus' eyes widened. "Maester Idrefe? How are you here? In that form?"

"One last demon to slay," Idrefe growled. "Lilana, your magic! Show us R'Nal!"

Lilana's tan human form vanished as her skin turned milk-white. Curled horns sprouted from the sides of her head, and the whites of her eyes turned pitch black. Yellow irises glowed as they studied the sky. "See what I see!" she commanded.

The backs of my eyeballs tingled, the sensation so strong that my face scrunched up and tears threatened to spill out. Around me, the elves reacted similarly, even Idrefe. Then, just as quickly as the strange feeling came, it was gone. High above us, a shape coalesced into a winged creature with iridescent skin and claws that burned with purple fire. The huge demon dove straight for us, his sparkling hide brilliant, even against the crystalline ceiling.

"By the queen's throne," Aelfus gasped. *"That's* the Mindless One?"

And he wasn't alone. Dozens of imps flew alongside R'Nal. "Prepare yourselves!" Aelfus shouted. The exorcist raised a shield around himself and his warriors. I did the same for Lilana, Idrefe, and Belnor.

At the last second, R'Nal changed directions and slammed into the power carriage's roof in an explosion of leaves and splintered branches. "He's going for the train's energy crystal?" Aelfus asked. "Has R'Nal ever shown interest in such things?"

I stifled a groan. *Of course, he would go for that.* R'Nal was little more than a mindless beast who desired to feed on the souls of clerics, exorcists, and other holy warriors. And right now, the essences of six of those warriors were feeding directly into the train's power source. Why go after snacks like Aelfus and Idrefe when the main course was at the front of the train?

The imps swooped in, their claws and teeth ready to tear flesh. Three struck my shield at the same time and went flying. Two regained their senses, but the third plummeted to the bottom far below. My magic wasn't much use outside, dealing with the undead, but it could at least defend against Veil piercers like these hellspawn.

More imps swarmed the train. While a few attacked us, the majority shattered windows and entered the train's interior. Shouts of alarm and cries of pain rose up from below. "Should we help them?" I asked.

"R'Nal is the bigger threat." Idrefe held out a hand toward Aelfus. "We have to stop him!"

Aelfus stared at Idrefe. "Maester, why did you—" He paused, his mouth twisting. "Maester, how could—"

Idrefe tried to float closer, but Aelfus backed away. She sighed, and didn't react as an imp attacked my shield, its slavering jaws mere inches from her aethereal face. "You have to trust me, Aelfus. You don't have the power to face R'Nal, not on your own. Let me help."

Aelfus blasted an imp out of the sky and watched as its burning carcass plunged into the depths. He opened and closed his mouth several times. He finally said, "Very well, but only because it's you, Maester." He glared at me. "My warriors will deal with the imps. Let's stop R'Nal!"

I had to admire Aelfus. Not many people could adjust to such a drastic change in circumstances, especially when it upended deep-seated worldviews. "Right behind you!"

We dropped our shields and started running. Aelfus's two warriors climbed back down to join their comrades inside the train. Belnor stayed with Aelfus, his sword glimmering as he struck down one imp, then another. Infernal flesh sizzled, and a sickly-sweet odor wafted back toward us.

As we jumped onto the lounge car, an imp flew out of the glass skylight and landed on the roof in a broken, twitching heap. I paused long enough to look down. The lounge had been trashed, its plush furnishings splintered and splattered with the purple blood of the imps. The dwarf miners struck down the remaining hellspawn with pickaxe and hammer. One of them looked up and waved. "We'll hold down the fort, laddie!"

"Gotta keep the ale safe!" another added.

"Save me a pint!" I called, then started forward again. I wished I'd been able to bring my necromancer's shovel, or at least my dagger. With a weapon, I could've fought against these imps, but direct magical attacks wouldn't affect them. Not my magic, anyway.

Up ahead, R'Nal ripped out a huge section of the canopy and dropped down into the exposed power carriage. A bright flash of light burst from the hole, followed by a scream of rage and pain.

The train lurched suddenly, and it started to slow.

"He's fallen into the circle!" Idrefe said. "We've got him— Adelvell, look out!"

An imp flew at me, claws raised. Something shoved me from behind, and I sprawled on the leafy canopy, a sharp branch stabbing my right palm. I cursed and yanked the splinter out. Blood welled up and dripped onto the leaves.

Lilana tore into the imp with her bare hands. The imp squealed in pain, but the succubus showed no mercy. She ripped its limbs off and cast it over the side before turning my way. Her black-and-yellow eyes fixated on my bloody hand. She licked her lips, then shook her head. "Keep going, Addy!" Her clothing melted away, and she unfurled a pair of large, black wings from around her tight little body. She beat them several times and took flight. "I'll deal with these pests!"

Aelfus and Belnor had ranged ahead of Idrefe and me, with one carriage separating them from our destination. I scrambled to my feet and ran. True to her word, Lilana kept the imps off my back. Whenever one got close, she swooped in and eviscerated it, her laughter pealing through the sky. "More! More blood!"

"Remind me never to get on her bad side," I murmured to Idrefe.

"You have no idea."

Aelfus and Belnor dropped down into the hole R'Nal had made, and their shouted commands mixed with the demon's howls of fury. Energy crackled and buzzed, and the sound of silver against claw rang out.

I jumped onto the power carriage's roof and looked down. A giant crystal took up the center of the carriage, its pulsing form encased in glass. Two elf sorcerers cowered on one side of it, their magic disrupted.

Aelfus and Belnor stood on the other side of the crystal, facing R'Nal. The demon crouched inside Idrefe's magical circle. The spell had created a confinement field too small for the demon's massive frame, and R'Nal's leg muscles bunched up as he struggled to stand.

Belnor tried to deliver a fatal strike, but R'Nal had enough strength to block each attack with his glowing claws. Even so, black blood wept from several minor wounds. R'Nal could be hurt, but it would take a lot more than that to kill him.

Aelfus leaned against his staff and chanted a spell. The force field surrounding R'Nal flashed and crackled as more energy poured into it. R'Nal growled and pushed harder. Idrefe added her power to Aelfus', and I encased their force field with a spirit shield. If R'Nal broke through one, he wouldn't have the strength for the other.

I hoped.

The severed head of an imp landed at my feet. Body parts rained from the sky, and Lilana let out a shriek filled with bloodlust. *It's good to see someone who enjoys their work,* I thought.

R'Nal roared in defiance and stood straighter. Sweat poured off Aelfus' face as he staggered. Belnor delivered a flurry of blows, but R'Nal deflected them. As skilled as the elf warrior was, his wounded arm hampered him.

"Incoming!" Lilana shouted.

A disemboweled imp dropped through the hole in the roof. It bounced off R'Nal's force field and crashed into Aelfus. Exorcist and dying imp landed in a tangle of slashing claws and ropy intestines. Belnor turned to aid the stricken elf.

A crack formed in the force field.

"What now?" I asked.

"In my current state, I can't hold it." Idrefe held out her hand. "Lend me your strength, Adelvell! I can channel your necromantic power through me, turning it into holy magic."

That explained why Idrefe had so willingly given me her anchor. I held up the ring. "Doing so will forever link us. Are you ready for that?"

"I've already broken faith with my kind by becoming undead in the first place." Idrefe scowled. "If we can defeat R'Nal, I care not what happens to me!"

"Didn't I tell you to have respect for your soul, elf?" I pushed the ring against the wound in my palm. The metal drank up the blood until its silver surface turned crimson. Idrefe's consciousness touched mine, a result of this new connection. I sent magical power into her, as I would with a spirit I'd made a formal contract with.

She hovered closer. "Yes, I feel it. Not as much power as I had in life, but much more than my current existence provides."

As if to prove it, she touched the wound on my hand with an aethereal finger. It closed up, the blood disappearing as my body reabsorbed it. "Thanks," I muttered. It felt weird, having my own power used on me.

She turned back to the hole in the roof. "Now, let's—"

The force field around R'Nal shattered. With a roar, he leaped into the air and broke through my spirit shield. I quickly raised another around myself, right as R'Nal struck me with a heavy shoulder. The smaller shield held, but the force of the blow sent me flying from the roof.

"Adelvell!" Idrefe shouted.

The train shrank from view as I plummeted past the half-cylindrical Root Way. I kept a death grip on Idrefe's ring and fought the urge to scream. *What a miserable way to go!*

"Addy, let go of your shield!" a voice cried from overhead.

I did as commanded, and a pair of slender arms wrapped around my waist. Hot breath tickled my neck. It smelled of jasmine. "Nice timing, Lilana."

"In my line of work, it's all about timing." Lilana beat her wings. We rose toward the train.

"We're going back? What happened to taking me someplace safe?"

"It wouldn't be safe, since I've smelled your blood," she said, her voice husky. "Besides, business before pleasure."

"Your business *is* pleasure!"

A translucent blur shot away from the power carriage roof. It was Idrefe, with R'Nal in hot pursuit. The demon opened his mouth and spat a fireball. The infernal flames harmlessly passed through the exorcist, and this infuriated the demon. His claws changed from purple to red.

I'll not let him devour me! Idrefe's defiant thought rippled along our spiritual connection.

I started to urge Lilana to fly faster, but a thought occurred to me. *Idrefe, get as close to us as you can, then turn toward R'Nal.*

What are you planning?

Something reckless. I gripped the ring. *Trust me. It's the only way to bring this to a satisfying end.*

There was a long pause. *Very well.*

Idrefe led R'Nal in a wide circle back toward the train. At my urging, Lilana positioned us right above the power carriage. Below us, Belnor and Aelfus climbed onto the roof and looked up. Aelfus pointed his staff at R'Nal, but I raised my hand. "Don't interfere!"

Idrefe sailed toward us, then spun in midair to face R'Nal. The demon roared in triumph and struck her with his claws. Idrefe shrieked as the demon opened its jaws and sucked her inside.

"Maester, no!" Belnor and Aelfus shouted in unison.

Maester, yes. I opened the well of my magic. It poured across the connection into Idrefe's soul. Black death energy suddenly blazed a brilliant white.

R'Nal writhed in agony. He clutched at his throat with one hand and scratched at his stomach with the other. Coughing, he tried to expel Idrefe's ghostly form, but she dove back inside. Her thoughts echoed in my head: *Die, foul monster! You don't belong in this world!*

Light shot from R'Nal's eye sockets and nostril slits. When he opened his mouth to scream, more light spilled out. His body glowed with the intensity of the sun. He let out one last shriek and vanished in a thunderclap.

My magic fled, and I slumped in Lilana's arms. The last thing I saw before passing out was Idrefe descending to join us. She appeared whole and hale.

Well, as hale as a loose spirit could be.

* * *

"I ds!" Mina threw her arms around Idrefe and pulled her into a tight embrace. Her blonde ringlets bounced about her face as she laughed. "It's been ages!"

"First Lilly, now you." Idrefe returned the embrace, then looked around the square before the Eternal Gate. "Is this how you welcome all the interred to your city?"

"Just good friends, and only if they're not leaking fluids." Mina sized up Belnor's bandages. "Bel, you might not make the mark."

Belnor bowed. "It's been far too long, Lady Grimina."

"Ever the formal one, I see. Lilana, couldn't you break him of his stiffness?"

"I tried, but no matter how many times it was, he never would—!" Lilana put a hand to her mouth, but I could see the smile in her eyes. "Oh, wait, you meant something else."

Idrefe coughed. "It's good to be here, much as I'm loath to admit it." She frowned. "I'm not sure what kind of welcome we'll receive, though."

"Better than you think," I said. "We don't have many elves here, but they all have similar stories to yours. They fled their homeland to avoid exorcism."

"We have living elves with us, too," Mina added. "They helped their undead loved ones escape and had to flee themselves."

Idrefe lowered her head. "I may have persecuted some of those families."

"That was before you met us, Ids," Lilana pointed out. "After you got to know Mina and me, you reserved exorcisms for out-of-control spirits and demons like R'Nal."

Idrefe still didn't seem convinced. I removed the lagola leaf pouch from my cloak and gave it to Belnor. "Give it a chance. There'll be trouble, no doubt, but there'll be opportunities. To forgive, to heal, and to help."

"Hey, since when did Addy become an optimist about anything?" Mina looked from Idrefe to Lilana. "What'd you do to him?"

Lilana threw an arm around my shoulder. "What didn't we do to him?"

My cheeks burned as I pushed her off. *If only that were true!* "I'm glad we're back and that Idrefe agreed to come with us."

And, of course, there was the fact that we had brought down a demon who had given Legion a run for its coins. Even better, we had saved the day deep in elven lands, with the three things the elves hated so much: necromancers, demons, and the undead. The gods really did have a wicked sense of humor.

Aelfus must have realized that, as well. He had agreed to let us go with no questions asked. To cover our tracks, he claimed victory in the battle against R'Nal, but he couldn't have done it without Belnor, who had valiantly given his life delivering the killing blow to the hated demon. There would be no mention of me or Lilana. I hated that the truth wouldn't get out, but if it spared me from extradition to the elf queen's court, I could tolerate it.

The stuffy elf had even promised to write Idrefe from time to time. Maybe exorcists weren't as bad as I'd made them out to be.

"I'm glad you're all here." Mina turned her red-eyed gaze on me. "Especially you, Addy!" She pulled a small notebook from her pocket. "Some things have piled up while you were away. Normally, I'd let you get settled in and relax, but these issues won't address themselves."

I thumbed through the notebook. Aside from the usual noise complaints from those unfortunate enough to live near the Banshee Borough and the turf skirmishes between the ashlings and the mummies, the most pressing concern was finding proper housing for the fifteen skulls illegally camped in Mr. Landas' mausoleum-apartment. "I took the bonus money from Idrefe's interment to pay their fees," Mina said. "I didn't think you'd mind."

That money was meant for me! I opened my mouth to protest, then closed it. If she hadn't done that, the skulls would've been cast out of Necrolopolis until they could afford the fee, and there was no telling what might happen to them out there.

What had I told Idrefe about respecting the value of a soul?

I sighed. "I'll get on it."

For a city of the dead, Necrolopolis sure kept me busy.

* * * * *

Benjamin Tyler Smith Bio

By day, Benjamin earns his bread as a necro-cartographer (which is a fancy way of saying he makes digital maps) for a cemetery software company, and by night, he writes about undead, aliens, and everything in between. He has two novels (Blue Crucible and Blue Salvation) in the Fallen World universe, with more planned. He also has short stories in various anthologies. He is currently writing a full length Necropolis novel.

# # # # #

The One You'd Least Expect by Chris Kennedy

"There!" Dantes said, rubbing his hands as he inspected the dire wolf trap he'd built. Although not an elf, he thought he'd done a reasonable job assembling it the way they'd shown him. It only required a knife to build, and the lack of anything artificial ensured the wolves wouldn't smell it before they sprang it.

A strange odor on the wind caught his attention and led him to a nearby path through the woods. A bundle in blue lay on the side of it fifty feet in front of him. The smell he was tracking had to have been the blood, which puddled near the blue shape.

Although excited by the scent, he didn't rush up to the human—he could see her face; it was definitely a human female—instead, he scanned the forest, looking for a trap. It wasn't an uncommon ploy for someone to fake an injury to draw unsuspecting victims in close, especially in the depths of the forest where there was nowhere to run and no one nearby to call to for aid. If that was what the human was doing, she would get more than she bargained for.

He didn't sense anyone else nearby—whoever or whatever had done it had obviously departed some time ago—so he cautiously approached her. The blood appeared real, and it didn't match the smell of any blood he was familiar with. Unfortunately, he'd never smelled human blood, so he couldn't tell if the aroma was that or

119

something used to distract him. Distract him, it did, however, as it aroused his senses and made smelling anything else difficult.

He made a slow circuit around the woman, who did in fact appear injured. Still not sensing anyone else in the vicinity, he stepped closer and rolled the woman over. Her clothes were slashed, and she had a variety of blade wounds across her arms and torso.

The woman moaned.

"Well, that complicates things," Dantes muttered. All his young life, his mother had taught him to stay away from humans. "They'll kill you," she'd said. The few times he'd seen them had been from the edge of the forest; he'd never been this close to one before.

Still, he couldn't leave her there. That would go against everything his mother had taught him about the 'beauty of life.' While he wasn't sure he believed in such a thing, his mother had a way of discerning when he was lying or hiding the truth; he was already late, and she would question him about it.

He sighed and broke open his pack. Blessed with a naturally high constitution, he didn't carry a lot of first aid materials with him—anything that could damage him would probably kill him—but you always wanted to be prepared in the forest, or so his mother always said, so he had some dressings and other supplies with him.

He packed the worst of the wounds with his limited supply of healing moss and bound them up, then tore his shirt into more bindings for some of the lesser wounds. He was sure he'd hear about that later, too. Having done what he could, he lifted the woman from the ground.

The motion woke her. She looked into his eyes and screamed, then fainted.

He sighed again as he picked up a ground-eating jog back to his house.

* * *

"Y ou're late!" his mother called as he entered. She came out of the back room, her mouth open to scold him, but saw the burden he was carrying before she could start. "What—no, *who* is that?" she asked as he set her on his pallet.

"I don't know, Mother," Dantes said. "I found her in the forest."

She drew up short. "Did you do this to her?"

"I had no choice, Mother."

"Dantes, I have told you, life is precious!"

"No!" Dantes exclaimed finally, realizing what she was asking. "No, I didn't hurt her. I found her in the forest, already hurt. I patched up her wounds as best I could, but she was in bad shape, and I didn't think she'd last much longer."

His mother stepped closer and put a hand on the human's shoulder. "No, she won't."

"Is there anything you can do for her?"

"Me? No. I don't have any of the healing arts."

"But we can't let her die."

His mother withdrew her hand and turned toward him. "Did she see you?"

"She opened her eyes when I picked her up," Dantes replied. "What does that have to do with it?"

"I've told you; you can't be seen by the humans. They'll kill you."

"But…but…but I couldn't just let her *die!*" Dantes exclaimed. "You wouldn't have wanted *that*, would you?"

His mother sighed. "No, I wouldn't have. Even for a human." She sighed again, then straightened her shoulders and stood taller. "I can't fix her, but there is someone who can." She walked to the door—still open—stepped outside the cabin, and trilled in a loud voice.

Dantes had never heard the call before. It sounded something like a bird call but was unlike any of the birds he'd ever heard.

"What was that?" he asked when she came back inside.

"I called Uncle Ehrdan."

"He can help?"

His mother smiled for the first time. "He can. It remains to be seen, however, whether he *will*."

"The woman won't last much longer," Dantes said. "I don't know if we can—"

"What is it, Caedara?" Uncle Ehrdan asked as he strode through the doorway.

Dantes' jaw dropped. He'd known the elder wood elf lived nearby, but had no idea how he'd been able to appear so swiftly. Although not much taller than Dantes' mother, Ehrdan moved with a purpose and had a confidence that made him seem much bigger and stronger.

She nodded toward the pallet. "Dantes brought home a gravely injured female. And no, before you ask, he didn't do it; he found her that way."

Ehrdan walked to the pallet and knelt next to it. He put his hand on the woman's shoulder, much like Dantes' mother had, and closed his eyes. After a second, he stood and turned. "Did she see him?" he asked.

"She may have," Dantes' mother said.

"*Why does that matter?*" Dantes asked. "She's hurt and will die if you don't help her."

"If I help her, and she lives, she may very well bring additional people here to kill you...and us for harboring you." He turned to Dantes' mother. "This is why I told you not to take the boy in. Now he has put us—and especially me—in a perilous position. I can either save her and run the risk of losing everything I love or let her die and run the risk of displeasing our gods."

She sighed. "I couldn't let Dantes die in the forest; he was just a child. Nor can you refuse to help the human. The gods put us in this position; I suspect they have a reason for doing so, and a way for us to get back out of it again."

Ehrdan stared at her for a few seconds. "You assume a lot," he said. His shoulders slumped. "Still, you're correct. I cannot refuse to help someone in need of healing." He turned back to the pallet and knelt again, then he placed his hand on the woman's shoulder and began muttering.

Although Dantes listened intently, he couldn't make out the words Ehrdan said, nor could he even tell if they *were* words. A blue glow rose in his hands and suffused out across the human, glowing brightly on her most grievous wounds.

The woman jerked, and her breath caught, then she slumped back to the pallet.

"Is she...dead?" Dantes asked.

"No," Ehrdan said, rising slowly. He stumbled, and Dantes' mother reached out to steady him, but he waved her off. "I'll be fine," he said softly.

Dantes' eyes widened. The vibrant man—whose aura seemed to fill the cabin the times he'd been there previously—now seemed a mere shell of his earlier self.

Ehrdan rolled his shoulders a couple of times. "It's been a long time since I healed a human. They take a lot more out of you." He looked back to the pallet. "She'll likely sleep for a couple of days, then will wake up hungry." Ehrdan turned back to his sister. "It would be better if she doesn't see *him* when she wakes," he said, then he turned and left the cabin.

* * *

Shaldan slowly came to consciousness, though she kept her eyes closed because her surroundings were strange. The last thing she remembered was fighting Alagar's minions in the forest and being overcome by them. Yet, she wasn't dead—she didn't think so, anyway, as it felt like she was lying on some sort of hard bed, not the ground. There was the glorious aroma of what smelled like stew, and she realized how utterly *famished* she was.

Yet, she couldn't remember coming to this place. She went back through the battle, and there was nothing, except for... "Monster!" she yelled, sitting up.

"I see you do remember meeting my son, after all," a woman's voice said.

Shaldan looked to her left and saw a gorgeous, yet slight, woman looking at her. If the copper skin and silver eyes didn't give away her parentage, the pointed ears certainly did. Wood elf. The elf handed her a bowl and spoon. "Here," she said. "Our healer said you'd be hungry."

Shaldan took the bowl and was so hungry she started eating before she realized she didn't know where she was or who it was handing her food. Her spoon stopped halfway to her mouth.

"It's fine," the elf said with a chuckle. "If I wished you ill, I could have easily killed you while you slept."

"True," Shaldan said with an answering chuckle. The spoon finished the trip to her mouth, and her taste buds exploded in ecstasy. "That is incredible! I don't think I've ever had anything so good."

"Thank you," the elf said, "although I expect it's because your body has expended so much of its potency healing itself."

"No, this is really good..."

"My name is Caedara," the elf said. "My son's name is Dantes."

"That *thing* was your son?" Shaldan asked between bites.

"Yes," Caedara said, "and you would do well to speak better of him. He saved your life."

"He…um…he did?"

"Yes. He found you in the forest and bound your wounds until he could get here. He kept you alive—and begged the healer to cure you when the healer didn't want to."

"Why would a healer not want to heal someone?"

"Because he was worried that you, having seen my son, would want to kill him. And kill the rest of us for harboring him."

"Oh." Shaldan used the cover of taking another bite to compose her thoughts. Her memory of the monster was somewhat hazy, but she remembered purple hair and horns. The horns were the giveaway. She cocked her head as she looked at the elf. "How is it that a wood elf gives birth to a teufling?"

"I didn't give birth to him, obviously," Caedara said. "I am neither human nor devil, so it is impossible for me to have done so. I found him one day when he was just a baby. He'd been left on a small island in the middle of a stream that runs through the forest."

"On an island?"

Caedara chuckled. "Yes, an island. Even at a young age, his skin could burst into flames when he was sufficiently aroused. It took some time for him to learn to control it, and whoever left him there apparently didn't want to burn down the forest." She sat down in a nearby chair and gazed steadily at Shaldan. "I notice you didn't answer the question about wanting to kill him."

"No, but it wasn't really a question; it was more of a comment you made." Shaldan held up her hand to stop Caedara. "Still, I understand what you mean. There are plenty of people who would kill him if they saw him."

Caedara nodded. "There are many elves who think similarly, which is why I live in a cabin in the woods and not in the elf city." She stopped and raised an eyebrow.

"No," Shaldan said, finally answering the implied question. "I am not one of those who would unnecessarily kill someone or something. I am in service to the Magistra, and our mandate is to keep order in the kingdom. It's hard to maintain the peace when people are killing each other out of hand."

"But even you are sure to realize there are people who *would* kill him if they saw him."

Shaldan nodded. "There are."

"And that's why we live in the forest, away from both your people and mine. He has a right to live, no less than anyone else. He wasn't able to control his parentage; all he is responsible for are his actions, which—to this point—have been nothing but honorable."

Shaldan nodded again. "Fair enough." She handed Caedara the empty bowl. "Can I see him?"

Caedara stared at her as if measuring her, then she finally nodded, the action nothing more than a small twitch. "Dantes, bring our guest another bowl of stew," she called.

The door to the cabin opened, and the boy in question walked in holding a bowl. As he crossed the room and offered it to her, Shaldan did her best to keep her reactions under control. It was difficult. The boy—no, *the man*, for he had to be 18 years old or so—had brick-red skin, a pair of thick horns on his head, and what appeared to be a prehensile tail. His purple eyes were especially disconcerting to look into, even if they did match his purple hair. There was no hiding his parentage; Dantes was a teufling—the offspring of an unfortunate mating between a human and a devil. Still, like Caedara had said, that didn't necessarily make him evil—only his actions and intentions did that.

"Thank you," Shaldan said, taking the bowl. "I understand I have you to thank for saving my life."

"You're welcome," Dantes replied. "Are you going to try to kill me?"

Shaldan laughed. "No. I make it a point not to hurt someone who saves my life."

Caedara laughed. "You make it sound like that's a recurring issue."

"It happens a lot more often than I'd like," Shaldan replied ruefully. "Part of the nature of the job, I guess."

"What job is that?" Dantes asked.

"I work for the Ministry, which is the Kingdom of Norlon's special police. We're responsible for solving the crimes local constables or city watches can't, usually because they involve magic."

Caedara pursed her lips. "Is that why you were attacked?"

"It is," Shaldan said with a nod. "I was tracking a very bad man. Well, not a man, really. A celemar."

"What is a celemar?" Dantes asked.

Shaldan smiled. "If there's a being that is directly opposite you, it would be him. At some point in his family tree, one of his progenitors mated with a celestial. Like teuflings, any difference in outward appearance may be minimal for generations, but eventually it shows up." She nodded toward his horns. "Any special abilities usually manifest at that time, too."

Dantes cocked his head. "But if he is the offspring of a god, wouldn't he be good? Why is he evil?"

Shaldan shrugged. "Who knows? Why is it that you—the offspring of a devil—are good?"

Dantes stopped and frowned and appeared to think it through. "I'm good, I guess, because that's what I was brought up to be. I still have urges to do things that would horrify my mother, but I control them and choose to be the person she wants me to be, not what the urges call me to be."

"I suspect Alagar is the same as you, except—like I said—he is your opposite. You both have predispositions for things, but you are sentient beings. And, while *you* choose to do good, *he* chooses to do evil. Perhaps he was raised that way, which calls into question who and what his parents really are. Hmmm…" Her eyes lost their focus as she pursued the implications of that thought further.

"Who is this celemar?" Caedara asked, dragging Shaldan away from her thoughts.

"Alagar is an uncommonly handsome and charismatic person, and taller than any other I've ever seen." She chuckled. "I have to admit, for a time, even I fell under his spell. Maybe it was his golden eyes; they were unlike anything I'd ever seen. Bad things always seemed to happen around him, but I didn't realize then—not yet— that he was actually the source of the events, not the cure for them he pretended to be. It was at the Battle of Rheams that I finally realized the truth. His armor was damaged, and I saw feathers growing on one of his shoulder blades. I knew immediately what he was—a celemar."

"And?" Caedara asked when she fell silent again.

"And everything fell into place for me," Shaldan continued. "I'd been having doubts about him by that point. He was from an aristocratic family, and I thought he just naturally treated his inferiors poorly because of his upbringing. What began to dawn on me was that he thought of *everyone* as inferior to him. When I saw he was a celemar, it all made sense; as a child of a celestial, he might very well see normal humans as lesser beings. The issue, however, is that where most celemar have empathy for other beings, Alagar does not. He has no empathy at all that I've seen. He sees everything—and everyone—as toys to be played with, and he will do anything he feels necessary to gain absolute power for himself."

"Does he know you're on to him?" Caedara asked.

"I don't know," Shaldan said with a shrug. "I don't think he knows I saw his feathers."

"Why did he leave you for dead then?"

"He didn't." She sighed. "What happened is that the youngest princess went missing, and one of her older sisters was killed. I went to Alagar's mansion to talk to him about it, but he'd already left, along with a number of his men-at-arms. I tracked them into the forest and found a sign that he had her, but he left a rearguard to watch for anyone tracking him. They surprised us."

"Us?" Dantes asked. "I only saw you."

"My partner ran off to get aid, while I held them off. Alagar's forces must have chased after her and left me for dead."

"But you don't know if she got away?" Caedara asked.

Shaldan shook her head.

"So what are you going to do?"

"Well, you don't have to worry about me hurting Dantes," Shaldan said with a smile. "I have bigger problems." She shrugged. "I have to recover the princess. I'm going to go back to where you found me and try to pick up Alagar's trail before he does something to her—if I'm not already too late. Hopefully, my partner, Ghorza, will bring help in time."

"And if you can't?"

"Then I'll do what I can."

"How are you going to get back to the trail?" Caedara asked.

Shaldan smiled. "I'm hoping your son—who, I repeat, I have no desire to harm—will lead me back there."

* * *

"Well, this is it," Dantes said as they came upon a path running through the forest.

Shaldan looked as Dantes pointed to a spot on the path where there were several darker patches. "Are you sure—" Shaldan stopped herself. "Of course, you're sure this is the right place. Unlike me, you're at home here."

"What do you mean?"

"If I didn't know you grew up with the elves, I would certainly suspect them in your training. You move more quietly than anyone I have ever seen, especially for someone your size. I think—"

Dantes grabbed her arm and steadied her as she stumbled, and he eased her to the ground.

She sighed. "I don't think I have all my energy back yet." *Not even close.*

He chuckled. "Very possible. You did nearly die a couple of days ago." He looked at her critically. "Let me build a small fire."

"But Alagar's forces—"

"Are long gone. Days ago. I don't sense anyone around." He shrugged. "Maybe your assistant will show up while you rest. It certainly doesn't look like you can go on any farther."

"True," she said with a sigh. She decided to give in to the inevitable. "I could use a brief rest, I guess."

Dantes gathered up some dead brush and arranged it on a bare spot on the path. "*Scintilla!*" he commanded. A spark shot from his pointer claw into the tinder he'd laid out. He blew on it lightly, and it caught. Within a couple of minutes, he had a small blaze going.

"You didn't say you had magical skills," Shaldan said, eyeing him critically.

He shrugged. "That? That's nothing. I've always been able to do that since one of the elves taught me the word. It's not very useful; I could do the same thing with flint and steel. It's not like I can conjure up food or water like the elves or anything worthwhile."

"No, that *is* something. Only people with magical abilities can cast Spark. It's the cantrip for people who are fire magic users."

"I'm not a fire magic user. I can just make a spark; that's all."

Shaldan chuckled. "I'm guessing you—based on your appearance—come from a long line of fire magic users." She looked thoughtful a second. "Let me ask you this. When you first used Spark, was it hard to get it to work, but now you can easily use it any time you want to, even back to back?"

"Well, yes, but Mother says that you get better at things the more you do them. Making a spark is no different."

"Oh, but it is. You're building up your mana—your ability to cast spells."

"But I can't cast spells. All I can do is make a spark. The elves tried to teach me some of their spell words, but nothing happened when I said them."

Shaldan smiled. "I'm going to guess wood elves don't know a lot of fire magic. It's not something they would need. I suspect they tend to be water and earth magic users."

Dantes shrugged and reached into the fire to adjust one of the larger sticks.

"Doesn't that hurt?" Shaldan asked.

"What?"

"When you reach into the fire? Doesn't that hurt?"

"No." He pulled his arm out of the fire, and flames danced on it momentarily. He watched them, and they disappeared. "Not unless it's a really big fire, and even then, not that much."

"You're a fire magic user," Shaldan said with a nod. "Well, maybe not a *user*—not yet—but you have the ability to become one."

"Like you already mentioned, I'm not sure how that's helpful, living in a forest."

"Maybe more than you know." She drew her sword. "Concentrate on my sword, point at it like you did with the Spark spell, and say *Calefacite.*"

"What will that do?"

"It's the Heat Metal spell the armorer uses when he's working on my sword."

"But you just said it and nothing happened."

Shaldan smiled. "I'm an air magic user. I couldn't even make the Spark spell work."

Dantes shrugged and pointed a claw at the sword. "*Calefact!*"

Nothing happened.

"The word is *Calefacite,*" Shaldan said.

"Whatever," Dantes muttered. "Calefacite." Nothing happened. "See?" he asked. "I'm not a magic user."

"Yes, you are. You just have to believe it and *command* the action. You don't just *say* the word, you *order* it to happen."

"*Calefacite!*" Dantes commanded. The sword began to glow. In a couple of seconds, it turned red, and Shaldan dropped it, shaking her hand.

She turned to Dantes, who was looking at the sword with his jaw agape. She smiled. "Believe me now?"

"Well, I, uh…"

"I'll bet your mind feels somewhat…empty now. Like something was there, but now it's not."

"How'd you know?"

"That's your mana; your ability to cast spells. The harder ones use more mana. When you're out, you can't cast spells."

"But I never had that happen before with the Spark spell!"

"That's because it's the fire magic cantrip; it doesn't use mana. First level spells and beyond do." She picked up her sword, which had cooled. It was now slightly bent.

"Oops," Dantes said. "Sorry about that."

"It was a victim of the learning process," she said with a shrug. "I can get the armorer to fix it when we get home, but it won't be much use until then."

"I could cast the spell again and fix it," Dantes offered.

"I doubt you could," Shaldan said. "You probably don't have the mana for it."

Dantes took the sword from her and said the command word, but nothing happened.

"You need time to build the mana back."

"Guess we'll have to do it the old fashioned way," Dantes said, grumbling. He stuck the sword in the fire and let it heat up, then pulled it out and bent it back into a nearly straight line. "That's the best I can do." He set it on the ground.

"Thanks," Shaldan said. "Once that cools, we'll have to go on."

"We?"

"I'm hoping you'll accompany me," Shaldan said. "You're at home in the forest; I'm not. I also have a feeling that I won't be able to do this alone. I was hoping Ghorza would get back, but I fear something bad has happened to her."

"I don't know what I could do to help with Ministry business. I only just learned I have some ability; I certainly don't know how to use it."

"Nevertheless, you're big and strong, and I could use some assistance, especially with scouting out where they've gone. After two days, I doubt I'll be able to track them."

Dantes looked back in the direction they'd come from. "Mother will not be pleased."

"I think your mother would understand, though. I fear for the lives of both the princess and my apprentice."

Dantes considered for a few moments, then he sighed. "Very well, I'll serve as your guide. I still don't know anything about magic."

Shaldan nodded. "Fair enough."

Dantes walked to the fire and scattered the sticks. As he moved them, the flames on them went out.

"Are you doing that intentionally?"

"What? Putting out the fire? Yeah, we can't leave it burning. Uncle Ehrdan and the other elves would get very angry at me if I did."

"No, I mean sucking up the flames."

"It's just something everyone—" He looked up. "Let me guess. Other people can't do this either."

Shaldan shook her head.

A strange look crossed Dantes' face. "I've never been able to absorb that much before. And, you know what? I don't feel as empty as I did."

"That makes sense," Shaldan said. "You just converted the fire into mana." She pointed to a still burning stick. "You missed one."

Dantes grabbed it, but it stayed lit. After a second, he set it down and crushed it out. "The ability stopped working."

"You're probably now full of mana."

"So I could cast the Heat Metal spell again and fix your sword?"

"Yes, but let's wait on that. Maybe we'll find a better use for your mana." *Although I hope it doesn't come to that.*

"So, which way do you want to go? Follow the trail or go after the group that chased your apprentice?"

"I don't want to waste a lot of time on it, but let's find out what happened to Ghorza, so we know if we can expect aid or not."

Dantes nodded. "I saw their trail while I was gathering wood. Follow me."

* * *

Dantes stopped as they came to a clearing. Shaldan stopped behind him and searched for what had caused him to stop. After a couple seconds looking around, he continued forward.

"This is where they caught her," he said, pointing at a patch of disturbed ground on the left side of the clearing.

"Caught her?"

"Yes, looks like she made her stand here. She injured at least two of them, and they injured her, then she was led off."

"How can you tell?"

"There are two types of blood. One is like yours, while the other is like yours, but not."

"That's Ghorza. She's a half-orc."

"What's that?"

"She's half human and half orc. It's another race." She grimaced. "One that most humans don't think very highly of."

"So, basically, another outcast like me?"

Shaldan smiled sadly. "Yes, but she's found a home in the Ministry. She is an air magic user like me. She may never be respected by all humans, but most of the people in the Ministry respect her for her talents, at least. And those that get to know her realize she's a good person once you get past her looks."

Dantes raised an eyebrow.

"She's got green skin and tusked teeth and tufts of coarse hair all over her body," Shaldan continued. "She isn't what most people think of as the traditional idea of beautiful."

"I'm guessing purple hair would set me apart from humans, too?" Dantes asked.

"Well, we can always get you a hat for that," she said with a smile. "It'll hide the horns, too, which are more of an issue." She nodded toward the site of the battle. "Back to Ghorza. They didn't kill her?"

Dantes shook his head. "They captured her and led her off. Her boot prints are much different than the rest of the men's."

"Can you follow them?"

"Absolutely."

"Then let's get going," she said with a frown.

"What's wrong?"

"If they got Ghorza here, before she made it back to the city, there isn't any help coming. We'll need to be careful, because we're on our own."

* * *

Dantes caught a scent on the wind and turned to motion Shaldan to stop. Although she was fairly competent—for a human—going through the woods, she sounded like a wild boar to his elf-trained ears, and he didn't want to blunder into Alagar's camp because he couldn't hear what was in front of them. He turned and whispered, "We're close."

"How do you know?" she whispered back.

"I can smell them. Stay here—and don't move—while I go scout."

She sank to the ground with a smile on her face, obviously needing the rest.

Dantes nodded and continued toward a clearing he could see ahead of them, now able to use all of his senses. In addition to the scent of humans and the not-quite-human smell of Ghorza, which he thought he'd picked up again, there was a second not-human smell that caused a fight-or-flight response the likes of which he'd never felt before. It was all he could do to keep the flames from bursting out on his skin.

Moving the way the elves had taught him, he approached the edge of the clearing and forced himself not to laugh out loud. The humans had set up camp in a clearing and had posted guards. It was an amateurish display, though; the guards were in the clearing and— with the fading sunlight still in their eyes—wouldn't be able to see him as easily as he could see them.

He moved a little closer for a good look at the camp. Several tents were set up, with one much larger than the others. While unacquainted with the ways of humans, he expected Alagar to be in that one, as well as—probably—the princess. There was also a cage in the clearing, in which a green-skinned demi-human—Ghorza from the description—was tied up. Her arms were behind her back, and something was in her mouth, probably to keep her from casting spells, although Dantes had no idea what sort of spells an apprentice air mage would use.

He watched the humans coming and going in the camp for a bit and then went to ground as he heard a commotion off to the side. Dantes watched in horror as Shaldan was led into the camp by a group of five large men. She was tied up and gagged like Ghorza. The men led her to the cage and tied her to one of the posts inside. They then set a guard, and the rest of them left.

A few minutes later, a group of several others, led by the tallest human Dantes had ever seen, came over to look at Shaldan. When Dantes caught a whiff of him, he got the same hackles-raising, fight-or-flight response he'd had earlier. Dantes couldn't understand what Shaldan had meant about Alagar being charismatic; he hated the man instantly and with all his might.

"I see my men lied to me," Alagar said to Shaldan. "They said they left you for dead, but I don't even see a scratch on you." He cocked his head. "I always thought you were a mage, not a cleric." Shaldan tried to say something but couldn't talk around her gag.

"I'll have to think about it," he said after a few seconds of consideration. "One thing I am not doing is removing your gag—not until you are dead, anyway. I had considered ransoming you back to the Ministry, along with your apprentice, but I think it's probably safer to just go ahead and kill you when we kill the princess tonight."

Shaldan jerked and tried to talk.

"What's that? You don't want me to kill her? Sorry, but the Ministry had time to ransom her; instead, they sent you two fools." He turned to one of his minions. "Make sure everything is set for the ritual at midnight. I'm going to go prepare myself."

Alagar turned and went to the largest tent, then he went inside.

Dantes looked at the sun; it was almost on the horizon. His stomach sank; there wasn't time to make it back to the elves for assistance. Not that they'd ever given him any indication they would deign to participate in the affairs of humans even if he could have. It was further to the closest human town, and he didn't have any idea how he would go about getting assistance there.

There was no one to help him, and they were going to murder three people right in front of him. While he knew he had to do something, he had no idea what that 'something' might be. As much as he might like to kill Alagar, he had no idea how to go about doing so, especially if the celemar had special skills or abilities, which Shaldan had indicated he did.

Shaldan—that was it. He had to set Shaldan free. She'd know what to do.

He had no idea how he was going to do that, either.

As the sun fell, he worked his way around to where the forest was closest to the cage, avoiding two of the wandering patrols as he did so. Splitting up had been a stupid idea, he realized; it had allowed one of the wandering patrols to grab Shaldan. *If only I'd known about the wandering patrols.*

He realized there was a lot he didn't know about humans and their ways. The couple of times he'd asked his mother about them, she'd put him off, saying she didn't know anything about them, having lived in the forest and avoided them all 500 years of her life. While probably true—the elves didn't want to have anything to do with humans—it hadn't prepared him for this.

Full dark fell, and the humans gathered around a bonfire to eat and tell stories. Dantes hoped the guard would join them, but he stayed put, and eventually someone else came and relieved him. Dantes realized he only had a couple of hours; he had to do something.

But what?

His options were few. He could try to sneak up and overpower the guard—and maybe even kill him—but that ran the risk of alerting the rest of the humans. Even if Dantes wasn't captured in the ensuing mayhem, he doubted he could overcome all fifteen or so humans. Plus Alagar. He didn't see how the *three* of them could overcome those odds, much less him by himself.

While the elves had trained him with a bow, he didn't have any other training in war, and he hadn't brought his bow with him. He needed to get Shaldan out. Quickly and quietly. The only thing he had going for him was that the guard wasn't watching her; he was watching the other people by the fire, probably wishing he could join them.

That was Dantes' opportunity.

Before he could talk himself out of it, he slithered forward into the clearing, staying as low as he could, and approached the back of the cage from where the guard sat. Shaldan's eyes grew large as he approached, and she nodded toward him to Ghorza. Both looked at him, and he made a motion for silence. Ghorza's eyes, if anything, were even larger than Shaldan's.

Arriving at the cage, he saw it had probably been brought to the clearing in pieces and assembled there; a couple of clasps held the pieces on his side together.

Dantes waited for the men at the fire to laugh at something—they'd been doing it all the time—and commanded, *"Calefacite!"* in a quiet voice the next time they did. The lowest clasp began to glow. After a couple of seconds, he reached up and pulled it apart. The pieces fell apart with a small *pop*. A weird feeling came over him, as if part of his mind that was solid rock had turned to water and created a lake in head.

Shaking it off, he looked at the pieces in his hands. They were hot, but not as hot as other things he'd held, and he blew on them quietly before setting them down on the grass. Gently, he pulled on the two pieces of the enclosure, trying his hardest to not make any noise or move it enough to get the guard's attention. He was able to make a gap big enough to slide through, and he crept into the cage.

He crawled over to Shaldan, using the humans by the fire as cover, and cut the ropes holding Shaldan's hands together. She removed the gag as he cut her free.

Shaldan motioned toward Ghorza and made a cutting motion, and he nodded as she crept toward the guard.

The guard, hearing something, jumped to his feet and spun.

"Dormi!" Shaldan commanded in a low voice. The man collapsed to the ground.

Dantes paused, waiting to see if anyone noticed, but Ghorza made a noise at him and nodded to her hands.

Right! Two magic users would be better than one! He quickly cut her free.

"Will that spell work to kill Alagar, too?" Dantes asked.

Shaldan chuckled. "No, it's just a Sleep spell. The guard isn't dead, although it will be a while until he wakes up." She looked at Ghorza. "We have to get the princess out of here before Alagar comes for her."

Ghorza shook her head. "She's in the big tent with Alagar."

"Well, that's going to complicate things." Shaldan turned to Dantes. "You need a combat spell. If someone attacks you, say '*Missilis Magici*' as you point to him."

"What will that do?"

"A missile will leap out and strike them. It may kill them, but probably not; hopefully, it will at least incapacitate them momentarily."

"I don't know if it will work." Dantes shook his head. "When I heated the metal of the cage, something happened, and my head all of a sudden felt emptier. Not like when I cast it the first time, but a whole lot emptier. I don't know if I can cast a spell now."

Shaldan and Ghorza both chuckled. "You just leveled up," Shaldan said. "What you felt is your mind expanding and your mana pool growing."

"So I can cast more spells?"

"Yes, but probably only one. It doesn't grow very much, especially for a beginner."

Dantes nodded. "So what do we do now?"

* * *

Dantes slid out of the cage while the two women held the opening apart, then he held it while the others slid out.

As Ghorza stood, Dantes heard a noise and looked to the front of the cage. A man stood next to the sleeping guard. "The prisoners!" he yelled. "*The prisoners are getting away!*"

"Gods!" Shaldan swore. She turned toward Dantes as the men by the fire began running toward them. "Ghorza and I will lead them off. I need you to rescue the princess."

"But—"

"No time for 'buts.' I will turn you invisible. You must do this, or the princess dies. You *must!*"

"I…whatever you say," Dantes said, having no real idea how he was going to do it.

"Better hurry," Ghorza urged. "Here they come."

Shaldan looked up and saw the men charging toward them. "Hold them a second!" she exclaimed.

Ghorza pointed at the man by the front of the cage. "*Abducete!*" The man drew his sword and ran to intercept the horde rushing toward them. "That won't hold them long," Ghorza said.

"Save the princess!" Shaldan said. "You must!" She stepped between them and the men racing toward them, turned back to Dantes, and commanded, "*Occultate!*"

Dantes looked down and couldn't see his body.

"Go!" Shaldan ordered. "Ghorza, with me!"

The two women ran off into the darkness beyond the camp, leaving Dantes in front of the mass of running men. "Gods," he muttered as he hurried to get out of their way. He looked down as he ran and could see the grass crush under his feet. *Got it—being invisible doesn't make me incorporeal.* The running men probably didn't see his movement, but he'd have to be aware that anything he interacted with might give him away.

"*Get the mages!*" a new voice roared, sending shivers down his back. Alagar had emerged from the large tent, wearing black robes. "Kill them if you must, but don't let them get away!"

If Alagar is outside the tent, that's my chance! Dantes realized.

He checked to see if anyone was looking in his direction—there wasn't—then he sidled around until the tent was between him and Alagar, and he raced for the back of it. The tent didn't have a back entrance, but he had his knife, and he slit the fabric at the bottom in the middle of the back panel and slid inside.

Dantes stood and looked around the tent. It was dark, aside from the minimal light coming through the rent in the fabric he'd made, but he could see in the dark as well as any of the elves, and better than most.

There was one person in the tent, obvious from the heat her body made. She appeared to be in a chair. *Probably tied to it*, he guessed. He moved toward her, careful not to knock over any of the furniture in his way.

He reached the woman and stopped to scan the room again from behind her chair, then he leaned forward and put a hand over her mouth. She struggled for a moment against his strength, until he whispered in her ear, "I'm here to rescue you."

She stilled, and he drew his knife.

"You know I can see you," a voice said from near the front flap of the tent, and Dantes nearly lost control of his bowels. "What? You thought I'd go chasing off after the mages like the rest of the stupid mortals? Not a chance. I don't know what you are, but I've known you were close by all afternoon, and I've been looking forward to our meeting…and your death."

While Alagar was speaking, Dantes eased his travel pouch off his shoulder. Just because Alagar *said* he could see Dantes didn't really mean he could. He'd fallen for that with the elves playing Hide and Find growing up. They had excellent hearing, and often tried to make the person hiding think they saw him, when they really hadn't. He was still invisible; even if Alagar could see in the dark, he probably couldn't see Dantes, although he might guess Dantes was present.

Dantes tossed the pack underhanded toward the opening he'd cut in the tent, keeping it low so that when it went visible, it was below where Alagar could see it, due to some intervening furniture. The pack hit at the base of the opening he'd cut and rolled out into the darkness.

"Aha!" Alagar cried, racing across the tent. He grabbed the sides of the tent and pulled them apart, making the tear big enough for him to stride through.

Without a word, Dantes cut the bonds holding the woman to the chair. As he did so, he jerked in horror—he'd become visible again.

"That was well done," Alagar said, filling the tear in the tent as he came back in. "But in the end, it wasn't good enough." He smiled and pointed at Dantes. "*Abducete!*"

Dantes felt a warm glow come over him. Alagar wasn't an enemy...he was a friend who should be listened to and obeyed.

No! Alagar is evil and wants to kill the princess! Dantes thought. "No!" he yelled, which helped push the charming thought from his head.

"Resistant to air magic are you?" Alagar asked. "No wonder Shaldan brought you along." He pointed at Dantes' feet. "*Vincula!*" Glowing chains of force appeared, locking Dantes to the floor. Alagar smiled. "I guess we'll just have to see how resistant you are to steel." He drew his sword and advanced.

Dantes looked down and tried to move his feet. Whatever he'd done to clear the spell that Alagar had tried to charm him with didn't work on the glowing chains. He held up his knife as Alagar approached, realizing it wouldn't be much help in a swordfight. He could try throwing it, but he'd never been very good at that, and if it missed, he'd be totally defenseless. *What was the spell Shaldan had told him?* Something about a missile... For the life of him—literally—he couldn't remember the spell, nor could he think of anything witty to say to delay his demise.

"Really?" Alagar asked, stopping a couple of paces away. He looked at Dantes' knife and frowned. "That's the best you have? A little knife and no spells? I would have thought Shaldan would at least have trained you in the use of magic."

That was it! Dantes pointed at Alagar's chest and commanded, "*Missilis Magici!*" A missile jumped from his finger and sped unerringly to Alagar's chest, knocking him backward. He tripped over something on the floor and went over backward out the hole in the tent. The chains on Dantes' legs disappeared as Alagar slammed into the ground.

"Quickly!" Dantes exclaimed, helping the woman from the chair. With more of the tent open to the night, he got a better look at her. She was probably in her teens, even younger than Dantes. "Run!"

"I can't!" she said with a whimper. "I've been in that chair so long, my legs are asleep."

"Gods," Dantes swore. He sheathed his knife, tossed the girl over his shoulder, and ran out the tent's front opening.

Where he was instantly surrounded. Men waited to the left and right of him, with the fire in front of him and the tent behind him. Although there were far fewer men than there had been, there were more than enough to stop him.

"Don't let him escape!" Alagar yelled from the depths of the tent behind him, and the men pressed forward from both sides.

"Hold your breath and cover your face!" Dantes yelled over his shoulder and sprinted in the direction the men hadn't expected— right through the fire. As he charged through, he concentrated on his legs and drawing the flames up into him, away from the princess. The fire was huge, and it was more than his legs could comfortably stand; he could feel his skin start to char, but then he was out the other side of the fire and sprinting toward the forest.

Although surprised at his avenue of escape, he could hear the men start after him. Still, he had an edge on them as they had to go around the fire, and there was at least ten feet between him and his pursuers as they reached the tree line.

Once into the woods, Dantes was in his element, while the men struggled to keep up as they got farther and farther from the light of the fire. He heard several shouts and grunts of pain as trees intercepted his pursuers. Dantes didn't have that problem as he was able to see where he was going and had spent all his young life running through the forest at night with the wood elves.

While he couldn't keep up with the elves, he was able to easily outdistance the men chasing him, and he heard them drop further and further behind. Not so Alagar, who—based on his shouts—was gaining on them, almost as if he knew where they were going. He reached a small clearing, and Dantes set the princess down to catch his breath for a second.

"Why are we stopping?" the princess asked.

"Although you aren't that heavy," Dantes said, "I can't carry you forever, especially if we're being chased."

"I thought you lost them."

"I lost the men, but I think Alagar can see in the dark."

"He can."

Dantes frowned. "That would have been nice to know."

"I really didn't have time to tell you. Besides, what would you have done differently if you'd known?"

"I—" Dantes couldn't think of anything he would have done differently. "I would have run faster," he said lamely.

"So, what do we do now?" the princess asked.

"I don't expect he'll stop looking for us?" Dantes asked hopefully.

The princess shook her head.

"Then we'll have to set up a trap." He reached for his pack and realized he no longer had it. "Gods." He did still have his knife, though, and he paused to scan the woods nearby. "Hmm," he muttered after a few seconds. "That just may work…"

* * *

Alagar wasn't particularly worried as he jogged through the woods at a ground-eating pace. He had a firm lock on the princess' dress with his Locate Object spell, so he knew where she was, as it was unlikely she'd be taking it off. He looked forward to catching her again and hoped the teufling would still be with her. He'd recognized what the creature was—the horns were the giveaway—before the darned thing had hit him with the magic missile.

The fact that the teufling was a fire mage was an unwelcome surprise—his air magic was weak against fire—however, based on the fact that there'd only been one missile, the teufling was only a beginner; Alagar didn't have to worry about walking into a fireball or something equally nasty. And—even if the teufling caught up with the two air mages, they were both lesser mages; there wasn't anything they could do he couldn't reverse.

He would kill the teufling—and the two mages, if possible—and still have time for the ritual with the princess. His plans might have been delayed slightly, but they had by no means been thwarted.

He could have cast light had he wanted to—an ability he'd gained from his heritage—but there was no sense letting them know he was coming. He could see just fine in total darkness. He smiled as he realized they'd stopped fleeing, probably thinking they were safe.

Fools.

It wouldn't be long now.

* * *

Dantes watched as Alagar stopped at the edge of the clearing and looked around. He had no idea how Alagar did it, but somehow he was able to follow the whereabouts of the princess like a moth drawn to a candle. It had to have been some kind of magic. *I just hope I live long enough to find out what kind.*

Obviously expecting a trap, Alagar said something too low to hear and rose a couple of feet off the ground, then he continued to cross the clearing. Dantes hadn't had time to dig a pit; if he had, he saw that effort would have been wasted. *Good thing I didn't bother.*

"I know you're around here, teufling," Alagar said as he reached the other tree line and settled to the ground. "I can feel your presence, and I know the princess is only another hundred feet into the forest. If you'd like to come out and give yourself up, I'll make your death easy and free from suffering. If you make me find you, that will not be the case."

"I don't think I believe you," Dantes said, stepping out of the forest about a quarter of the way around the clearing. *"Missilis Magici!"* he commanded, and the missile once again sprang from his finger.

Alagar was prepared this time and didn't try to dodge the missile. Instead, he braced himself and allowed it to hit him in the chest. It staggered him slightly, but while he gasped, he didn't seem in mortal peril. "Is that the best you've got?"

"Missilis Magici!" Dantes commanded again. Somehow, he knew he still had enough mana to make the spell happen, and it did. Once again, a missile raced across the clearing and slammed into Alagar.

This one—or, more likely, the cumulative effects of the two missiles—rocked him backward but didn't knock him from his feet.

Dantes' jaw dropped. "By the goddess."

Alagar rolled his head around once, then glared at Dantes as he started forward. "You're out of mana now," he said. "My turn."

He started to point, and Dantes jumped back behind a tree like a startled deer. Whatever spell Alagar cast either missed or didn't affect him; Dantes had no way of knowing. All he knew was that it was time to run. He raced into the forest, and, with a yell, he heard Alagar coming after him.

He'd only made it a few steps into the trees when he heard Alagar cast another spell. He didn't catch the word, but all of a sudden, everything in front of him went blurry and out of focus. It was like running in a dream, where the objects around you seem to shift and waver. He thought he knew where he needed to go, but he slammed face first into a tree after three steps.

Stunned, he fell to the ground.

"Really?" Alagar asked as he came to stand next to Dantes. He stuck the toe of his boot under him and flipped him over.

Dantes blinked as everything came back into focus. Whatever the spell was, it had been broken when he ran into the tree, and he was able to see clearly again. The view, however, was terrifying: Alagar stood above him with his sword drawn.

"Any last words before you die?" Alagar asked. "Perhaps I can get you to scream a little so the princess knows what's coming for her?"

"Not hardly," Dantes said, recognizing where he lay. He gathered himself and sprang backward as Alagar chopped downward with his sword. The stroke that should have caught him in the chest ripped through his leg, and pain exploded in front of his eyes the likes of which he'd never seen before.

His arm still worked, though, and he pointed to a patch of leaves between Alagar's legs. *"Scintilla!"*

A spark leaped from his pointer claw, and the leaves caught fire. A small blaze sprang up.

Alagar jumped back and laughed. "Oooh, I'm scared," he taunted, laughing. "Is that little fire going to get me?"

"No," Dantes said with a grunt as he struggled to see through the pain. "It was just to get you to move back a step." He swung his knife and cut the vine next to him.

Alagar heard motion and spun, just in time to have the dire wolf trap spring forward, driving a wooden spike through his chest. Alagar fell backward, sliding off the spike, and hit the ground next to Dantes.

Alagar gasped and raised his sword. Dantes tried to move, but when he went to push off with his injured leg, the pain incapacitated him. He watched in horror as the sword started down toward his chest.

Only to be knocked away as the princess slammed a thick branch into Alagar's arm. The sword flew off into the forest as the princess dropped the branch, grabbed Dantes' knife, and drove it through Alagar's heart.

"That's for my sister!" she screamed into Alagar's face, then crumpled to the ground in tears.

Dantes started to close his eyes, but he heard the unmistakable sounds of footfalls coming toward them. He opened them again, but everything was blurry. He found his knife—still in Alagar's chest. He crawled over but wasn't able to pull it out. He collapsed back to the ground. An out-of-focus object appeared, which moved closer, until it resolved into Shaldan's face.

"Well done, teufling," she said. It was the last thing he heard.

* * *

"I'm getting too old for this," a voice said as consciousness returned. "Not once, but twice in the same week? Bah."

"Oh, Ehrdan, you're barely even 600 years old," Mother's voice said in reply.

"That's six hundred and *twelve* if you please," Ehrdan said.

"Well, you have my thanks for both of them," Shaldan said.

"I ought to," Ehrdan replied, grumbling. "Especially since one of them *was* yours."

"You also have my thanks," the princess added, "and I'm sure my father, the king, will be most appreciative as well."

"Huh. King's thanks, too? That and a couple of copper pieces, and I can get myself a good cup of wine."

"Oh, Ehrdan," Mother's voice was back, "you know you love being the center of attention."

"You'll have to share some of the attention, I'm afraid," Shaldan said. "Dantes was quite the hero, and we'll all need to thank him, too."

"Well, don't bother waiting," Ehrdan said. "He's awake and listening to everything you're saying about him. Bah."

Dantes couldn't help but smile at the elder elf's continued grumpiness in the face of people trying to voice their appreciation, and he opened his eyes to find himself in his pallet back at his mother's cabin.

"Told you," Ehrdan said. He moved back as everyone crowded around Dantes' pallet, and Dantes saw him slip out when no one was watching. Dantes may have been mistaken, but it had almost looked like Ehrdan had winked at him.

"Well done," Shaldan said.

"Thanks," Dantes replied. "I suspect I have you to thank for getting me here in one piece?"

"You do." She smiled. "We couldn't let the hero bleed out all over the forest floor now, could we? Besides, I owed you one."

"It was a close thing, though," the princess said. "I'm glad we were able to get you back in time and that the elf—" She looked around for Ehrdan and shook her head when she couldn't find him. "I'm glad your uncle was able to heal you."

"Me too," Dantes said with a smile. "I'm just glad we were able to get you away from Alagar."

The princess nodded. "You have my thanks, of course, but that's not enough for someone who risked all—especially when they had no reason to do so—to save my life. What would you have from me as a boon?"

"A boon? Nothing. I just did what I thought was the right thing to do."

"But what is it you desire? Money? Land? A title?"

Dantes shrugged. "I don't need any of them. We don't really have a need for money here in the forest, and land or titles are pretty useless, too."

"I have an idea," Shaldan said.

The princess raised an eyebrow.

"Make him a member of the Ministry. He has magic, a good heart, and a definite sense of right and wrong. We need more people like him." Ghorza nodded behind her. "Besides, this is the one job where his looks might actually be able to help him. He'd be the one you'd least expect to be one of our team."

"I'd make him a member, but then Dantes would have to come into the city, and I know—based on his looks—things would not be easy for him there." She turned to Dantes. "Well, Master Dantes, what is it *you* desire? Would you like to be a member of the Ministry? There will be many who ridicule you, despite what I decree."

"Many," Ghorza added. "There are many people who are too close-minded about what people look like."

"Still," Shaldan said, "you will have a chance to grow in your magic and make a difference in this world, even if you have to put up with shallow-minded people periodically. What do you say?"

Dantes looked at his mother. "Will you be all right if I go to the city?"

She smiled. "I will...but only if you come back periodically to visit."

"I will, Mother."

"So you'll come?" the princess asked.

Dantes nodded.

Shaldan smiled. "Welcome to the Ministry."

* * * * *

Author Bio

A Webster Award winner and three-time Dragon Award finalist, Chris Kennedy is a Science Fiction/Fantasy/Young Adult author, speaker, and small-press publisher who has written over 30 books and published more than 200 others. Chris' stories include the "Occupied Seattle" military fiction duology, "The Theogony" and "Codex Regius" science fiction trilogies, stories in the "Four Horsemen," "Fallen World," and "In Revolution Born" universes and the "War for Dominance" fantasy trilogy. Get his free book, "Shattered Crucible," at his website, https://chriskennedypublishing.com.

Called "fantastic" and "a great speaker," he has coached hundreds of beginning authors and budding novelists on how to self-publish their stories at a variety of conferences, conventions, and writing guild presentations. He is the author of the award-winning #1 bestseller, "Self-Publishing for Profit: How to Get Your Book Out of Your Head and Into the Stores," as well as the leadership training book, "Leadership from the Darkside."

Chris lives in Coinjock, North Carolina, with his wife, and is the holder of a doctorate in educational leadership and master's degrees in both business and public administration. Follow Chris on Facebook at https://www.facebook.com/ckpublishing/.

# # # # #

Oathbreaker by
Melissa Olthoff

"**B**y the angels, this is awful," I gasped in between sneezing fits. I took a small sip of water from the canteen on my hip, trying to wash the taste of dust out of my mouth. I spat it over the side of the wagon before taking a deeper drink. It still tasted like dust.

"Aw, come on, Kratt, don't be like that," Higgs replied with an easy smile. "Could be worse. At least we got to spend a few days in the capital while they got the supplies for the fort in order."

"Oh yes, a whole two days being nagged at by my mother. It was magical," I replied dryly.

"That'll happen," he said, wincing in sympathy. "Well, at least it's a beautiful day."

Higgs liked to look on the bright side of things.

There hadn't been a good rain in weeks, and it was so hot that wearing leather armor was miserable. Or it would be, if we still wore it.

I launched into another sneezing fit, this one so violent, I slammed into the unyielding backrest. Higgs winced, then slapped at a bird-sized mosquito on his arm.

I squinted at him through watering eyes. "Oh sure, we're living the dream right now."

He boomed out a laugh, and a grin spread across my face.

Still smiling, he cast a critical eye at our horses and twitched the reins to encourage them to pick up the pace. Instead, they slowed further, ears flicking back and forth, broadcasting their unease. I scanned the tree-covered hills on either side of the road, but saw nothing to cause alarm. It was quiet.

It was *quiet*.

My eyes widened, and I placed a hand on my sword hilt, the feel of the worn leather comforting. "Higgs," I said softly, "When did the birds stop singing?"

"Dunno," he replied just as quietly.

The corporal pulled the horses to a full stop, the overarching branches of an ancient maple casting dappled light and shadow across us. He reached behind his seat and pulled out his crossbow.

The larger draft, Rufus, stomped a front hoof and snorted, while Zoe shook her mane and pinned her ears. For the placid drafts, this was the equivalent of a full-on outburst.

The piercing cry of a hawk cut through the oppressive silence, drawing my eyes upward reflexively. I caught sight of the bird just before it dropped below the tree line, fleeing a much larger predator. I sucked in a startled breath.

Higgs followed the direction of my gaze. "What's a birdman doing all the way out here?"

I reluctantly tore my eyes away from the angel in flight. "I don't know, but I don't like it. Put your armor back on."

"Best idea you've had all day," he agreed absently, still staring up at the unusual sight.

I snorted. "You said the same thing when I told you to take it off."

"You know I'd take it *all* off for you, Kratt," he replied automatically, but his leer was halfhearted at best as he strapped on his armor. Despite what the angels had done for us, seeing one this far from the realm gate was alarming.

"I don't think I'm missing much," I shot back, giving Higgs a dismissive once-over as I hurriedly jerked the reinforced leather cuirass over my head and tugged the side straps tight.

I shrugged a couple of times to settle my armor into place. It hugged my body like an old, trusted friend, exactly as it should. There wasn't much to do at Mountain Home outside of drink and train, and there was only so much beer to go around.

"Let's get gone, Higgs."

"You got it," he said, no trace of his smile remaining. He flicked the reins and got the horses moving again.

I cleared my throat. "So, when we tell everyone this story, how about we leave out the part where we were hauling supplies without armor?"

The corporal snorted. "Do I look dumb to you? Billings would have us *both* running laps. In full gear."

"Glad we understand each other."

* * *

We didn't stop until we reached the Willow River. The horses nickered eagerly as we unhitched them and led them down to the bank for a much-needed drink.

"Not too much now," Higgs cautioned. "We don't want them cramping up on us."

I rolled my eyes. "Yes, Higgs, believe it or not this isn't my first time—"

I froze. Tucked under the bridge, out of sight of the road—or the sky—was a man curled up on his side. I elbowed Higgs. He hefted his crossbow, narrowed eyes scanning the trees.

Bandits loved the injured-man ploy.

With Higgs guarding my back, I soundlessly drew my sword and stepped closer. The poorly wrapped injuries were real enough. He looked like he'd been through hell. It also looked like he was out cold. I signaled to Higgs, and he walked up behind me, peering over my shoulder.

"Are you seeing what I see?"

"Is that really…" Higgs trailed off.

"Angel armor," I confirmed.

"The angel army only takes the best of the best."

I rolled my eyes at the awe in his voice. "You mean the most powerful. They don't care if you have the fighting prowess of a potato so long as your magic is strong."

"Doesn't look like it did this poor bastard any good." Higgs frowned in concern. "Think that angel was looking for him? What if he's a deserter?"

"Does it matter? We can get his story later. Right now, he needs our help, so move it, Higgs."

Higgs hustled back to the horses as I stepped closer to the wounded soldier.

I lightly kicked his boot. "Hey, buddy, I don't know if you can hear me, but I'm here to help."

When there was no response, I sheathed my blade and crouched down next to him. I reached out and touched his arm. Before I could blink, I was flat on the ground with a dagger to my throat. The soldier crouched over me, teeth bared in a wild snarl. His face was filthy, and ten years older than when I had last seen it. It didn't matter. I'd know him anywhere.

"Michael," I gasped.

His snarl faded as his eyes widened in recognition. "Nora?" Then his eyes rolled up, and he collapsed on top of me. Heavy bastard.

"Higgs!" I bellowed.

The corporal skidded down the bank at my shout. He swore and sprinted over, grabbing Michael's shoulder to pull him off. I stopped him with the one arm I had free.

"Wait! Look at his face, Higgs!"

"Murphy? But how?" His eyes narrowed. "It could be an elven trick."

I shook my head. "It's really him, Higgs. He knew my name. Now help me get him to the wagon."

Higgs sucked in a deep breath but picked up the smaller soldier without arguing further. He settled him in the back of the wagon, and I hopped in after, moving supplies out of the way to make room.

"Get us moving, Higgs. I'll keep him alive until we get home."

As Higgs urged the horses to their top speed, I grabbed the small healer's kit and used every bit of it on Michael. He had a multitude of minor injuries, but it was the deep slice in his side that worried me. He groaned as I cleaned and bandaged, and I gripped his hand without thinking.

He was missing a finger.

I winced and tried to release his hand, but his remaining fingers tightened on mine. I didn't have the heart to pull away. It looked like an old injury. From what I could see without removing his armor, he had a lot of those.

"What have they done to you, old friend?" I murmured as I brushed a lock of black hair out of his sweaty, dirt-smeared face.

By the time Mountain Home's gray stone walls came into sight, I was reduced to softly encouraging Michael. "Hang in there, brother. We're almost home."

I steadied him as we ascended the final hill where the fort guarded Glacier Pass. The exhausted horses plodded through the gate, the back of the wagon barely clearing the portcullis before they came to a grateful stop with drooping heads and heaving, sweat-slicked sides.

There were a few soldiers in the bailey and up on the parapet, but the only one alarmed at our appearance was Brennan. "What did you do to my babies?" he demanded hysterically, stroking Zoe's neck soothingly.

"I need the healer out here *now*," I bellowed over his theatrics.

Brennan took one look in the back of the wagon and sprinted into the keep, horses momentarily forgotten. His heartfelt curses were enough to tell me he recognized our wounded soldier.

"Help's almost here," I urged Michael, keeping my hands clamped on his side. "Don't you *dare* quit now."

Higgs rushed to the back of the wagon and moved supplies out of the way. He was quickly joined by Billings, our sergeant. Built like a rock, the man gave the impression that if something got in his way, he'd simply go through it. The supplies never stood a chance.

Brennan charged back out of the keep, dragging the protesting healer with him. Pemberton had just enough elven blood to give him a real talent for healing and more than enough arrogance to land him a posting out here with us. To give him his due, the healer stopped complaining the instant he realized he had a real patient.

He imperiously pointed at Brennan and Higgs. "Carry him to the infirmary. Keep pressure on his side. Quickly now!" He scanned me with a clinical eye as I scrambled out of the way. "You are not injured?"

"I'm good, go take care of Michael…"

I trailed off, the healer already gliding away at top speed. I stretched my stiff limbs and slowly climbed out of the wagon, desperately hoping I wasn't about to faceplant onto the rough cobblestones.

"What do you need?" Billings asked.

That was it. No questions. No demands for an explanation. The man was worth his weight in beer, and I'd never been more grateful.

"Get this place buttoned up tight. Set a watch for angels. If we see them flying, I want to know about it."

If Billings was confused by the unusual order, he didn't show it. He just nodded his bald head sharply. "Why don't you get cleaned up? I'll handle things out here."

I looked down and realized I had blood—Michael's blood—on, well, everything.

"Appreciate it," I replied with a nonchalance I didn't feel.

I marched across the bailey and ducked into the narrow entrance of the keep. The dark, claustrophobic passage, with its sharp turns and murder holes, never failed to motivate me to move faster. I didn't slow until I emerged in the crowded great hall.

I desperately wanted to go directly to the infirmary, but Billings was right. I needed to get cleaned up, then go check on the state of our defenses. As if anything we had could fight off even a single angel!

I fought back a tidal wave of despair and frustration as I turned my steps to my room. Of all the places Michael could have gone for help, why did he head for Mountain Home? We weren't a combat posting. We were a single throwback company holding down a fort meant for a battalion.

What exactly did Michael think we could do?

An errant thought stopped me in my tracks. Maybe Michael hadn't been coming to *us* for help at all. But he'd looked relieved when he saw me. That had to count for something.

* * *

It took longer to clean my armor than to clean myself. Fully cleaned up and on a mission, I charged out of my quarters to hunt down my sergeant, only to nearly crash into the man himself.

"How do you *do* that?" I demanded.

Billings lifted an eyebrow. "Do what?"

I wasn't buying his innocent act. "How do you always know when I'm looking for you and find me first?"

"It's a talent honed by all sergeants," he replied dryly.

I rolled my eyes and briskly led the way back to the great hall. "How're we looking?"

"I've got a full watch posted under lockdown orders, with Emerson in command," he said as we entered the suspiciously empty room. I looked around in confusion.

"I also decided this would be a great opportunity for a barracks inspection," he added nonchalantly.

Keeping everyone too busy to be overly curious about our unexpected guest. Scratch that earlier thought. The man was worth his weight in *whiskey*.

I arched an eyebrow. "Did you now?"

Billings flashed a grin, there and gone so quickly, I would have missed it if I had blinked. "Cadre are assembled and awaiting your orders."

I snorted. "You mean, they're hanging around and drinking."

"Potato, potahto."

I followed the faint sound of voices to our barracks. My cadre was spread out around the tables. Drinking.

"Nice of you to finally join us, Kratt," O'Reilly called out with a grin and a raised mug.

I flipped him off and collapsed into the nearest empty chair. These people were family. I didn't have to pretend to be anything other than what I was—absolutely exhausted.

Griff slid a full plate of food in front of me. I blinked up at him in surprise and got a scowl in return.

"Eat. You look like crap."

"Oh good, you're still a jerk. I was worried there for a moment."

I grinned at his huff of exasperation and looked around the table, noting the empty chairs as much as the full. We were all that was left of the original throwback training class. The army promised they could bring out our latent magic. They never promised we would all survive.

"I filled them in for you," Higgs said around a yawn.

"Good. Any word on Michael?"

Brennan leaned back and crossed his arms. "He's stable, but Pemberton said to stay the hell out of his infirmary until he's finished the job."

I gritted my teeth and reminded myself that punching my healer in the face while he was in the middle of a healing was a bad idea. It took everything I had to stay seated when I so desperately wanted, no *needed*, to see Michael with my own eyes.

Higgs smiled, but it wasn't up to his usual standard. "Don't worry. He said he'd be done soon."

"Right before he kicked us out," Brennan grumbled.

Midnight approached with no word, but we all stayed. I zoned out, listening to the chatter with half an ear and pushing food around my plate. I snapped out of my exhausted haze when a frazzled Sergeant Emerson ran into the room.

"Healer Pemberton just rode out the postern gate. I'm sorry. I thought we had it locked down."

Brennan lurched out of his chair. "Which horse did he take?"

"I don't know." Emerson scowled. "Does it matter?"

"Hell yes, it matters," Brennan snarled and ran out of the room, a confused Emerson following behind.

Bitter recrimination slapped me in the face. I should have anticipated the healer running to the Magnum Concilium. He desperately wanted a better post, and what better way to get one than to report a potential deserter. And from the angel army no less.

Anders shrugged dismissively. "If he's a deserter, wouldn't we have to turn him in anyway?"

West smacked him on the back of the head before I could say a word. "We don't betray our own."

Griff shook his head slowly. "And you all say *I'm* an arsehole."

"Well, he's not wrong," a new voice chimed in. "Though I prefer the word *escaped*."

I whipped my head around. Michael stood in the doorway, pale, but upright. The tight band around my heart loosened by slow degrees until I was finally able to take a deep breath again.

"You're alright!" said Higgs.

"Good to see you on your feet!" added West.

"You look like crap, Murphy," growled Griff.

I shot Griff a look of disbelief at that one, but he just shrugged and grinned.

Michael smiled at me and Higgs. "I'm alright, thanks to you two dragging me back here. And your excellent healer. Who, unless I'm mistaken, is heading to the capital to report me."

"That'll happen," Higgs replied with forced cheer.

I watched through narrowed eyes as Michael carefully sat next to me. He was still favoring his injured side.

O'Reilly slapped a full plate of food and a mug of what should be water—but was probably beer—in front of him. "Eat up, brother; you look like you need it."

"Thanks."

They briefly clasped hands, then Michael attacked the food like a starving wolf. I slid my half-full plate over to him and got a wink in return. I took the time to study him. He was physically fit, but underneath the armor and the scars, he looked worn thin. Haunted.

As Michael polished off my food, I gradually became aware of the pointed looks everyone kept giving me. I sighed and waited until he was done eating.

"Alright, Michael. Spill it. What the hell is going on?"

My old friend raised his head, and for just a moment, I saw a stranger. Then the ice thawed, and a rueful smile spread across his face.

"Blunt as always, Nora. You haven't changed."

"You have," I challenged. "Now, start talking."

"It's better if you don't know."

"How can we help you if we don't?"

Michael's hands tightened into fists. "I never asked for help."

Everything hit me all at once. The exhaustion from the trip back from the capital. The fear Michael would die before we could get him help. The shock of Pemberton's betrayal. And now, Michael's pigheaded stubbornness. I exploded.

"Well, it's kind of hard to ask for help when you're dying in a ditch!"

Higgs coughed. "Technically, he was dying under a bridge."

I ignored the scattered laughter. "Why come here if you didn't want help?"

"I wasn't coming here," Michael replied shortly, irritation coating every word.

My heart sank. I knew it.

West raised an eyebrow. "Where were you going?"

"It's better if you don't know," Michael repeated stubbornly.

He shoved himself up from the table, and his legs buckled. I lunged upward and wedged myself under his shoulder before he hit the floor. It brought our faces close together. Too close. I froze, staring into a pair of eyes that used to be as familiar as my own.

"I need to go, Nora," he said, his voice softer.

I felt an old pain I thought long buried shiver to life, stabbing me all over again. It pissed me off.

"You need to sit down," I snarled.

"The bastard took Ace!" Brennan shouted as he ran back into the room. He skidded to a halt and stared at us. "Awkward."

Billings cleared his throat. "Son, I get that you want to protect your friends. I tried to keep your presence here quiet, but that ship sailed the second Pemberton ran." The older man paused to make sure he had Michael's attention. "Now, the way I see it, you've got two options left to you. Either accept our help, or convince us we can't. And good luck with the second."

A beat passed. Defeat and a hint of exhaustion broke through Michael's stony mask, and he nodded once. I eased him back into his seat before retaking my own.

"How long do we have before Pemberton reaches the capital?"

Brennan paused in thought before slouching in the chair next to Higgs. "About six hours."

"Six hours! It took us over twelve," Higgs protested.

"With a heavy wagon and drafts. Ace is elven-bred. He can do it in five with a good rider. Lucky for us, Pemberton isn't."

I glanced at Michael. "How long would it take an angel to fly up here?"

I could see the struggle on his face, but at last he said, "An hour, maybe two."

"Let's go with six hours then," O'Reilly remarked, then glanced at Michael. "Assuming the angel is motivated."

"Consider him motivated," Michael replied grimly. "And I already said I don't want your help. What I need to do is leave before the angel gets here and kills you all."

Sanderson, our best archer, frowned. "Mountain Home is a big place. Why can't you just hide until the angel leaves? You know we'll cover for you."

Frustration tightened his eyes. "You don't understand. He can sense me if he gets close enough. I need to get through the pass and into elven lands. He won't be able to sense me past their barrier."

Disappointment swelled. "So you *are* running," I said quietly.

His head whipped around. "You're damn right I'm running! Do you know how many of us come back from the angel realm?"

"Not enough," I admitted.

Michael bared his teeth. "Try none. The Magnum Concilium keeps it quiet, but once you're on the other side of the gate, you find out real quick that it's a one-way trip."

I tried to think of anyone I knew who had come back and came up blank.

"And then you find out why the angels *really* gave us magic," he continued, voice growing harsh with pain. "It isn't so we can help them fight the demons. It's so they can rip it out of us when their own runs dry on the battlefield. I lost the only person I cared about because of it, and I'll be damned if I'll fight a second longer for those bastards!"

Everyone fell silent for a moment.

"Okay," I finally said, nodding briskly. "Then we get you to elven lands."

Michael stared. "Just like that?"

"Of course," West said with a smile. "You didn't think we'd let you go alone, did you?"

"This is the most exciting thing to happen since training," Griff added as he grabbed a map and spread it across the table. "Look here. The smart thing to do is go east and round the tail end of the range, but if the angel can track you, we don't have time for smart."

"There's always time for smart," Brennan objected.

"Not this time. It's Glacier Pass or nothing."

Dealing with the elves would be bad enough, but that was nothing compared to the monsters that hunted the pass. They were the real guardians. We were just window dressing.

Oblivious, Michael shook his head stubbornly. "I can't sense magic in any of you. With an angel hunting me, it's too dangerous for you to help. I can get through the pass on my own."

I flinched at the familiar stab of hurt at the dismissal. As if lacking magic made us completely useless.

Griff snorted derisively. "You'll never make it through alone. We need eight—large enough to fight, small enough to sneak. And we'll need one of the dogs, which means Brennan has to go." He ignored Brennan's muttered curse and looked around the suddenly quiet room. "The question is, who else is going?"

Everyone's eyes landed on me. I looked back at my friends, my family, and fought a rising sense of panic. I mostly succeeded by replacing it with anger. "I hate you all."

Higgs grinned. "We love you too. Now, who's going on a suicide mission through the mountains to go visit the nice elves?"

"Fine! Let's skip past the part where you all volunteer. Griff, you know the mountains better than any of us, you're lead. West, Sanderson, you're my best shots; bring twice the arrows you think you'll need. Higgs, you're attached at the hip to Griff and West. If I don't include you, you'll just follow."

Higgs shrugged his massive shoulders but didn't deny it.

I hesitated, but I needed another basher. "Anders, you're up."

Anders smiled his happy smile, lazily pulling himself out of his chair. The man was an absolute beast and towered over all of us. "Been awhile since I punched a troll in the face."

Michael jerked his gaze to me. "Troll?"

O'Reilly narrowed his eyes. "That's seven, including Murphy. Who's the last?"

I smirked. "Me, of course. Billings, you have charge of Mountain Home until we return."

I left the 'or until they send up a replacement' unspoken. He gave me a solemn nod. Once again, he had my back.

"Get ready. We leave in twenty."

Michael grabbed my arm. "*Troll?!*"

* * *

Traveling in mountainous terrain at night, even with an experienced guide like Griff, was not something I ever wanted to do again. The drizzling rain did not improve the experience.

We had ascended well past the colorful leafy trees that gave the Firebrand Mountains their name and into the sparser evergreen forests when Griff called a break.

"We're nearly to the middle of the pass. We need to wait for daylight before we go further."

"Why?" Michael demanded.

Griff glanced back. "Trolls don't usually hunt during daylight."

There were no more objections.

We followed Griff under the drooping branches of a massive evergreen. Padded with a thick carpet of dried needles, it was large enough for all of us to sit if we were friendly. Best of all, it was dry.

I found myself wedged between Michael and Griff. Poor Sanderson had the misfortune to be stuck between Anders and Bear, Brennan's massive German Shepherd.

"Brennan, did you *have* to bring the drooly one?" she complained as she swiped at her damp shoulder.

Brennan scratched Bear behind his ears. "Don't you listen to her. You're the bestest boy, yes you are." He shot Sanderson a glare. "Nova's senile, Dargo limps, and the two pups aren't trained. Bear's the best troll sniffer we have. Deal with a little drool."

She rolled her eyes but didn't comment further.

Everyone ate quickly and settled down to get what rest they could. I bit back a smile at the sight of Sanderson snuggled up to Bear. I shifted around, trying to get comfortable, and noticed Michael was still awake.

I nudged his side. "Hey, you should get some rest," I said, voice hushed.

Michael slowly turned to me, eyes haunted. "I lied. I *was* coming to you for help. But you, *none* of you, ever found your magic. You have to promise, if the angel catches up, you'll leave the fight to me. I've probably already cost you your command; I won't have your death on my shoulders, too."

I laughed, not bothering to hide the bitter note. "Do you really think they gave *me*, a throwback without magic, command of Mountain Home?"

Michael awkwardly rubbed the back of his neck. "I feel like there's no right answer to that question."

Griff snorted before slitting his eyes open. "What she's trying to say is our illustrious commander, Sir Brookston, drank himself into liver failure last year and had to return to the capital for healing."

West yawned and added, "Last we heard, his wife beat the crap out of him for drinking too much. He needed healing for that, too."

"And even if I had command, I still would have helped you, dummy." I gave him a mischievous grin. "I can still kick your butt, you know. No magic required."

He grinned back, that dormant spark flaring in his eyes. "You think so? I'm willing to bet I've learned a few new tricks."

Griff groaned obnoxiously. "Would you two quit flirting already? We're trying to sleep here."

I jabbed an elbow into his side. "Would you stop being a jerk for five minutes?"

I turned back to Michael, still smiling, but it faded at his look of raw grief. Oh. I knew that look.

"Who was she?" I asked softly.

He was silent for so long, I didn't think he would answer. "Everything."

I pretended I didn't see the wet shine in his eyes.

We rested until the grey dawn light shone through the branches.

"Alright, listen up if you don't want to die," Griff announced with his usual tact. "Stick to the middle of the pass, and stay away from the rocks. The trolls blend so well, we'll never see them coming."

Once again, they all looked at me. I heaved a sigh. "Do you really need me to say *let's move out?*"

Higgs smiled. "It makes us feel better."

I rolled my eyes but smiled back. It was Higgs, dammit. I couldn't help myself.

One by one, we crawled out from under the branches. Anders held up a hand before we got too far.

"Time," he grunted.

I was fairly certain the man couldn't count to a hundred, yet he possessed the inexplicable ability to mark time nearly as well as one of the fancy clocks in the capital. Our six hours were up.

We picked up the pace until the rocky high point of the pass came into sight. Troll hunting ground. Bear slowed, growling low and looking to his handler for reassurance.

Griff glanced over his shoulder, grim as I'd ever seen him. "Weapons out, eyes open, and pray to whatever god you hold dear the trolls hunted well last night."

I drew in a deep breath, feeling the first twinges of doubt. But, unless we wanted to hand Michael over to an angel, turning back wasn't an option. Our only way out was forward.

Bear stopped abruptly and snarled, pivoting to his left, hackles raised high. We all froze, scanning the rocks. My hand turned white-knuckled on my sword hilt.

We were staring right at the troll and still didn't see it until it was too late. A terrifying bellow ripped through the pass and then it was on us. Bear leaped in front of Brennan, snarling, but the troll swept him out of the way with a bone-crushing hit.

"Michael!" I screamed as the tail end of the blow sent both him and the dog rolling down a gully.

A sharp scream of agony jerked my head back around in time to see Brennan fall to his knees, his guts decorating the ground in front of him. I drew my sword with a curse and looked up. And up. The troll was fifteen feet tall and nearly as wide. It was as if a piece of the mountain itself had broken free and decided to go on a killing spree.

I hesitated. I *hesitated.*

Griff didn't.

He charged right in, longsword gleaming in the rain. His first strike glanced off the troll's stone-like skin, throwing him off-balance. The troll snatched him up before he could recover, one massive hand wrapping around his head, the other ripping his sword away. Griff tore at the troll's hand, thrashing wildly as he was lifted into the air.

West desperately fired an arrow. It ricocheted off the bony ridges of its forehead, just missing the vulnerable eye.

Fear forgotten, I charged in from the left. I made it all of three steps before the loud crack of Griff's skull breaking brought me stumbling to a halt. I could live a thousand years and never forget the sound.

The troll snatched Brennan's body off the ground with his free hand and vanished into the rocks. The speed of the attack and its abrupt ending left me dizzy.

I stared at the pieces of Brennan the troll left behind and vaguely wondered why my sword was shaking. An errant breeze brought the stench of blood and gore to my nose. I doubled over and vomited.

West fell to his knees. "*No.*"

Michael charged up out of the gully, blood trickling down the side of his face from a gash near his hairline, a sword in each hand.

Too slow. We were all too damn slow.

This wasn't a training exercise or an adventure. Brennan and Griff were dead. My fault. All my fault.

The sharp whine of a dog in pain brought me out of my shock. I stumbled over to the side of the gully and let out a shout of surprise. "Bear's still alive!"

Anders frowned. "We don't have time to save the stupid dog; we gotta get moving."

Higgs shoved past him, scowling. "It's what Brennan would have wanted." He slid down the slope, carefully cradled the wounded dog in his arms, and climbed back up. When he was close enough, Anders leaned down and offered his hand.

"Careful, his leg's broke. And his ribcage doesn't look right," Higgs warned.

"I've got him," Anders grumbled, taking the dog with surprising gentleness. Bear whimpered once and fell silent.

The sound of rocks tumbling, rising and falling in a distinct cadence, echoed off the sheer walls of the pass. Troll-speak. We tensed, expecting another attack. But the sound didn't repeat, and the attack never came.

"What did it say, West?" The archer didn't answer, face still slack with shock. I strode over and grabbed his shoulder. "West! What did the damn troll say?"

The archer swallowed a few times. "He said…the toll is paid."

Oh god. Brennan. Griff. I wanted to cry.

"Let's move out," I ordered hoarsely.

We marched single-file through the rest of the pass, weapons ready. But true to their word, the trolls didn't bother us again. We had paid.

* * *

The descent on the far side of the range took nearly as long as getting through the pass. I could practically feel the angel breathing down my neck, but Michael assured us he would sense him before we could see him.

We slowed to a stop at a shallow creek. Elven lands began on the other side.

Anders stretched his back after gently setting Bear down. "Well, that was fun."

"Fun," West repeated in disbelief. "We just lost two of our friends, our *brothers*, and that's the word you go with?"

Sanderson defended him. "He doesn't mean it like that. He just sucks at talking."

Higgs actually growled and stalked closer to Anders. "And thinking and pretty much anything that isn't fighting. Speaking of fighting, where the hell were you back there?"

Anders looked down. "Back off, little man. Now."

"Stop it!" Michael shoved himself between them, iridescent magic sparking off his fingers. "If you want to blame somebody, blame me. I'm the reason you're out here."

Higgs stepped back, shaking himself sharply. Anders flexed his fingers.

"Tingly," he commented with a grin.

I pinned Michael with a hard look. "You're right. We're here because of you. Are you ready to tell us what we're really doing out here?"

"I already told you—"

I stomped over and got in his face. "You told us a load of crap. The man I knew would never run from anything."

Michael scowled down at me. "Maybe I'm not that man anymore."

"Would you two get a room already?"

"Shut up, Anders!" Michael and I shouted in unison.

Higgs crossed his massive arms. "I think she's right. You always were a bad liar, Murphy. Tell us the truth."

Michael scrubbed at his face. "Like I said from the beginning, the less you know the better."

I searched his eyes. "How can you still not trust us?"

"It's not about trust," he growled in frustration.

I threw my hands up. "Then what is it? Just tell us!"

"Griff and Brennan are gone," West added softly. "You owe us that much."

The silence stretched painfully, broken only by faint whimpers from Bear. Sanderson dropped to the ground and stroked his fur, murmuring nonsense words. Just like Brennan would have.

Michael glanced down at the dog, and his shoulders drooped. "Very well." He pulled something out of his belt pouch and held it up for our inspection.

Anders scratched his head. "Uh, nice rock?"

We all stopped and stared at him for a moment. It was clearly not a rock.

"Seriously?" Sanderson muttered.

I rolled my eyes and studied the angular gemstone. Nearly translucent, it was crisscrossed with the faintest of lilac wisps that seemed to curl and twist in time to a beat I couldn't hear.

I leaned closer, fascinated. "What is it?"

"It's—"

An arrow buried itself in the ground next to his foot. We stared at the arrow for a split second before diving for cover as several more flew over the creek. Sanderson threw herself over Bear, protecting the wounded dog as best she could.

"Peace!" I screamed in passable Elvish.

Crouched behind the same tree, West shook his head. "Your accent is terrible."

The archer called out something in Elvish and got a shouted reply in return. West took a deep breath and nodded at me. Together, we stepped out into the open. When we weren't immediately shot, the others emerged from hiding as well.

On the other side of the creek, a trio of elves flowed out of the shadows. There could be dozens more hidden within the trees, or none. Impossible to tell.

West held out empty hands and spoke, the lyrical words spilling off his tongue easily.

The centermost elf stepped forward with what could only be described as a pained grimace and cut him off. "I think it best if we speak in your tongue."

Ha! Maybe his accent wasn't any better than mine. My amusement faltered at the elf's unfriendly expression.

"Understand this, I am only speaking with you because of *her.*" He tilted his head at Sanderson. "You protected the animal instead of yourself. Bravery such as yours should be rewarded. So, I will hear your words."

Sanderson faltered for a second when she realized he meant literally, then rolled her shoulders back. "We've come to request sanctuary for our brother. He's being hunted by an angel."

The elf snorted, already turning away. "Your people were the ones foolish enough to invite them in. Deal with the consequences."

"If the demons make it to our realm, we will *all* pay for the mistakes of our ancestors!" Michael called out, urgency sharpening his words. "The angels are losing their war. I've seen what happens when demons overrun a realm. We can stop that from happening, but I—we—need your help."

The elf turned back, eyes narrowed on Michael and the swirling purple gemstone he held out in his hand. "I recognize your armor. You swore oaths to fight the angel's war. And yet, here you stand, with the keystone to our realm gate."

Michael met his gaze unflinchingly. "Sometimes, doing the right thing is more important than keeping your word. I don't need sanctuary for myself, I need it for the keystone. Without it, the demons can't reach our realm."

The elf raised a thin eyebrow. "And the angels can't steal away humans for their army," he retorted. "Humans who would become powerful mages that would allow your kind to steal more of our lands. Why would we help you?"

"Because as bad as humans can be, the demons are so much worse. They're like a plague, and they don't stop until everything is laid to waste."

The elf snorted. "The same could be said of your people."

"You said bravery should be rewarded," Michael snapped, desperation seeping into his voice. "A lot of good people gave their lives to get us this far. But we can't get any further, not with an angel trapped on our side of the gate. He will never stop hunting the keystone, and I can't protect it from him. But your people can."

The elf considered Michael and the keystone he still held outstretched for a long moment. "The words of an oathbreaker mean less than nothing."

Michael's hand slowly dropped to his side, shoulders slumping in defeat. The elf sighed and leaped across the wide creek. He stopped a bare step away from my friend.

"Actions are what matter. I know nothing short of extraordinary effort could have wrenched a keystone from the angels' grasp." Michael drew in a shaking breath and dropped the keystone into the elf's outstretched hand. "Know this. The demons have other ways to reach worlds. What you have given us is time, nothing more."

Grief flashed across Michael's face. "Sometimes, you'd give all you have for just a little more time."

The elf nodded solemnly as he tucked the keystone out of sight. He took a step toward the creek when Sanderson's hand shot out toward him. The other elves snapped their bows up, arrows ready to fly.

"Wait!" she cried, oblivious to the threat. "Bear was hurt defending us. Can you...can you take him with you? He'll die without a healer."

The leader looked at the wounded dog, and his expression softened. Then his head snapped up to the sky, searching the clouds. When he looked back down, his face was grim.

"Very well."

Sanderson gave Bear one last scritch behind his ears and rose to face the elf. "Take care of him, please."

"Unlike some, we keep our word," he replied, not unkindly.

He gently picked up Bear and leaped back over the creek as if the dog weighed nothing at all. Then the elves were gone, and we were alone again.

There was a moment of silence, then Anders grunted. "Now what?"

Michael turned to us with an oddly peaceful expression on his face. The sight filled me with dread, though I wasn't sure why until he spoke. "Now, we say goodbye."

My pulse thundered in my ears until I could barely hear my own voice. "What?"

"The angel is close. It's too late to run, and there's no hiding for me," he replied, gaze drifting upward, tracking something we couldn't see. "The keystone is safe; that's all that matters."

"You matter," I burst out. "What are you going to do when the angel gets here? Tell him you gave the keystone to some random elves and just apologize?"

"I was thinking of telling him to go to hell," Michael said as he drew his twin swords, iridescent magic spiraling up the blades.

"Cute magic, Sparkles." Higgs snorted.

"Why not just tell him the elves have the keystone?" West asked, brow furrowed. "Maybe he'll leave you alone."

"One, the elves need time to get further away. I'm not sure their barrier will keep the angel out, I only know it'll block him from tracking it."

"And two?" I demanded when he hesitated.

"Angels are all about rules, and I broke...a lot of rules. They like to make examples of rule breakers. Keeps the rest of us in line."

I nearly screamed in frustration. "And you expect us to hide in the bushes while he *makes an example* of you?"

Michael scowled at me, his own frustration rising. "You have no chance against an angel. None."

Anders bulled forward. "Do you, little man?" he rumbled.

Michael didn't answer.

Higgs drew his battle axe. "We already lost two brothers today. You're an idiot if you think we're going to stand by and watch another die."

West stepped up beside him, absently checking his bowstring. "Stop trying to save us, Murphy."

"Maybe stop being an idiot while you're at it," Sanderson added.

One by one, they all looked at me. Just like they always did. And I was done hesitating.

I lifted my chin. "West, Higgs, take right. Sanderson, Anders, left. Cover your archer, and if you see an opening, take it."

I glanced at Michael, eyebrows raised. He actually growled. Then he stopped, staring at his blades.

"You're all throwbacks," he whispered. He jerked his head up and stared like he was seeing us for the first time. "You need to get to cover!"

Not that again. "We're not hiding—"

"You don't understand," he interrupted excitedly. "Not to hide, to ambush! He can't sense you if you don't have magic!"

I blinked. "Well...crap."

Everyone just stood there for a second, until Anders snorted. "How 'bout we stop wasting time and *move*."

"Wings and eyes. Those are your vulnerable points," Michael called after them as they vanished into the brush. I stayed exactly where I belonged. Guarding Michael's back.

He frowned at me. "What are you doing, Nora?"

"Something stupid, probably."

Dread stamped his features, wiping out his momentary excitement and making him look years older. He needed a reminder of what we once were together, what we could be again.

A team. Even if it was only for one battle.

I held out my fist, offering a half-smile. "Never quit."

An answering grin spread across his face, and he lightly bumped his fist to mine. "Never die," he finished.

* * *

I f I expected the angel to make a dramatic landing or immediately launch a devastating attack, I was both disappointed and more than a little relieved. He lightly touched down next to the creek and slowly folded his massive wings.

I could see why some humans worshipped them. The angel was so much more than a man with wings and shining armor. Power rose off him in near-visible waves, and his eyes shone with an inner light that was difficult to look at directly.

He was terrifying.

"Where is the keystone?" he asked mildly, attention locked on Michael. I was more than happy to be ignored. "You've hidden it somehow."

Michael just stared back in grim silence, feet set and swords raised in a fighting stance. I stood several paces back on his weak side, my sword steady even though I was shaking inside.

The angel considered us silently for a moment. I didn't like how his eyes fixed on me, as if he saw me as a weakness to exploit.

"You will give me the keystone. We will reopen the gate and return *home*." For a moment, emotion bled into his voice. I felt a twinge of compassion for him, cut off from his realm and his people. It died at his next words. "Where you will be executed for your crimes against the host."

Michael finally broke his silence. "What about your crimes against humans? You steal our magic, our *lives*, for your endless war. If the Magnum Concilium knew—"

The angel drew back in affront. "Your leadership is fully aware of the cost of the bargain they struck. Magic for all humans in exchange for conscripts for our army, to be used in whatever way we deem necessary."

Michael faltered, and my mouth dropped open in shock. No. They couldn't—wouldn't—have done that. Except…stuck between an invading orc horde and powerful elves, maybe they had.

"Normally, we just harvest the excess magic from your kind to bolster our own." The angel drew his broadsword with a rasp of steel and stretched out his free hand toward Michael, fingers open and grasping. "But in those sentenced to die, we rip it out at the root. Why waste it?"

The iridescent magic coating Michael's blades stuttered, then streamed over to the angel's hand where it was absorbed without a trace. My old friend's face stretched in a silent scream of agony, and he fell to his knees in the mud, weak and shaking, where seconds ago a deadly warrior stood.

"Now, you're as barren as she is," the angel remarked coldly.

Fury erupted, and I did something really stupid.

I attacked an angel.

I think I surprised him with my idiocy, scoring a direct hit on his outer thigh before he responded. I held my own for a moment, but I was tired and slower than I used to be. The fight would have been over in seconds if Anders hadn't engaged, nearly clipping a wing with his own broadsword.

The angel spun away, protecting his wings, and I slammed a blow into his side. His armor held without so much as a dent, and the angel completed his spin, smashing his broadsword into my smaller blade. The tip of my sword sheared off, and I felt the shock of impact as his blade glanced off the bone in my upper arm.

I should have died then, but Higgs was there, dragging me away from the fight. "Don't worry, Kratt. I got you."

I forced my eyes open—when had I closed them?—and watched as Michael staggered to his feet just as Anders was knocked aside.

Michael and the angel raged across the small clearing, blades moving so quickly they were a blur. Arrows flashed out of the trees, slamming into the angel's wings.

His scream of pain was deafening, even from where I was propped against a tree. Higgs winced but didn't stop wrapping my arm in a desperate bid to keep me from bleeding out.

The angel screamed again, and power rose so thick, the air was choking with it. It built up until I could practically see it shimmer in the air around him. Then it detonated.

A silent wave of power rippled outward from the angel in a perfect circle, knocking down trees and sending Michael and Anders flying. For a moment, even the rain stopped. The small clearing was suddenly a lot bigger. It left the archers exposed.

The angel barked out a command and pointed his sword at West. He flew backward, slamming into the shattered remains of a tree. I could hear the crack of his bones from where I lay, but he didn't fall. The jagged branches pinned him in place, driven through his armor. His head lolled, gone before he could even make a sound.

Higgs stared at West and gave a cry of pure anguish.

The angel sent another blast of power at Sanderson, but Anders slammed into her, knocking her out of the way.

"Get off me, you dumb ox!" Sanderson yelled, the tiny sergeant pinned by his much larger weight.

Higgs rushed the angel, battle-axe low at his side. I struggled to push myself to my feet, but I tried to use my injured arm. It didn't go well.

Across the clearing, Sanderson was still thrashing beneath a frighteningly still body. "Martin? *Martin!*"

Somehow, she pulled herself free. Her bow had snapped in the fall, so she drew her short sword and threw herself at the angel. She was fast and drew blood, but the angel instantly recovered and drove her backward. She stumbled. That small mistake was all it took for the angel to drive his blade through her chest. She fell, half-lying across Anders.

Higgs roared, lurching up from the ground and throwing a handful of mud in the angel's eyes as he parried a strike from Michael. The angel sent out another pulse of power blindly, catching Michael full-force. He landed in the creek and was still.

Higgs ducked the blast and came up swinging. But the angel's broadsword was there to meet the strike, and his axe blade shattered. For a moment, both man and angel were still, their momentum checked. Then the angel brought his hand up, rested it on Higgs' chest, and blew out his heart.

Higgs dropped, his smile gone forever.

Michael slowly got back to his feet, stalking out of the creek one measured step at a time. Blood ran down from a gash in one arm, and his side was soaked. His old wound had reopened. He staggered and almost went down to one knee.

He pulled himself back up. He threw himself back into battle, dancing with the angel once more, but there was no hope in his eyes.

I braced my back against the tree and pushed to my feet. I stalked past Sanderson and Anders, past West and Higgs, dragging my broken sword through the mud behind me. Blood soaked the hasty bandage and dripped in a steady stream from my fingers. I gritted my teeth and kept moving. They hadn't quit. Neither would I.

I attacked from behind, aiming for those precious wings. The angel spun before I could do any real damage. He knocked my broken blade aside with his armored forearm and hammered a blow to the side of my head. I slipped in the mud, my legs threatening to give out.

Michael snarled, his twin swords a blur as he drove the angel back, giving me a chance to regain my footing. My head rung, and I could feel a warm trickle down the side of my face. None of that mattered when the angel landed a brutal hit on Michael's side, right over the open wound where his armor was already weak.

My old friend collapsed with a scream, and I didn't think. I attacked. The angel snorted in contempt. In quick succession, he disarmed me, grabbed me by the throat, and jerked me into the air. I found myself eye to eye with the angel, but he wasn't looking at me. He was looking down at Michael, lying in the mud and blood. So much blood.

"Tell me where the keystone is, and I'll kill her quickly."

Michael grimaced through bloody teeth but didn't say a word.

The angel unsheathed a small, razor-sharp dagger and shoved it into my side. Slowly. I gasped at the icy pain before gritting my teeth.

"Last chance, little mortal," the angel hissed, twisting the blade. This time, I couldn't suppress my scream.

I saw the conflict in Michael's eyes, and the moment he wavered.

I struggled but could barely breathe through the grip the angel had on my throat, let alone talk. My eyes filled with tears. If the angel got to the keystone, this was all for nothing. Our friends *died* for nothing.

I jerked my eyes away from the angel's implacable face.

They landed on the black and silver fletching of West's arrow, still buried in the angel's wing.

"The keystone…" Michael coughed, blood flecking his lips.

It couldn't end like this.

I wouldn't let it.

I reached over the angel's shoulder, grabbed the arrow, and twisted as hard as I could.

The angel dropped me, screaming in agony, and I screamed with him. The dagger ripped free in the fall, and I lost my hold on the arrow. It didn't matter. The damage was done. Dark red blood soaked the beautiful white feathers, just like it soaked my side. I clamped a hand to my wound, trying to stem the flow.

The angel fell to one knee, fingers clawing at his crippled wing. Michael threw himself into a desperate lunge and stabbed him in the eye with his dagger.

It should have been a killing blow, but the angel just wouldn't die. I looked up in despair as the angel ripped the dagger out of his ruined eye, tossing it aside in favor of his broadsword. Michael slumped back to the ground next to me.

We had nothing left.

The angel towered over us, sword raised high, and I could only be thankful we'd angered him enough to kill us quickly. The keystone would be safe. Our *world* would be safe.

Without warning or fanfare, arrows flew out from the trees. From *beyond* the elven border. Most ricocheted from the angel's armor, but one sunk into his thigh. The angel grunted in pain and leveled his broadsword at the hidden elven archers. The ensuing blast of power didn't even ripple the leaves on the far bank. The elven border held.

The angel roared, frustration and rage battling for dominance. He swept his broadsword in front of his face, barely deflecting an arrow that would have taken his remaining eye. It wasn't until an arrow grazed his previously uninjured wing that he admitted defeat and fled the battlefield.

It was over.

I laid there for a moment, just trying to breathe. It was hard. A quiet gasp from Michael reminded me I wasn't alone, and I found the strength to crawl to his side.

"Is he dead? Did we do it?"

I watched the angel escape and lied through my teeth. "We did it."

"Good."

I grasped his hand with fingers that were growing cold and held on until there were no more breaths. I was alone. It didn't hurt anymore though.

An elf melted out of the shadows and knelt in the mud. He closed Michael's eyes with a gentle hand and turned to me. "No fear, brave one. We will never allow the keystone to fall into his hands."

I smiled through the darkness creeping into my vision. Good enough. I closed my eyes.

* * * * *

Melissa Olthoff Bio

Melissa Olthoff spent her youth daydreaming about riding dragons and slaying monsters. After joining the Air Force, she spent years having real adventures before becoming a responsible adult. Sort of. She now works as an accountant (seriously) and is back to daydreaming of adventure. Sometimes, those daydreams even make decent stories.

# # # # #

Changes by
Kevin Steverson

Chapter One

"Alright. Those are the rules," the old man said. He sat back in his simple wooden throne and stared at the six people standing in front of him. Several faces were hidden within the recesses of the hoods on their cloaks. On his left hand, a coin moved across his knuckles, seemingly without effort, the lights from overhead lanterns striking a dance of their own as they glinted off it. The King of Sneak Thieves may have been old, but the dexterity in his good hand was as sharp as ever.

His other hand, and the side of his body it was on, was another story. The healer could do nothing for him after he was found on the floor of his bedroom, one side useless from *the fit* he suffered sometime in the night. It had improved over the last year, but he still had trouble walking.

"But Brantle," the youngest of them asked, "why now? The healers say you shouldn't have another...fit. You lost weight and are in better shape now." The look in her eyes was enough to hurt the old man's heart, regardless of his health. "Why give up the throne?"

"Because it is time, Kelly," Brantle said. The coin disappeared, and he reached up to run his hand through his white hair. "I have led the family for a decade longer than I should have. It was necessary, I admit, but it is time to step away."

"It had to be you on the throne," another said. "No one else could've done what you did. Before you, some were being noticed as they grew bolder. Others thought they could go rogue. They had no respect for tradition...or for the family."

"Ye pulled us back into the shadows," a tall middle-aged woman added. The accent from YayLok was unmistakable. She smiled. "I agree. It was necessary. I donnae know that I agree with ye stepping away now, though."

"Well, I think it's time for someone to take your place," stated a short, pock-faced, red-haired man. "A lot of different things could be done to make us all richer."

"And who should that be?" a large man asked. Traces of Orc blood showed in his facial features and size. "You, Trent? Bah! You'd get caught by the newest recruit on a small town's watch. You only have what you have because you operate outside the walls of the King of Gar-Noth's palace. Gar is a city full of fools. What you need to concentrate on...is stopping the unauthorized activity there."

"Whatever," Trent said. "I can't know about everything happening in the slums of that place, Karn. How about you mind your own and just worry about the Baronies. We never hear of anything happening there."

"Precisely," Karn said. "Yet I add more to the family's hoard than you do in a much more populated kingdom."

Trent gave the mixed breed man a hand gesture. Karn's eyes widened, and he stepped toward the smaller man. He reached for the steel fist-grip hidden within his traveling cloak.

"Stop," commanded the Sneak Thief King.

Karn stepped back and took his hand from the inside of his cloak. The fist-grip remained in its hidden pocket. He nodded to Brantle in apology.

Brantle gave the man running the family's business in the city of Gar a look invoking no nonsense. "If you cannot gain control of your own city, perhaps you should not be standing here, vying for the throne."

He reached up, rubbed his chin thoughtfully, and sighed. "But I did ask for those who feel they can sit on this throne. I will not change that now."

"I am only here to beat Trent," Karn said. "Were he to rule us, the family would come to ruins."

The short man stared daggers at Karn.

"I didn't choose to be here," Kelly stated. "You asked me to come."

"Yes," admitted Brantle. "I did." He looked around the room, daring anyone to challenge his decision. "Your skills are better than any I have ever seen. Ever. This room included."

The look on Trent's face pleased Brantle, though he did not show it. "You may be the youngest of this group, but from the day I found you in a basket on my kitchen table, I have known you were special. You will compete for the throne with the others."

"On your table?" the tall woman asked. She folded her arms. "I've not heard this story, to be sure."

Brantle shrugged. "Not much to tell, Shayna. I woke up one morning twenty years ago and found her in a basket on my table. She was a little thing wrapped in wet cloth. I learned to change a baby right then…and to warm milk." He smiled at the memory.

"Where did she come from?" Karn asked.

"Someone was able to enter my home without disturbing me."

"Your home?" another man asked. "With traps set and you in the prime of your life? Who could do such? We all know there are no Tarlok Hunters in the family and their skills are best suited for the forests. Who else might have the stealth?"

Kelly dropped the hood on her cloak and showed herself. It was something she rarely did, for obvious reasons. She wasn't hiding her looks, for she was beautiful, with dark hair hanging in soft curls. She did it to hide the shape of her eyes. If anyone payed attention, they could see. She was part Elf.

"Oh," Kane said. "My apologies, Kelly."

"A half-breed," Trent said.

* * *

Trent woke up minutes later to a pounding headache. He stared at the ceiling, blinking, trying to remember how he wound up on the floor. He drew a blank.

"Get up," Brantle ordered.

Trent staggered to his feet, holding his head. "Why did you hit me?" he demanded of Kane. "I wasn't talking about you."

The large man laughed. "You deserved it. But if I had hit you, you would not be awake yet." He grinned at the young woman beside him where she stood with fists balled. "Kelly knocked you across the room with a kick to the side of the head. I had to restrain her on Brantle's orders. You're lucky she didn't pull a blade and gut you. There is no place for that in the family."

* * * * *

Chapter Two

After the others left to go back to their cities, Kelly sat down beside Brantle and slid a bowl of stew over toward him. He grinned in the lopsided way she was used to seeing this last year, picked up a spoon with his good hand, and dug in.

"Slow down," Kelly said. "I made a big pot. There is plenty, and you will have some for tomorrow, too."

Brantle paused long enough to say, "I missed your cooking. I get tired of eating at Tayner's Inn. It's good, mind you, but I can't get a bowl of goat stew."

"You have the recipe," she admonished. "Use it."

"It's not the same, even if I do it almost like you wrote it."

"That's because you don't put enough red roots and peas in the pot." She shook her head sadly. "When you make it, it's all meat, taters, and onions."

"I don't like them. I pick around them even when you make it."

"You need the flavoring anyway." She gave him a direct look. "Don't change it. Change isn't always good, you know."

"Sometimes change must come, Kelly. Look around you. Look at me. Everything changes. I admit, sometimes the change is for the worse." He wiped his mouth. "Take King Westell, for example. Since he took over the throne years and years ago, things are worse. I mean, it's easier for us, since those with plenty to spare are busy with backstabbing, maneuvering, and politics. They are easy marks, but the people suffer."

He paused with his spoon in the air. "That is why I have discouraged the family from taking from those who desperately need what they have. Yes, there are those operating outside the family and doing it anyway, but they are taken care of when caught."

She smiled. "Trent sure hasn't liked that. I think he gets a cut from turning a blind eye to unauthorized activity in his city."

"Yes, and yet he makes no attempt to get into the nearby Halls of Magic where untold treasure awaits," Brantle said. His voice conveyed the disappointment. "Maybe with the throne as the prize, he will finally attempt it."

"Do you think that is his plan?" Kelly softy blew across a spoonful of stew.

"You know the rules," the King of Sneak Thieves said. "Whoever pulls off the biggest job in the next year wins. It must be one job. Otherwise, Trent will show up with a year's worth of small jobs."

"And who's to know if half of what he brings wasn't part of the family's cut from those below him," she added.

"I will know," Brantle assured her. "I have no less than three people I can turn to who own truth stones. Favors are owed."

Kelly grinned. "You'd turn to the use of magic to ensure no one cheats. I like it."

"Of course, I will," Brantle said. "We have a couple of magic users in the family. No mages, mind you, but a few who, at least, attended the Halls of Magic. One must use what is available. It is not as if I can ask a Cleric to use a prayer spell to determine who followed the rules. What god will grant one on a thief's behalf?"

Kelly laughed. "None. Not Saint Minokath Lord of the Seas, and Saint Gronthon rules over the plants and crops, and surely Saint Lenae would have nothing to do with thieves. There may be gods and minor deities for nearly everything in this world, but not us."

"That has always troubled me," admitted the old man. "The Creator did not plan for us thieves."

"You can be assured," Kelly said, "if there is a creator, whatever plans there are for us are not good. We don't live a life deserving of anything other than what we make for ourselves."

"You do not believe in the Creator?" Brantle asked. He put his spoon down.

"No," she said. "Wait, that's not right. I guess I do. I mean, I've seen the blue glow when Clerics cast spells, so I know there are gods. I know the Creator made everything, including deities and demons; I just don't think there is a grand plan by the Creator. Maybe everything was put into place, and the Creator stepped away."

"I believe," Brantle said. He gave her his sternest look. "There had to be a reason a daughter I would never have was given to me. You were the reason I worked to change so many things. So you would have a better life. It was not just to put the family's activities back into the shadows. It was also to keep you safe."

Kelly reached out and held the old man's hand. "I know. Thank you for that. I also know of the three different times you had Elves searching for a rumored Half-Elf disposed of."

"That is all part of being a father," he dismissed. "You keep your family safe...your real family. The only time those cursed Elves have come through the swamps in the last hundred years or more is to send in their death squads to kill any who dared to have Elven blood. Not that many escape Zar. They are normally killed at birth when an unlucky slave has one."

He shrugged his shoulder again. "Besides, they came in the night, attempting to be unseen. They never stood a chance. I called in a favor from one of the Unspoken."

Kelly raised an eyebrow. To hear the man she thought of as her father say the name surprised her, even in his position. The fact that an assassin owed him favors was also impressive, but she remained silent. She went back to spooning warm stew into her mouth for a few minutes.

"They haven't sent one in years," Kelly observed. "Maybe they learned their lesson."

"I doubt it," Brantle said. "I think it is because you have successfully disappeared into the shadows."

"Such is the life," Kelly said. "It's all I know."

"It's all I could teach you," Brantle said. "I am sorry."

"Don't be," Kelly said. "It's a great life."

"Do you know what you will do?" Brantle asked in an attempt to break the somber mood.

"I do," Kelly said. She blew a puff of air upward to move a strand of curly hair away from an eye. "You just gave me a great idea…and no, I'm not telling you."

"I did not think you would," Brantle said. "Will you fill my bowl again?"

* * * * *

Chapter Three

Six months later

Kelly sighed and put the grey robe on. It was as thick and itchy as always. She made sure the hood was all the way up and pulled over her face before she left her small room. She didn't do it these days to hide who she was. They learned the first day, it was to hide who they were as an individual and become one of the acolytes of Saint Darvon, patron saint of the poor. Anonymity was encouraged.

Before she left the room, she bent down and felt along the inside edge of her simple bed frame. Her sword was still in place where she had secured it with melted wax from her candle. She didn't bother to check her daggers, hidden under the base of the rough wooden stand with pegs to hold her two robes. She had checked those before she laid down the night before.

Tucked deep within the hay mattress were her thin sheepskin climbing gloves and slippers. They were thin enough to ensure she maintained the ability to feel what she gripped, yet thick enough that she didn't cut her hands on sharp edges of blocks and stone. She wasn't quite sure if she would need them, but it was best to be prepared.

Like the others slipping into the long passage leading to the meal hall, she remained silent. Once she entered, she followed the others to the line for her morning bowl of mush. It was terrible, but there was a large portion allotted to each acolyte, and she needed it. She took advantage of every meal because she kept up her stretching and exercise every night in her room. Working an angle to get the score was no excuse to get lazy.

She finished her meal quickly and looked discreetly toward the far end of the hall. What she saw bothered her. It had from the first day she entered the seminary to work toward becoming a Sister, a Cleric. Not that she had any intention of attempting that. She went through the motions everyday and never actually did the constant praying they demanded. It was all about working the angle.

On the far end, Brother Amdil, head of the order, and the senior Clerics sat at a table fit for royalty. The small, empty cups hanging on their necklaces were made of gold, the symbol of Saint Darvon gleaming brightly. The plates, cups, and silverware were extravagant. The food looked and smelled wonderful. Kelly was sure it was all bought with the tithing and donations of the city's poorest residences. It was, after all, their church. Saint Darvon was their Saint.

She now had an idea of how much treasure the church had squirreled away in the locked storeroom. Brother Amdil and his cronies sure didn't use much of it to help the poor. They talked about it, but never did any of it. Those who attended the services were none the wiser.

"I don't understand how they can do that," Londar whispered.

Kelly could see only his chin. She had seen his face a few times since they started together five months ago. "I agree," she said quietly. No one could hear them as they sat at the end of a long table, as was their custom, so they could talk without reprimand.

"Think of the families they could be feeding with all of that, Leena," the skinny man said. It was the name she had been going by since she had started this score.

"Think of how much they spent on the silverware alone. That's real silver, you know," Kelly said. "They waste coins." She reached up and touched the small, thumb-sized cup on her own necklace. Like the others in seminary, it was carved from wood.

"Sinful," declared Londar. His hood moved back and forth as he shook his head.

Kelly grinned underneath her own hood. Not at him, only at his seriousness. Londar was a true believer, and Kelly had no doubt that, one day, Saint Darvon would accept him as a Cleric. It was only right. The man came from the poorest of the poor, straight from an orphanage where he grew up and later helped out. If anyone deserved a god's favors, it was him.

"Do you know our assignment for the day?" Kelly asked, changing the subject.

"Yes," Londar said. "You and I go with the exchange wagon today. After our morning reading and prayers, of course."

"Of course," Kelly agreed.

She rolled her eyes. She had already read through the copy of The Book of the One she had been given when she joined the order. She had read it twice for something to do to fight boredom. There were some interesting things in it, but it wasn't for her. She was there to pull off the biggest job of the year. She would empty the storeroom of all the tithings.

At first, she thought she might have waded in over her head. She helped collect the tithes at the main church in the city. It was nearly all coppers. They weren't worth much individually, but they added up. The smaller churches all around the city brought their weekly coin in to the main church.

She soon found out that, twice a month, the exchange wagon left the grounds with guards to go to a coin changer. After taking his cut, the coin changer swapped all the coppers and the few silvers for gold pieces. A wagon load of coppers returned as a small bag of gold. Acolytes drove the team pulling the wagon.

Kelly could get away with a fortune if she could get to the gold. The value of the gold was one thing, but the way she got it would be the decision maker. Something like this had never been attempted by any in the family. Not here in the city of Gar, the Kingdom of Gar-Noth, or any other kingdom or barony on Kerr. There was no way Trent would beat her, and to make the victory even better, she was operating under his nose…in his own city.

It had taken months to work her way up to being one of those trusted to drive the wagons with all the coins. Soon, she would be one of those taking the gold to the store room and, perhaps, taking inventory as it was put away. Then, she could plan the removal of it, make the score, and disappear. The title of Sneak Thief Queen sounded good to her.

The fact that the head of the order hoarded most of it and wasn't taking care of the poor only made the decision to take it easier in her mind. It wasn't as if she was the one taking it from the poor.

She turned her gaze to the corner where four of the guards stood. Two leaned on their tall bladed spears in boredom while the others laughed and joked. She was glad there were never many, and the ones she saw were the dredges of their profession. They were either beyond their prime or barely sober enough during their shifts to stand watch. It was one of the reasons she chose this sect over other religions. All of the other churches had adequate security.

When the time came to leave with the haul, she hoped to avoid the guards, but if they confronted her, she wasn't worried about the outcome. None of them even carried a crossbow. It was ridiculous.

She wondered why no one else had ever thought of emptying this church's coffers or any other, for that matter.

* * * * *

Chapter Four

K elly and Londar hitched the draft horses to the wagon and moved it around the back of the main building. Like the other times, the guards stood near their horses waiting. It was up to the two of them to go inside and carry the bags of coin out. The guards weren't paid for that.

It wasn't a long walk down the back hallway from the storeroom, but it usually took several trips. It wasn't made any easier since the two guards posted up the hall never bothered to move or help.

This time, they carried twelve bags of coppers. Kelly noticed several of them were half to three quarters full. Those came from some of the smaller churches in the city. It gave her an idea. She looked over to see if the partially filled bags concerned Londar. He didn't seem to notice. Armed with the information, she knew her plan could work.

They made their way across the city without incident and were able to carry on a conversation without fear of a Cleric ordering them to silence. The guards never paid attention to them, anyway. The two up front rode close together, engaged in their own conversation, and the two in back passed a wineskin back and forth as they trailed behind. They stayed far enough back that the sergeant in charge couldn't see what they were doing. Not that he ever looked back.

"When we get there, you go in and let the coin changer know we are here. If he is busy selling any of the junk in his shop, it may take a little time," Kelly suggested. "I'll pour the coins from the half empty bags into the others so we don't have to make as many trips."

"That's a good idea," Londar said. "Be efficient in all you do."

The last was a quote out of The Book of the One. Kelly knew it was from the fourth, maybe fifth, chapter. It had to do with making the most of the time the Creator has gifted in this life...or something like that.

She muttered the proper response, "Sayeth the One."

Londar nodded approvingly. "Maybe one of us should speak to the Sister in charge of accounting to do the same before we take them from the storeroom."

Kelly grinned beneath her hood. She made sure not to show her emotions when she said, "You're right, Londar. I'll speak to her. Perhaps she won't take offense with the suggestion. It's not as if she is the one doing the carrying."

"No," Londar said. "Though she could do with the exercise."

"Londar!" Kelly exclaimed, though it was all she could do not to laugh as the image of the rather large woman came to mind.

"You're right. I am sorry. May Saint Darvon forgive me for my judgement of another."

"Pray upon it," Kelly suggested. "I won't speak of it."

"Thank you."

"But you're also right in your assessment. Were she to make this trip with us, neither of us would be able to ride up front on the wagon seat."

"Now who needs to pray?" Londar asked, trying not to laugh.

"I merely state fact," Kelly said. "I am not judging. The man who raised me for many years was a large man."

"Raised you?" Londar asked. "Were you orphaned like me? It is strange. I have noticed of late you never speak of your youth. I am not trying to pry, but know that if you ever want to talk, I am here."

"I appreciate that," Kelly said. And she meant it.

They rode the rest of the way in silence, each lost in their own thoughts. Once again, Kelly made sure she had memorized the route. She also took notice of intersections and alleys wide enough for the wagon. She had finalized her plan in her mind by the time they reached their destination.

When Londar came back out of the rear door of the coin changer's shop, Kelly had the coins consolidated into eight bags. They were not all filled to the top. This was also part of her plan.

"Very good," Londar said. "Did the guards question you?"

"The sergeant asked me what I was doing opening the bags out here," Kelly said. "When I explained, he shrugged and said it made sense to him. They're over in the shade of the building across the street. See their horses tied up?"

"They always are," remarked Londar. "It looks like the sergeant is drinking with them." He looked at the bags waiting for them. "At least until we come out with gold in the bag. Let's begin carrying."

* * *

When they returned to the compound, Kelly carried the half bag of gold into the building down the hall and put it on the shelf with others in the storeroom. Londar put the empty bags on another shelf. Kelly quickly placed a strand of her hair on the folded top of the bag.

Once the guard locked the room, they left the building. Kelly paused to adjust the rope acting as her belt. She heard the outer door lock and the guards walking down the hall toward the room they stayed in.

They led the horses and wagon away. Like always, they would do it again in two weeks. Kelly doubted anyone would come into the room during that time. The accountant kept some coins with her at all times, should the High Priest call on her for some. She had left the hair to ensure herself of it.

* * * * *

Chapter Five

The next two weeks passed as usual. There were the normal chores, lessons given by Clerics, and time spent studying. For the first time, they were introduced to some of the prayer spells and the small sacrifices needed for them.

Each of those accepted by the Saint carried a small spell book. These kept the prayer spells everyone in the order had as well as some room for a few more that would be learned later. Kelly had heard that, occasionally, a deity compelled their Clerics to write down a new spell or a change to an existing one.

Common among the ones known by all were the spells for simple healing. Cuts, minor burns, fractures—all could be healed if the Cleric were granted the gift of the prayer spell. Usually these spells worked, and the common people often brought those hurt to the church. Of course, an offering was expected. In this church, anyway. Even though she had no intention of actually trying to become a Sister in the order, this bothered Kelly.

"It doesn't seem right," Kelly said in a low voice.

"I agree," Londar said. "The gifts of Saint Darvon are gifts, not something bought. One day, when I am accepted, I will question Brother Amdil about it."

"Someone should," Kelly said. She meant it. "Why do we never see him and the senior members during the days anyway? They are never the ones praying for healing."

"I was told they are teaching, trying to grow the numbers of clergy by planting the seed in the young."

"Really?" Kelly asked. "I suppose that is one way to do it."

* * *

When it was time to retrieve the bags of copper coins, Kelly stepped near the thick shelf containing the bags of gold. She noticed the long strand of curly hair was right where she had put it. There were twelve bags of coins for them to carry again.

They both went back and forth six times each, determined not to carry too much weight at once. As Kelly thought they would, the guards grew bored waiting on them and shuffled down the hall a bit to continue their conversation.

"That was much easier," Londar said. "I must say, you appear to be stronger than I am. You had no trouble carrying two bags last time. I am glad you suggested more trips, though I wish the accountant had taken your idea of consolidating bags."

"I have a feeling they will next time," Kelly said.

"How can you be so sure?" Londar asked as he leaned back, stretching before urging the horses to move.

"It's time for a change," she answered. "Things will be a little different around here, I suspect."

"I will pray for it," Londar said. He was serious.

* * *

Two weeks later, Kelly opened the wooden shutter to her room. With the eave of the building directly above the opened window, not much moonlight was available to brighten the room. Kelly didn't care. Wearing the clothes she came to the church in, with her own dark, hooded cloak covering most of her, she pulled her tight gloves on and slipped out the window.

The wing housing the rooms for the clergy and those in training was built like the main church, of stone blocks roughly cut into shape. There were occasional sections with raw stone stacked and secured with mortar. These were mostly over doors on the ground floor and for the multiple chimneys, the largest of which warmed the wing occupied by the High Cleric.

It was a simple task for Kelly to find finger and toe holds on the wall, and in no time, she was standing in the shadows of the building. She held still, listening. Other than the rustle of drying leaves in the trees nearby, she heard nothing. The air was brisk with the onset of an early winter.

Because of the dry leaves already on the ground, Kelly only lifted her feet slightly and stepped through the grass, careful not to crunch any of them. With no more than a whisper, she moved around the main building toward the back door she was so familiar with.

As she suspected, it was locked. With a shrug, she felt along the front edge of her cloak. Even through the gloves, she found what she was looking for. From each side, she extracted an eight-inch piece of firm wire. She knelt in front of the lock and, using the wires like a seamstress would use knitting needles, she went to work in the keyhole. After a few minutes, she heard the sound of the tumbler's final click.

After a quick look around, she eased the door open and stepped into the dark hallway. Far ahead, she could see a flickering glow coming from under the guardroom's door. She shook her head in disgust. These were no guards. They merely wore the armor and the uniform and played at it.

Still, I am merely playing at becoming one accepted by Saint Darvon, so who am I to judge? she thought as she went to work on the next locked door. The storage room was easier to unlock. She locked it back once she was in. This she did in the complete darkness of the windowless room.

Kelly felt her way across the room, careful not to trip over the bags of coppers she knew would be there. She took two of the empty bags off the shelf and blocked the bottom of the door, then she pulled the small stump of a candle out of her pocket and lit it with a small piece of fire striker and steel. It only took a few tries. Once she could see in the dim light, she went to work. One more trip from her room before daylight, and she would be ready.

* * * * *

Chapter Six

The next morning, she yawned a few times during breakfast. Londar noticed and asked, "Did you not sleep well either?"

"I stayed up late," Kelly admitted.

"I did, too," Londar said. "I have been troubled of late at things I now see and know here in the church. I was up praying about them."

"Did you receive any wisdom?" Kelly asked. She knew he hadn't. They were too new to the training and everything else to have been accepted by Saint Darvon already.

Londar looked around the room, his eyes moving wildly, as if he had a secret to share and wanted no other to hear. He spoke even quieter than normal. "I think I did. As Saint Darvon is my witness, I think I did."

Kelly's eyes widened, though no one could see. Having seen healing spells work lately and knowing how devout Londar truly was, she was intrigued. "What?" she asked. "Tell me."

"All I heard was 'changes come.'" Londar paused a moment. "I lay awake half the night wondering, waiting to see if I would hear it again or if it was my mind playing tricks."

Kelly pondered what it could mean and if it would affect her plans. Either way, there was no changing them. Things had already been put in motion, and there was no way out now. She was startled from her thoughts when Londar nudged her.

"Look," he whispered. "There, at the head table. I hear he is the one bringing the children to learn from Brother Amdil. It happens more often these days."

Kelly looked and barely controlled her surprise. Trent was seated beside the High Cleric, engaged in conversation. Londar noticed the reaction.

"Do you know him? Londar asked. "I thought you came from Noth, by the sea. At least the way you speak tells me so. Is he from there?"

"I thought I recognized him," Kelly said, recovering from her surprise. "I was wrong. We should go and finish our morning lessons before we go to the changemaker."

* * *

When they entered the storeroom, there were only four bags waiting for them. The bags were doubled up and stuffed so full, the sides bulged. They were tied tight at the top. The shelves around the room held the normal bags seen every time.

"The accountant took your advice," Londar said. "All the coppers are in only four bags. It means less trips, but they do look heavy."

Kelly put a hand on his bony shoulder and said, "I will carry them. Why don't you go check the back hoof on the grey? He seemed to limp when I led him out of his stall. It wouldn't do to injure the poor beast with a loosened shoe."

"A good idea," Londar said. He spoke to the closest guard as he left the room. "She'll get them; I must tend to a horse." The guard didn't bother answering.

Kelly squatted and got her fingers underneath the first bag. Using her legs, she lifted and held it close to her body, taking advantage of her center of gravity. Londar had no idea how heavy the bags actually were when he said it. Kelly had doubled the four bags and left some of the gold in other bags, mixed with coppers. She knew four trips, while walking normal, would be all she could manage under the load. It would still be an incredible haul. More than she had ever heard of.

On her fourth trip, she was sweating underneath her robes, but the guards paid her no mind and shut the door behind her when she walked out. Londar was up front with the horses when she managed to get the last bag up high enough to slide it into the back of the wagon. She placed the tailboard between the slots and wiped her hands off, breathing heavily.

Londar came around the side holding a small pebble. "He had this wedged in his hoof. Poor thing. It's a good thing you noticed his limp. It would have been terrible and might have caused permanent damage. I pried it out with a stick. I wonder where it came from. There are no stones in the stalls of the barn."

"It could be from anywhere," Kelly said as she leaned back, stretching. "Who knows who uses the wagon when we are inside studying all day and most evenings?"

"If you are done being a blacksmith or farrier or whatever, get on the wagon and let us be done with it, brother," the sergeant said as he rode by. The man urged his horse toward the front of the wagon.

"That was the first time he called me brother," Londar remarked. He touched the symbol on his thin leather necklace. "I haven't earned it yet, but it sounded right."

"It fits you," Kelly said. She urged the horses to follow the two guards up front.

When they pulled up to the back of the moneychanger's shop. Kelly said, "I'll carry them again. You go inside and see if he is ready for us or if it will be a while. I'll be sure to wait until you return before I start."

As Londar climbed down from the seat, the sergeant raised a hand toward Kelly and slowly rode across the wide street to the shade. He dismounted and tied his horse with the others. When his back was turned and the wineskin was against his lips, she snapped the reins, urging the draft horses to move.

Kelly had the horse turn as soon as she passed the building into an alley. She snapped the leather across the horses' backs and then broke into a run. It was now or never, and she was determined to make several turns before the lackluster guards could figure out what was going on and give chase.

She turned several times as the horses ran for all they were worth, fearful of the snapping reins against their backs. Following the route she had memorized months ago, she finally turned them into a high-fenced, run-down estate. This part of the city had many of them; most were occupied by homeless people, even though some had no roofs. The owners had long ago given up on the neighborhood. She owned this one and had it watched to keep it from becoming occupied.

She called for the horses to stop and pulled the brake up to lock a wheel. She jumped from the still moving wagon and ran to shut the gate. The horses trotted into the open barn in front of them. She shut the barn door behind them.

Kelly pulled the itchy grey robes off, tucked the necklace under her own clothes, and pulled up the hood of her cloak. She slipped out the gate of the estate and stood with her hands on her hips, looking down the road. She heard the horses coming around the corner behind her. She turned as if startled.

"You!" the sergeant shouted, pulling up near her. His horse spun in a circle as he tried to regain control of the heavily breathing animal. The others fought their own mounts to stop.

"Did you see a wagon come by this way?" he demanded.

"Aye, and I did," Kelly said, putting on her best Yaylok accent. "Nigh ran me down right here in the street, it did. The red-headed woman driving it looked crazy, I tell ye. Wild eyes that one had. One was looking sideways. Lock that one away when ye catch her, I'm to be saying."

"Red hair?" the sergeant asked. "Thank you for that. I've never actually seen her hair...or her face. Which way did she turn?"

"It went up on two wheels, as sure as I'm to be standing here, it did. She turned to the left not three streets down."

"Hah!" the sergeant shouted, urging his horse to move again.

Kelly watched them go and turned and saw a small girl watching her from across the street. The girl stood in a dirty dress, holding a doll of sorts. It was actually a piece of cloth tied to look like a dress on a bundle of straw.

Kelly knew the girl. Her father had been paid a silver to ensure the place stayed empty. She raised a finger to her lips and made a shushing sound. When the little girl nodded, Kelly reached into a small pouch tied to her belt and flipped a small piece of copper to her. The girl's eyes lit up when she heard it hit and roll toward her, and she grinned. Her two front teeth were missing.

Kelly closed the gate behind her, walked to the barn, and entered. Using the light filtering through the missing pieces of roofing, she moved the back board and dragged the bags off the wagon. She hid them in the hole she had prepared and placed the broken pieces of roofing back over it. She scattered old hay over those.

She pulled her sword and daggers from underneath the seat, strapped them on, and felt like her old self. She unlocked the brake and led the horses through the doors on the other side of the old barn and out the gate into the street behind.

Kelly climbed up, turned the horses away from the house, and slapped the reins lightly. Once the horses were walking at a leisurely pace, she jumped quietly off. The horses continued down the wide street, pulling the empty wagon.

* * * * *

Chapter Seven

Kelly waited for about a quarter hourglass. She stepped through the gate and closed it behind her. She started to turn and walk up her side of the street when she heard the clatter of hooves. The guards were riding hard back up the street. She stopped to watch them go by, and time slowed.

She could see the riders coming out of the corner of her eye and the little girl across from her. The girl had a much smaller boy by the hand as she led him toward her. Several things went through her mind at once. She knew the girl wanted her to give the boy a coin, too. It happened often. Those from the streets looked out for each other. It started young and was encouraged. She also knew the guards would not slow for ragged children in their way.

Kelly held up her hand and shouted, "No!" But it was too late.

The guard closest to the children never bothered to pull back on his reins. Kelly saw it all in slow motion as it happened. The girl flung her arm back, dragging the boy from the path of the horse, but she was unable to get out of the way herself. The front hoof of the horse clipped her head and sent her sprawling. She slid several feet before coming to a stop. Time flowed again as Kelly rushed across the street.

She heard the sergeant shout back that it served the girl right and to stay out of the streets. The four of them rounded a corner and disappeared out of sight. When she glanced the way they went, she saw familiar robes coming toward her.

Kelly dropped to both knees, sat back, and cradled the little girl's head on her thighs. She ignored the blood running from the child's nose and ears onto her leather breeches. She softly brushed the girl's hair back and looked at her innocent face through the tears in her eyes.

Suddenly, without hesitating, Kelly reached into her shirt's collar and pulled out her leather necklace with the symbol of Saint Darvon on it. She closed her eyes and prayed.

Saint Darvon, I do not deserve your blessing. I know I don't. This one...this little one does. Will you hear me?

* * *

Kelly found herself in a small home. The furniture was sparse, and there were no curtains on the windows. By the fireplace, a bald man stood stirring a large pot. When he looked at Kelly, his eyes spoke of centuries, of time unmeasurable, and of the here and now.

"Hello, Kelly," he said. The tone of his voice was soothing, yet provided strength unlimited.

"So, now, in your time of need, you decide to actually pray?" He shook his head in dismay. "All this time in my church, and you never once truly meant the words you uttered. You simply went along to blend in."

He turned toward a dark corner and spoke. "What did you call it, Anthone? 'Working an angle,' I believe."

"Yes," a raspy voiced answered. Kelly looked hard but could not quite make out the figure seated in the darkest corner away from the light of the fireplace and windows.

Kelly found her voice. "I...I am sorry. I will give it all back. All of it. Please. Will you heal the girl? She did not deserve to be run down in the street like a stray dog."

"Caught red handed, by me, no less, yet your only concern is for the child. You, my dear, are a hard one to figure out," Darvon said. He blew softly on the spoon and then tasted it. "Perfect," he declared.

He set the spoon aside. "Can't use that one now. That would be rude of me. I'll get another to dole it out." He pointed to the table where three chairs were. "Have a seat."

"She hasn't much time," Kelly said, the tears coming again. "I think she's dying."

"Time is irrelevant right now," the Saint said. "We must talk before anything happens. Sit."

Kelly moved stiffly over to the table and sat down. Saint Darvon brought over three bowls; two he balanced in one hand, though the bowls clearly were wider than his palm.

Saint Darvon sat down in front of her and looked into her eyes. She had managed to stop crying. He glanced over toward the corner and then up as if listening.

His mind made up, he turned back to her. "Anthone is going to join us for a bowl of goat stew. I would ask that you not be alarmed when you see him. All is well."

Anthone stepped out of the shadows, and Kelly inhaled sharply. She didn't utter a word as he settled into the empty chair. She found herself looking at what she could only think of as part demon.

His head and upper body were like hers, or even Saint Darvon's. His lower half retained the legs and hooves of the demons as described in the Book of the One. She had seen its like on tapestries and works of art, some of which she had removed from the owners' homes over the years. Good quality art always sold well in another kingdom. There were members of the family who specialized in it.

"I don't understand," she managed to say.

"Well, it's simple," Saint Darvon said. "Alright, I admit, it is not. You asked for my acceptance when you prayed for the life of the child. We hear all the prayers to us, you know. We then decide if we wish to grant the prayer spell or not. There are always a number of things to consider. Things like: Is there a true need? Is the one asking worthy to be granted a prayer spell? Will it be for the good of all involved? And…and in a situation like this one, will our Creator answer my prayers?"

He smiled. "I see the confusion on your face. We all answer to the Creator. The most powerful spells come from on high. Even I must pray for them."

"All belong to the Creator. Verily, I say to you, even the saints and gods," Anthone said reverently.

"Indeed," Darvon agreed. "Well said."

Kelly knew the thing sitting beside her quoted from the Book of the One. She had read the passage several times. She wondered why a demon would do so.

Saint Darvon put his spoon down. "My child, I cannot help you. Though you reached out to me, you are not mine. You…are a thief. That is something I would struggle with. I am the God of the poor, the downtrodden, the homeless. Not thieves."

"No one is," Kelly said, a little more forceful than she intended. The tears had started again when he said he would not help the girl.

"I agree," the God said. "That is where Anthone comes in."

"You would have me pray to a Demon?" she asked. "I will do no such. Elves…Elves worship Demons. They are evil!"

"Which one?" Saint Darvon asked.

"Both," Anthone answered for her. "Both."

"Eat your stew," Saint Darvon said. "It has the peas and red roots you love. I will tell you a story."

"Once, long ago, there was a Demon. Like all Demons, he resided in the fiery pits, only to come forth when called by those who worshiped such. Such is the way our Creator designed the reality in which we live. There is good, and there is evil."

"Deities and Demons," Kelly said.

"Yes. And all thinking beings have the free will to choose between the two. The Deities are here to aid, and the Demons are here to tempt. One's choices in life determine what happens when their time here is done."

He pointed at her and then to Anthone. "All have free will. Even one such as Anthone has free will. Long ago, the Demon decided he did not want to be evil. I know, right? It shocked all of us. Us, meaning my brothers and sisters. I am pretty sure our Creator knew it would happen, but we are not privy to all things. Many things, but not all.

"It took some getting used to. We watched, and we waited, for these things cannot be rushed. When the next opportunity arose, and the Demon was called forth, he acted. He acted in a way the Elf did not expect. You see, he was called to accept a sacrifice. A baby. These are the types of things Elves do."

He took a bite of a soft roll. "Anyway, the Demon grabbed the baby and vanished with it, breaking the boundaries holding it to the place it was called. Apparently, that was a dangerous act. Once free of the Elf, he never went back, and he did not go to the fiery pits."

Enthralled by the story, Kelly asked, "What of the baby? Where did he take it?"

Anthone spoke in his raspy voice. "I took you to someone I had never met but could relate to. I took you to the home of the King of Sneak Thieves."

* * * * *

Chapter Eight

"It was me?" Kelly asked, her voice now a whisper.

"Yes, child," Anthone said. "I could do no other."

"Our Creator had mercy on Anthone and changed part of him," declared Saint Darvon.

"The Creator gave me the strength to break free from the boundaries," Anthone said. "I am no longer a full Demon. All things come through the Creator."

"In infinite wisdom," Kelly said. She surprised herself by quoting from the Book of the One.

"Yes," agreed Saint Darvon. "Now, Anthone has been staying with me. After all, I am the Patron Saint of the poor, the downtrodden, and the homeless. He is, without a doubt, homeless. I have also been teaching him, so to speak. I feel honored our Creator has tasked me with it. Proud, if I am being honest. I need to work on that. My pride." The last he said to himself as he stared into the distance, contemplating.

Saint Darvon shook himself from his thoughts, looked directly at Kelly, and said, "Our Creator has decided. Anthone will be the Patron Saint of Thieves."

Kelly sat up straight in her seat, unsure whether she had heard him right. She reached up and pushed her hood back to see better. Anthone smiled at her.

He said, "There will be some things that must be known. First of all, violence must be avoided. I understand there are times it cannot be, but those who follow me must try. Actually try. Half of what is taken must go to the people. To the poor. More is better, but I will accept half for now. Sneak Thieves will continue to stick to the shadows. They will not be brazen and open. As Brantle has said, so shall it be."

"We are to continue to steal? Stealing is evil. The Book of the One says so," Kelly said. She was confused as to where all this was going.

"That's what I say," Saint Darvon added. He looked up and raised his hands in apology. "But I am not the one in charge. We must trust in the plan."

"It is evil," Anthone agreed. "But…when coupled with giving, it is reduced. The lesser of two evils, shall we say. Though I strive every day to fight the evil within myself, it is always going to be within my nature. My followers will fight it too. Our Creator has spoken."

"In infinite wisdom," Saint Darvon said.

The room was silent as Kelly thought about all she had learned. The sound of the fire crackling was mesmerizing. She looked long and hard at the one who wished to no longer be a Demon. The one who saved her so many years ago. *Freewill. I have freewill.*

"Saint Anthone," she said. "Will you hear me? Will you save this child?"

* * *

Kelly looked down at the child's face and saw peace come over it. The little girl drew a breath and then she drew another. Her eyes fluttered open, and she stared up. Fear showed in them. Fear for another.

"My brother? Where is my brother?" the little girl asked.

"He's right here," a voice said behind Kelly. "He is alright."

Kelly helped the girl stand, bent over, and retrieved the doll. She handed it to the girl with a smile. She turned to face Londar. He set the child on the ground, and he ran to his sister.

Kelly reached over the boy's head, brushed the girl's hair out of her eyes, and handed her the coin purse. "Take this to your father. Let him know he has my thanks for watching my home. Tell him to use some of the coins to repair the house. It's yours now. Can you remember all that?"

"Yes, Sister. I'll remember. Thank you." The girl ran off with her brother.

"Sister," Londar said. "It fits you, Leena."

"It's Kelly," she said. "My real name is Kelly."

"I don't understand," Londar said. "And where are your robes? Why did you take the wagon? Where is the…"

He stopped and looked closely at her, her face now visible to him. The glow from the symbol on her necklace lighting it from beneath. "Your pendant glows. It is not Saint Darvon's. It looks like a mix of fire and ice, swirling around each other. How did that happen? I mean, I saw the glow from your hands when your prayer spell was answered."

He paused and reached for his own pendant. "I thought it came from Saint Darvon."

"I do not follow the same god you do," Kelly said softly. "I have been accepted by another."

"I know. I can see the glow. Wait. I can see the glow of it at all times," he said. He dropped his hood and smiled.

"Yes," Kelly said. "And I can see yours glowing. You have been accepted by your god."

Londar closed his eyes, thanking Saint Darvon. He opened them and asked, "So, what do we do now? You stole the coppers from the church. You *stole* coppers!"

"Shhhh," Kelly said. "You're going to give me away. It wasn't coppers. Come with me." She looped her arm in his and walked him across the street.

* * *

Six months later

The Queen of the Sneak Thieves and High Cleric of Saint Anthone sat back. "That's what happened. Those are the rules. We now have a god watching us. It is up to us to do right. Once we start this, the people will depend on us. We cannot let them down."

Karn stepped forward. The big man spoke loud enough for all those in the room to hear. "I, for one, am willing to do it. What I now have is too much for any one man. I'll give away half upon my return to the Baronies."

"Aye, and I'm to be doing the same," Shayna said. "And I'll bust a knot on the head of any of those in me city who don't follow the new family rules."

"I'll do what I can," Brantle said. He wiggled the fingers on both hands. "Now that I can move freely again, I'll get Gar where it needs to be before I truly retire. Trent has it in sad shape. I've never seen the like."

"*Had*," Kelly said. "He is no more." She paused before continuing, "The Book of the One tells us we are not to murder, nor kill unjustly. His death was not unjust. He and those child-abusing clergy members now burn in the pits. The things they put children through demanded it."

"The new High Cleric of Saint Darvon will provide shelter when needed. Brother Londar is a good man. Go. All of you. Go to your cities and guide the family. We have many others to save. Changes come."

"And…things to acquire," Brantle said with a grin.

"There is that," Kelly said. "There is that." She toyed with her necklace.

* * * * *

Kevin Steverson Bio

Kevin Steverson is a retired veteran of the U.S. Army. He is the author of the Amazon best selling science fiction novels, the Salvage Title Trilogy, which are now optioned for feature film. He is a published songwriter as well as an author. When he is not on the road as the Tour Manager for the band Cypress Spring, he can be found in the foothills of the NE Georgia mountains, writing in one fashion or another.

# # # # #

What the Eye Sees by Quincy J. Allen

The Eye of Tuluum, an obsidian sphere dangling on a silver chain, went slack in Rellen's hand. It had once again served its purpose. Unfortunately, Rellen had no idea what that purpose was.

He lifted his gaze past the doors of a time-worn tavern to the carved bear claw symbol hanging above them. The deep snort of a thick-chested horse broke the morning silence, coming from a livery beside the tavern. The street, if one could call it that, was barely a hoof-wrinkled mud stain running between a few dozen weathered, wooden buildings.

It wasn't the first time the Eye had led him to a tavern. In Rellen's experience, most trouble started in a tavern or crossed one's path. This was, however, the first time it had led him to a battered dump in a nameless village nestled squarely in the dirty creases beyond civilization.

Rellen let out a resigned sigh and slipped the Eye into an inner cloak pocket. "Really? You couldn't come up with something better?"

The Eye, ever silent, seemed to laugh at him.

"I guess I'll go inside and see what's what," Rellen said.

Shaddeth, Rellen's black war horse, twisted his ears back and snorted in disgust.

"You're right," Rellen said as he dismounted. "This place is a shit hole." He patted Shaddeth's shoulder. "Protect the gear, and I'll see about getting you stabled and fed."

The horse stared at him expectantly, as if to say, "Get on with it."

Rellen shrugged the black, woolen cloak around his shoulders, checked the blades at either hip, and strode up the single step to the double doors of the tavern. Twisting the latch, he stepped into a lantern-lit interior as badly battered as the exterior.

A half dozen worn wooden tables and chairs filled the center of a wide room. Four long tables and benches lined the left side, and a brightly polished bar occupied the right. Tattered and faded banners covered the walls. Rellen, surprised to see them, recognized two from wars fought over a hundred and fifty years earlier.

The most recognizable was a red and gold standard for the Lissian Army, not seen since Pelinon forces had pushed south and wiped out the Lissian forces. That war had been fierce and bloody, ending in Lissia's defeat and annexation into Pelinon.

Another banner, only slightly less faded than the others, was the black field and silver dragon of the Cabal of Suria. Eighty years earlier, they had attempted to overthrow Pelinon with wave after wave of life-stealing magic users, but, like the Lissians, had been defeated.

He couldn't put a name to the other standards, although several seemed familiar. He had to wonder why in the name of the Five Hells the Eye had brought him here.

He shrugged. "There's only one way to find out," he said under his breath.

"What did you say?" a burly man asked as he kicked open a door at the back of the room. The newcomer eyed Rellen as he strode toward the bar with five pewter tankards in each massive hand.

The man, as tall as Rellen, was broader across the chest, with tree-trunk arms, and only the suggestion of a neck. His shaved head contrasted with bushy, black eyebrows and a heavy beard reaching the middle of his chest. Colored patterns of red and black tattoos peeked from beneath the beard where the man's jerkin was partially laced open.

What surprised Rellen the most was the sinewy, winged creature perched on the man's shoulder.

A dragonette!

This one, its glittering scales the color of midnight, had its tail coiled around the man's neck. Its tiny green eyes never left Rellen.

"Nothing, good sir," Rellen replied. "Just muttering to myself. Hazard of traveling alone as much as I do."

"You came here alone?" the man asked, with a raised eyebrow. He sized Rellen up. Rellen couldn't tell if the man was impressed, worried, or merely considered Rellen a fool.

"Indeed." Rellen smiled. "Well, alone, save for the horse outside, and he's a poor conversationalist. I was wondering if I might stable him in the livery next door during my stay."

The man got an odd look, as if he'd concluded Rellen was a fool. "It's a silver a day for the livery and two silvers for a room. I have no one to feed or water the animal, so that's on you... assuming you stay. It's dawn. You should consider going back the way you came. There's no law this far south. You rode from the northeast, yes?"

The question surprised Rellen. "I did. How did you know?"

234 | KENNEDY & HOWELL

"Because the brigands who own this town went southwest two nights ago, the road only goes in two directions, and if you'd crossed paths with those thirteen bastards on the road somewhere, you wouldn't have made it here at all."

"Brigands?"

The man nodded. The dragonette seemed to nod as well, which Rellen found a bit peculiar.

"And that's their best quality. They're as rough as they come…a hungry pack of jackals who take what they need rather than working for it."

"And yet, you're still here?"

The man gave Rellen a grim smile. "I retired here long ago, after the original inhabitants moved on to greener pastures and well before these vermin arrived. When Kurm and his crew showed up, I refused to leave. They couldn't pry me out, no matter how hard they tried. I guess you could say we came to an arrangement. As much as it pains me to say, they're my only customers." The man got a strange look on his face and added quietly, "Not that I really need any."

"I assume these brigands are the reason you suggested I move on?"

"You catch on fast."

"Sometimes." Rellen stepped up to the bar and held out his hand. "I'm Rellen, of Corsia."

"Staggin." The man wiped a hand on his leggings and held it out.

They shook, and as they did, Rellen caught sight of more tattoo work running up from Staggin's wrist. He would have sworn the tattoos moved. He glanced at the man's neckline, just behind the beard. He spotted the ink-work he'd seen before, but it was more blues than reds this time. The idea of shifting tattoo patterns stirred Rellen's memory, but he couldn't quite place it.

"What brings you here?" Staggin asked.

Rellen paused, considering his reply. He rarely mentioned the Eye, for relics made greedy people hungry for its power. He didn't want to mention being a bounty hunter, either, because Staggin might decide he could get paid for handing Rellen over to the brigands. And telling people he was one of the thirteen Guardians of Pelinon was out of the question. Such secrets were best left unrevealed.

"Simply meandering after too many years under the yoke of military service," he replied. The answer had the merit of being mostly true.

"That, I understand," Staggin said with a grim nod. His expression held a bit more interest than a moment before. "I've seen enough butchered bodies and burned souls to last an eternity." He pulled a rag from his waistband and wiped down the bar. "Under whose banner did you serve?"

Again, Rellen paused. Would it do him harm to admit he served in Pelinon's army? "I served under King Saren II in a number of campaigns," he finally said.

"I, too, served Pelinon." Staggin cocked his head to the side. "I guess that makes us comrades, of a sort. If you truly want to stay, I'll only charge you two silvers a day for the stable and room, but I must warn you, I can't guarantee your safety beyond the walls of these two buildings. That was the accord I reached with Kurm. He and his men have held to it for four years, now, and I doubt they have the courage to renege at this point."

"Then I'll stay at least the night," Rellen replied.

"Go stable your mount," Staggin said. "I'll have food once you return. On the house."

"Thank you, Staggin."

"If veterans won't look out for each other, who will?"

"There's a lot of truth in that."

"You'll find fresh hay in a bin by the stable door. Take what you need."

Rellen waved over his shoulder and walked out the door. "Come on, old friend," he said, pulling Shaddeth into the livery.

There were a dozen stalls within, with only one occupied. The occupant was a gray and black roan almost as tall as Shaddeth, broader across the chest, with a white mane and tail. The horse looked old, with a swath of white and gray running down its face and around its eyes. Black symbols ran down the center of its face in an unrecognizable script.

Rellen couldn't tell if they'd been inked there, but it was unlikely the horse had been born with them. The runes elicited yet another vague memory from Pelinon's distant past. Behind the horse was a great chest, closed and secured with a padlock. Beside it, on a railing, lay a weathered saddle the color of blood. There were also several weapons hanging on the wall, shrouded by black cloth.

He placed Shaddeth in one of the stalls and removed the bundle of books, saddle bags, and saddle, hanging them on hooks set into the wall. Pulling a small iron rod from a pouch on his bandoleer, he concentrated for a moment, made a quick gesture with his hand, and spoke an incantation. The rod evaporated in a pale flash of light that then surrounded his gear. The spell locked everything against the wall and would send a searing shock through anyone who touched it. Satisfied his gear was safe, he grabbed a pitchfork and placed some hay in the stall. As he worked, he heard the growing sound of hooves coming in from the southwest. He quickly finished with the hay, filled a large wooden bucket with water from a nearby barrel, and set it down for Shaddeth to drink from.

Rellen checked his blades again and stepped through the stable doors. Three riders had gathered in front of the tavern. In the center sat a stern-featured man with a silver-trimmed black cloak and long, black hair. On either side were two rough-looking riders wearing red-trimmed black cloaks. More riders approached in a long line.

Riding beside the men were three battered-looking women with leather leashes around their necks. They wore nightgowns and looked as if they'd been dragged from their beds. Strangely enough, there was a stain of blood in the center of each woman's chest, as if they'd been stabbed, yet still lived.

Slavers. No wonder the Eye brought me here, he thought.

He was surprised to see a pale woman with gaunt, angular features holding the leashes. She had parchment-dry skin that looked like it had been pulled taut over her skull. Her black hair, cascading down a crimson cloak, had a white streak running from her left temple all the way back. Her bright blue eyes narrowed at the sight of Rellen's bandoleer. She wore fine, green cloth with silver trim. She also had a bandoleer of pouches across her chest, as well as several more along her black leather belt.

Not just a slaver, a magic user, he thought.

The riders turned wary eyes to Rellen as he strode toward the tavern doors. He spotted several hands move toward sheathed blades, but did nothing. They were all what Rellen had come to expect from thugs and brigands—lean, hungry-looking, with deep-set anger in their eyes. Most wore ill-kept leather armor, chain mail, or a combination of the two. The designs were haphazard, as if each piece had come from a different artisan.

The outlier was the leader, who wore a fine suit of half chain mail that looked like it had just been fashioned. "Who in the Nine Hells are you?" he barked.

Rellen paused a few steps away from the tavern doors and stared back, an unconcerned look upon his face. "I'm Rellen, of Corsia," he finally replied.

"Your business here?"

"Not that it's any concern of yours," he said in a patient tone, "but I'm here for breakfast."

"You better enjoy it. It's likely to be your last."

Rellen smiled. "Of course it is. I never have more than one breakfast. I hate feeling full so early in the morning." Rellen gave the leader a wink and stepped through the doors.

Once inside, he pulled a small crystal from a pouch, made a quick gesture, and muttered a short incantation. A soft white glow momentarily encompassed his body. He felt a tingle that quickly subsided. The spell would remain in place for several hours, at least, and it gave him some comfort in case things got nasty.

He took a seat at the bar just as Staggin strode out of the kitchen, a pewter plate heavily laden with scrambled eggs in one hand and a pitcher in the other. He placed them in front of Rellen. He filled a tankard with water from the pitcher and set it next to the plate.

Rellen got another look at Staggin's arm above the wrist as he poured, and the tattoos there had shifted once again.

"It's not much, but it's fresh and should fill you," Staggin said, reaching beneath the bar and placing a fork and knife beside the plate.

"Thank you." Rellen started in on the eggs, wracking his brain to dredge up any memory of moving tattoos. "The eggs are perfect." As he scooped up another mouthful, the dragonette unwrapped its tail from Staggin's neck and flapped down to the bar. It landed a few inches from the plate and eyed Rellen expectantly. Rellen swallowed and then smiled at the small creature. "Can he have some?"

"She," Staggin said. "And she'll eat whatever you give her."

Rellen pushed a few bits of egg to the edge of the plate nearest the little black draconian. "Go on," he said.

With an excited screech, it darted forward and snatched up a piece, swallowing it quickly. It prepared to snatch another bite and paused, lifting its head. It looked at Rellen for several seconds. Its head slid forward on a long sinewy neck and stopped just over his left breast, where the Eye of Tuluum lay in a pocket. It sniffed several times and then gave Rellen a blinking, green-eyed stare. A moment later, it returned to the plate, gazing hungrily at the scrambled eggs.

Wondering if it had somehow sensed the Eye, Rellen pushed a few more pieces to the side and took another bite. The dragonette's head darted in several more times, gulping hungrily.

"By the way," Rellen said, taking a swig from the mug, "it looks like your brigands are back. Ragged bunch led by one with silver trim, right?"

"That's them," Staggin said.

"There's at least thirty out there, not thirteen, including a woman I believe is a mage. I suspect your accord is about to crumble." He watched Staggin's reaction closely, and he found the dragonette staring at the big warrior as well.

Staggin's eyes shifted to the doors for a moment. "I heard riders coming into town." He seemed unconcerned. He glanced at the dragonette, held its gaze for several heartbeats, and then it seemed to nod at him. "And if they doubled their numbers, you're probably right."

"That doesn't worry you?" Rellen asked, surprised. He took another bite.

A strange chuckle escaped Staggin's lips. "Everyone has their time, Rellen of Corsia. Me. Them. You. If it's one thing I've learned, it's that our deaths don't amount to much over the course of decades and centuries. Sometimes, people are just food for wolves. And soldiers like us…we're usually just fodder for kings, queens, and despots. Either way, none of it matters much."

"You can't believe that."

"I've seen it with my own eyes…over and over again. The kings of Pelinon, in all our great wars and battles, merely painted the illusion of the higher moral ground when it came to the lives spent achieving victory."

"Pelinon has never been the aggressor," Rellen said a bit defensively. "We defended our borders and eliminated threats to both the people and the Crown."

"That's not entirely true, but even if it were, the hoarding of gold and power always breeds avarice in one's neighbors. Always." Staggin glanced again at the banners behind Rellen. "Pelinon has hoarded quite a bit of both over the centuries." He drew in a deep breath, his features thoughtful as he spoke. "Kings covet. Their soldiers die. That is the way of kings." He fixed his gaze upon Rellen. "Let me ask you a question. In the aftermath of our victories against those *aggressors*, did the kings before Saren III claim the nation-states that attacked them? You know the answer is yes. The many have become one, bought with the blood of men like you and me, regardless of banner."

"Are you saying the kings of Pelinon should have done it differently?" Rellen felt his ire rising. "That they should have merely held our borders and let neighboring nation states regroup and attack again?"

Staggin blew out a weary breath. "You misunderstand me." Scratching the dragonette's head thoughtfully, he continued, "I'm not saying it's wrong. I'm not saying it's right, either. Knowing what I know of men…and kings…I doubt we're capable of doing anything else. The desires of kings rarely translate into anything but spilled blood for those who fight for them. Do farmers and merchants really care which king or queen receives their tribute?"

The question stopped Rellen cold. He'd never been able to offer his father, Saren II, a good reason for why he didn't want the throne. When his father passed, the High Council asked him again to take up the mantle of king. His only answer had been it wasn't for him. He'd been grateful his brother was willing to occupy the throne. Until this very moment, he hadn't realized he'd always understood what Staggin was getting at. "I think I see your point," Rellen finally admitted.

"You've killed in battle? Killed in the name of the King?"

"More than I can count," Rellen replied.

"Did you know who you were killing? Know anything about the lives you took? Their mothers, fathers, children? Was every person you killed evil? Or were they just nameless enemies set upon you by their own king or queen?" He stared into Rellen's eyes. "How many had ever done you harm before the battle in which you took their lives?"

Rellen leaned back, thinking hard about that litany of questions. Maybe that was the reason he'd chosen the path he was on. Fighting soldiers had come to feel like fighting with himself. There had been good reasons for the battles he'd fought, but what he did now— going from place to place, seeking out evil and bringing an end to it felt, somehow, more...*righteous?*

He glanced at one of the banners hanging on the wall as a wild notion began to take shape. He looked thoughtfully at Staggin as he took another bite and chewed. Staggin had spoken of Rellen's forefathers as if he'd known them, or at least served in their armies. But it was impossible...unless. He eyed Staggin. "Can I ask you a personal question, one veteran to another? There's no judgment in it. I'm just curious."

"Go ahead, but I don't promise to answer."

"Those brigands outside, they eat and drink here, right?"

"That's right." Staggin looked like he knew where the question was going.

"You obviously don't like them, and I get the feeling you don't like brigands in general. I can only assume it's because they prey upon the weak and defenseless."

"I suppose that's the gist of it."

"And yet, you reached an accord with them. Why help them prey upon the weak? Why not do more than just hold them at bay? If you can do that much, do you not have the wherewithal to end them? Or at least keep them from preying upon the people of this region?"

Staggin blew out a weary, almost frustrated breath.

The dragonette stared at Rellen with its head cocked to the side. Rellen couldn't explain it, but he felt as if the little creature somehow agreed with him.

Rellen pushed what little remained of his breakfast toward the dragonette and nodded to it. It squeaked in delight and dove in hungrily.

"As much as I hate to say it," Staggin replied, "it's a fair question." He looked toward the doors of the tavern, gave the dragonette an irritated glance, and then fixed his gaze upon Rellen. "Who am I to insert myself into that natural order?"

"What?" Rellen was appalled by the question. "You're not serious." The dragonette snorted at Staggin, a tiny jet of smoke erupting from its nostrils.

"I've—" Staggin started but stopped as the dragonette moved across the bar and tentatively crawled up Rellen's arm. When Rellen smiled and nodded, it scampered up and took a seat on his shoulder, its tail coiling around his neck.

"Xilly likes you," Staggin said, "and I've never been more serious." There was a strange calm to his features. "The people we're talking about, in the isolated farmsteads, hunting lodges, and tiny burghs that are spread for miles in every direction, they *choose* to live out here, beyond the reach of civilization, the reach of the King. They made their choice, despite the dangers, for reasons only they can know and generally choose not to share with outsiders. Does it then fall upon me—upon *anyone*—to risk life and limb to kill men and women who have taken up their own place in that natural order?

"Predators and prey *are* the natural order. Everywhere and always—and let's face it, the same applies to the kingdom itself." Staggin snorted. "Gods, even the alliance with Kumal—" he nodded toward a green banner behind Rellen, "—was only because one of Pelinon's kings developed an appetite for Kumal's seaports in the northwest. Few know this, but early in his reign, King Saren gave Kumal an ultimatum: sign a treaty that granted free access or face invasion to achieve the same result. He sent a company of warriors who then laid waste to several Kumalian forts along the border as a warning."

For just a moment, Rellen froze at the accusation. Not because it wasn't true, but because it *was*. "I can't help but wonder how long it's been since you served," Rellen said. The answer lay there. He watched Staggin closely.

Staggin's eyes fixed on one of the banners behind Rellen for several moments. "It's been longer than I care to remember," Staggin said. "Those years are not something I like to think about."

Rellen glanced over his shoulder to where Staggin had been looking. It was the silver dragon and black field of the Surian Cabal.

Could one of Staggin's ancestors have been there? Eighty years ago? What forces had been involved in the war with Suria? The regular infantry and Pelinon's renowned cavalry had been involved. Pelinon emptied the magic schools, creating a potent battalion of mages to counter Suria's Life-Stealers. Dozens of mercenary companies had been integrated into Pelinon's ranks, as well as troops from several allied city-states. Who else...?

The memory of it struck him like a lightning bolt. The Strakhanni were a company of magically imbued warriors from the northern mountains, warriors whose magic was derived from swirling tattoos covering their bodies. He fixed his gaze upon Staggin and traced his eyes from the man's rough features, down to the tattoos beneath his collar and those at his wrist. As impossible as it was, it all fell into place.

It hadn't been an ancestor....

Just as Rellen took a breath to speak, the front doors slammed open.

"Staggin!" the man in black and silver shouted from the doorway. "It's time we had a conversation."

"What do you want, Kurm?" Staggin asked as the leader strode in with a line of brigands in tow. "I guess you're not here to eat?" The mage stepped out from behind Kurm, a faint smile upon her thin lips. Staggin's eyes went wide when he spotted her, and his expression turned to one of disgust. "What's she doing here?"

"The same thing we are," Kurm growled. "The treasure stashed in this lousy tavern, somewhere."

Staggin shook his head. "She's using you, Kurm. Azeera uses everyone…" He fixed steely eyes once again on the woman. "You miserable wretch."

Her smile reminded Rellen of a mummy, bared teeth and taut skin, but with crazed blue eyes.

"I don't know what you're talking about," she replied innocently. Her voice sounded far younger than the crone standing before them. "When you ran out on me, you left with enough Surian wealth to set up your own fiefdom." She raised an eyebrow. "Why, in the name of the Nine Gods, are you living like a pauper in a mud-hole like this?"

Staggin cast a sidelong glance at Rellen that seemed to say, *See? Wealth only attracts greed.* He returned his gaze to her for a few heartbeats. "Why am I here?" He laughed, but it wasn't a happy sound. "To get away from *you.*" He blew out a disgusted breath. "And you know damn well there's no treasure."

"Liar!" Kurm shouted.

A faint smile flickered across Azeera's face. Rellen knew a lie when he saw one. She was after something else, but he couldn't imagine what it might be. *Revenge, maybe? A jilted lover?*

"As she pointed out, Kurm, I have no need for wealth in a place like this."

"It's here! I know it is." Kurm seemed obsessed by the idea of gold hidden nearby. "I'm going to make this easy for you. Get on that big horse of yours and ride out, or we'll kill you and your new friend there. There are thirty of us now, Staggin, and you *know* what she's capable of. You don't have a prayer. We'll get that gold whether you're alive or dead."

Staggin shook his head. He glanced at Rellen. "When this gets started, slip out the back and ride away from here as fast as you can."

Rellen smiled at Staggin. "If veterans won't look out for each other, who will?"

Staggin looked as if he wanted to say something, but Rellen pushed his chair back and stood, facing the brigands. He locked eyes with Kurm, "He doesn't need a prayer. He has me." He slowly released the leather thongs securing his falchions and tilted his head left and right with loud pops.

"You sure you want to do this?" Staggin asked, pulling off his shirt. He shifted his gaze to the mob that filled the far end of the room.

"As it turns out, I think it's the reason I'm here," Rellen replied.

Staggin gave him a confused look. The old warrior's upper body, from waist to neck and down to his wrists, displayed a hodgepodge of intricate, shifting tattoos. Smoke and fire danced along one arm. Ice and stone tumbled down the other. A red demon shifted over one breast, an armored warrior upon the other. A menagerie of beasts, both wild and magical, slid across his skin in a slow swirl of images.

Staggin *had* to be a Strakhanni, perhaps the last. Rellen focused his attention on Azeera. She was his primary concern. A mage in the mix could be the wildest card of all.

"Enough!" Kurm shouted. "Kill them both!"

Several things happened at once.

The brigands attacked.

Kurm moved back a step, fading behind them.

Azeera and Rellen raised their hands and made quick gestures, beginning incantations.

Xilly flew from Rellen's shoulder as Staggin leapt over the bar like a hungry predator.

Rellen and Azeera released their spells just as Staggin reached the closest of the brigands.

A small bolt of black lightning shot from Azeera's finger, striking Rellen in the chest. A sharp tingle coursed over his body, carrying with it a strange miasma, as if the spell had been designed to rip the life-force violently from his body.

The mitigation spell he'd cast when he entered the tavern did its job. It was a simple, but potent, defensive spell that dissipated magical energy into whatever lay beneath his feet. Azeera surely had the same wards, but Rellen's spell wasn't meant to affect her. The leather strap of her bandoleer came to life, unbuckled itself, and slithered across the floor, headed toward the still-open doors. The pouches, opened by the spell, spilled their contents along the way. Azeera shouted in surprised rage. She chased after it, shouting curses at Rellen's ancestors.

Several strange thwacking sounds to Rellen's left drew his gaze. He couldn't believe his eyes. Three brigands had struck at Staggin simultaneously. Staggin held one of the brigand's blades in a right hand covered by the stonework tattoo. The armored warrior tattoo, solid but translucent enough to see through, had partially lifted off Staggin's chest. It held its sword high, crossed with the scimitar of an attacker. The crimson image of the demon stretched out ghostly, with clawed hands that were now wrapped around the blade of another brigand.

Rellen had never seen anything like it.

Staggin twisted his body, driving two of his attackers back, while the demon ripped the blade free from the hands of the third. In a flash, Staggin crouched and lashed out with his left hand. Tattooed flames coursed down his arm and along his fingers, igniting the leggings of the nearest brigand, who fell to the floor screaming.

Three brigands came at Rellen, weapons held high.

Rellen parried a slash from the first and then the second as he stepped back. With a well-practiced motion, he jerked a small vial full of black powder from his bandoleer. He parried another slash. Barking out a one-word incantation, he threw the vial straight at the furthest of his three assailants, leaping back with his eyes closed. The vial exploded with a sharp thud, pushing him further back.

The detonation drove the brigand before him staggering sideways. It sent another backward into several of his compatriots, while the third fell to the floor. Rellen slapped the staggered one's blade away and thrust his own into the man's throat. Yanking it free with a twist, Rellen stepped forward and drove his blade into the back of the one on the floor.

Meanwhile, Staggin snatched the stolen blade from the hands of the demon tattoo and waded into the remaining brigands like a berserker. They slashed and parried at him to no avail. He blocked with the stone tattoo on his left hand and slashed with the blade in his right. The tattoo knight deflected one swing after another, while the demon clutched and clawed at anything within reach.

Three more brigands shifted their attention to Rellen and charged.

Rellen grabbed a vile of green liquid from his belt, spoke an incantation, and threw it at their feet. The vial shattered. The contents erupted into an expanding cloud of thick green smoke that quickly enveloped them, giving them all horrific coughing fits. Rellen sucked in a breath and leapt forward. He slashed at the nearest leg and sent that man screaming to the floor. He thrust and impaled the next through the belly, wrenching the blade free. He spun, brought the blade around, and decapitated the third.

Grabbing the edge of his cloak, he spun again and spoke another incantation. A powerful gust of wind pushed the cloud straight into the mass of Kurm's brigands.

"Toreth!" Kurm screamed at the back of the tavern, "Light it!" He glared at Rellen. "Everyone outside!"

Kurm raced through the front doors, followed by the brigands in black and red.

Staggin and Rellen didn't let up. They charged forward, hacking and slashing at the remaining brigands bottlenecked at the door.

Staggin impaled one and severed the arm of another. The tattoo demon grabbed a brigand and ripped out his throat. Rellen drew his second falchion and engaged a pair of brigands, driving them back, their eyes full of fear.

"You don't think I'm going to let you get to those doors, do you?" Rellen growled.

He slashed with one blade and was parried. He blocked a slash with his off hand and riposted into the side of a brigand. He muttered an incantation, and the second brigand's cloak flew up and covered his head. Rellen drove his blade through the cloak and the chest behind.

Azeera stood at the door, her empty bandoleer in hand, and her eyes full of fury as she cast a spell. "*Kava thulai*!"

Rellen recognized the spell and braced himself as best he could. A smoky wall of force exploded into existence before her, expanding as it moved. What magic remained of Rellen's mitigation spell caught a piece of it as it crashed through the room. Tables flew in its path. The bodies of the dead and wounded lifted off the ground and went sailing. Rellen was tossed back and slammed against a rear wall. The force of the impact drove the falchion from his off hand.

Staggin, on the other hand, leaned into it as the demon tattoo lifted almost completely off his body, put its hands together, and pierced the force wall. The spell passed mostly around Staggin, ruffling his hair and pants, as if he merely stood in a strong gust of wind.

Rellen slumped as he came down off the wall. One of the brigands had landed at his feet, and Rellen dispatched him with a thrust through the back. He looked down to find that several vials in his belt had been shattered by the force wall. He cursed the loss of those spells just as Azeera grinned triumphantly at him and slammed the front doors closed. He heard her utter another spell, and a pale wall of red energy gleamed through the doors. He recognized the spell. It would kill anyone who touched it.

Flames crackled at the back of the tavern.

A loud *WHUFF!* erupted outside the front of the building, and smoke instantly seeped through the seams between the boards of the front wall.

"Damn it!" he barked. "It seems they mean to burn us out."

Staggin gave him a bland expression. "You think?"

Azeera's voice rose over the sound of the flames as she concluded another spell.

As Rellen and Staggin watched, smoky, black tendrils seeped through the front wall, racing toward the corpses that littered the floor.

"Death magic!" Staggin shouted.

Rellen gave a confused look just as tendrils touched the first body. They coiled around it, then around another...and another. The bodies, covered in blood, convulsed, arched their backs, and let out horrific, mindless howls as, one by one, they got to their feet.

"She's a Life-Stealer," Staggin snarled. "Don't let the zombies touch you!" He reached down and picked up a second blade.

"Zombies?" Death magic was forbidden in the schools where he'd studied. All he knew for sure was that they had to be burned or decapitated. He picked up his second falchion and sank into a low fighting stance. He didn't have time for any magic as the nearest zombie charged him, hands outstretched and mouth agape in hunger.

Rellen slapped its arms away with the blade in his left hand, stepped out of its path, and swung with the blade in his right. It chopped through an already ruined neck with a wet *THUCK!* of steel through bone.

Another zombie came at him. He ducked and tumbled to the side, came up, and cleaved off a leg. It slashed at him with an outstretched hand as it toppled sideways. He stepped back and cut its hand off with a quick slash.

Three more zombies were coming for him while Staggin did his best to fend off four that were clambering over each other to get to him. The knight and demon tattoos grappled with the clutching arms of the undead. Staggin hacked and slashed, hewing an arm off, then a head.

Rellen coughed as the room filled with smoke. He could already feel the heat coming from the front and rear of the building.

"We have to get out of here!" he shouted.

"Destroy these damn things first," Staggin yelled back as another head came free of its body.

The two zombies nearest Rellen charged straight for him, while the one with the missing leg and hand dragged itself across the floor to get at him. Rellen leapt sideways and swung. The arm of the first charging zombie came off just above the elbow. He slashed again, removing the other arm. It screeched in rage and leapt at him, its mouth wide open to bite. He stepped back as it landed face-down on the floor.

That's when the one behind it swiped at Rellen and clipped his left forearm. Freezing agony coursed up the limb, and the blade fell from his hand. Rellen screamed and staggered to his right, barely dodging another slash from the zombie. His left arm dropped to his side, lifeless. His right arm felt like it was made of lead. The zombie shifted, ready to pounce. Rellen knew he wouldn't be able to get out of the way.

A piercing screech filled the room as a black shadow darted down from the roof beams and latched itself onto the back of the zombie's head. The small dragonette reared back. An instant later, the zombie's head was engulfed by a stream of flames jetting from the dragonette's mouth.

The zombie stopped in its tracks, flailing its arms over its head, but the dragonette had already fluttered out of reach.

"*Kill it!*"

The voice slammed into Rellen's mind. It was small, feminine, and Rellen didn't hear it so much as sense it somehow. He staggered upright as the zombie howled, batting at the flames that now engulfed its head and shoulders. He felt like he was moving through molasses, but he summoned a last bit of panicked strength, drew back, and swung for all he was worth.

His blade passed almost completely through the zombie's neck. The zombie's head flopped sideways, dangling on a thin ribbon of flesh, and then its body fell forward slowly to collapse on top of the flailing zombie already on the floor.

Rellen forced his frozen muscles to work and finished off two zombies crawling toward him.

He could barely see Staggin through the smoke, but he saw enough. Three zombie bodies lay on the floor at the big warrior's feet. The demon tattoo, roaring in silent rage, held the arms of the last zombie at bay.

"*We go now!*" The feminine voice filled Rellen's thoughts. He couldn't think clearly, but he understood the urgency. He focused on his falchion lying on the floor, leaned over to snatch it up, and barely kept from falling over. Taking a deep breath, he steadied himself and picked up the weapon. Sliding it back into its scabbard, his senses reeled. He nearly toppled over.

Staggin swung with both weapons as he stepped backward. The zombie's arms came free, still clutched in the demon's claws. Staggin crossed the blades in front of him, the edges against the zombie's neck. He spread his arms with a quick jerk, and the head came free, tumbling to the floor with a thud.

The body crumpled in front of him and writhed.

"Get behind the bar!" Staggin shouted as the knight and demon tattoos sank back against his skin.

Rellen coughed and staggered across the room. Staggin leapt over the bar and disappeared behind it. As Rellen stumbled around the bar, Staggin rose again, revealing a large, wooden trap door and a set of stairs that descended into darkness.

"Quick," Staggin said, nodding toward the opening.

Rellen strained to lift a falchion aloft.

"*Lumitavay*," he muttered, barely able to get the word out. The falchion glowed, giving off as much light as a torch. His head reeling, he made his way down the stairs, steadying himself against the wall as he descended. With each step, he grew dizzier. The chamber below, stretching away into darkness, faded before him. He felt himself tumbling forward.

The world went black.

* * *

Rellen lay in frozen darkness for an eternity.

Without warning, a pinprick of light drew him up. Bright, soothing warmth flowed through his body, melting the ice enveloping him. He sucked in a deep breath. His eyes shot open to find Staggin and the dragonette staring down at him. The big warrior held a burning torch that illuminated a small room.

"You let one touch you," the big warrior said in a mildly accusing tone.

Rellen blinked several times as his mind registered the source of the warmth. He looked down. The tattoo of a golden snake with emerald eyes had coiled itself around Rellen's right arm up to the elbow, while the rest of Staggin's tattoos were flattened once again against his body, swirling in slow motion. The snake's body, however, pulsed in time with Rellen's heartbeat.

"You're one of the Strakhanni, aren't you?" he asked weakly.

"I believe I'm the only Strakhanni left," Staggin replied flatly. "The last of my brothers gave his life almost eighty years ago."

"How old are you?" Rellen lay there, stunned.

"I've lost count." Staggin chuckled. "What year is it?" he asked, a curious expression on his face.

"It's the twelve-hundred-and-fifty-first year, in the Second Age of Kai."

"Then I've been in this burgh for twenty-two years, and I am—" he paused for a moment, "—two hundred thirty-seven years old."

"How—"

"The Strakhanni were made to be nearly immortal," Staggin said, cutting him off, "falling to the perils of our enemies but not time. The price for this *boon* is that we foresee the moment of our demise."

"Is this—" Rellen started, looking up at the ceiling where crackling flames flickered through the floorboards above. He couldn't help but wonder if Staggin hadn't seen a fiery death beneath a burning tavern. He'd never heard that about the Strakhanni. Such magics were beyond his learning, but he had to admit, such an existence must be difficult to live with.

"No," Staggin said quickly, with a pained smile. "Although part of me wishes it had happened long ago." The golden snake dimmed, uncoiled itself, and slid back up along Staggin's body to disappear up over his shoulder.

Rellen looked around. A single rectangular hallway yawned at him, ending in darkness. He realized it went toward the livery.

"So, what happens now?" he asked, struggling to sit up. He felt better, although he wasn't certain he could get off the floor.

Staggin stood, helped Rellen up, and clapped him on the back.

Rellen swayed but managed to stay on his feet.

"We must get out of here," Staggin said, turning. He strode through the darkened hallway, his torch illuminating a passage that ended at a set of wooden rungs built into the wall.

Retrieving his falchion from the floor, Rellen followed as Staggin climbed the rungs. There was a faint scraping of wood as straws of hay and thin streams of dust fell to the earthen floor.

Staggin disappeared through the trap door above.

Rellen climbed slowly, collecting his wits as the remaining warmth of Staggin's magic pushed away the last vestiges of ice. When he reached the top and stood on the dry hay of the livery floor, he found himself in an empty stall at the back of the building. Staggin had already moved into the stall with the strangely marked roan and was rummaging around in the large chest. The roar of flames consuming the tavern filled the air, and they could hear timbers creaking. Smoke seeped through the cracks of the livery walls, but the building hadn't caught fire yet.

"Saddle your horse," Staggin called out.

Rellen moved to where Shaddeth slowly chewed on some hay. The horse snorted and shook his head in greeting.

"Sorry, old friend, but it looks like we won't be staying." Rellen patted Shaddeth's neck as he passed. With a single word and gesture, he dispelled the enchantment protecting his gear. He returned the saddle, saddle bags, and books to Shaddeth's back, securing everything. He turned to lead Shaddeth out when he froze in his tracks. It was a sight he'd never thought he'd see.

Staggin led his massive horse, unsaddled, out of the stall.

The last Strakhanni stood resplendent in a magnificent silver helm with a tall black crest rising over his head. The warrior's entire body was bare, save for black leather sandals laced over his calves and a silver, scale-mail loin piece falling to his knees. He held a five-foot spear with a curved blade on one end and a straight blade on the other.

"You ready?" Staggin asked, his voice full of grim warning.

"Of course," Rellen replied. "This is sort of what I do."

"What do you mean?"

For a moment, Rellen thought about telling the big warrior who he was, but there wasn't much point, and the flames engulfing the tavern were licking at the side of the stable.

"It doesn't matter. I just like a good fight is all."

"Well, this is likely to be one. Azeera *was* a Surian Life-Stealer. You didn't happen to see any young women ride in with them?"

"Yeah, three," Rellen replied. "It looked like they'd been stabbed."

"Ghasts." Staggin spat disgustedly. "Azeera steals their hearts and enslaves them. Ghasts are fast, deadly, and possessed by a limitless appetite for human flesh. Oh—" he eyed Rellen, "—and you don't want them touching you more than you didn't want those zombies touching you."

"Understood." Rellen opened a small pouch on his bandoleer and pulled out a tiny bamboo cage with a sharply horned beetle inside. He spoke a familiar incantation, made three quick motions with the hand holding the beetle, and then crushed the beetle onto his leather breastplate. He felt the spell flow over his body. With a chitinous clattering, thick plates formed around him with swirling light. Moments later, he was encased from head to toe in thick, horny plates that would keep the ghasts from touching his flesh. "That should do the trick."

Staggin raised an impressed eyebrow. "Indeed." He turned and stepped up to the stable doors.

"How do you know Azeera?" Rellen asked.

Staggin paused, his hand hovering over the latch to the doors. "She was my wife a very long time ago." He cracked the door open a hair and peered down the street.

Staggin's shoulders rose slightly, as if some weight had been lifted. He let out a long, relieved sigh.

"It's time I ended this." There was a strange finality to the statement.

"You mean we," Rellen corrected.

"No," Staggin said firmly. "I wasn't sure until just now. You're taking Xilly here." He nodded to the dragonette perched on his shoulder. "When I give the signal, you need to ride out as fast as you can."

"But—"

"No buts," Staggin said. "Xilly must live, and I know now I must die. My time has come, Rellen of Corsia."

"What are you talking about?"

Staggin smiled. "My vision has come to life out there. As for Xilly, I only know that Azeera wants her." He turned and stared into Xilly's eyes. "You knew this would happen, didn't you?"

The small creature nodded and rubbed her head along Staggin's cheek.

"Go, my friend. It's time for you to travel with a new companion."

Xilly licked his nose and then fluttered over to Rellen's shoulder.

"I need to go out there and get them all to surround me, including Azeera and those wretched ghasts." He locked eyes with Rellen. "Whatever you do, stay at least thirty feet away from me. Now, mount up."

"Why thirty feet?"

"Just do it," Staggin barked.

Rellen hauled himself into the saddle. Xilly fluttered but managed to stay in place.

"Are you ready?" Staggin asked, placing his hand against the stable door.

Rellen locked eyes with Staggin, wanting to push the question, but the set in Staggin's jaw made it clear there was no point. He nodded once and gripped the reins tightly. "I am now."

"Ghasts will come for me. Be ready."

Xilly's thought slammed into Rellen's mind. He wondered if ghasts could outrun a warhorse. He knew for certain they wouldn't tire. Ever. He thought about Staggin's plan to get them all around him. He suspected what was about to happen, but if the ghasts came for Xilly and not Staggin, they'd probably rip Rellen from his saddle eventually. He opened a pouch and pulled out a small piece of curved glass. Palming it, he thought his reply. *Don't worry, little one, I'm ready.*" He visualized what he had in mind.

Xilly cocked her head to the side, nodded once, then licked Rellen's cheek.

Staggin kicked the stable doors open and marched out with his warhorse in tow.

"Kurm!" he shouted as he marched into the middle of the street. He pointed his spear at the mass of brigands gathered in front of the burning tavern. "You want me? I'm right here."

Rellen stayed hidden inside, but he had a clear view of Staggin.

"You don't think we're going to let you ride out now, do you?" Kurm shouted back.

Staggin turned his horse away from the brigands and promptly slapped it on the ass with the flat of his spear. The horse whinnied angrily and shot off down the street at a full gallop. Staggin stared after it for a moment and then turned to face Kurm and the rest. As Rellen watched, it galloped about thirty yards and then quickly faded out of existence.

Rellen blinked his eyes, not believing what had happened. He heard a few surprised shouts from the brigands.

"Where's the other one?" Kurm asked, unphased.

"That bitch's zombies got him. They're all burning in the fire. You happy, Azeera?" Staggin asked, turning his head slightly. "You ruined yet another life, you malevolent bitch."

"We'll just see about that." The crone's voice came from well out of sight. Three distinct screeches filled the morning, and there was a scampering of clawed feet racing across the dirt.

"Rellen!" Staggin shouted as he charged forward. "They're coming for you!"

Rellen urged Shaddeth through the doors and looked down the street.

A thick pillar of smoke rose from the roaring flames consuming the tavern. A smoky haze filled the street, slightly obscuring where Kurm stood amidst the brigands. They all had their blades drawn. Azeera sat upon her horse, well past the brigands, glaring at Rellen and the small dragonette upon his shoulder. Three young women raced toward him with glowing white eyes, but they were women no longer. Their bodies had transformed, decayed like mummies, with mouthfuls of sharp teeth and long, black talons tipping their fingers.

Staggin charged straight into the middle of the brigands, slashing mightily with his spear as the demon and the knight rose from his body to protect him. He was completely surrounded.

The three ghasts had halved the distance to Rellen and were headed straight for him.

"*Cuum stava sym!*" Staggin's booming voice filled the street as he drove his spear into the ground. Three brigands drove their blades through Staggin's body as thunder clapped with the impact. In an instant, a swirl of color erupted around Staggin's body, like a tornado of bright ink caught in a maelstrom. The tattoos covering his body expanded, grew to impossible sizes, and began tearing the brigands to pieces.

The swirl of ink turned more crimson with each passing moment as it chewed into them. They screamed in terror as it shredded their bodies. They were done for.

The ghasts, however, were nearly upon Rellen. He waited patiently as they raced toward him. He hadn't known what Staggin was going to do, but he'd suspected the outcome and had prepared accordingly.

The three ghasts, black talons and white fangs nearly upon him, shrieked their hunger.

Rellen focused upon the glass lens in his hand. He shifted sideways in the saddle, adjusting the intended trajectory. With a sweeping motion, he directed his magic into the lens and shouted *"Kava thulai!"*

A wall of force, identical to the one Azeera had used against him, shot away from his body, smashed into the three ghasts, and sent then hurtling back into the churning maelstrom of blood filling the street. The ghasts' howls were silenced as they disappeared into the swirling tornado.

Moments later, the twister shrank and disappeared, leaving only a bloody stain upon the ground. There was no sign of Staggin or the brigands.

Rellen focused his attention on Azeera. He prepared a defensive spell, drew his second blade, and urged Shaddeth toward her with Xilly perched upon his shoulder.

"You ready to die?" he called out. "You're all alone, now."

The gaunt woman glared at him. For a moment, it looked like she was going to stand her ground. Rellen tensed, preparing himself for whatever spell she might cast.

She hissed at him like an angry animal and jerked on the reins of her horse. She kicked the animal's sides and it took off at a full gallop.

Rellen watched her ride away as the heat from the burning tavern warmed his skin.

"She'll be back," Xilly's faint voice echoed in his thoughts. *"She'll never give up on me while she lives."*

Rellen turned his head and peered into her tiny, green eyes. "Can you tell me why?"

"I know not why. I only know she will."

"Well," Rellen said tiredly, "she isn't the only person I have to look for over my shoulder."

Shaddeth's ears shifted nervously as the tavern continued to burn. Xilly fluttered down and landed on Shaddeth's head, and it seemed to calm the big horse.

Rellen shook Shaddeth's reins and got him moving down the street, headed toward the southwest.

"Shaddeth, that's Xilly. Xilly, Shaddeth."

Xilly sniffed at the horse's head and then licked him between the eyes. Shaddeth snorted lightly as he walked down the street.

"Xilly, you don't happen to know the nearest city to the southwest, do you?" Part of him felt a little strange talking to his new companion.

"Sabatar."

"Then we're off to Sabatar. Hopefully, we won't run into Azeera—or anything else—along the way. I need a bed and a bath."

"Me too!"

Rellen let Shaddeth find his own pace as they headed away from the pyre that had been the Bear Claw Tavern. He looked over his shoulder just as the burning roof caved in with a thunder of breaking timbers and snapping boards. A gust of wind, fire, and smoke blossomed, and, as it did, the real reason the Eye had led him to it became clear. It hadn't been to kill Kurm. It obviously hadn't been to save the last Strakhanni, or even face down Azeera. He stared at the small dragonette as she peered down the road ahead of them. For whatever reason, the Eye of Tuluum had brought him there to find Xilly. He didn't know why, but he sensed it as the truth.

He gave the small creature a gentle scratch along its neck and then let out a long breath. He would do what he'd always done since becoming a Guardian of Pelinon. He would travel, find evil in the world, and see to its end. He would just do so with another mouth to feed.

"*Yes!*" the small voice chirped in his head. "*Food!*"

* * * * *

Quincy J. Allen Bio

National Bestselling Author Quincy J. Allen is a cross-genre enthusiast with a growing number of titles under his belt. His media tie-in novel *Colt the Outlander: Shadow of Ruin* was a Scribe Award finalist in 2019, and *Chemical Burn*, a sci-fi noir thriller was a Colorado Gold Award finalist in 2010.

Blood Oath, book 3 of his Blood War Chronicles series, debuted in February of 2019, and he is currently working on the fourth book in that six-book fantasy steampunk series, entitled *Blood World*. He coauthored the fantasy novel *Reclaiming Honor* with Marc Alan Edelheit in their Way of Legend series, released in October of 2019, book 2 is due out early in 2021, and he is currently working on book 3. In November of 2019, he and Kevin Ikenberry published the novel *Enforcer*. Set in the Four Horsemen Universe, it is part of Ikenberry's Peacemaker series. He is currently working on a novel for Kevin Steverson's Salvage Title universe based upon the short story "Vorwhol Dishonor," as well as one for Jamie Ibson's Myrmidon universe based on the short story "Cradle and All."

His short story publications are numerous, including "Sons of the Father," appearing in Larry Correia's *Monster Hunter: Files* from Baen, as well as a growing number of novelettes appearing in Chris Kennedy Publishing's anthologies both in and out of the Four Horsemen Universe.

He works out of his home in Charlotte, North Carolina, and hopes to one day be a New York Times bestselling author.

# # # # #

Songbird by Jamie Ibson

...Oh, the year was sixteen twenty and four,
How I wish I'd been in Westlocke then!
A Venator Knight came from the east
Riding eighteen hands, a magnificent beast

Gods curse them all!
He was told he'd hunt the swamps for that Greyskin gold
He'd smite them down, in the moor
But the victory cheer was premature
The Alfar's bounty just a lure

The Alfar Lords revealed their plot
How I wish I'd been in Westlocke then!
For twenty damned elves ambushed the knight
But found themselves in a helluva fight

Gods curse them all!
He was told he'd hunt the swamps for that Greyskin gold
He'd smite them down, in the moor
But the victory cheer was premature

The Alfar's bounty just a lure

F lint's baritone voice made him sound older than he was. The hall's many patrons drowned him out as they joined in for the rest of the song, most of them singing badly off-key, but to the miners, stevedores, and porters, enthusiasm was vastly more important than pitch. The "Alfar's Lure" was one of those songs that could get every human in Clifftop Hall clapped in irons, locked in the stocks, or worse, but the tune remained one of the most popular in the few human-only drinking holes in all of Westlocke. The room fell silent as Flint took over for the final verse, traditionally whispered solely by the voice leading the song.

It's been three hundred and twenty year
How I wish we'd been in Westlocke then!
If we'd known then what we know now
We'll take this city back, this we vow!

And then the crowd came roaring back for one last repetition of the chorus, slowing on the final line.

Gods curse them all!
He was told he'd hunt the swamps for that Greyskin gold
He'd smite them down, in the moor
But the victory cheer was premature
The Alfar's bounty just a lure.

The hall erupted into whoops and cheers before Flint's voice had died away, and the older men raised their mugs of ale in salute. Flint took a bow and retired to his seat. "Grand, lad," one of the old miners said. "They still adding the years to that last verse?"

"That's how I was taught, aye," Flint replied, and the miner raised his stein in mock salute.

"Good. First time I heard that tune, we was only up to the two 'undred seventies. Made the verse kinda awkward-like." The miner moved on, bought himself another dram of whiskey, and threw it back before stumbling out the door.

No one had a thing for Flint, though. As a boy, he'd sung for his supper and been well rewarded for a night's entertainment. He'd grown into his voice as it deepened until he had just as much range as Reverend Bartholomew at the Respitoreum. He knew dozens of songs, every verse, start to finish and could stay on key when most of these mopes couldn't carry a tune if it were piss in a chamber pot, but the crowd was stingy tonight and had no spare coppers for him. They were drinking it all away. The clink of coin on the bartop kept the proprietor, Julius, in a constant state of motion. The barkeep's daughter, Patience, brought Flint a half bowl of stew and a chunk of bread and laid it before him with an embarrassed flush to her cheeks before fleeing back to the kitchen without a word. He turned the bread over and saw part of it had already gone grey with mold. He grimaced, cracked off the moldy bit, and tossed it into the hearth. He scooped the stew—watery and thin, with little more than celery and mutton fat to thicken it—with the bread.

Then again, maybe not even Julius. There'd been days, when Flint was younger, where he'd gotten a whole loaf of bread fresh from the oven, and the stew had been thick and hearty. Clearly, Patience knew she was serving him little more than slop, and she'd retreated before he could complain.

Disgusted with the whole thing, Flint slipped from his bench at the table and made his way out the door, bowl in hand. It was chilly outside, and the stench of rotting fish and sea salt replaced the odors of spilled ale and hearthfire. Mutt got to his feet when he saw Flint coming and wagged his tail. Flint unlooped Mutt's rope leash from the hitching post and knelt next to the dog. "Heya boyo," Flint said and patted the dog's flanks while Mutt headbutted him and licked at his face. Flint laid the mostly empty 'stew' bowl down in front of the dog. Mutt buried his nose in the bowl and slurped at it greedily. Patience stepped out of the hall as the dog finished.

"Father's mad, Flint. He wants that bowl back," she said.

"Of course," Flint replied. "I'm just going to—"

Julius burst from the doorway, almost knocking his daughter over. "Give that bowl back, thief!"

"Gods and daemons," Flint swore, "I'm not *stealing* it! I just gave the last of that slop you called stew to Mutt, and then I was going to—"

"What? You're feeding that mangy thing from my good bowl?" Julius interrupted. "How dare you—"

"I'm washing it!" Flint yelled. He moved to the flowstone trough that followed Blackwood Way, the thoroughfare outside, and dipped the bowl in to let the clean water sluice over it. "I'm not stealing your stupid bowl!"

"Return it now, or I call for the Garda," Julius demanded. Patience's eyes went wide, and she fled back inside.

"Over a stupid bowl of watery stew and moldy bread? Get ploughed, ye hal'far turncoat." Flint gave the bowl a flick to rid it of the water from the trough and threw it like a discus at the barkeep. It clattered off the wall next to Julius and tumbled to the cobblestones. "I can get shite food and naught to drink anywhere I like!"

"You'll not be coming back to Clifftop Hall, ya wee prick," Julius snarled. "Yer not welcome, not no more."

"Clearly," Flint growled back. "You've poured enough draughts tonight, you're welcome very much. See how much watered-down whiskey and fizzy piss ya sell when you've got nobody whetting your crowd's appetite!"

He scooped up Mutt's leash and turned to depart. He nearly collided with the young lady waiting silently, a few paces back, and had to dodge to the side so as to not run her over. He froze. She was *stunning*—strawberry blonde hair in curls down past her shoulders, flawless skin, white linen blouse, a snug red vest embroidered with silver, and a matching full-length skirt. "Pardon, lady," Flint said and stood aside with a deep bow. "Seems the proprietor's got a full-blown case of raging arsehole. I'd be careful, were I you. C'mon, Mutt."

Flint made his way down Blackwood Way as it wound down the cliffside in a series of hairpin turns. Front doors of cavehomes, built right into the cliff's face, dotted the way. He had no idea how they'd managed to hollow them out—probably some kind of damned alfar magic.

He rounded one of the switchbacks and grimaced. The smell preceded the gallows. Three new victims hanged, and the carrion feeders had been hard at work. Flint kept going, head down. He didn't want to know if he knew any of them. It was all too easy to wind up dancing on Hangman's Row. He was probably pushing it just singing "Alfar's Lure." Neither the alfar nor their half-breed spawn had any sense of humor about the song. The only thing that saved him was that *everyone* in the hall was guilty of singing along.

The switchbacks finally flattened out into Downtown proper. The starlight was enough for him to see his way between the shanties and shacks to his lean-to. His belly grumbled and complained, but that was nothing new. He pulled a ratty fur pelt over him for a little warmth, Mutt flopped down next to him, and he went to sleep.

* * *

"**O**i!"

Flint awoke early the next morning to a kick in the shins, cursed, and kicked out by reflex, but didn't connect. He pulled the fur back, and sunlight pierced his brain, eliciting a groan.

"Don't be like that, Flintie," Kaeso said. Kaeso was such a turd; Flint wasn't even upright yet, and he could already tell the day was going to hell. "Dog squad's comin'."

"Gods 'n daemons," Flint cursed. "Why'd you care?"

"They're bloody hal'far, mate," Kaeso replied. "I need a reason now, do I?"

Flint crawled out from beneath his lean-to and tugged on Mutt's leash. "Ugh, where are they?"

"They's comin' up from the dockside. Get that doggo away lickety-split, or you'll never see 'im again."

"Thanks," Flint said and slipped away down a weed-strewn alley, Mutt following dutifully at his heels. "Whaddaya say, boyo? Where are we going to disappear to?"

He passed Old Missus Decarius' perch, the only three-story building in all of Downtown, heading for Blackwood Way again.

"Och, don't ye be goin' up thataway, Songbird," Decarius crowed from her balcony. "Ye don' be wanting to go thataway."

"Why's that?" Flint asked. "And my name's not Songbird, Missus."

"Suits ye better'n Flint," the elderly lady replied. Her left hand hung in a sling across her front, as it always had, and she pointed with her right. "Head down t'wards the cliffs above the waterfront. The mutt wranglers be about."

"I know about the Dog Squad, Missus," Flint replied. "They're down that way. I'm looking to stay ahead of them."

She shook her head. "They ain't, I seen 'em afore the sun lit that little hovel you claimed. Stay off Blackwood, Songbird, lest ye regret it."

Decarius was old and likely senile and had been for some time. Flint ignored her warning and set off again in the same direction as before. "I take it back," Decarius shouted. "Flint'll do ye fine, rock fer brains. Don't say I never warned ye!"

Flint had never trusted the old crone on her perch. She seemed a bit...touched. He made it all of two alleys over before he regretted disregarding her warning. A hand of hal'far squaddies, led by an Overseer, rounded the corner moments before he reached it, and Flint froze in his tracks.

The hal'far patrol wore broad leather hats, with one side pinned up, and a red-and-white bloodhawk feather standing proud to indicate they were, indeed, the Garda. Their leather jerkins and boots were dyed a deep green and done up with bright brass buckles. The green contrasted against the white linen of their gambesons and trews, all neat and clean. If the uniforms and armor didn't give it away, the flintlocks, basket-hilted swords, and needle-fine daggers did.

"Oh ho, what 'ave we 'ere?" the Overseer laughed, and the squad spread out to fill the lane. Flint took a step back and tightened up on Mutt's leash protectively.

"Bite me, wanker, this' my Mutt and I care for 'im. I feed 'im, he ain't no trouble to no body, and ya can't 'ave 'im."

"Oh, *sorry*, sir, beg yer pardon!" the Overseer replied. "Hey lads, did you see this new directive from Lord Bjornsen?" The others shook their heads in the negative. "Apparently, it's the *serfs* wot gets to decide wot dogs we takes. D'ja know that, gents?"

"Naw, sorry 'Seer, but I ain't seen nuttin' like dat," one of them replied. He wore a broad grin, but his eyes were cold. "Last I 'eard, the Downtownies were nuttin' but the turds at the bottom o' the dung 'eap."

"Now," the Overseer said with a predatory gleam in his eye. "What say we come to an understandin'?" Flint glared at him suspiciously and clutched Mutt's leash tighter but didn't object. "What say we don't take that mangy fleabag with us, and in return, you 'elp us track down one Felix Maximus, reputed to be something of a healer in this festering shithole?"

Flint distrusted hal'far as much as the next Downtowner, but seeing as they outnumbered him lots to one, he didn't have much choice. Everyone knew the Dog Squad took the dogs away, and no one ever saw them again. He couldn't let that happen to Mutt.

"You promise you won't take Mutt?" Flint asked.

"Absolutely," the Overseer said. "On my oath of office."

Flint turned, then froze and looked back. "And the rest of your squad, too?"

The Overseer smirked at the beggar's suspicions and nodded. "None of us will take your dog anywhere. Half-elf's honor."

Half-elf's honor? That's not worth a bucket of spit, he thought. "Fine. This way."

Flint threaded his way through the mishmash of lanes, alleys, and paths and considered simply fleeing, but if they got even the slightest chance, they could volley fire their flintlocks into his back. That, of course, assumed the Overseer didn't command some kind of magic that would strike him down in an instant. No, they had him over a barrel, and he knew it. He led them on until he came within sight of the nondescript shack.

"There it is," Flint said, nodding his head slightly toward the house. He didn't know who was watching, and Felix was a well-loved member of the Downtowner community. Even if the Garda didn't kill him, someone else might, for the crime of breaching 'etiquette.'

"You're sure?"

"Sure, I'm sure, Overseer," Flint snarled. "You think I'm too stupid to know what'll happen if I take you to the wrong house?"

The impertinence earned him a cuff upside the head from one of the squaddies, and Flint accepted it without complaint.

"Remain here."

The Overseer and his squad crept down the lane, and he sent two of his men around to the front. They paused a moment outside, then on some unseen signal, they threw the rear door open, almost tearing it from its hinges, and stormed inside. Flint heard some shouting and a crash. Mutt whimpered and whined, and Flint shushed the poor boy. Mutt was a big softie and didn't have an aggressive bone in his body.

Soon, the squad exited into the lane, their quarry bound and gagged. Flint tried to remain stoic as Felix's eyes locked on his, accusing, but failed, flinched, and looked away.

"Thanks for the help, boy," the Overseer said as he approached.

"Much obliged. Old Felix here's been a thorn in our side for some time now. Off you go, lads, we'll catch up."

Three of the squad continued past Flint, dragging Felix toward the Blackwood switchbacks with a rope much like the one Mutt wore. Flint swallowed hard. "What are you going to do?"

"Oh, that's up to the magistrate. *Technically,* he hasn't killed anyone, so it's an interesting case, but he's *saved* a few lives we'd rather he hadn't. You'll know if he turns up dancing on the Row. And if not…" he left that unstated threat hanging in the air.

"What 'bout the dog, 'Seer?" the one remaining Garda squaddie asked.

"What? You can't!" Flint protested and stepped between the Garda troops and Mutt. "You gave your word you wouldn't take him!"

"True. I did say that, didn't I?" the Overseer replied. "On one hand, you did help us locate Felix, who has been wiley like a fox and escaped us until now. On the other hand, you've been insolent, disrespectful, and are in no position to start making demands, *human.*"

In one smooth motion, the Overseer drew what Flint had taken to be a dagger from his belt. It wasn't. It was a polished length of oak with a granite pommel the size of a jay's egg, and opposite the pommel, a colorless, translucent blade winked into being. The Overseer plunged the blade deep between Mutt's ribs.

"NO!" Flint shouted, lunging for the Overseer, but the squaddie tackled him from behind. Mutt collapsed, Flint went down, and the Overseer piled on, laying into him with boot and fist.

Flint was utterly outweighed and outmatched, but he was furious and hateful, and barely noticed. He turtled, lashed out with knees and kicks and punches of his own. The squaddie swatted his hands aside and wrestled to control him, but Flint's ragged clothing just tore when he grabbed a handful.

Flint's hand closed on something on the squaddie's belt, and he tugged it free. In desperation, Flint drove the blade up with a wordless scream of anger and hate. The squaddie's scream faded away, replaced by a gurgle. The squaddie's hands clutched at the stiletto that pierced his chin to the hilt.

"Murderer!" the Overseer hissed and lifted the bladewand for a downward strike as the translucent *force* projection shimmered back into existence. Flint didn't hesitate. He lashed out again and struck the Overseer in the wrist. The bladewand tumbled away, and the blade disappeared. Flint scrambled backward on his hands and feet, like a sandcrab. The Overseer stalked closer, reaching for Flint with his bare hands. "You're going to regret that, boy."

Flint turned over onto his front, clawed his way to his feet, and ran.

He ran past the huts, down the alleys, and across pathways. He vaulted over half-broken walls, past Madam Neredia's brothel, flophouses, and Missus Decarius' Perch. Somehow, the Overseer managed to keep pace. He knew each turn, each double-back, and each trick Flint employed to shake him.

Decarius stepped out from her front door just as Flint dashed past, blundered into the Overseer's way, and the two went down in a heap. She hurled some creative curses at the Overseer, and Flint felt terrible for the poor old lady, but he couldn't exactly go back and help her. He passed the crematorium and was sucking wind hard, stumbling over cobblestones and holding onto shack walls for support.

When he turned around and walked backward to look behind him, the Overseer was gone. Flint turned back just in time to notice a translucent staff swing out of the alley, bash him in the shins, and then he collapsed when his legs exploded in a fiery ball of pain. The Overseer's backstroke smashed him on the crown of his head, then the hal'far raised the wand two-handed and brought the force-staff down across Flint's gut. The staff struck just below Flint's ribcage and knocked the wind from him. Flint's eyes grew blurry with tears of agony. The force staff's long shaft shortened into a chisel-tipped point, and Flint scrunched his eyes against the knife blow.

It didn't come.

His belly finally cooperated, and he drew breath. Then he wiped a dirty forearm across his brow to clear his tears away and looked up. The narrow wand with the granite pommel clattered to the cobblestones, followed by the Overseer's knees, then shoulders. The hal'far grasped his throat, and bright red blood pumped with each heartbeat between his fingers.

An old, wizened man stood just beyond the dying half-elf, with a length of fine wire ending in a loop dangling from one fist. Wisps of white hair fluttered in the wind, bushy eyebrows rode his brow like grey caterpillars, and liver spots mixed with pockmarks on both of the man's cheeks.

"Thank you," Flint wheezed and got to his feet on unsteady legs. Blood trickled from his scalp where the staff had struck him, and

Flint wiped the blood away. He felt for the wound and winced as he found it and applied pressure. He didn't recognize the old-timer. "I don't believe we've met, grandfather, but I fear you've likely just condemned yourself to the same death as I."

The old man's voice was strong and clear. "That's where you're wrong, boy. Flint, is it? We've met before," he said, and before Flint's eyes, he *changed*. His old, reddened, hooked nose shrank and became sharp and predatory. His scruffy grey eyebrows became dark, trim, and neat. The pockmarks on his cheeks filled in, his eyes lost three dozen years in age, and his wispy grey whiskers transformed into a neatly trimmed goatee. His shabby clothing became a fine brown cloak, tan linen shirt, breeches, and calfskin boots.

"Nero?" Flint gasped in astonishment. Flint did indeed know the man; they all did. Everyone knew the King of the Downtowners.

"Aye, lad. Check the thug for valuables, bring the wand, and follow me. If you're to unplough this mess you've created, you'll need some guidance."

"*I've* created?" Flint echoed. "What in all the ivory towers is that supposed to mean?"

"It means you sold out one of the bravest men to have ever lived Downtown to the hal'far over a dog they were going to kill anyway, and you were too naïve even to see the double-cross coming," Nero spat. "Now hurry up!"

As instructed, Flint checked the Overseer's belt pouch and turned up more coin than he'd seen in his life—a handful of copper hawks, two silver gyrs, and even a golden eagle. Those alone would keep him well fed for weeks. He patted the body down and found something heavy hanging from the corpse's neck. Flint fished it out and let out a long breath.

The amulet hung on a dainty silver-colored chain. Three triangular blue stones, the color of the sky at noon in June, lay arranged with their tips touching with some kind of leather and sinew woven around them in an intricate knot. The metal seemed heavy like quicksilver made solid. With his clothes little more than tattered remnants and rags, he had nowhere to put his newfound riches, so he draped the amulet around his neck and claimed the belt and pouch.

"Grab the wand and help me with him," Nero ordered and hoisted the body up, heaving one arm over a shoulder as Flint took the other.

"What...where are we...going?" Flint asked. Nero chinned toward the cliff's edge, beyond the next row of shacks. Whitecaps crashed against the rocks below, as the wharves and jetties stretched out into the bay off to their right. Nero counted to three and heaved. The body tumbled limply over the edge and disappeared into the foamy seawater.

"Won't someone notice?" Flint asked. His gaze lingered on the harbor below.

"Probably, aye," Nero replied. "So we'd best be gone by the time they come to investigate."

Nero led him back through the warrens until Missus Decarius' three-story tower came into view. Nero entered like he owned the place and pulled the door shut behind them. Decarius was nowhere to be seen. Nero opened a closet door, stepped in, and vanished.

"Uh...hello?" Flint asked cautiously. Nero's arm emerged from the back of the closet, grabbed him by the collar of his shirt, and yanked.

The closet had a false back, and once he was past the jackets, coats, and robes, he was on a descending spiral stairway. Nero waited for him at the bottom.

"What do ye know about magic, boy?"

Flint gulped. "That it's a one-way trip to the gallows, sir."

"Wrong," Nero replied. "Try again."

"That...that's all I've ever been taught, sir." Then he inhaled sharply. "But *you* know how to use it, right? That's how you changed and snuck up on the Overseer!"

"And do I look like I'm on my way to the gallows, Flint?"

"No, sir."

The stairs led to a chamber of stone walls and a ceiling with lanterns hung from hooks. There were a table, some chairs, two bookshelves flanking a heavy door, and a weapons rack. Flint gave it a wide berth, as he wanted nothing to do with it. Like many other prohibitions in Westlocke, to be found in possession of a sword, dagger, or other weapon meant at least a flogging, perhaps even hanging on the Row. Missus Decarius rummaged through a trunk in one corner.

"Where's Kiara?" Nero asked. Before Missus Decarius could answer, the door opposite opened, and Flint's jaw dropped. He recognized her instantly. She was the strawberry blonde from outside Clifftop Hall the night before, except now she wore a charcoal leather shirt and pants that, aside from the color, could have passed for standard Garda armor. Over the armor, she wore a mottled cloak with a hood, which hid most of her curls in shadow. Her reddened eyes and blotchy cheeks suggested she'd been crying, but she wore a grim, determined frown on her face and clenched her fists into tight balls. She strode into the room, crossed directly to Flint, and slapped him on the cheek with a piercing *crack*.

"We aren't even, not in the slightest." She marched to the weapons rack and retrieved a dagger that went into a sheath she already wore on one hip. "But it's essential you understand *precisely* where you stand."

"Who—?"

Missus Decarius laughed. "Oh, that's right, it's been a while! Songbird, this is Kiara Maximus. You remember, Felix Maximus' daughter?"

Flint was astounded. True, he hadn't seen Kiara in years, but the awkward, straw-haired girl he remembered from too-many seasons ago had matured into a stunning young woman.

"*Songbird?*" Kiara asked, with a moue of distaste on her lips.

"Don't let the threadbare rags, skinny legs, filthy hands, bare feet, scraggly hair, weak mustache, patchy beard, and scars fool you," Decarius said with a twinkle in her eye. Flint cast his gaze down at his bare feet and felt his cheeks flush. "The boy can sing."

"Alright, Ceres, that's enough," Nero said. "We don't need the boy hating us too. But it's true, Flint, you look a mess. I daresay if you didn't *look* so much the part of a beggar, you wouldn't find yourself begging for watery stew and moldy hunks of week-old bread. Give Kiara that bladewand you took off the Overseer and follow me."

Flint nervously handed the wand over to Felix's daughter, retracted his hand like she was a viper about to strike, and fled into the next room. Nero pulled a kettle off a woodstove and took a washbasin off a shelf.

"Strip and sit." Nero gestured to a chair with a thick towel over the back. The chair sat in front of some kind of winged armoire. When Flint hesitated, Nero flicked open a straight razor. "Sit!"

Flint pulled off his ragged shift, no more glamorous than a knee-length potato sack, tucked the blue stone amulet into the folds of the fabric, and wrapped the towel around his waist. "What...are you doing?" Flint asked.

"Saving your life, and maybe Felix's too. Quiet."

Nero daubed shaving soap all over Flint's face, expertly shaved his cheeks and neck, and swapped the razor for shears. He trimmed Flint's too-thin mustache and shaped the hair on his chin.

"Much better," Nero said absently, then went to work on his shaggy mane of hair. He stopped abruptly. "Ugh. You have lice. Did you know you have lice? Never mind."

Nero kept working, tugging on lengths of Flint's hair and shearing them off until they were all of reasonably equal length, hanging just to his jawline. Flint squirmed but didn't complain when Nero ran his fingers over the goose egg where the Overseer had bashed him. Nero finished a few moments later, and he passed Flint a scented bowl of oil.

"Run your hands through that, then through your hair. The oil will kill the lice in a day or two. Ideally, you'll even still be alive to appreciate it. More warm water there to wash up, pumice stone for scrubbing, and there are clothes in the drawers there."

* * *

When they emerged, Kiara wore a furious look on her face. "Are you sure the Overseer is dead?" she began, without preamble.

"Entirely," Nero said. "Garotted him, opened his arteries, bled him out, and threw him into the sea for shark chum."

"I can't bond with this accursed wand. It's inert." She offered the bladewand back to Nero. She glanced at Flint. "That's quite a change, did Nero glamor you?"

"Ouch," Flint replied. "I wasn't that bad...was I?"

"You were," Nero said. "Shave and a haircut, clean clothes and a wash, they'll change a man. Now, what is this about the wand? That hal'far is dead as can be, his soul's departed, no question unless..." Nero looked at Flint in sudden horror. "You! Come here, boy."

"Him?" Kiara asked.

"I'm such a fool," Nero cursed. "Head wound. He bled like a butchered swine."

"Bollocks," Decarius complained. "How did you not notice?"

"I was busy!" Nero raised his voice. "Now, there's only one way to know for sure." Nero passed the bladewand back to Flint. "Hold this."

Nero fished out a keyring from a pocket and slipped one of the keys off it. He held it out on his palm before him. "Try to take the key. Imagine a hand, your hand, reaching across the gap between us, closing the key in its fist, and returning it to you," Nero said. "Concentrate. *Hard.*"

"This is foolish," Flint said. "I can't use magic. I'm no wizard."

"You think, therefore you can," Decarius said. "But only with the aid of a bonded focus. If Nero's right, you accidentally bonded to that wand. Do as he says, Songbird."

Flint stared at the thing in his hand. The shaft was solid oak, about as long as his forearm, with half of it wrapped in some kind of pebbly leather. One end bore a perfectly smooth granite stone the size and shape of a chicken's egg, held in place by a tiny net woven out of some material he didn't recognize. The net came together at the wand's base and tucked away under the leather wrap. The exposed wooden end was blunt and sanded smooth. Flint did as he was told and pointed the wand at Nero's waiting palm.

"You have to visualize it," Nero said.

"I am," Flint replied. He imagined himself reaching out, grasping the key, and pulling it back. It was silly.

"You have to *want* it," Nero said.

"I…don't, though," Flint said. He lowered the wand. "I—"

"How about this," Nero interrupted. "A focus can only bond with one soul at a time. I'd hoped Kiara could bond with it. She knows what she's doing, but if you've bonded to it, she can't. Do as I say, so I don't have to toss you to the sharks like I did that blasted half-elf. Refuse, and you follow the Overseer into Tritonia's embrace. Does that make this little test rather more urgent?"

Decarius got between them. "No, Nero, it's fine, if he—"

"It's not fine! Until Kiara's ready to take over, Felix is irreplaceable. Either Flint wants this badly enough, or the sharks feed well today." Nero caught Flint's attention once more with a snap of his fingers. "Try again."

Kiara sat, fear etched across her perfect features. She was the most beautiful girl Flint had ever seen. What was she—or her father—doing living Downtown? How had he never seen her before? Or, at least, not since she was a plain little girl, not the absolute *vision* that sat across from him now.

A hollow pit of fear approaching panic formed in Flint's belly. He pointed the wand at the offered key, and the wooden tip wavered and danced like a fisherman's bob on a lure. Flint took a breath. Then another. The pounding in his ears came down to a dull roar. He imagined his hand reaching out for the key, grasping it—he imagined the long fall to the seawater below Downtown's cliffs if he failed—and he *pushed*.

The key leaped of its own accord from Nero's hand and clattered to the chamber's stone floor.

"Hah! I knew it," Nero shouted, and Flint jumped back in fear.

"He bonded with it?" Kiara asked.

"He bonded with it," Nero confirmed. "Sorry, Luv, we'll get you one next time."

"But I don't want it! Honestly! I couldn't even pick up the key. Can't I unbond with it somehow?" Flint asked, but Kiara was already shaking her head.

"When an unbound focus tastes a soul, the soul instinctively bonds to that focus until it departs for the heavens," she said. "The only way to break that bond is for the bonded person to die."

"Tastes?" Flint repeated, confused. "How does a soul *taste* something?"

"The brain is the center of the intellect," Nero said, "and the heart is the center of the soul. The soul is found, therefore, in the heart, blood, arteries, and veins—"

"—and I had my blood on my hands when I picked it up," Flint finished.

He didn't like where this was going, not one bit. The amulet sat heavily against his chest, unnoticed by everyone.

"So now you're all-in, Songbird," Missus Decarius said. "We aren't going to let someone with a bonded focus go to waste. Welcome aboard."

Flint wasn't at all sure he wanted to be 'aboard' whatever it was they were planning. His mind whirled. How could *he*, of all people, be using magic? He'd been a copperless beggar when he went to sleep last night, with naught but a dog to his name. Now, even Mutt was gone.

"Now just a minute," Flint said. His voice wavered, and he swallowed hard. "Nobody's asked me whether I want to be any part of this. I didn't want Kaeso to send me right into that Dog Squad patrol, and I didn't want to take them to Mister Maximus' house!"

"And I didn't want a know-nothing beggar bonding with one of the more powerful earth foci we've ever managed to acquire, but here we are," Nero replied evenly. "Not to mention, Ceres warned you about not heading up toward Blackwood Way, a warning you ignored."

Flint's eyes betrayed his shock, and he opened his mouth to protest, but Missus Decarius just shook her head disapprovingly. Nero continued. "You went all-in the moment you pinned that squaddie's mouth shut with his stiletto, boyo. What else can you do? Hide away in the sewers until disease and plague claim you?"

"I—I mean—What can I do?" Flint asked. He hated the whining tone in his voice, so he stopped and tried again. "I don't know anything about magic. I'm no fighter, never swung a sword nor shot no flintlock."

"You have until tomorrow night," Nero said, "to practice a few simple effects with that wand. That it's as powerful a focus as it is should let you pick up a few tricks. Kiara will teach you—"

"No, I won't!" protested Kiara.

"Yes, you will, and Ceres will supervise. I have other arrangements to make in the meantime. Tomorrow night, we're busting Felix out of Stormford Gaol, and you're going to help." Nero shimmered, and the liver-spotted, frail old man was back. He hobbled past them without another word and headed up the stairs to the ground floor closet with the false back.

The moment the King of the Downtowners was gone, Kiara growled at Flint. "Ordinarily, we'd spend at least a week going over five element theory before you tried the slightest effect on your own. But we don't have a week, thanks to someone being an idiot."

"Start with what's most essential, Luv," Missus Decarius offered. "It's an earth focus. Start there."

Kiara took a deep breath and began again. "Earth elemental magic protects you, or pushes, pulls, twists, anything you could do with your hands. A skilled magician could conjure up an entire tower shield that would stop arrows, bolts, or bullets equally well, or hand weapons like a dagger or sword. You can pinch out a lantern wick at a distance, turn a key in a lock, or lift the key off a desk. So let's start with that. I'm going to put that key in the lock, and you're going to turn it in the mechanism without touching it."

Kiara placed the key in the lock separating their main chamber from the room where Nero had cleaned him up. She positioned him just barely out of reach of the door and circled behind him. She leaned in close, close enough that Flint could feel her breath on the back of his neck and ear.

Flint held the wand loosely down at his side and raised his empty hand in front of him. "You can point it at the key if it helps you visualize," she said, "but you don't need to if it's distracting."

"*It's not the* wand *that's distracting me*," Flint thought, but he kept his mouth shut.

"You do have to be in physical contact with the focus to use it though. The focus opens the channel from your soul to the real world. It's up to you to direct it.

"Good. Now imagine a hand, twisting the key in the lock; see it in your mind's eye," she whispered, "and *push.*"

Flint imagined putting his thumb on the upper half of the key's bow, and his first finger on the lower half, and twisting them in opposite directions. He'd never really thought about the mechanics of turning a key before, but at that moment, when he conceived of exactly how he would turn a key in its lock, there was an audible click, and the bolt dropped down into place. Flint released a breath he hadn't realized he was holding and felt cold sweat erupt all over his back.

Kiara blew out a breath. "At least, you're not completely without talent."

Missus Decarius came over from behind them. "No, did he? Truly? Already?"

"He did. Let's see if he can unlock it."

Flint accepted this challenge and reached out with his hand again. He flexed his will like a tangible thing and found it was easier this time. The bolt latch lifted away and retracted back within the door. "Good," she said. She wore a stern look on her face, but it had softened, if only slightly. "Do it again."

* * *

When Nero returned that night, Flint rested on a thick straw mattress with a splitting headache, and his teeth hurt from clenching his jaw too tightly.

"How'd it go?" Nero asked. Flint grimaced, drew the wand, and pointed it at the key on the nearby table. He flicked his wrist, and the key leaped off the table as though Flint had tossed it underhand. It sailed clear over Nero's shoulder as he stared at the young beggar on the straw mattress—but it didn't clink when it hit the ground. Nero glanced behind him, and the key hovered there, mere inches above the stone floor, then it gently floated up and placed itself neatly in Nero's hand.

"It went well," Ceres said. "He's willful, determined, talented, and he's utterly smitten with Kiara."

"Am not," Flint protested weakly from his pallet of straw, but the older woman laughed.

"Am too. The teacher is gorgeous, and the student is willing. He's figured out lifting, throwing, twisting, pulling, and pushing with that force wand of his and was able to manifest a simple truncheon. The moment Kiara came at him with her flame blade, it collapsed, of course, but that was more from panic than anything else. She hadn't told him she had a fire focus. *Redheads.*"

Nero rolled his eyes but seemed pleased. "Where is she?"

"Pouting in the next room," Ceres answered. "She's been teaching him all she can, but she's also a tad miffed the lad got that focus, and she still hasn't forgiven him for Felix. There might be a bit of tension there. The Songbird's a natural."

"At this rate, this magic shite is going to kill me anyway," Flint moaned from his mattress. "I feel like a hand of squaddies beat my brain into pudding. Then she can have the bloody thing."

"You'll be fine in the morn, dearie," Ceres said. "You've had a big day."

Flint buried his head under his cloak and wished the world would just go away and leave him to his suffering. They hadn't warned him magic would hurt!

* * *

The next morning, Flint had to admit he did feel better. The clenching in his jaw was down to a dull ache, and his brain no longer felt like tenderized goatchops. The morning's practice, this time under Nero's merciless supervision, rendered him insensate again by the time Ceres brought down a hearty lunch for them all. Flint ate, slept the afternoon away, and dragged his sorry self from the straw when Ceres served them a last, late dinner of broiled rabbit, greens, bread rolls, and rice with herbs and shallots. It was more food than Flint had seen at one sitting in his entire life.

"Thank you, Lords and Ladies, for your wisdom and guidance," Missus Decarius intoned before they ate. "Thank you, Galeria Uxor, for the bounty of this meal, and thank you, Umbria Legatus, for your wisdom as we move against the hal'far openly. I beg the Noctis Raptor's watchfulness when we are hiding and the Centurion's strength in combat. Let us move quickly, strike with precision, and disappear before any more harm can come to Felix Maximus, our protector, our leader, our friend. To Deus Maximus and all the gods and goddesses, we pray."

"We pray," Nero and Kiara echoed.

Flint did not; he'd never prayed at a meal before, nor had he heard anyone ever do so. "Who were they?"

"The old gods," Ceres replied. "I don't think we have time for a lesson on them tonight, but perhaps tomorrow, if we're all still here."

"I'd like that," Flint said. It was strange, eating at a table with other people, and he found he rather enjoyed it. When all their plates were bare, Nero stood. He took a belt with a thin blade from the weapons rack, looped the belt around his waist, and hid the knife beneath his cloak. Kiara did likewise, while Ceres merely took a dagger. Her left arm was free of her sling and moving fine, but her hand was covered by a leather gauntlet that bore multiple overlapping bloodstains until the whole thing was a reddish dark brown. She passed Flint a dagger of his own, then they headed up the stairs. They emerged from the perch to a coal-black night-time alley. Clouds hid the stars, and the only light was from the everlamps that lined Blackwood Way.

At the base of the Blackwood switchback, Nero knocked on one of the cavehome doors. The door opened, and Nero led them inside without a word. At the rear, another false-backed wardrobe led to a stairway that ascended into the guts of the cliff itself. Kiara summoned a light with her flamewand, and up they went.

Up and up, they climbed, and Flint's legs burned. They reached a landing, and the stairs doubled back. Then another and another until they ended on a small round landing and no more stairs. Kiara's light illuminated the shaft above them. Twenty or thirty feet above them, Flint made out the underside of a trap door set with a thick brass ring along one edge, and Kiara leaned close. "Use your focus and knock."

Flint stared up at the trap door for a moment in wonder, then grasped what he had to do. He envisioned his hand seizing hold of the brass ring and rocking it against the flat of the trap door. With his wand clutched tightly in his left hand, he reached up with his right and pantomimed the action he desired. The brass ring thumped twice against the underside of the trapdoor.

It worked.

The door lifted away. A rope ladder tumbled down. Nero climbed first, Kiara followed, and then Decarius. Flint couldn't help but notice how awkwardly she grasped the rope with her gloved hand. She hooked the rungs with the hand like a claw, like the fingers didn't work. She managed safely, though, and Flint followed.

Strong hands pulled him over the edge at the top into a small storeroom. Those hands belonged to Julius, the proprietor of the Clifftop Hall. He didn't appear to recognize Flint. Patience closed the trap door, and she paid him no mind either. There was a din coming from the front, where someone was mangling an off-key rendition of "The Cobalt Passage," a sea shanty almost as old as the "Alfar's Lure." Flint followed the others through to the front room of Clifftop Hall and found the offending singer was none other than Kaeso.

Flint felt his heartbeat quicken and his face flush with righteous anger, but Kiara stepped in front of him, breaking his gaze. "Later," she hissed, and when he opened his mouth to object, she pressed a finger to his lips and leaned in close. "*Later.* We both owe him, but not tonight. Tomorrow, we flay the bastard an inch at a time."

They made their way further up Blackwood Way, past the Respitoreum, and into Central Park. Flint had never been this far up. He crept through the park, moving between the bushes and trees, always careful to keep his distance from any passing hal'far citizen who might recognize him as lacking elf blood.

At last, they reached the edge of the park, and Flint could see the long cobblestone walk path that led to the front of the gaol, with a moat to either side. They crouched in the shadows beneath a fireoak and waited.

And waited.

And waited.

Flint shifted uneasily. He didn't know how long they'd waited, but he felt exposed. Atop the battlements of the ivory-walled prison, he could pick out the guards, marching back and forth on their patrol.

Two blocks uptown, a granary detonated. Flaming chunks of pottery flew into the air. In seconds, hal'far came running from all over—including the street-level Garda standing in front of the prison's entrance. There was more shouting, and the Garda on top of the outer barbican began turning a great wheel to raise the portcullis. Garda troops ran up the path to the flaming wreckage of the granary in ones and twos. The guards up top locked the portcullis at its highest point, and another wave of Garda followed the first.

A second granary exploded on the far side of the first. An Overseer, judging by his bloodhawk feather hat, jogged down the path after his gaolers. Nero broke from the brush and headed after him. The Overseer had only taken two or three steps alongside the moat when Nero's blade found his back. He collapsed without a sound, and Nero waved them forward. By the time they arrived, he'd already patted the dead half-elf down and passed a wand, much like Flint's, to Kiara. "Told you we'd get you one," he said, and Kiara smiled. She rolled up a sleeve and Ceres made a tiny incision with her dagger. Kiara touched the wand to the welling cut and closed her eyes a moment.

"Is that all?" she asked. Nero nodded, and with a flick of her new focus, the Overseer's body skidded across the cobblestones and into the moat, where it disappeared beneath the pond scum.

Nero was leading the way to the open portcullis when it began lowering again.

"I got it!" Kiara said and grunted with effort as she manifested a wedge of pure force in the portcullis' track, preventing it from descending any further. Flint could see the guards' mechanism above them, a wheel and ratchet that locked the iron gate in place. Flint drew his wand and flicked, slamming the ratchet lock into place and holding it there.

"*I've* got it!" Flint shouted, and Kiara gasped in relief as she let her conjured wedge drop. The portcullis dropped another two inches, but the ratchet locked in place. Then they were through the gate.

"Split up," Nero ordered. "Kiara, with me. Ceres, Songbird. Ceres, you find Felix, you *message* me and get him out. Meet back up at Varthas' cavehome at the bottom of the stairs if we can. Keep moving if you're followed. We'll find each other."

Missus Decarius didn't acknowledge the orders; she just took off. Flint suspected she was nowhere near as old and decrepit as she made herself out to be. She entered the guardhouse at the base of the barbican, with Flint on her heels. Inside, she jogged up the stairs, leading with her dagger, and burst out onto the top of the barbican. The Garda gaolers were just entering the other gatehouse, but the one trailing spotted them and tapped his partner on the arm. They returned to the rooftop and drew their swords.

"Rats," Ceres cursed. "I'd hoped they had pistols. A fire focus does a wonder to their priming pans if you can catch them before they've drawn. Now we do this the hard way."

She drew a gnarled wooden thing from her belt and pointed it at the approaching hal'far. With a flick of her wrist, a green glob of what looked like pond scum struck the first hal'far square in the face. He clutched his eyes, screaming, and toppled over the edge.

The second gaoler raced toward them.

"That amulet you never told anyone about," Ceres said. "Now might be a good time."

Flint gaped for a moment and stuttered an excuse, but Ceres shook her head. "Ice! There, now Songbird! Now!" she pointed. Flint hadn't even experimented with the blue-stoned amulet yet, but he stretched his hand out and willed the moisture on the ivory barbican to freeze solid. He pushed with his mind until something gave. The Garda slipped on the ice mid-sprint and skidded across the sheet out of control until Ceres plunged her dagger into his throat.

"We make a good team, Songbird. Let's keep going."

The barbican pathway descended a few steps to more battlements that encircled the prison, which in turn was enclosed by grey basalt cliffs. They could see down into the center of the courtyard as they ran. Prisoners began streaming from the structures set against the cliffs. "A moment," Ceres said and held Flint's arm. She scrunched her eyes shut, then shook her head. "No, he's not found him. There's far more prisoners than he'd expected."

They descended a stone stair to the courtyard and went inside, following the trail of open cell doors like breadcrumbs. "Ahead!" Ceres shouted suddenly. "Up a level."

They sprinted up the stairs, just in time for Flint to hear Nero shout at someone, "...just open the door, blast you!"

"Not bloody likely." Flint reached Nero's side and discovered one gaoler had locked himself *inside* Felix Maximus' cell. They'd manacled Felix to the wall at the wrists and ankles. Shirtless, his body bore scars, fresh bruises, bloody cuts. The Garda was inside next to him with a pistol to Felix's head. "I know I've only got the one shot, but you can't get in here without this key. If you kill me here, you'll never be able to reach it." He lowered the pistol for a moment. "Give up, you Downtownie scum, you won't—"

The pistol fired, its barrel pointed harmlessly at the adjacent cell floor, and the Garda stared at it in dumb shock. "Gets 'em every time," Ceres said. Another flick of her gnarled taproot thing, and vines sprouted from the cracks in the cell floor, wrapping the hal'far's wrists, arms, waist, and legs tight. The vines pulled him against the back wall of the cell, a mirror of how they'd trapped Felix.

"If you'll allow me?" Flint asked, and he reached for the key on the hal'far's belt. It floated across the gap between them, between the bars, and came to rest in Kiara's palm. "My lady, the key to your father's cell."

"*Smooth*," Ceres said, and everyone let out a quick, relieved laugh, even Kiara. She threw the door open and went to work, freeing Felix from his manacles. He stumbled before he'd taken two steps.

Ceres pulled the gauntlet off her left hand, and Flint recoiled. Her hand was a rigid mass of angry welts and glossy scars, poorly healed into near uselessness. She drew her dagger and cut deeply across her palm. She placed her bloody hand on Felix's shoulder and closed her eyes. "They've broken you proper, have they, Luv?"

"Afraid so," Felix said. "You shouldn't have come for me."

"Bollocks," Ceres replied. "Kiara's a force of nature; she gets it from her Da. Don't act like that was even an option."

Then Felix screamed in pain, and his daughter went to him. "It's alright," Felix sobbed. "All the agony of a broken ankle healing compressed into one second."

"There's too much damage. I can't heal it all, not like this," Ceres whispered.

Nero's eyes flicked up at the Garda, still trapped by the vines. "There's him."

"I'm no reaver," Ceres said, "no matter what you're thinking."

"We didn't come all this way just to lose him now," he argued.

"There's always another half-elf thug where this one came from."

"Don't," Felix protested, desperate. "Don't become one of *them!*"

"Don't listen to him, do it!" Kiara snarled. "Do it now! We have to go!"

"*Gods and daemons forgive me,*" Ceres whispered. Then, with her damaged hand still on Felix's shoulder, she plunged her dagger into the hal'far Garda's chest. She screamed and seemed to grow *brighter* somehow. Whatever energy she was drawing boosted the healing magic. Felix's scars melted away, bruises faded, and wounds closed. Felix screamed with her as bones visibly knit themselves together under his skin.

A moment later, he stood under his own power. His right hand was still a mass of scars, however. It looked much like Missus Decarius', but less severely so.

"Forgive *us,*" Felix said. A sheen of cold sweat covered his bare torso, but he looked strong and healthy again. Nero passed him the thin blade he'd taken from the weapons rack. "We need to go. Now."

* * *

They were almost through Central Park when Flint heard their pursuers. The others ran for all they were worth, but Flint allowed himself to lag behind and then turned to face the squaddies who'd given chase. There were ten of them; too many, far too many. He could buy the rest some time, at least. No Overseers that he could see—at least, none of them were wearing the feathered cap. Maybe he could draw this out even longer.

"You'll have to go through me," he declared.

"Your terms are acceptable," a hal'far squaddie said and drew his smallsword. Flint flicked the wand around, and as it circled, he *willed* the staff into being. The translucent glow blurred for the barest of moments before it struck the advancing Garda in the temple, laying him out cold.

That changed things. The Garda grew wary.

"Who's next?" Flint challenged, far more bravely than he felt. The others drew their swords and closed in, cautiously, trying to get a feel for his reach. Flint slipped aside at an angle, toward the oak, so the hal'far had to get past each other to reach him, while he only had to deal with one at a time. He bashed another one in the wrist with the staff, sending the soldier's sword flying, and followed up with a vicious stomping butt-end into the trooper's throat. Flint ducked under a branch and willed the grass beneath it to freeze. Frost nipped at the grass's tips, but the next hal'far to advance just crunched right through it and slashed at him. Flint had to skip backward to stay out of range. He was breathing hard already, exhausted from all the magic he'd been using up.

He stayed low, keeping his hands out to his sides as he circled to prevent them from surrounding him. He stepped over the first unconscious half-elf he'd laid out when yet more of the Garda came running through the trees.

Blast, he thought. *Now they really can just rush me.*

Fiery darts soared past him and struck the closest Garda, who cried out in pain. Flint risked a glance behind.

"I suppose you think you're bloody brave, sacrificing yourself for the young miss?" Ceres Decarius asked.

"I was trying to do the right thing for once," Flint replied. One of the hal'far edged closer, and Flint lashed out with his force staff again, but this time, his concentration failed before impact, and the wand flicked uselessly. "It was my fault Mister Maximus was in there."

A few of the hal'far edged closer, and Ceres lobbed more caustic green goo at them. Then she unleashed a fan of flames that ignited two. They screamed and collapsed as their comrades tried to put the fire out.

"Do an old blood knight a favor, Songbird?" Ceres asked. "Take care of her, and do what you must to free the city. In forty years of fighting, I've never had to reave a soul before. Tonight, they forced my hand. I'll do it once more and call it square. Go, Flint. Take care of my niece and do right by her. I don't have all that much time left anyway."

Flint felt tears stinging his eyes, but he did as she ordered and fled. He'd almost cleared the edge of the park when he heard Ceres scream one last time, a scream of defiance that echoed through the trees and caught Flint in the gut. Her shriek reached an inhuman pitch and blended into an ear-rending explosion that rocked the park and knocked Flint to his knees. All fell silent again.

The others waited for him at the edge of the park. "She's not coming," he said, and he wept. Felix stared at him with haunted eyes, and Kiara cried openly. Nero caught Flint by the shoulder and wrapped him in a hug.

"No blood knight worth her blade dreams of an uneventful life and dying in bed," he told Flint. "She believed in you. Now, all you have to do is live up to that."

"Is that all?" Flint asked.

"That's all. Now come. You have much to learn, young squire, before you can call yourself a shadow knight. But you will."

* * * * *

Jamie Ibson Bio

Jamie Ibson is a new writer from the frozen wastelands of Canuckistan, where moose, bears, and geese battle for domination among the hockey rinks and igloos, fueled by the great alchemists of Tim Hortons. A retired soldier and RCMP officer, Jamie has been publishing short stories since 2018, and his first novels came out in 2020. His website can be found at ibsonwrites.ca. He is married to the lovely Michelle, and they have cats.

# # # # #

One More Flight by Sarah A. Hoyt

There comes a time in a woman's life—and probably a man's too—when something deep and fundamental, something that had once been an animating principle and a reason to rise in the morning, breaks. And then, no matter how old or young that person is, they go away. Some go away inside, and some go away far away. And no matter how many years it takes them to die, no matter what else they're doing, the people who retire in that way spend those years doing one thing only: composing their death dirge; their goodbye to the world that defeated them.

I'd broken five years before. I was not who I'd once been. In fact, I'd killed that identity so thoroughly, sometimes I, myself, forgot it.

"Lady in Blood," he said from the doorway of my tent at the same time his broad shadow fell across the brocade I was sewing.

Without looking up, I said, "I am not one."

Before I plunged the needle back into the fabric, I heard his not-quite-chuckle. And then his voice became familiar, as he said, "Alda, really!"

I looked up, and of course I knew him. His name was Bran. He was in truth as dead as I was, both of us having died on the same day, in battle, over the perilous crossing between Aquitaine and

Garumna, dragon against dragon, and both our spouses and their dragons, flaming and falling to the thick forest below. But he hadn't gone away—though he might, for all I knew, have gone away inside—and he stood in my tent's opening, fully kitted out as a Wing Knight: dark blue riding leathers, his hood fallen back, and the goggles pulled down below his chin, as though he'd arrived on dragonback and just stepped in.

My heart sped just a little because I'd changed my name, moved far away, and taken up a new occupation—or if you prefer my first one—and now, if a dragon had flown all the way here, and a Wing Knight had come to visit me, people would know. People are not usually as stupid as we wish them to be. And after Madeleine's death…well, it wasn't safe.

"My name is Ambre," I said, looking back down at the red and golden fabric in my hands, and blinking rapidly so that no tears would fall, the tears that threatened when Madeleine's death—only six months ago—came to mind. "And I am a seamstress with the King's Troupe."

Without looking up, I felt his shoulders sag, his face set in a kind of despairing tiredness. He sighed. "I wouldn't break your solitude for the world, old friend, but your grandchildren need you."

And that caught me, and made me look up, because Madeleine had died before giving birth. Dead, and the babes she carried with her. And I knew by whose hand, but you can't get justice against the throne. The throne I'd once served.

I tried to form words, but none came, and Bran made a little huff of impatience, which I remembered from when we were all young and stupid and in the king's service, and he knew something about a sortie or a battle that the rest of us didn't know or were ignoring.

He walked fast into the tent and dropped to the floor with the ease of a much younger man, though his hair was as gray as mine, and he would not see his fiftieth summer again. There, close to my chair, he whispered, "The babes live. They're due to be born tonight. You must come and protect them. Or would you lose them also, and the throne with them?"

My mouth was dry, my tongue glued to the top, and what he said was impossible anyway. Madeleine had died, stabbed in front of the theater in the capital city of Vascone. She'd bled out as I watched and tried to summon a healing magician who never came. She died. And the babes in her, unborn.

Bran touched my hand, his fingers calloused from the reins. "There is a magic," he said. "So powerful and forbidden, so rare…well, we get it from the dragons. Only wing knights can perform it. We knew the babes were the heirs to the throne. We've kept them alive, fed them with the magic, but they must be brought out tonight, or they will perish for real and finally."

I blinked. The idea was obscene. Oh, I'd done some magic, dragon-aided. After all, the very dragon fire is magic, and I'd directed it when I was Lady in Blood. But this? Keeping alive children after their mother died? Keeping them growing in the cold womb? It seemed obscene, profane.

And then, in a second, it turned in my mind. Obscene it might be, profane it was. But the children were Madeleine's. Madeleine's and…the king's.

"Please, Alda," he said. "We need you. The effort to keep them alive was great, but they are alive. And they are yours. And the only hope of the kingdom. Or do you want the throne we have protected all our lives to fall to that family? To the evil ones of Garumna?"

You see, the king, then the prince heir, was married, forcibly and without his opinion being consulted, to Myriene, Princess of Garumna, as part of the peace deal. The accord was such, the war still fresh, that our prince never told his lord father, the king, that he'd married my daughter Madeleine a year before, in secret, as the daughter of two dragon knights, no matter whether they've grown up together and been each other's first love, is not a suitable spouse for the future king.

All might have been well had his father died before the new bride arrived. The king had, after all, been old and expected to die, and once he died, the prince, Luca, could repudiate his bigamous marriage, and Madeleine could be queen.

But the king had lingered on. I didn't know and couldn't tell if Myriene, the prince's official wife, was embittered by her husband ignoring her or if she found Luca's younger brother more attractive, but the would-be-queen and her brother-in-law had fallen in love and put Luca under some kind of spell, and his mind had withered day by day. Before he knew that Madeleine was with child, he'd descended to the level of an imbecile, and his brother had taken over as regent and had also taken over the princess Myriene, whom he'd married, her marriage to Luca having been annulled.

Before that, Madeleine had become an actress, an occupation that allowed her to be near the palace but not live there, not calling attention to herself.

It hadn't done any good. Someone, likely Myriene or the prince Regent Ancellus, had Madeleine killed and thus, they thought, eliminated the only legitimate line of descent from Luca: my two grandchildren Madeleine was carrying.

I stuck the needle securely into the brocade and folded my hands upon it. "They are alive?" I asked.

He nodded. "They are alive. They are to be born tonight. But we fear Garumna might have gotten word. We fear they might come and try to kill them. Or prevent us from rescuing them."

"They would come this far into the land? They would dare?"

"We have word they're on the way, with the usurper's help and cover."

* * *

Dragon leathers are heavy and padded. Though dragons themselves are warm-blooded, the atmosphere high up is always cold. Most of the leathers worn by Royal Wing Knights are scuffed and dirty, with spots of blood and mended rents. I used to mend mine and Bernar's leathers late at night. My mother was a seamstress and taught me sewing early, before my father presented me for selection to the knights at twelve.

When I asked Bran how he planned to get to the cemetery, he gave me his rueful grin. And when I asked him where my leathers were, if he expected me to go out, dragon back, he went outside and came back with a roll.

They were new and crackling, these leathers.

I was suddenly taken with the thought that, if I were to be gone, the costumes for tomorrow unfinished, I needed to tell someone. But I didn't wish to call attention to the dragon—Bran's dragon, Yvenant—who he said was behind a copse of trees near the camp we'd set up for this stop in our performance tour.

I remembered my apprentice would be in sometime in the evening. Soon enough. I'd either be back by morning to finish the costumes she couldn't before the performance, or I'd not be back at all. The costumes were irrelevant in the long run, I suppose, but a Wing Knight does not shirk his—or her—duty. So I shooed Bran out and wrote a fast note to my assistant on a scrap of paper, which I set atop the unfinished work, and then I took off the broad skirt and tunic that were now my day attire and slipped on the leathers.

They were strangely cold and unfamiliar. They also fit me, which meant nothing but that someone had kept track of me, and that this operation had been planned for a long time.

Walking to the copse of trees, Bran spoke in a low voice, "Most of us are retired wing knights. Some of the new ones were sworn in by Ancellus, and we cannot trust them, not with this. I don't know that they'd outright side with Garumna, but they'd not be with us."

"But if they know what's taking place, and when, would they not be at the cemetery before it happens?"

He shrugged. "We have people stationed," he said. "Ombe, Sene, Nescat. Plus we have a spell to confuse location. They've been searching for months. They've desecrated other cemeteries thinking they'd found the right one."

And, suddenly, I remembered hearing stories of cemeteries profaned and graves opened, the corpses of recently dead young women thrown out of their coffins, and I gasped.

"I know, it is terrible," Bran said. "But it was necessary."

I nodded. I'd gasped, not because it was terrible, but because it had suddenly become real. It became more real when we came face to face with Yvenant.

People talk of dragons as either things of horror or things of beauty. The number of times I've heard poets and others rhapsodize on the beauty of a dragon in flight cannot be counted, nor can the number of times I snorted and suppressed a laugh.

Very few people come close enough to dragons to actually see them, and I swear those who do are blinded by either fear or bards' tales. Perhaps I would have been too, if I hadn't first met the beasts at twelve after being accepted for training by the knights.

In sum, they don't look a thing like winged serpents, nor even like serpentine winged horses. They're low-slung beasts, with powerful haunches and forelimbs, and vast membranous wings. Their faces are flat, somewhat like a crocodile's, only not quite that flat, with curiously intelligent eyes, which makes sense, as it is said they are smarter than humans. I don't know about that, as we have no means of talking to them, but I suppose they are smarter than some humans.

Their colors range from white through grey to green, and as they age, just like humans, they take on a mottled and wrinkled appearance.

Yvenant had always been mottled: whiteish grey, with flecks of green and brown, and an unusually large head, with unusually smart eyes. He flicked his tail and semi-unfurled his wings at the sight of us.

He was fully saddled, bridle in place, like in the old days, though I knew that he, like my own Glydra, had been living in retirement in the royal stables.

I said, "Hail, noble Yvenant." We've never known if they actually require us to give them titles, but we spoke to them as though they did, and Yvenant seemed to understand and appreciate my words. He inclined his head, and I touched his nose, as I would have if he'd been my own dragon. We were, after all, old friends, and I'd ridden him into battle a few times, when Glydra and Bran chanced to both be incapacitated.

This close, the smell of him came to me. I hear people who've never worked with dragons say they smell bad. I've heard them described as "smelling like a hot snake." Since I've never smelled a snake, either hot or cold, I don't know if that's true.

They had an animal smell, the kind you know if you've ever been near penned carnivores. They're clean creatures, who use a corner of their quarters for excreting. Cleaning that part was not the duty of the Knights, but the orderlies, but still, they smell like animals. But the battle dragons also smell of oil, which we rub on their skin to keep it supple, because it is not natural for them to spend many hours in the air in all weather. And they smell of the old leather of the saddle and the human sweat and blood that was shed on that saddle.

Perhaps it is unpleasant. To me, it smelled like coming home.

Yvenant extended his leg, so I could step on it and grab the handholds on the side of the saddle and hang on. He made a rumbling sound. They don't talk. No, they don't mind-talk the riders, either. But, like any human working with another species, people who have long been around a dragon sort of understand what he means or says.

Bran patted Yvenant's shoulder before he, too, climbed on the saddle behind me and put his arms around my waist.

This was a shock. Not because Bran touched me. Because *someone* touched me. I realized how isolated I'd been since Madeleine's death.

Bran said, "Yvenant is impatient to get to where we left the other dragons waiting."

And, suddenly, I was impatient too, as Bran had said Glydra would be there.

Leaving Glydra behind had been difficult, as difficult as losing Bernar. But it had been thought, particularly if Luca ascended soon, that it would be better if Madeleine's mother wasn't the Lady in Blood of the Wing Knights. Because, if I were, it would look too much like a coup d'etat, and Garumna might have cause to renew the war.

And then, when Madeleine had to leave because the king was yet alive and her marriage had to remain secret, I had to stay away. But it had hurt. I suddenly felt like a specter who, coming back to life, realizes how much she's missed the world of the living.

We flew in a northeasterly direction, as the night grew darker, and a bitter wind started to blow. Before we reached the dragons, there was snow.

They waited in a mountain pass, hidden in the shadow of rocks. I jumped down from Yvenant and ran to Glydra, as though I were again the young woman and she the young dragon who'd been paired by the whims of the Lord in Blood, the commander of the time.

It seemed to me that Glydra was more beautiful than any other dragon. Her light green skin had freckled with age, and her teeth snagged in a more disorderly way out of her mouth, but her golden eyes were intent and opened a little wider when she saw me, and she gave a little snort, the same snort with which she used to greet me after a long absence.

I stroked her shoulder as she extended her leg. She was saddled with my old saddle.

As I climbed aboard, I felt it all come back to me. There are commands you can tap on the back of the dragon's neck, commands they're trained over years to obey instantly.

Before we rose, I looked around. There were twelve knights. In the dark, with their hoods up, I couldn't identify all of them, but I could tell they were all my age and older.

Bran lifted the glowing lantern, burning with mage fire, that we used for communication at night and waved it with gestures that said, "We'll follow your lead, Lady in Blood."

Like that, I was back in command. Perhaps because the operation was about my family. Perhaps because there was no other lady or lord in blood in the group. I didn't know. I responded with my glow stick, acknowledging. Then I gave quick instructions. We'd fly to the Cimetière des Perdues, where Madeleine had been buried, a usual burial ground for actresses, gypsies, and other itinerant folk with no regular parish. And then we'd land.

Bran had explained we'd need to exhume the body to free the babes. Though he'd also told me that Madeleine's body had been kept in a static state of pseudo-life, I feared seeing her again and re-living my loss.

I felt like I had no emotional strength left in me, nothing to rely on to perform this most difficult of missions.

My father, who was a Wing Knight, said that it was a state given to you not because you had done great things, but because you promised to risk your life in the service of the throne. And while this was not in the service of the current occupants of the throne, it was in the service of the real king, Luca, and of my daughter's children, who would inherit the throne.

I would do it, even if I had no strength left.

* * *

The Cimetière des Perdues was on desolate ground, surrounded by a half-ruined wall of stones. The gate, if there had been one, had long since fallen off the opening in the wall, leaving only a gap, like a missing tooth in an aging mouth.

We left our dragons outside, not tied, as they didn't need it, and walked in.

Madeleine's grave was at the back and, next to it, two figures stood. I recognized Belex and Angele and was taken, for a moment, by surprise at how aged they looked. It wasn't that five years had made so much difference, but that in the time I'd been away, I'd started thinking of them again as the young man and slender woman I'd first met in training. Their hair was white, their faces lined, but they smiled at me, and they stood with as much pride as I'd ever seen in them.

Each held a shovel, and their smiles at me might have held hints of apology, as though they felt guilty for doing this. I nodded, partly giving assent and partly absolution, I suppose. I couldn't really complain about disinterring my daughter and profaning her grave, if this was done to save my grandchildren. Worse, by far, if they should die now, after so much magic had been expended to save them.

They dug out the grave with swift strokes, especially if one considers that, after being buried for six months and the setting in of winter, the soil was compacted and frozen.

As the coffin appeared—a plain pine coffin, bought cheaply, since we had to make it a quick burial—there was a pale nimbus of light around it, the hallmark of magic. And it made sense, since there would have to have been transport of air to the sealed coffin, or the babes would have died.

I had not thought deeply about how this could have happened, or what they meant by giving Madeleine the semblance of life, so I was surprised when they pulled up the lid, and she lay there in the white gown I'd chosen and sent to the undertakers for her to be buried in—the same gown she'd worn at her secret wedding—and looked alive. Her cheeks were rosy, her chest rose and fell, and her blond hair, carefully arranged on either side of her face, made her look like she'd just laid down to sleep.

Bran laid a hand on my shoulder. "We couldn't bring her soul back. We got there too late. It had flown. Even all of the combined magic of our practitioners couldn't save her, any more than they could save King Luca's mind. They are gone somewhere where the evildoers can't reach them. But we could get the babes back. And we could keep them alive."

I nodded and looked away because I couldn't bear to see Madeleine seeming to breathe, knowing I was going to lose her to death, stillness, and silence again.

It was good that I looked away, because I saw the flicker in the air.

With the light of the lanterns, I didn't need the glow stick, and, anyway, they were all packed in close, the twelve of them, watching the grave. I said, "To dragons, knights."

And as one, we moved, pulling up our hoods, running to the entrance, mounting on dragons.

My bow was in the saddle bags, as were the throwing axes. This was good and showed Bran's foresight, as I'd not thought to ask.

I put the bow across the saddle and secured it on the hook for that purpose, and I signaled with the glow stick that the enemy came from the south, and we should fly wedge formation, till we could access a better strategy.

It wasn't till we were in the air that I realized the enormity of the problem.

There were at least thirty dragons approaching, flying in a wide formation which would keep us from surrounding them. From their flight speed, and the way their wings glistened in the moonlight, they were young dragons, with young riders. They gave off the cry, "Saint Seguin and Victory," of the knights of Garumna.

We responded with, "Saint Amour and Glory."

And the battle was joined. I signaled to go full speed, still wedge shaped. Our only hope was to scatter their formation before they could think. Thank whatever saints attended my birth, at fifty-four, I was still keen of eye. Which was good, because I realized that going fast, there was neither time for the bow and arrows, nor for sighting carefully.

Instead, I pulled out the bespelled throwing axes, one in each hand, and as we flew through the formation of startled invaders without stopping, I threw them at the knights of Garumna.

Whatever they expected of old knights, that wasn't it. My right-hand ax hit a knight in the face, eliciting a scream as the knight fell, and the suddenly riderless dragon plunged after the human it had been bonded to, screaming its grief.

It was hard to keep my mount, to close my ears to that scream. I'd heard it so many times, in so many battlefields, when dear friends—and once the love of my life—died.

My left-hand ax brought only the startled and scared scream of a dragon, which meant I'd missed the rider and hit the beast. But it lost control and dropped from formation, its rider a shadow in the night, trying to pull it up.

This meant the two riders behind me in formation could hit a knight on each side. And so forth. I held out my hands, and my spelled axes returned to them, the handles hitting hard enough to sting, even through my padded leather gloves.

Without realizing it, I'd been counting in my head the twelve seconds for each of my knights to pass through the formation, and on precisely the count of twelve, I started climbing. We had to make use of surprise, while we still had it, and go above. If we were lucky, we'd taken close to half of their number out of the melee, which meant the battle would be more even when it came to singular combat. Which it always did, when it came to dragon fights in the air.

These men and women had all fought under me, and they all climbed with me, not needing to be told, to thinner and colder air. There was somehow a tinge of blood in the air, though there shouldn't be.

Far below was the light of lanterns by the tomb, but also a couple of fires burning in the night, where falling dragons had panicked and self-immolated in the explosions that often signaled the death of their kind.

Battle time is a strange thing. I felt as though I'd been flying forever *and* for less than a breath. As we climbed, a dragon of Garumna climbed just as fast. Just one, directly in my path. I could see the rider's green leathers, her slightly turned head, the movement of her body, which inexplicably reminded me of Madeleine.

Maybe that's why I didn't swing, though my arms lifted with the ax.

But Bran must have had better presence of spirit than I, because, as I saw the rider smile and raise her arm, an arrow came from my right—arrows being better at greater distance—and impaled her through the chest. She gave a keening scream. Her dragon screamed, too, and lost purpose, weaving erratically. I barely managed to coax Glydra higher, but not so high that I didn't feel the wind of the other dragon's fall. Its scream was deafening.

It was still close enough when it burst into flames that the heat of its last fire and the smell of charred flesh enveloped us. Glydra keened softly, as though in memory of her many lost comrades, and then we were high enough for me to look around and see which of my knights were in trouble. Bran was besieged by two knights, each lifting ax to throw. I got my bow and arrow, with the speed of years of practice, and managed to hit the one on the right. Bran dodged the one on the left, and then let loose his own arrow. Two more enemy knights fell, and their dragons flamed in the night.

A yelp from Glydra told me she'd been hit, and I saw the arrow sticking out of her shoulder, but there wasn't a vital organ there, and her scream hadn't been of deathly pain. I saw the knight who'd done it and threw my ax as he approached for another hit. I had a pang of sorrow at killing a young man, but I was going to save my grandchildren and the throne of Aquitaine.

It was at that moment that I realized a knight was flying straight at me, screaming, "Seguin and Victory."

I didn't waste breath on screaming. Let the young do that. We, who know how many of our breaths are counted before death, will just fight. I had my bow in one hand but judged the distance was closer and better for axes, so I grabbed those from their pockets on the saddle bags. Then, holding on with only my legs and my feet in the spurs, I signed Glydra to rush at the other dragon.

There is a name for this game, and it's one that children often play their first time on a dragon.

You rush at the other as fast as possible, counting on the other to drop first.

When you play this as a child, you learn pretty quickly whether the other one is going to drop, or you'll have to. Not that some idiots don't manage to collide midair, and not that some of them aren't stupid or unlucky enough to have their very young dragons explode beneath them when they panic.

But at my age—

I knew two things: the other dragon wouldn't drop. And I wasn't going to drop. Which left only one way to go: up.

I realized that the other rider had also ordered his dragon up, so I wheeled right, throwing both axes in quick succession, one at the rider, one at the dragon's neck.

Before I saw if I'd hit either, I felt an impact on my shoulder. In the moment of confusion, I felt Glydra drift, and I held the reins tight with my good hand, while looking over my shoulder to confirm that the other rider was falling out of control.

I had an arrow in my shoulder, but could still move my arm. Glydra appeared unharmed beyond the arrow in her shoulder. There were no fights around me anywhere. There were no knights of Garumna. There were six left of mine. My eyes filled with tears for lost comrades, and I noted, with relief, that one of them was Bran, riding stoutly at my right hand, though blood soaked the left side of his suit.

I guided Glydra gently to the place by the Cimetière des Perdues, near the still glowing light by the grave of my lost daughter. We left the dragons and headed to the unbarred opening in the wall.

The two people by the grave were re-sealing the coffin, and for a moment, I thought it was all for nothing, then I heard the thin wail of the newborn and followed the sound to two blankets and the bundles within them by the grave.

"Felicitations, Lady in Blood. They're a boy and a girl and both healthy."

I took a step toward them, when first the disturbed noise of the dragons and then screams reached my ears. Turning, I saw a party of six people rushing at us. They were dressed in the metallic—bronze really—armor of land knights, and there were the arms of Garumna upon the chest, the dragon rampant, devouring the lion.

They carried swords, and a young woman rushed at me, luxuriant red hair escaping from beneath her helmet.

I had time for two thoughts. The first was that she was not a professional fighter, because no professional fighter gives the enemy an easy handle by which to grab and hold. The second was that I'd stupidly left my weapons in the saddle bags. It was obvious the others hadn't. I could see, out of the corner of my eye, Bran's axes flashing in the light, but he had his own attacker to deal with.

If I lifted my hands and called my axes; they wouldn't come in time. My opponent had a huge battle ax and was screaming in fury. In the light of the lantern, her eyes were a very bright green.

I felt a handle in my hand and realized that, before joining the fray, one of the diggers had handed me one of the enormous shovels.

I took it in both hands and parried the ax with it. Metal rang on metal with a deafening din. My arms hurt as though they'd been struck, particularly the point on my shoulder where the arrow had wounded me.

Without even thinking, without pausing, I struck back with the shovel, the sharp edge, meant to cut through frozen soil, aimed at the slender white neck.

It cut through easily, and the ax fell from the girl's hands. She swayed a moment, her neck fountaining blood. And then she fell, even as around me the fights resolved, and Bran turned to me, round-eyed and wild, and said, "You killed the queen!"

I stared.

"The would-be queen," he said. "You killed Myrienne of Garumna."

I swayed on my feet; I was so tired, and my shoulder hurt like living fire. And it all seemed to matter not at all. I heard myself spit out, "Well, then, she was a fool for coming into the fight herself." And I turned on my heels to go tend to my grandchildren.

They were indeed a boy and a girl, wrapped in warm blankets and crying their outrage at the lack of meal to compensate them for being expelled from the womb.

I picked them both up, one in each arm, though the left hurt. They were well grown and had Madeleine's blue eyes and something of Luca in the set of their tiny mouths. "Madeleine and Luca," I said, proclaiming the names, so they would be known.

Bran, smiling, with a squint, and his eyes looking impossibly tired, nodded once. "It is fitting," he said.

"They'll need a nursemaid," I said.

"We—I have something I'd speak to you about," he said, "but we should leave here."

I looked around at the rag-tag band of eight, feeling gratified we'd lost no more. "Where will we go?" I asked.

"How about Bayne?" he asked, naming a small town near the cemetery. "You and I. We'll regroup there. Give me Luca," he said, taking the child from my weak left arm.

"The others," I said, feeling so dizzy I might almost fall over.

"They must stay to hide the bodies, or we'll be tracked."

I didn't ask how they intended to hide the bodies. There are things I'd rather not know. Yes, the dragons were carnivorous, and, though scrupulously trained not to eat human flesh, they'd been known to break training after a battle.

I climbed on Glydra's saddle and had the odd thought it was for the last time. We climbed up to the dark sky and flew on her wings through the night. Against my heart, snuggled tight, while I steered with my left hand, Madeleine snuffled, her heartbeat small and steady.

We landed on the outskirts of Bayne. Bran climbed down from his dragon and sighed, holding Yvenant's reins lightly in one hand, Luca nestled in his other arm. He approached. He looked suddenly as awkward and gangly as he had when we'd met at twelve.

"What is the plan?" I asked. "For the children. I don't want to let them go. I could take them back to the theater and—" I paused. "No. You tracked me there; they might also."

He nodded. He was beet red. "I meant to talk to you in the tent, but we were in a hurry, and then there seemed to be no time. The attack came so soon."

"I don't want to let them go," I said.

"No," he said. "And I wouldn't want you to." He cleared his throat. "I thought...I have inherited a farm from a great uncle. No one knows who I am there, except old Jean's nephew. He had a sheep farm. No one will..." He foundered, then seemed to take his courage in both hands. "It was left to me," he said. "And to me alone to determine where the children should go. I don't think the locals would care if an unassuming older couple appeared, carrying their young grandchildren, whose parents had died. We could...That is, understand that the farm is profitable enough, if nothing out of the ordinary. When Luca dies, or the usurper does...When the children are grown, we can—" He must have seen something in my eye I wasn't aware of transmitting, because he added hurriedly, "We don't need to, actually, you know, live as husband and wife. Or...Or we could be an older brother and sister."

My laughter surprised me; it was light and young as it hadn't been in far too long. Bran was dark-haired, with dark eyes, while my hair was blonde and my eyes as blue as the children's. While such differences do occur among siblings, they made us stand out more. And anyway, I'd known Bran most of my life, and my Bernar and his Aralie were both long dead.

It wasn't love, but we'd fought and bled together; we'd shared sweat and tears and our last crumb of bread too many times to count. And having someone to stand by you as the cold winds of old age blew was better than not having it.

My voice sounded surprisingly rich and bashful as I said, "I don't mind being your wife."

It wasn't a love declaration, but his face lit up.

Moving very quickly, he extracted a bag from Yvenant's saddle, and from it he took a normal round skirt, an unremarkable blouse, and cloak for me, and a tunic and breeches for him.

We dressed quickly, and he helped me coif my hair in a respectable bun.

We looked like not particularly prosperous, but not penniless, farmers.

"We'll get the children a temporary nursemaid who will travel with us, and then we'll find them some local girl, unless this one wants to stay," he said. "I have…money put by, in case of need."

We said goodbye to Yvenant and Glydra—I cried on her warm muzzle—who would go back to their place in the royal stables as though nothing had happened, to live in happy retirement. Glydra keened a little into my shoulder, before withdrawing.

They took off into the night sky, and we watched them go, our youth with them, before we set off on foot toward Bayne.

Sometimes, you break, you change, and you go away, or go deep within yourself, and start contemplating your death song.

And then life calls you and needs you, and you have to save the kingdom and the future.

What can you do but answer?

Bran and I would continue answering.

* * * * *

Sarah A. Hoyt Bio

Sarah A. Hoyt was born in Portugal and lives in Colorado. Somehow, along the way, she acquired a husband, two kids (now grown, though one still lives in the house), and a bunch of cats. (The number varies. She's down to two and feels like there must be something wrong, somewhere, with the universe, so expect a beggar at the door any day.) Also, inexplicably, she seems to have written thirty-some novels, at least one of which (she really doesn't feel like checking) hit the best seller list and two of which won major awards (Darkship Thieves won the Prometheus and Uncharted (with Kevin J. Anderson) won the Dragon for alternate history.)

She's currently in the middle of at least three projects, one rather unexpected, and REALLY should be writing.

# # # # #

A Quaint Pastime by Casey Moores

Wislig, despite being a pioneer of aviation, had a tremendous fear of heights and wished he could fly lower than he did. However, the gnome feared being shot at more than he feared heights. Soldiers of *both* armies had an increasing propensity to indiscriminately shoot at anything whatsoever that flew overhead. Granted, most mud puppies had no concept of aiming at where an aircraft *would be* as opposed to *where it was*, but his bowels still clenched every time he saw puffs of smoke on the surface. Numerous holes in the fabric of his wings, discovered after every landing, confirmed the danger.

Deep in his soul, he'd prefer to return to studying dragons and wyverns, like the great Archibald. Wislig's great passion lay in designing machines inspired by their wings and maneuverability. He'd made requests for such so often, he'd been ordered to stop. Unfortunately, the War Staff had decided that those with knowledge of aerodynamics were best suited to fly alone, unarmed and unarmored, over Naught Land to scout enemy positions.

His eyes caught another aircraft, approaching from the opposite direction. It was a biplane, painted in the black colors of Fersang. Wislig's sense of terror reached a new zenith as he feared what the enemy aircraft would do. When he observed the friendly wave of the enemy pilot, he relaxed and returned it with a shaky hand.

Thank the great gnome goddess Yutaeris that we still honor the unwritten code of the sky—Thou Shalt Not Shoot At Another Pilot. That, for the time, was one small blessing.

He turned his attention back to the ground below. The gray, dismal space on Naught Land morphed into the haphazard, yet organized, lines of the layered enemy trenches. He'd arrived at the joyous moment in which he got to hold the controls steady while drawing stick figures on paper strapped to his thigh.

As he identified something new, he felt consternation mixed with a strange excitement. Excitement in that there was something different to report; consternation in what it was. Large tents, which indicated a collection of giant creatures, and stacks of large iron shields. In the weeks since fighting had begun over the border town of Kusen, few of the larger creatures had fought.

A great line of shielded giants would roll over the Lutetian defenses like waves upon sandcastles. Lutetia and the Isles would lose The Greatest Conflict of All Time.

In the time Wislig spent drawing the positions of the Bigs on the chart tied to his knee, he found he'd put himself into a right bank and nosed down uncomfortably close to the ground. He jammed the pencil into the leather loop on his leg strap. Carefully, he divided his attention between Not Crashing and folding the observation chart up enough so that he could stuff it into his breast pocket. As he did so, he nosed up just enough to avoid Terra Exitium and banked the plane over to reverse his course and head home.

His gluteus maximus clenched tight as he witnessed a large boulder fly past him on the right. Instinctively, he jerked the stick left.

Another boulder flew past on his left, so he pushed the stick down for half a second and then pulled up and right. Although his mind told him not to, he looked at the surface, where he found a group of Bigs launching stones. Farther in front of his flight path, flashes and puffs of smoke rolled out like a blanket. He heard the rapid fire hammering noise of a chain gun. His heart threatened to explode from his chest.

He jammed the throttle forward, pitched the aircraft to aim just above the horizon, closed his eyes, and recited a prayer to his goddess.

Minutes later, when the buzzing sound of bullets dissipated, his heart calmed. He'd cleared enemy lines. After a sigh of relief, he checked his aircraft for damage. An uncomfortable number of holes dotted the fabric of his wings. Thankfully, all the control surfaces responded normally to his inputs. It might have been his imagination, but he thought he heard a grinding sound somewhere in the engine, paired with an occasional sputter. Hopefully, no greater issues would appear during the most critical moment—landing.

Scanning about for landmarks, he found the chewed up, black remains of a large forest. A few hundred yards to its north was a smaller grove of surviving cottonwood trees. He analyzed the wind by watching flower blossoms float and maneuvered to land into the wind. First, he overflew the airfield, wagged his wings, and peered down to ensure the Lutetian flag still flew. Chances were he would already know if Fersang had overrun the field, but one could never be too careful in such a brutal war. The flag also confirmed the wind direction. He spotted Enchtur, his goblin mechanic, and gave a slight wave, which the goblin reciprocated. He leveled the wings and counted.

"One candle, two candle, three candle…" Wislig banked left and eased the throttles back. At this point, if the engine cut out, the airplane could *probably* glide safely to the surface. If the controls locked up, however… he cleared the thought from his mind and focused on the turn.

As always, his heart and mind screamed with joy when he felt the wheels lightly kiss the flattened earth.

He loved aircraft. He *hated* flying.

* * *

The spindly green-skinned miracle-worker mechanic trotted out to the bird with an intense gaze and stern frown.

"What've you done to *Archie's Whelp* this time, you wrinkled elf baby?" Enchtur asked in his high-pitched, grumbly voice.

Wislig feigned confidence and patted the sides of his plane, where a small gold dragon head and the aircraft's name were painted.

"Nothing short of superior pilotage, my gobby friend," Wislig replied, with a strong grip on a strut to keep his hand from trembling. He swung over the edge and climbed down. "In the face of certain death, I did what we pilots do and…"

A tall blond elf with a stern look marched toward him. He wore a well-pressed dress uniform bearing a major's rank that was cleaner than anything Wislig had seen in months. The gnome pilot concluded the messenger had arrived straight from Vestige, Lutetia's capitol. He had few guesses as to what sort of message would be delivered in such a manner.

"Leftenant Wislig, I presume," the elf messenger stated. Wislig hopped the remaining distance to the ground and straightened up. He looked the elf in the eye and saluted.

"Yes, sir." *And you are?*

The elf returned the salute and produced a sealed envelope. "I present to you a message with a new assignment."

An "assignment?" Well, that narrows the possibilities to two, and it's well beyond my wildest dreams that they'd assign me back to aircraft design, so...

"Thank you, Major," Wislig replied. He received the letter, stuffed it into his pocket, saluted again, and walked toward the telegraph tent.

"That message requires your immediate attention, Leftenant!" the Major shouted. Wislig stopped and spun about.

"I understand, Major, but I must make my report immediately," he replied. "The Fersang army is mounting an offensive of Bigs at this very moment, and I must make the Generals aware of it. Would you prefer our army was unprepared for a major assault...*Major?*"

The blond elf walked back up to Wislig and looked down at him.

"The assignment contained within that envelope is far more important to the war effort than making a report about a common daily attack, *Leftenant*," the Major said, and poked a finger into Wislig's chest. "Now...Read. That. Letter."

Wislig gave another, much more obnoxious, salute. Then, making a great show of stuffing his hand into his shallow pocket, he rummaged around for a bit. At length, he ripped the crumpled letter out and fumbled about with the envelope. Finally, he shook the letter itself open and read. The assignment was exactly as he'd guessed. He snapped his boots together and saluted again.

"Sir!" he shouted. "Leftenant Wislig has received his orders and will execute them with vigor! May I request permission to make my report before I depart?"

The elf returned the salute and walked back to his carriage.

Wislig closed his eyes and sighed. Continuing toward the telegraph tent, he considered his new assignment.

At least it gets me away from the Front. I hope I don't get eaten.

* * *

Wislig breathed in the sweet, clean countryside air. As assignments went, it was, so far, a welcome holiday. His three-wheeled powerpony sputtered along the dirt road, raising a cloud of dust. His gaze swept the open fields, with their softly rustling stalks of wheat. Birds danced around playfully in the sky, with no fear of bullets or boulders. He caught the scent of a distant fire, which reminded him of home.

He pictured his mother by the hearth, feeding wood pellets into the steam oven to cook a rabbit dinner, while his father smoked a pipe and poured over ancient texts in search of forgotten inventions to recreate. Those texts had contained the knowledge that made heavier than air flight possible. The development of that knowledge had dominated his life, for better or for worse, ever since.

His attention returned to his peaceful surroundings as he approached the craggy rocks and steepening slopes of his destination. Another long, deep breath carried the taste of sulfur. The powerpony slowed as he navigated the tight switchbacks up the mountain. Trampled over centuries by actual ponies, horses, and goats, the trail was ill-suited for his powerpony, but he had faith in his design.

Two-thirds up the hill, the nose wheel caught in a small crack in the ground. At the same time, his rear left wheel slid on a spot of loose gravel. The whole trike tipped sideways. When it reached a vertical tilt, he accepted his fate, kicked his feet free, and pushed himself off. He slammed into the ground in a dusty heap.

The big, triangular contraption banged, bounced, and tumbled down the hill. A great crash of metal echoed with each bump. Broken and bruised, he stared at the poor machine.

Perhaps two wheels, if I could stay balanced, would work better…

"Who dares disturb my slumber?" a great voice boomed from above. The ground rumbled, and a few small boulders spilled down the mountain after his powerpony.

Wislig grimaced and turned around. An enormous, golden-scaled wyrm crept angrily over the ridgeline. One of its clawed hands, whose individual talons easily dwarfed the diminutive gnome, reached up and grabbed hold of a mountain peak. The other grabbed another peak. The great crested head of the beast emerged. Its eyes narrowed, and its massive jaws hung slightly open, as if it contemplated raking the entire mountainside with hellfire.

"Apologies, Archie, I'd intended for a quieter arrival," Wislig said.

"My name is Archibald the Tremendous Terror!" the dragon shouted. Its great head slid back and forth, like a snake preparing to strike. "By rights, I should devour such a disrespectful interloper!"

"Tremendous, indeed, *Archibald the Tremendous Terror*," Wislig replied. "I can see the villagers keep you well fed. They also seem to keep you quite lonely if you're this desperate for some drama."

The dragon gave a thundering laugh and pulled himself higher into the sky.

"Please, Archie, you're splitting my eardrums, and you're likely to start an avalanche that'll crush a poor little soul like me," Wislig protested. "Does everything have to be *enormous* and *loud* and *thunderous?* Can't we just have a nice, quiet conversation among friends? Is that too much to ask?"

Steam erupted from Archibald's nostrils as the great dragon sighed.

"Fine," he said, much quieter and sounding a little bored. He rumbled further over the ridgeline, exposing another hundred feet of his body, and he reached down the hill toward the broken contraption. "Here, I'll help you with your—"

"No, wait, Archie—"

It was too late. The dragon's claws closed around his smashed up powerpony and crushed the remains.

"Oops, sorry Wiz," Archibald said. "I always forget how delicate your machinery is. Tell you what, I'll give you a ride home when we're done talking. It'd probably be good for me; it has been a long time since I stretched my wings."

"I guess I have no choice but to take you up on that," Wislig said.

Perhaps that's for the best, I can claim success, and then, maybe, when he sees the front...

"Come on inside, my tiny friend, you can tell me what's brought you out here," Archibald said.

* * *

The tiny gnome followed as the great wyrm meandered down the tunnel, far quieter than most would guess a dragon could move. Wislig knew that Archibald only stomped and rumbled when he chose to, and usually just to scare off unwanted guests.

The main cavern of Archibald's lair was filled with the characteristic treasure hoard, neatly organized into chests of matching coins, jewels, etc. The dragon hoarded no paper money, as he believed it a "curious arrangement which will not stand the test of time." Wislig found an impressive armory in one expansive side room. *Antiques now, almost completely useless. Though, they might be valuable to collectors someday.* Another side chamber was loaded with artwork and sculptures, and another was an expansive library. Other than a great deal more dust, things had changed little since Wislig's last visit.

"Over here, good friend, over here," the dragon said. Archibald squatted back on his haunches and motioned Wislig to a raised dais with a set of comfortable looking chairs. "I'd offer you tea or a snack, but, alas, I let my servants go ages ago. Didn't seem worth the money when no one visited for years."

"I've got my own provisions. I'll make myself a snack, not to worry."

"Well, here, I can light a fire, and there's a kettle right there if you've got the tea leaves," Archibald offered.

"I do, actually; that would be splendid."

With a slow, controlled exhalation, Archibald lit some prearranged logs in a campfire. Wislig made himself tea and extracted rations from his pack.

"So, have you come to reminisce on old times, or are you here to ask another favor?" Archibald asked and settled down to the ground like a scaly, gargantuan, fire-breathing dog.

"A favor, of course, I'm sad to say," Wislig said, as he tended the teakettle. "But we'll get to that. Must observe the niceties first and all. How have you been?"

"Bored. Lonely. Not too much to challenge one such as me in this world and few whose company I prefer."

"Well, then, I am quite honored," Wislig said. He spent a few moments laying out some crackers and cranking open a tin of meat, deep in thought. *How do I approach this?* "You remember that affair in Vervast? Did you consider *that* a challenge?"

"So, it is to be reminiscing, hmm?" Archibald answered. "Very well, and I'll say *somewhat*. The orcs and goblins, not one bit, no disrespect to you smaller creatures, even with those loud and smoky little cannons. The orc and ogre shamans, well they had quite a few tricks, but nothing too serious. The ballista and those ogre archers were a pretty big deal; they gave me a few close calls, but their numbers were such that I learned to dodge those great bolts and arrows. Heh. Hahaha."

The dragon smiled and chuckled as if digging up some hilarious memory. Wislig poured himself a cup of tea and raised an eyebrow at his immense friend.

"Sorry," he said. "I just remembered you and that whirligig contraption of yours. You gnomes always have such clever little creations. The goblins tried their hands at their own versions, too, didn't they?"

"Yes, but the Vervast versions were always rickety little death traps, more like poor, flimsy copies of what we did," Wislig explained. "You know, you're the original inspiration for those designs."

"But none of them flap like I do, do they?" Archibald asked.

"Well, yes, but flapping contraptions never worked out," Wislig explained. "We did, however, copy your wings. That *whirligig* contraption was a slender simulacrum of your wings, perhaps more like wyverns' wings, but they spin about fast enough to produce lift. They have their uses, but they're a bit slow and, well, somewhat complex. A lot can go wrong with those. We've got something new now."

"Curious." Archibald's eyes drifted away in thought.

"Yes, well, anyway, we *all* have quite a few new things," Wislig continued. "Our capacity for war has gotten quite—"

"Do you remember the enemy dragon the Vervastians enlisted?" Archibald interrupted. His eyes became big, and his face looked giddy, almost childish.

"Uh, well, yes, uh, Fireheart, was he?" Wislig replied. He stuffed a meat paste-covered cracker in his mouth.

"Feuerherz, actually, was *her* title, along with Kaiserin, which means 'Empress,'" Archibald explained. "Her full name is Kaiserin Brünstiglena von Feuerherz. Quite the feisty filly."

"*Her*, is it?" Wislig asked while he chewed. Never before had he witnessed such a twinkle in the dragon's eye. "I never realized. That's a Fersangian title, isn't it?"

"Yes, that's where she's from," Archibald answered. "My little fire-hearted Fersang Empress. You ask where I've found a challenge, well, my tiny friend, *that's* where. I've dreamt of those emerald green scales in the decades since that little war. I made a wager with her, you see, at the outset. She put up a hell of a fight, but when I, sorry, *we*, when *we* won…heh, well, as they say, 'To the Victor go the Spoils.'"

Oh my. Wislig gulped down his food. While he blocked awkward imagery out of his mind, Wislig envisioned where the conversation would lead.

"This is something dragons do?" Wislig asked in wonder.

"It is the *only* way dragons do these things," Archibald said. "The male must prove himself worthy. The wager is his death matched against her...*compliance.*"

"I never knew."

"Quite the feisty filly," Archibald repeated, with a foolish grin. "I'd give anything for another chance to delve into that crevasse."

"Please, Archie!" Wislig protested. "Really, you can stop detailing your conquest to me."

"Sorry, Wiz," the dragon said. "It's just, as I said, I've been quite lonely. That's a tale I've desperately wanted to tell for quite some time. Anyway, Wiz, let's get to it. What favor are you here to ask?"

With a trembling hand, Wislig smiled and retrieved the pipe from his satchel. He stuffed some leaves into it and stuck the pipe in his mouth. Archibald waited while Wislig lit a thin stick in the fire and used it to light the pipe.

"There's another war going on, my old friend," Wislig said as he nuzzled into the chair. He drew in at the pipe and released a puff of smoke.

"Against who?" Archibald asked with great curiosity.

"You must understand, as I said, our war machines and weapons have come quite a way since that last, uh *scrap,* in Vervast."

"Who are you fighting? The Marriens?" Archibald asked.

"No, and they're *Lutetia* now," Wislig said. "Have been for quite some time. The Lutetians are our allies and, to be honest, it's their war, really. But, what I'm trying to say is that those *smoky little cannons* have come a long way, along with our ability to make them. Now, whole armies are armed with them. War is quite different than it was."

"Haha, you smaller creatures are always saying things like that," Archibald said. "*This war is unlike any other.* You're quite excitable every time anything at all changes. Wislig, I've been fighting in these quaint little pastimes of yours for centuries, perhaps millennia. The weapons change a little, periodically someone thinks they've found a better way to kill dragons, but it never amounts to much. Throw a hail of arrows at me, and I need but sweep my wings to knock them from the sky with a mighty gust. Fire a massive ballista at me, and I'll snatch the bolt from the air and throw it back. No, this new little war of yours concerns me little—Now! What I want to know is, *who are you fighting?*"

Wislig sighed and took another puff of his pipe.

"We're killing each other faster than we've ever—"

"I've swept down enemy lines and burned a hundred soldiers in a single pass," Archibald said, irritated. "Who. Are. You. Fighting?"

A hundred soldiers die the moment a whistle is blown, before they've even left the trench. But the Tremendous Terror cannot hear me. No avoiding it…just get it over with.

"Fersang."

Archibald pushed himself up, raised his massive head, tilted his head back, and roared with laughter. The entire cavern rumbled and threatened to collapse.

"So!" he shouted. "Fate has come calling! Just as my desires reach the limit of sanity, the world presents me with a new chance to encounter Brünstiglena, that's 'Fireheart' to you, on the battlefield. Another chance to *rekindle*, if you'll pardon the expression."

"It's not that simple, Archie...you don't understand..."

Smoke poured from Archibald's nostrils, and he sighed in delight. Wislig puffed the smoke out of his mouth in frustration. The dragon stomped about in excitement and lowered his head back in close to the gnome.

"I understand the signs of the world, my dear friend. I've been reading them for eons. Fortune smiles upon me, bringing a great adventure to break me from this torpor. And you, its herald, I shall not soon forget what you have given me this glorious day. Come! Let us fly forth! Let the Great God of War charge out to rain death and terror on the battlefield once more! Let us remind the smaller creatures who truly rules this world!"

I hope you're right, dear friend, I truly do.

* * *

Wislig and Archibald alike stared at the newly delivered biplane. Long gray fabric stretched over numerous spars on both wings. At the front of the machine was a large, well-polished oak propeller. The gnome inventor recognized the design as his own, as were all the designs which his mentor, Knaphauser the Great Tinkerer, claimed.

"I hope you don't mind, but I've named her *Archie's Teeth*," Enchtur said. "But I haven't had the chance to get it painted on yet."

Twin chain guns sat on the top wing. A simple drawing of a dragon's head adorned the sides. Enchtur stood behind the biplane, as if hiding from the dragon.

"Magnificent!" Wislig exclaimed. "They're finally trying my designs." His smile switched to a frown. "Are those *guns* on top? Why are there guns on top?"

"Strange," Archibald said. "Those wings look too rigid. I still don't understand how you fly, if the wings don't flap. And it has another of those whirligig contraptions on the front, only much smaller. How does that do anything at all?"

"That's the propeller," Wislig explained. "The engine makes it spin amazingly fast, and it pushes all the air behind it, to gain enough speed so that the air flow under the wings pushes us into the sky."

"Ogre dung," Archibald replied. "Admit it, you use some kind of air magic."

"Nothing of the sort, in fact, air mages are one of our biggest problems," Wislig said. "They can kill our lift in an instant, drop us out of the sky. Thankfully, though, they are few. Fire mages are more common, but only dangerous up close. Anyway, Enchtur! I ask again, why are there guns on top? If we start carrying guns, they'll start carrying guns!"

"Oh, sir, we're well past that, I'm afraid," the squeaky goblin explained. "One of them popped off with a shotgun, just after you left. Things spiraled fast. Now, anyone who goes up, goes with guns. 'Shoot first' is the new orders."

"My lord!" Wislig exclaimed. He focused on keeping his hands steady, but his foot twitched. "So, all decency has left the skies. I wasn't gone *that* long. Anyway, how am I supposed to shoot with the trigger all the way up there? Or aim, for that matter?"

"You'll get used to the aiming, so the other pilots tell me," Enchtur said. "And we'll raise your seat up a bit so you can reach the trigger. Sorry, but our newest batch of pilots—elves and humans— are all taller than you. Not so many gnomes up there anymore. Apparently, they're all skeered of flying, and it's only gotten worse now there's more shootin' going on."

Wait...claiming I'm too scared is an option?

"What's it called?" Wislig asked. With great focus, he ceased the twitch in his foot and fought to keep his nerves from manifesting elsewhere. As he did, a female elf and a male human walked up, both wearing fur-lined leather jackets which matched his. Both were considerably taller than him and wore Leftenant's rank.

"'Knaphauser's Iron Drake', sir," the human said. "But we call it a 'Kid' for short. Captain Wislig, I presume?"

Knaphauser's, is it? Miserable, thieving sod. Wait...did he call me "Captain?"

"No, it's...oh, I suppose it *is* Captain, now, isn't it?" Wislig replied.

"Ha-ha-ha!" Archibald boomed. "Forgotten our meeting with the Archministress already? Not used to cavorting with royalty, or whatever passes for it these days?"

"Not hardly, if I'm to be perfectly honest," Wislig replied. "Can't even remember whatever titles it was they bestowed on both of us." Wislig extended a hand to the elf leftenant. "But yes, I am *Captain* Wislig. And you are?"

"Lieutenant Sefyre, Captain," the elf lieutenant answered in a soft, Lutetian accent, as if every word would rather have been a kiss. She took the hand, locked eyes with an intense gaze, and gave a solid handshake, as if fighting to prove herself. "Cismi Sefyre. And this is *Leftenant—*"

"James Rought, sir." The man took his hand next and gave a gentler, friendlier handshake paired with a respectful nod. "Good to see another fellow of the Isles."

"Well met, both of you," Wislig said, and swept his arm toward the large golden dragon. "Might I introduce Archibald the Tremendous Terror, Bane of Vervast, Vanquisher of the Fireheart, and now, Grand Marshal of the Skies."

"Vanquisher of the—" Sefyre started, with a raised eyebrow.

"Grand Marshal of the Skies, is it?" Rought spoke over her and shot her an angry glance. Wislig wondered at the meaning.

"Yes," Archibald said. "Grand Marshal. So, I suppose that means all of you fall under my command, am I right in that assumption?"

"Yes, Archibald," Wislig answered. "But we still fall under the purview of the Generals. As your liaison, once I'm sorted out here, I suggest we go the War Staff next, so we can receive their orders."

"Nonsense!" Archibald boomed. "I've come to win the war for you and win the war I shall. The Archministress would not have bestowed the title if she did not trust me to lead this new aerial force to victory. So come, masters of the sky, launch your planes and watch me raze the armies of Fersang. Let me show you why this noble gnome rousted me from my slumber!"

The three pilots looked around at each other, dumbfounded. Wislig pleaded with his eyes for help.

After a moment, Sefyre shrugged and smiled. "If the Grand Marshal demands, then who are we to argue?"

"But the Generals...it should be coordinated, right?" Wislig asked. "That's still the way of things here, is it not?"

"Well, we've got his orders, Captain," Sefyre replied and maintained her confident grin. "We'll send word to the War Staff, leave it to them to take advantage."

"I'll just be stretching my wings, getting the lay and all that," Archibald said. "Announcing my presence, causing some mischief...and then I'll return to let the word fester." The great beast nuzzled his head down to Wislig and winked. "Wait for word to make its way to Brünstiglena's ears."

Sefyre turned and raised her chin toward the dragon as if to speak, but Rought took a step and shouldered into her. They shared a look, which Wislig pretended not to notice.

"Well, Archie, if you just want to go and have a look, we certainly can't stop you, can we?" Wislig asked in resignation.

With a grim expression, Rought grabbed the gnome's arm. "May I presume to make a suggestion, Captain?"

"Please."

"Authorized by the War Staff or not," Rought said, "we should launch to support our Grand Marshal. Wouldn't want to lose him on his first day."

He thinks that's a possibility?

"I suggest we take two flights of five. Sefyre will take her flight, and I'll take mine, to include you. Fly on my wing so you can get the hang of the formation tactics we've developed. Just do what you can to stay outside my wing and slightly aft. Should anything threaten our *Grand Marshal,* I will give the order to break up, like this." He flashed a hand with fingers outspread. "Then, you find and shoot whoever you can, be they wyvern or biplane."

Wyverns? Oh my...

"Are you sure?" Wislig asked. "I haven't any experience with the new birds, and if we're shooting at each other now..."

"Sir, you're the Grand Marshal's advisor, are you not?" Rought asked. "And a bit of a legend here as one of our early pilots. I would've thought you'd be excited to try the Kid out."

Gods, no! Wait...did he say I'm a legend?

"Yes, of course," Wislig said. "Anything I should know about them?"

"If that's settled, I'll see you at the Front!" Archibald laughed, kicked himself into the sky, and beat his wings until he gained altitude. The aircraft rocked and dust swirled about in the maelstrom he created. He shot into the sky and circled for a bit. "Hurry up, you fools, if you'd witness this!"

Rought and Sefyre shouted orders, one of which included an alarm. A loud buzzing noise sounded from somewhere, and, in moments, pilots rushed from tents toward the aircraft.

Rought pointed at *Archie's Teeth*. "Once you're started up, pull up behind me and follow at all costs! There's no time to teach you how to drakefight, but you'll figure it out!"

Drakefight?

* * *

Wislig found his hatred of flying outmatched by his eagerness to try out the new aircraft. In fact, it proved his greatest thrill in weeks. Quite a feat, as his previous weeks included visiting a dragon, meeting with the Archministress, receiving all sorts of accolades, and attending a ball with the finest souls in Lutetian and Isles aristocracy.

The monoplane he'd flown on reconnaissance missions had been a flimsy thing, whose wings he feared would snap off with every bout of turbulence. Riding on Archibald's back was equally terrifying, as there was little to hold onto, and the dragon insisted on sweeping about to examine everything that caught his fancy.

The Kid, on the other hand, felt sturdy, reliable, and unbreakable. He understood it wouldn't stand up much better to bullets. On the other hand, he knew that it would turn, roll, pitch, and accelerate better than anything he'd flown. He also knew, better than those who'd been flying it, where its limitations lay.

Unfortunately, the dangers of the Front had increased exponentially since his last flight, not the least of which was flying in formation.

Wislig's wide range of emotions vied for attention with a newfound fear of crashing into other aircraft. Rought would periodically throw up some simple hand signals which Wislig learned to mean up, down, left, and right. Immediately after, he would maneuver as indicated, and Wislig found himself in danger of *over*-controlling the magnificent aircraft in order to follow.

So focused was he on Rought's aircraft, that he forgot he feared heights, or that there would be ground fire directed at them. Nowhere in his mind did it occur to him that enemy aircraft might be searching them out. Worst of all, he completely forgot their purpose was to follow and support his friend, the Grand Marshal.

When Wislig gained some confidence in maintaining formation, he spared some attention to look down. They were higher than he'd realized, and his stress increased. Naught Land seemed darker, muddier, and more chewed up than he remembered. A great collection of small mounds had appeared near the Lutetian lines. A great ridge had inexplicably sprung up further north. For a moment, he doubted whether they were where he *thought* they were, but he found other references. The location was correct, but the terrain had changed.

Earth mages?

Reality returned when his peripheral vision caught a blast of fire ahead and below, tracing its way across the enemy trenches. Puffs erupted from Fersangian rifles.

Archibald jerked sharply to his right, lined up on a long stretch of trench, and unleashed another rending stream of hellfire. The sight gave Wislig great hope.

The enormous golden dragon climbed into the sky and turned toward Wislig's formation.

Coming to crow in triumph, no doubt.

Rought's hand shot up and made a gesture like a talking sock puppet followed by two fingers. Confused, Wislig followed the pilot's head when Rought looked right. Past the other aircraft, just forward of their wings, he spied birds. The birds had remarkably long, thin wings, bodies, and tails.

Wyverns!

The diminutive dragonkin had not been a part of the war before his journey.

They're up here with the sole purpose of killing us.

His greatest nightmare had become reality. Wislig felt himself go white with terror.

Rought's hand went up again and pointed toward the wyverns. The formation turned.

Abruptly, Rought dove down, and Wislig realized the man's hand was up, fingers spread. The other aircraft turned away to their respective sides.

Though trembling, he forced himself to think rationally. Wislig reasoned he preferred more altitude, not less, in order to dive on the enemy. While climbing, he searched to visually reacquire the wyverns.

Half a dozen wyverns, all carrying riders, fluttered into battle. Though no match for the speed of the ingenious aircraft, they were infinitely more maneuverable.

Three of them dashed in on one of his fellows. The biplane threw a furious, but ineffective, spray of bullets as the wyverns closed on it. As Wislig turned to help, he watched the wyverns attach to the Kid and break it apart. One of the wings snapped, and the aircraft plummeted without hope.

The gnome's eyes went wide. He'd never even considered the thought that a plane might be broken apart in such a manner.

Rought zoomed in and unleashed a stream of metal at the cluster. Two of the wyverns dropped. One was clearly dead, and its rider struggled in terror. The other, wounded, dove for the ground to escape.

A series of high pitched shrieks drew his attention up. Another cluster of miniature wyrms dove toward Wislig's plane. They'd placed the sun behind them to hide their approach. Frantically, he searched for friendly aircraft, but found none that could help him.

They were too close. If he tried to turn toward them, they'd be on him immediately and tear him up. A few bullets, from their riders, tapped against his wings. He jammed the throttle, banked hard away from them, and accelerated away. When he was clear, he started a climb.

The tremble in his hands stopped as he clung to both his control stick and the throttle knob with a death grip. His vision tunneled, and his thoughts focused on escaping the aerial hell.

You can't just run. Archie will know.

Wislig glanced back just in time to witness Archibald dive on the cluster of wyverns. He roasted two with fire, grabbed one in his jaws, and slashed a fourth with his claws as he flew by. The last two broke off their pursuit and dove for the ground as well.

See? With Archie here, you'll be fine. It's just a quick in and out, right? Go show the dragon you're worthy of his friendship, and we can fly back.

He forced a breath out and focused on a slow inhale. Then, he wiggled his fingers, rolled his shoulders, and tried to clear his head.

The gnome rolled the aircraft inverted and pulled a half loop toward the ground. The ground approached fast, but he leveled back off with plenty of altitude. At the end, he was upright and well-oriented to chase down one of the fleeing wyverns. With a hand up on the trigger of the twin chain guns, he fired a few rounds that went well wide. The wyvern danced about, and its rider twisted to shoot backward. A bullet tore a hole in Wislig's left wing.

Wislig exhaled slowly, focused, and read the wyvern's movements. The aircraft became a part of him. When he'd gotten close and felt confident he could anticipate the next move, he jerked the trigger. Bullets stitched across his target. The winged critter spasmed and fell like a dead bird. The rider screamed as they plummeted.

Regaining his bearings, he found Archibald chasing a wyvern who was chasing Rought's Kid. As Archibald reached out for the wyvern, it dropped.

A scattered sphere of wyverns collected around the dragon, and the riders poured fire into him. More gunfire erupted from below as well, as Archibald lay quite close to the ground. Wislig banked toward the group.

The dragon blasted flame in an arc around himself, which frightened a few off. He committed to dashing at the closest one. It dropped evasively, but Archibald anticipated the action, catching the wyvern and its rider in his jaws. He crunched hard and spit the dead pair out.

A stream of bullets from another Kid ripped through one of the wyverns. Wislig smiled.

If we can protect Archibald, perhaps he truly can break Fersang once and for all!

Suddenly, the other Kid whipped up, spun, hung for a moment, and then slid down, tail first, toward the earth. Halfway down, it rolled and twisted so the propeller pointed down, but the spin continued uncontrollably until it smashed into the ground. The pilot could not have survived.

An air mage.

Gusts and swirls of wind hunted for him before he found any sign of the mage.

"Go, my friend! I will find this mage!" Archibald shouted, his voice booming over all else. "Black and white robes, yes?"

Wislig nodded and raised an upturned hand to indicate affirmation. Archibald flapped around to search and quickly dove again. Another Kid flipped. Its wings cracked, and it tumbled down.

You can do nothing for him. Get away and watch for more wyverns.

The gnome accelerated away from the dangerous area and climbed. He scanned the horizon for friendly aircraft and for more threats. No Kids seemed to be anywhere nearby, but a collection of dots approached from the Fersang side. Glancing up, he flew a climbing arc to place himself between the sun and the approaching aircraft.

A burst of flame announced that Archibald had located the air mage upon a hilltop. The dragon hovered and poured death all around it, but was, in turn, engulfed by a storm of metal from below.

The dots resolved into black-painted biplanes. Still collected in formation, they raced toward Archibald. The dragon appeared unaware and struggled to climb away from the ground. Wislig realized the bullets had taken a toll on his friend. If Archibald climbed away from the ground fire, the fighters would tear him up. Even a dragon could only take so much.

Careful to keep the sun at his back, Wislig turned the Kid and descended toward the enemy planes. Fully aware his aim with the chain guns was miserable, he held his fire. With a hand ready on the trigger, he strained to watch the individual pilots in order to discern when they observed him.

One glanced up at him and seemed to shout. Closing fast and diving nearly head to head with the group, Wislig pulled the trigger tight and raked bullets across the formation.

One kicked up and returned fire as the others banked to the sides. He heard a single pinging noise in his engine, but it seemed to hold.

As they roared past him, he continued straight and craned to see the result. One aircraft rolled uncontrollably until it crashed. Another aircraft's engine bellowed smoke.

When he felt he had sufficient speed, he pulled back in an upward half loop. Inverted at its zenith, he rolled upright and searched again. The leader of the formation wobbled lazily and flew straight down into Naught Land. The aircraft bounced into the ravaged terrain until it flipped over forward.

Archibald flew low over Naught Land, retreating. He flapped his left wing twice as hard as his right in a desperate struggle to stay airborne. Two more Fersang biplanes, line abreast, zoomed toward him.

Wislig oriented his Kid toward the two planes, but they unleashed another torrent of bullets on Archibald long before Wislig could catch them. The gold dragon snapped his head up, and Wislig noticed his friend held one of his eyes shut and clutched a clawed hand to his side.

Archibald loosed another stream of fire into the air. One of the aircraft burst into flames, the other banked off and ran. The dragon flapped miserably a few dozen feet off the ground. As he got closer, Wislig could tell that ground fire still riddled his poor friend.

With another glance, Wislig discovered the last Fersang plane had banked in a teardrop to return to Archibald. The gnome worked out the vectors in his head. He aimed behind the aircraft at first, and then sharply reversed his bank to align himself straight behind it.

Before he closed, the enemy pilot spotted Wislig and began to jink in every direction to frustrate Wislig's aim. The gnome pulled up, leveled, and accelerated. Something popped in his engine, followed by a ratcheting noise. Thankfully, the propeller kept spinning.

As the Fersang aircraft closed on Archibald, Wislig dove at a sharp angle and fired when the wings grew large. He held the trigger until the chain guns clicked empty.

The Fersang pilot twitched. As Wislig shot past and pulled up to avoid crashing, the Fersang aircraft pushed over and dove straight down.

A loud ringing from hundreds of tiny whistles echoed through his ears. Looking down, he discovered a great light blue and gray mass had erupted from the friendly lines and charged across Naught Land. It appeared the Lutetian and Isle Generals sought to take advantage of the chaos Archibald had sown.

Thousands charged forward. Hundreds fell every step of the way. The Fersang soldiers were not as distracted as the War Staff had guessed. The Fersang lines, those not obscured by the black smoke of Archibald's handiwork, disappeared in the white smoke of gunfire.

As the ratcheting in his engine worsened, Wislig scanned in search of more threats. A fresh set of dots appeared to the Northeast. Without ammunition, the best he could do was try to lead a few off.

Five light blue flashes raced past him, led by the female elf lieutenant. She waved as she passed.

Content someone else could handle any inbound enemy planes, Wislig turned back to find Archibald.

The dragon had cleared Lutetian lines to safety. Oddly, Archibald snapped his head, turned sharply toward a low ridgeline, and landed in a field. Wislig found a spot nearby where he could land.

* * *

The engine on Wislig's Kid sputtered in anger as he lined up on the field where Archibald sat. The propeller froze for a moment, sputtered, spun, and then froze again. It ceased entirely as the wheels hit the ground. The plane bounced up and leaned right. After a few more disconcerting bounces, the aircraft settled and slowed.

By the time it stopped, the gnome had unstrapped and torn off his goggles. He jumped out of the aircraft, collapsed, picked himself up, and sprinted on stubby legs toward his enormous friend.

Archibald crouched low with his eyes closed. His wings were a torn, tattered mess. Dark fluid leaked out from hundreds of pinholes all over his torso. A thick, gelatinous secretion collected along the base of Archibald's eyelids. In his mud-caked claws, he held up the head of another dragon, mostly buried in the dirt. It was the new long, low ridge Wislig had spotted earlier. The dragon buried in the ridge was emerald green, just as large as Archibald, and completely lifeless.

"Did you know?" the golden dragon asked.

"I suspected," Wislig said, panting. "The others danced around some secret, and I couldn't think of what else it might be."

"And you feared to ask, for if they'd answered, you would have felt compelled to tell me."

"Yes," Wislig replied and remained silent for a moment. "I'm sorry, Archie. I tried to explain how this war is...I didn't know how...oh goddess, this must have happened after I—"

"Quiet."

The giant golden dragon nuzzled the corpse of Kaiserin Brünstiglena von Feuerherz.

"I fought in the Soul Wars against the Death Mages. I was there when the Great Horde erupted from the Deep. I've seen many other wars as well. Never, in all that time, have I seen this much devastation."

"I feared as much," Wislig said. "But I still hoped…"

"I have become nothing but a great target, who feels his mortality more than ever before. I'm going home, my dear Wislig." The declaration hung in the air as the greatest the dragon had ever made. "My dear friend. The greatest tinkerer I have ever known. Would you come with me and leave all this behind?"

Wislig's gaze dropped.

"I wish that I could, my old friend," he answered. "But I have a duty here, to the Isles, and to all my fellows to see this through." He took a long moment to parse his next words. "Though others may not, I understand. Take care of yourself…Archibald the Tremendous Terror, Bane of—"

"Stop. I am none of those things." The golden dragon set the green dragon's head gently down and rose up on his haunches. "Today, I learn all my titles are for naught. There is a word among your kind I have never understood before, but today I do. Humility."

Tears streamed from Wislig's eyes. He closed them in a vain attempt to hold the tears in.

"After this day, if I will be called anything, it will be Archibald the Humbled. If this war is to be won, it will be by brave, brilliant souls such as you…not big, bloated beasts like us."

The golden dragon nuzzled the face of his dead love once more.

"Enjoy your war, my dear friend."

* * * * *

Casey Moores Bio

Casey Moores was a USAF rescue/special ops C-130 pilot for over 17 years—airdropping, air refueling, and flying into tiny blacked-out dirt airstrips in bad places using night vision goggles. He's been to those places and done those things with those people. Now he lives a quieter life, translating those experiences to fiction. A Colorado native and Air Force Academy graduate, he is now a naturalized Burqueño, retired in New Mexico.

# # # # #

Backup by
D.J. Butler

"You really shouldn't rely on me to say anything that sounds remotely intelligent in this meeting," Indrajit warned his partner.

"Believe me," Fix said in his high-pitched voice, "I know. You're just the backup."

Both men wore togas. Indrajit's was a dark orange, and Fix's was a rich purple, with strong notes of blue. They weren't the false togas that were really just robes, easier to move in and adopted by the merchant class when they wanted to appear wealthy, but wrap-around-the-body-and-pin-over-the-shoulder togas. They weren't uncomfortable; if he were compelled to pronounce on the comfort of the garment, Indrajit would even have said that it felt good. Air flowed around his thighs, as it did when he wore his customary and preferred kilt, and under his arms, as it did when he wore the loose tunic he liked, and he felt at ease.

But if he ran, he worried the toga would slip and trip him. And there was no room in the toga to hide his legendary sword, Vacho, so Indrajit was reduced to wearing a stiletto on a belt wrapped around his thigh.

The thought that he would be unable to either fight or run made the Recital Thane nervous.

Also, he was wearing perfume. It was a floral scent, though he didn't know the name of the flower.

A bright blue-skinned wine peddler on the other side of the street caught Indrajit's eye and started across, the tray hanging at the level of his sternum from a strap around his neck jostling only slightly, the cups not even rattling. He raised a jug in one hand, and his face fell when Indrajit waved him off.

"I'm probably being too harsh on myself," Indrajit continued. "I mean, when we were investigating those indoors traders last month—"

"In*side* trading," Fix corrected him. "Not in*doors*."

"Yes, and I was the one who realized what they were up to."

"To be fair," Fix said, "I knew something was off, since the inside traders in question had already tied me hand and foot and dropped me into a hole underneath their offices."

Indrajit nodded. "Fortunately, I was able to put two and two together, realize exactly what they had been up to, and come to your rescue."

"Yes. If by put two and two together you mean you overheard Samwit Conker say, 'I am very excited to get rich by this inside trading scheme, just as soon as we kill that fellow Fix, whom we have stashed in the basement.'"

"Not in so many words."

"But almost."

"I was very pleased to be able to rescue you."

"I was pleased, too," Fix said. "I remain pleased. I hope that, in the future, every criminal we come up against will have the decency to confess in your presence. It really simplifies the investigative process."

"Also, when a high level of general culture is required, I'll contribute." Indrajit cleared his throat. "But if we need to say something about the horoscopes that were provided to us, I'm right out."

"Projections," Fix said.

"Right." Indrajit nodded. "Papers telling the future."

"Yes, but not by stars or entrails." Fix, too, had to forego his usual falchion, hatchet, and knives, and wouldn't be carrying a spear, either. Indrajit didn't think he had so much as a knife on his person. Still, arms folded over his chest, he seemed at ease. "But the real question is whether what we got is a bottom-up or a top-down projection."

"I assume we prefer top-down." Indrajit put on his thinking face, the one he wore to communicate that he understood, that he was taking the conversation very seriously, and he knew the answer to the posed question was likely something sophisticated and nonobvious. "But I am anxious to hear your view."

"The real point is, did someone just bump the revenue number up five percent each year, or did they actually analyze the underlying business on a contract-by-contract basis, in light of recent Auction House trends, to determine what they thought would happen, and, by chance, arrive at a round five percent figure?"

"Correct." Indrajit touched a finger to his pursed lips.

Fix snorted. "Don't worry, I'll do the talking."

"I'm just showing you that I can fake it," Indrajit said. "For a little while, at least."

The two men waited for their palanquin to arrive. The sedan chair was being sent by their master, Orem Thrush, the Lord Chamberlain of Kish, but it wouldn't bear his horned skull emblem. It would look luxurious and anonymous, as Fix had specified.

To be precise, the palanquin was being arranged not by Orem Thrush himself, but by Grit Wopal, the Lord Chamberlain's Yifft spymaster. Indrajit and Fix reported to Wopal, not as members of the Lord Chamberlain's espionage organization, the Ears, but as their own separate unit. They formed a two-man jobber crew, nearly anonymous, with the flexibility to undertake a wide range of missions in and around the Paper Sook.

Of all the places and institutions of Kish, the Paper Sook might be the one Indrajit hated the most.

"You must realize that I value you for qualities other than your understanding of how the Paper Sook works." Fix raised a hand as the palanquin hove into view around a corner. It was picking them up at a swanky tavern in the Lee, as arranged, rather than at their quarters at an inn in the Spill.

"But I do know how the Paper Sook works."

"Yes," Fix said mildly.

The palanquin stopped. Its six bearers were all thickly muscled men with scaly shoulders and four arms. They ran on their legs and on their middle set of arms, which had horny, callused knuckles. A short, thick tail swished back and forth behind each bearer.

Fix crossed to the far side of the palanquin to enter, and Indrajit climbed in where he stood, settling himself with a bolster behind his back and a cushion under his raised knees. With his widely spaced eyes, Indrajit could face forward and still see out the door of the palanquin with his left eye, while his right rested its gaze on Fix. Fix, who had a very ordinary Kishi arrangement of his facial features, looked out his door as the six-limbed palanquin bearers picked them up and began to jog toward the Crown.

"What qualities?" Indrajit asked.

"Hmm?" Fix seemed distracted. Outside the palanquin, the Kish evening was lit with torches, oil lamps, and fires. A three-armed juggler tried to rush the sedan chair, perhaps hoping for a gratuity, but the bearers hurled him back into shadow.

"What qualities do you value me for?" Indrajit pressed.

Fix cleared his throat. "Well, for one, you're not needy. You feel very confident in your contributions to our joint enterprise, which makes it always easy to deal with you. I don't have to be gentle to your wounded vanity, or overstate your excellence. I think it's easy to underestimate how attractive that quality is in a partner."

"Yes." Indrajit nodded. "What else?"

"Well, you're tall. And you have good peripheral vision."

"Those traits could prove extraordinarily useful. There are also my poetics."

"Though I understand those sound better in the original Blaatshi."

"Everything sounds better in Blaatshi."

"You're good in a fight," Fix pointed out.

"We're not going to get into a fight tonight," Indrajit said. "We're going to pretend to be investors, considering funding the joint-stock company of a new jobber band, while actually investigating the promoters."

"Listen to you," Fix said. "Talking the language of joint-stock companies so well."

"You are trying to distract me."

"We might get into a fight. This is supposed to be a private pitch session, part of what is sometimes called a *road show*, so it should just be us and the promoters."

"And we think they're from out of town."

"Wopal thinks they're foreigners, gathering up local money to pay for an assassination attempt on Orem Thrush."

"Why not just outlaw joint-stock companies?" Indrajit suggested. "Nip this whole thing in the bud?"

"That would have other consequences." They passed the Spike, with its cluster of five temples. They were nearly at their destination, now. "Legitimate businesses would be hurt. And the assassination organizers would just raise money some other way. And besides, the Lord Chamberlain can't just make things illegal by decree, he's not a king. He'd have to get the heads of the other Houses to agree, or at least four of them, and that never happens. And if it did happen, then they'd have to pay the Auction House to inscribe the new law into the legal code."

"We might get into a fight tonight if the promoters really are crooked, and they conclude that we work for Thrush."

"Correct. And one way they might be led to conclude that is if there are real investors there, and they recognize us. We're anonymous in many places in this town…"

"But not in the Paper Sook. Frozen hells." Indrajit sighed. "If I could pick one place in Kish to be well-known, it wouldn't be that one."

"Because all they do in the sook is yell and trade chits, and that gives you a headache."

"I know what they do in the Paper Sook. They trade shares in companies, and they make bets on the future prices of company shares, and they trade currencies, and…hey."

"See?" Fix elbowed his partner. "You *do* understand the Paper Sook."

"Like I said, it still gives me a headache."

The palanquin stopped; they had arrived. The two men climbed out.

"But this road show meeting," Indrajit said, straightening his toga and looking up at the rectangular palace above them, "it's not being held anywhere near the sook."

"That would be entirely too unimaginative," Fix said. "The promoters are trying to convince rich men to invest some of their wealth, so they want to radiate wealth and success themselves."

From within his toga, he drew the letter of invitation Grit Wopal had given them. "Ergo, we meet in an elegant building in a fine old neighborhood."

The palace porter looked at the seal on the letter and waved the two men toward a staircase at the back left of the building's inner courtyard. There stood two tall men, bright yellow in color, with narrow eyes, blue on blue, tall feather headdresses, and long spears. The smaller of the two, who had a bent nose and one eyebrow permanently arched high on his forehead, took the letter.

"The Bilzarian Partners?" Bent Nose asked.

"Obviously," Fix said.

Indrajit snorted his contempt for the process.

The palace was four stories tall and six at the corners, so Indrajit was dreading a long and breathless climb. They shuffled up two flights of stairs to a landing where two more of the tall, blue-eyed yellow men with spears stood. They patted down Indrajit and Fix both, but the search was perfunctory; another beauty of the toga was that it tended to communicate *harmless noncombatant* and therefore discouraged the searchers from carrying out their task with too much zeal.

Indrajit followed Fix under an arch, passing from the landing into an airy, high-ceilinged chamber. A low table in the center of the room was laden with food—roasted tamarind, coconut, mango, rose-apples, apricots, cubes of lamb and goat meat on skewers, a soft white cheese, flatbreads. A pitcher of chilled tea sat surrounded by huddled stone cups. Surrounding the low table were reclining couches and divans piled high with cushions. To Indrajit's left was a taller table, on which rested an open ledger beside an ink pot and a quill.

Two yellow spearmen stood in each of two arches exiting the room.

Beside the low table stood two Xiba'albi men, one wearing a gold collar and the other wearing multiple gold rings. Both had gold hoops in their ears.

Beside the ledger stood a lavender-skinned Zalapting, with a small hump on his back and a gray beard. He wore a simple tunic and kilt, gray in color, and the gray of his tunic and beard and the fading lavender of his skin blurred into a nondescript gray smudge. Beyond him and the table bearing the ledger was an open doorway leading to a balcony. Potted palmetto plants on the balcony muffled the street sounds rising from below.

"Mr. Bilzarian?" one of the Xiba'albi asked.

"Yes," Indrajit and Fix both said.

Oops.

"We're brothers." Indrajit smiled.

"Different mothers," Fix said to the immediately raised eyebrows.

"And we're an exotic race of man," Indrajit continued. "Our appearance varies widely."

The Xiba'albi both bowed deeply. "We are but the subscription agents," one of them said. "Give us a few minutes, and we will bring the issuer out to meet with you. In the meantime, please refresh yourselves. The tea is delicious."

The Xiba'albi swept from the room in a tinkle of gold.

The Zalapting cleared his throat.

"Do we know each other?" Indrajit asked.

The Zalapting inclined his head, a stiff gesture. "I have some familiarity with many of the professionals of the Paper Sook."

Indrajit smiled, but he wasn't sure whether the Zalapting was intimating that he might be a threat. Was he saying he knew that Indrajit and Fix were not who they said they were? Or was the Zalapting bluffing? Or just being polite?

"Perhaps the Bilzarian Partners would care to examine the company's registry while they wait?" the Zalapting suggested, tilting up the book beside him to show the present page.

Indrajit waved fingers, feigning indifference to cover the fact that he couldn't read. This was a good sign, though—it might mean the Zalapting didn't really know who he was.

Fix peered at the page. "I see."

The Zalapting replaced the book on the table and shifted from foot to foot.

"So…you don't work for the issuer, then?" Fix asked.

"I'm a notary's clerk," the Zalapting said. "I'm just here to witness in case any shares are transferred tonight."

Indrajit stretched himself out on a divan and took a handful of apricots. Fix glared at him.

"What?" Indrajit asked.

"We just ate…and drank," Fix growled. "How can you still be *thirsty?*"

"Just having a few pieces of fruit," Indrajit said. "To be polite. This is Kish: eat when you can."

His words seemed to irritate rather than calm Fix and then the shorter man was stalking across the room. "Perhaps you would like to read the register yourself," Fix grunted.

Fix knew very well that Indrajit couldn't read. Indrajit was an oral poet, who could spin out thirty thousand lines of his people's Blaatshi Epic on the toss of a coin but couldn't read a word of any language. Fix knew this and had mocked Indrajit repeatedly for it.

What was Fix getting at, suggesting Indrajit might like to read?

"Fine," he said, and as he stood, he reached for the tea.

"I'll get that." Fix knocked the pitcher over, spilling tea across the table.

"How clumsy," Indrajit said, waving fingers again to feign...being rich, basically. "We shall have to subscribe to more shares to make up for the tea we have spilled."

The large yellow men looked impassively at him.

"Yes," Fix said, "that's no problem. But first, come take a look at this."

The Zalapting stepped aside, and Fix drew Indrajit close to the registry volume.

"What are you trying to say, Fix?" Indrajit murmured under his breath.

"That it's past time you learned to read, for one thing!" Fix snapped.

"This is an awkward time and place to have this argument." Indrajit looked over his shoulder at the nearest yellow spearman and smiled.

Fix jabbed his index finger into the blue ink swirls written on the page to which the registry was opened and lowered his voice. "What our new Zalapting acquaintance here has written is, 'The tea is drugged.'"

"Frozen hells."

"The Bilzarians." These words came from behind them, but they were spoken by a familiar voice.

"Samwit Conker." Indrajit turned around.

Conker was a Wixit, one of the most common races of man in Kish. If Wixits walked on all fours and kept their mouths shut, they might easily be mistaken for some forest-dwelling species of beast or pets of Kish's wealthy. Wixits were furred and looked rather like ferrets. Some might even find them cute.

But Conker stood upright, on his hind legs, on the back of a divan. His hands were on his hips, and he was definitely in no mood to keep his mouth shut.

"Fix *Bilzarian*," the Wixit said. "The last time I saw you, I was locking you in my basement, while I decided what to do with you."

"Apparently, you decided to sell me shares," Fix said.

"Wrong." The Wixit shifted his gaze to Indrajit. "And Twang *Bilzarian*."

"Indrajit is my first name," Indrajit said, "if you care." He longed for his sword.

"I don't. I do care that my rather elaborate plan to drug you and feed you to my lizards has been thwarted."

"You were exiled from Kish," Fix said. "Kish can stand its share of murder and robbery, but your insider trading scheme made the Lord Stargazer lose a lot of money."

"I was too enthusiastic." Conker curled his lips back to show his teeth. "I got greedy."

"I bet he just put a leash on his own neck," Fix continued, "and had one of those Xiba'albi walk him through the gate like a cat."

Samwit Conker arched his back and hissed. "I am no one's pet."

"Or just curled up on some prostitute's lap, pretending to be a handbag," Indrajit continued. "You'd be a good handbag."

"Kish is as porous as a sponge," Conker said. "Nothing easier than to move in and out."

"Welcome to Kish," Indrajit said, quoting one of the dozens of epigrams featuring the ancient city's name. Some bore wisdom, others humor, but most of all, they told hard truths about the hard city. "Or not, as you please."

"Today, the answer will be not." Conker raised an arm and spun one finger in a quick circle. This gesture summoned the yellow spearmen to surround Indrajit and Fix. More of the men slipped from the arched doorways in the process, and Indrajit and his partner found themselves detained by eight warriors.

"You came in underground, didn't you?" Fix asked. "Through the tunnels?"

The Wixit squinted at him. "Why do you say that?"

Fix shrugged. "You stink."

Samwit Conker laughed.

"Welcome to Kish," Indrajit said, "hold your nose."

"Kill the Zalapting," Conker ordered.

One of the spearmen turned and took a step in the clerk's direction, but Indrajit reached out and touched the man on the chest to restrain him.

"Hey," Indrajit said.

Three spearpoints pressed into the flesh of his chest and arm.

Indrajit swallowed, his throat dry. "You don't need to kill that guy. He's not going to tell anyone anything, and he can't stop you. No point in making more enemies than you have to."

Conker stared at Indrajit. "So, the clerk is one of Wopal's Ears, too?"

Indrajit shook his head. "None of us are the Lord Chamberlain's Ears. Fix and I are jobbers, you know that. The *Protagonists*."

"Ah, yes." Conker's smile was cold. "The heroes. And you don't want me to kill this innocent registry clerk."

"Just let him go. Or tie him up if you need to."

"He's only a Zalapting. In the time it takes me to kill him, they'll have bred a thousand more."

Indrajit grinned. "Just because he's short doesn't mean his life is worthless."

Samwit Conker snarled, but then his snarl broke down into a tittering laugh. "You've got wit, Twang. Perhaps when we are done, I'll keep you. Blinded and gelded, chained to a pit in my throne room, forced to entertain me until you die."

"When you say 'throne room,' I imagine you squatting on a hat box."

"Tie them up all up," Conker said to one of the yellow men, a fellow wearing a taller headdress than the others, full of white and purple feathers. "Leave them conscious, if possible."

Indrajit ground his teeth as the yellow men bound his hands behind his back. The fabric of the toga at his shoulder tore around the pin of the brooch as they handled him, but it didn't rip all the way through. "Good move," he told the Wixit. "Hold us for ransom. And you can use the registry clerk as a little kicker during negotiation, if the Lord Chamberlain doesn't want to meet your demands."

"Yes," Samwit Conker said. "Something like that."

Then spears in his back prodded Indrajit forward.

The captain of the yellow men went first, followed by Fix. Two yellow men held Fix, one gripping each arm, while a third walked behind him, holding a knife to his kidneys. Then a single yellow warrior dragged the Zalapting, and, finally, three brought Indrajit along.

"Where are you brightly-colored fellows from, anyway?" Indrajit asked.

"Why do you care?" Samwit Conker snapped. He must be bringing up the rear.

"Indrajit is probably trying to compose an epithet," Fix said.

"I'm wondering whether I already know one," Indrajit countered. "I don't recall anything about men with yellow skin, but there is an epithet that goes, *tall men and feathered, who sail the Sea of Rains.* So I would be interested to know if you guys are from Thûl or Xiba'alb or somewhere near the Sea of Rains."

"On second thought," Conker said, "I'm going to have to kill you. Nothing else will shut you up. Do you never tire of this, Fix?"

"When it seems tedious," Fix called over his shoulder, "I just try to imagine how Indrajit feels when I explain option contracts to him."

"I understand option contracts," Indrajit protested. "That's the one where you sell something you don't actually own, right?"

The Wixit cackled.

"Close," Fix said.

They passed through several rooms with weighted silk curtains. Indrajit could smell the sea. At the back of the apartment, a blank door of solid *yetz*-wood was held shut by a thick iron bar. The captain heaved the bar up with visible effort and set it aside. When the door opened, it revealed a narrow chute lined with orange bricks, leading down. Iron ladder rungs bolted into the bricks provided a means of descent…

For a person with free hands.

"Do our ways part here, then?" Indrajit asked.

For answer, the yellow captain pushed Fix into the chute.

Indrajit's short, muscled partner fell but landed on his buttocks on the floor, legs jammed down the chimney and hands behind him.

"Get a move on," the Wixit growled.

"His hands are tied," Indrajit protested.

"He has shoulders and feet," Samwit Conker said. "And I only need one of you to survive, anyway, so if he falls and dies…it's your lucky day."

Fix scraped his way down the chute, grunting with effort and pain. After a minute of listening to his partner's efforts and imagining flesh being scraped off by old brick, Indrajit heard the dull thud of Fix falling to the floor at the bottom of the shaft.

The yellow captain went next, much easier.

"It isn't far!" Fix called up from the pit. "When the wall starts moving away behind you, just drop!"

Indrajit seated himself at the chute before he could be forced to sit. There was only one yellow warrior in the chamber below—if Indrajit could get his stiletto into his hand and surprise the man, this might be his and Fix's best chance to make their escape. He felt the cold weight of the weapon and the pinch of the belt around his thigh as he scooted forward.

"At least untie the Zalapting," he said as he probed with one sandaled foot for his first hold. "What's he going to do, attack your eight huge mercenaries?"

"We are a ferocious people," the registry clerk said, "driven by our inborn wildness to war. War proves which Zalapting men are fit mates, and war also keeps the population down. All our poetry exalts war, all our childhood play trains for it. We are driven by our mad bloodlust until the Turning."

"Then what happens?" Samwit Conker asked.

"We become even more ferocious."

The Wixit laughed. "Twang is right. Untie the Zalapting, or he'll break his neck."

Indrajit heard the cords around the clerk's wrists being snipped as he lowered his weight onto his iron-rung footholds and sank into the chute. He felt the skin of his shoulders being scraped raw as he used them like feet, inching downward with his weight first on one shoulder and then on the other.

He didn't feel especially self-conscious about another man seeing up his toga, except that today he wore a secret knife wrapped around one thigh. He tried to keep his legs together, without appearing like he was trying to keep his legs together.

It almost made him lose his foothold twice.

Then, when his head was maybe three cubits below the surface of the floor above him, he felt the wall behind him begin to bow out and away from him. Smooth, time-gnawed brick gave way to a rougher surface that cut into his flesh. The chute was opening into a room.

"Drop!" Fix called.

Indrajit let himself fall. He landed on his feet, feeling the hard impact through his soles and his legs and crashing into his pelvis, knocking him to one knee. But the knife stayed in place and his toga stayed on.

He stood.

"Get up," the yellow captain said, prodding Indrajit in the shoulder.

Indrajit stood. He and Fix and the yellow man were in a brick chamber that seemed to suffer from centuries of neglect; bricks lay heaped in the corner, and gaps in all the walls showed where the bricks might have fallen from. Light came from an oil lamp that burned in the corner; the slight flicker of its flame testified to the presence of an air current, but there were no windows, and the only other opening was the mouth of a second chute in the floor.

"We are from Boné," the yellow captain said in a low voice. "We are Udayans. We come from the hill country, and we serve only the greatest noblemen."

"Why are you satisfying my curiosity," Indrajit asked, "if you only plan to kill us?"

"They don't plan to kill us," Fix said.

Indrajit snorted. "We aren't worth much ransom."

"They want us to do something," Fix continued. "My guess is an assassination."

The captain of the yellow warriors gave no hint that the guesses were at all correct. He stepped to the other side of the steel rungs bolted into the bricks, keeping his spear pointed at the Zalapting clerk for the last few cubits of his descent.

"That's sort of a funny joke on Conker's part," Indrajit said. "Luring us to this meeting, thinking we were going to prevent an assassination, then trying to make us carry one out. Do you think the Lord Chamberlain is the target?"

"It's a good guess," Fix said. "Maybe they hold one of us prisoner to force the other to kill Thrush."

"Or maybe they send the Udayans with us, we commit the murder together, and then the Udayans leave, and we're left behind to take the punishment."

Fix watched the yellow man closely. "Or they kill us on the scene, so it looks like the Lord Chamberlain killed us in self-defense."

"These scenarios all sound bad for us." Indrajit sighed. The Zalapting clerk reached the floor and padded over to join Indrajit and Fix. The captain didn't retie the clerk's hands. The yellow warrior stayed beneath the chute, looking upward and calling instructions to someone who was now beginning to climb down. "I apologize for not asking earlier, but what's your name?"

"Tufo," the clerk said.

"What was that you were talking about, the Turning?" Indrajit asked. He kept a close eye on the yellow captain, who, for his part, was looking up the chute. Indrajit's hands were tied behind him, but he was able to gather up a large handful of toga material, which was coming loose from movement and from the brooch pin tearing through the toga fabric. Leaning forward slightly and yanking, he managed to ruck the cloth up around his hips, exposing his thighs and, he hoped, the dagger strapped to one of them.

Which he couldn't mention verbally.

Fix helped, though, raising one foot off the ground to point at Indrajit's weapon.

"You smell nice," Tufo said.

"It's a flower," Indrajit said. "I forget the name."

"It means," Tufo said, "that when we become too numerous, so that war does not prune our numbers and our warrens can no longer hold us, something happens to our births. Our males are then born overwhelmingly homosexual."

Tufo missed the stiletto in the dark and started patting around on Indrajit's thigh.

Indrajit felt exposed. "I...ah..."

"What an interesting way to keep your numbers in check," Fix said. "'Homosexual' means that the men are attracted to other men, Indrajit."

"I know what homosexual means." Indrajit cleared his throat. "Can't you see it?" he hissed. "A little higher. Not there. Are you saying—is that happening now, the Turning?"

"No. The warrens of Kish are large, and there is much violent work among the jobber companies to keep the numbers of our males pruned. We have relatively few homosexuals in these times." Tufo finally found the stiletto and drew it. "I am one, of course."

Indrajit let his toga drop around his legs.

"You said you become more ferocious in the Turning," Fix said.

"We homosexuals are noted for our savage prowess in combat." Tufo cut through the rope around Indrajit's hands with a single firm motion, then moved to stand behind Fix. Indrajit held the sliced bits of cord around his wrists, trying to maintain the appearance that he was tied.

The person coming down the chute was Samwit Conker himself. He was nimble, as Wixits generally were, but the iron bars were large for his small hands, so the yellow captain took care to stand beneath him, prepared to break his fall. Conker focused on his hand- and footholds.

Tufo walked around to stand beside Indrajit, hands behind his back, presumably holding the stiletto there. Indrajit couldn't ask for his knife back, but he was about to reach over and take it when Conker dropped to the floor, and the Wixit and the yellow Bonean both turned to face Indrajit and his companions.

"They almost figured it out," the yellow captain said to the Wixit. "But then they got distracted, talking to the Zalapting about how ferocious Zalaptings are."

Samwit Conker laughed. "Oh? How ferocious *are* Zalaptings, then?"

Tufo attacked without warning, leaping at the yellow warrior. As the larger man tried to step aside, Tufo reversed the stiletto and slashed it through his right hamstring. Shrieking a string of syllables in some foreign tongue, the warrior sank to his knees. He tried to bring his spear into play, but it was too big to get between him and the Zalapting.

Conker leaped forward...

...and Indrajit kicked him against the wall.

The Wixit bounced, snarling and yapping. Indrajit's brooch pin chose that moment to finally eat its way through the cloth of the toga, and the garment collapsed around Indrajit's body, tangling his legs and tripping him.

Indrajit stumbled. He stood at the edge of the shaft in the floor, arms flapping as if he might take flight.

Tufo wrapped his left hand in the yellow warrior's hair, stepped onto the man's thigh to raise himself, and plunged the stiletto up to the hilt in the man's throat. Blood spattered across the brick floor, the Zalapting, and Indrajit.

Fix grabbed Indrajit's toga and yanked. He pulled the poet back from the edge, and Indrajit reeled across the room into the far corner. The toga pulled away from Indrajit's body into Fix's hands, and Fix turned, holding the cloth up.

Tufo grabbed the dead man's spear and looked up the chute. A second warrior was descending, yellow legs vivid in the flickering lamplight. Above them, shadowed movements suggested the presence of a third, coming down the shaft. Tufo braced himself.

Samwit Conker leaped at Fix, fangs bared and limbs splayed, a raucous war-shriek unrolling from his lungs.

The second yellow warrior dropped and was impaled through the chest on Tufo's spear. He died with no sound other than a heavy thud as he and the Zalapting fell over sideways.

Fix swung the toga like a net. He wrapped it around Conker, snatching the little furry man from the air and wrapping him entirely into a squirming bundle.

Indrajit found himself wearing only a loincloth and sandals, with an empty knife sheath strapped to his thigh. Tufo climbed out from under the dead yellow warriors' bodies, straightening his disheveled clothing, and Indrajit started to laugh.

A voice called down from above in an unknown language.

"Your two friends are dead!" Indrajit yelled back up. "And we have your employer tied up in a sack. Time for you to go home!"

He eyed the shaft that descended. Presumably, it must drop below the level of the street, into the sewers and other passages that honeycombed the enormous hill, part-natural and part man-made, built of the accumulated detritus of millennia, beneath the city of Kish. Presumably, the yellow men or the Wixit knew a route through that maze that would have let them attack Orem Thrush, which meant that they probably also knew a way out, but Indrajit didn't want to put a single foot down there if he could help it.

At least, if he had to, he'd go armed. He unbuckled the sword belt of the yellow captain and then rebuckled it around his own waist. He took a spear in hand, too, though in his life, he had mostly used spears for fishing.

Tufo kept the stiletto, saluting Indrajit with it by touching it to his eyebrow.

Fix handed Indrajit the bundle of toga cloth. Indrajit gripped the balled top firmly, letting the excess material fall over his elbow; the Wixit squirmed inside, and Indrajit buffeted him gently with the knuckles of his other hand. "I've got a blade now, Conker," he whispered. "Hold still, or I will cut you."

Fix armed himself, pulling the bloody spear from the yellow corpse and belting a sword around his shoulder.

"Let the Wixit go," a voice from above called, "or we'll come down and make you regret it."

"Oh, yeah?" Indrajit laughed. "We killed two of you armed with just a knife! How much damage do you think we'll do to you now that we have your friends' weapons, too?"

"Counteroffer!" Fix shouted. "Get out of here, and we'll leave you alone!"

"No!" Conker shrieked, the sound muffled by the toga. Indrajit boxed the bundle lightly and was rewarded with an angry hiss.

The murmur of discussion drifted down from above.

"What do you think came of those Xiba'albi?" Fix whispered.

Indrajit frowned. "I assumed they were just hired to lure us in and then left. You don't think maybe they're down there, do you?" He pointed at the shaft leading down.

"We have no idea what's down there," Fix said.

"Right." Indrajit nodded. "And we don't know the way."

"But Conker probably does," Tufo said.

Indrajit stared at the Zalapting. "What kind of *notary's* clerk are you?"

"I work for Wopal," the clerk said. "I was here as your backup."

"Backup?" Indrajit harrumphed. "Do we *always* have backup?" He looked at Fix for an answer. "When did we ever have backup before?"

Fix shrugged.

"All those things you told us about Zalaptings," Indrajit said to Tufo. "You know, warrior poems, and the Turning, and you being...an especially ferocious sort of Zalapting."

"All true," Tufo said.

"We'd better be more careful around Zalaptings," Fix suggested.

"You two are also quite ferocious," Tufo said. "I wouldn't worry too much."

"We're not ferocious," Indrajit objected. "We're the good guys."

Conker snarled and thrashed about in his cloth cage.

"We haven't been paid," a voice called down. Indrajit peered up the chute and saw light from the floor above, unobstructed by any bodies, so whoever had been in the process of climbing down the shaft had thought better of the idea.

"Not our problem!" Indrajit called back.

"It *is* your problem, because you're holding the man who owes us!"

Indrajit rapped a loving knuckle where he thought Samwit Conker's head was. "Don't think that we're going to just let him come on up to you. We like having him as a hostage!"

More murmuring. "We could allow you to ascend. We would promise not to hurt you."

Indrajit met Fix's gaze and frowned. "The more you talk, the less I trust you!" he yelled. "You could just stab us as we climb up!"

"I'll pay you myself!" Conker shrieked. "Ten Imperials. I'll lead you out through the tunnels and then you let me go!"

"Well, that's odd," Indrajit said softly. "Why would you pay us? I'm pretty sure you planned to kill us."

"Because, if we give him to his yellow boys," Fix said thoughtfully, "he knows they'll shake him down for more. Since he hasn't got the assassination he wanted, he's just trying to get out alive at the cheapest price."

"But he might have more fighters in the tunnels," Indrajit said. "The Xiba'albi or someone else."

"I have no fighters in the tunnels," the Wixit said.

"Maybe a trap," Fix suggested.

"I have no traps, either."

"It would be nice to get paid," Indrajit said.

"Twelve Imperials!" Conker cried.

"We could climb down in there with you!" an upstairs voice called. "You could leave the Wixit with us and climb out!"

"I don't trust you not to attack us as soon as you have Conker!" Indrajit shouted. "I'm pretty sure that's what he'd want!"

"The hole in the floor is looking better all the time," Fix said.

"What if you all climbed down unarmed?" Indrajit yelled.

"That's not going to happen!" the unseen yellow warrior called back.

Indrajit lowered his voice and stepped in close to Fix and Tufo. "We seem to be at an impasse."

"We can take our chances with the hole in the floor," Fix murmured.

"I'll still pay you ten Imperials!" the Wixit squeaked.

"I have a plan," the Zalapting said. "Perhaps we should be careful to bind the Wixit's mouth shut before I say any more."

* * *

Cho'ag Yoom was the youngest of the eight Udayan warriors who remained in this ancient, rotting city. They had been the bodyguard of a pasha, once, but he was dead, and their numbers had dwindled from their former thirty-six (to match the thirty-six houses of the night sky) to eight, as the pasha's enemies had driven him from his lands across the Serpent Sea, and then to this city, and then had made repeated assaults on the pasha before he finally took his own life, leaving his prized Udayan warriors to become mercenaries.

And, perhaps, only six remained, if the fish-headed man and his companions were to be believed. The gods had hated the Bonean pasha so much, they had not been content to kill him alone, but were now sating their last appetite for vengeance upon his bodyguard.

Leaning on his spear and waiting, with his five companions, for the fish-head's answer, Cho'ag shook his head.

Cho'ag was a member of the band, only because his uncle Zhan had chosen him and sworn him in. Zhan was the headman of the band. Cho'ag had survived under Zhan's protection, only gaining tentative acceptance, if that, from the other warriors, and now Zhan was likely dead.

A scream sounded from the chamber below. "No!" a voice shouted. "Don't leave me here, they'll kill me!"

"That doesn't sound like the fish-headed man," Hakk said. Hakk was the senior surviving member of the band and had been their spokesman in communicating down the shaft. He had a bent nose and low cunning.

"Please!" the voice called up the shaft. "The two jobbers are running! They're fleeing down into the tunnels with the Wixit, who promised them ten Imperials! Please don't hurt me!"

"This could be a trap," Churt suggested.

"Yes," Hakk said. "That is why we will send Cho'ag."

Five spears dropped to level at him, and there was no arguing. Cho'ag took his spear into his left hand and looked down into the shaft. Seeing the Zalapting looking up at him, covered in blood, he eased himself into the chute and rapidly descended into the chamber below.

A flickering lamp sat on the edge of a second shaft that dropped further in one corner of the room. Near the foot of the ladder, obscured by shadow and blood, lay two bodies. Cho'ag couldn't see their faces, but he saw their Udayan headdresses; one bore the purple and white headman's feathers.

"Uncle Zhan," he murmured and sighed.

The Zalapting pointed down the hole. "They left me!"

"Do you live, mighty Cho'ag?" Hakk called down from above.

Cho'ag did not appreciate the sarcasm. "So far!"

He knelt to examine the corpses. These were the bodies of his uncle Zhan and of his former fellow guard, Ferut. Strangely, Ferut's loincloth was missing. Barbarians. "Safe sailing, Uncle," he murmured. "I will sing for you when next I see the Celestial River."

Hakk now climbed down the ladder. "Why are you not pursuing the fish-head down the hole?" he demanded.

Cho'ag stood. "I was saying farewell to my uncle." He crossed to the opening of the second shaft and began to climb down it. His feet descended below him into darkness, and he imagined the feeling of spears stabbing into his flesh with each step.

"Shall I kill the Zalapting?" Hakk sneered.

"As you wish," Cho'ag said. "But if you want to be useful, hold the lamp so I can see where I climb."

He didn't wait for Hakk, continuing his descent into darkness.

* * *

"They are gone," Tufo whispered.

Indrajit and Fix dropped the toga. They'd been holding it up to screen themselves from view, standing in the darkest corner of the chamber and counting on the orange dye in the toga and the orange brick of the wall to blend enough, in the shadow, to escape notice.

It had worked.

Samwit Conker's muzzle was bound shut with the loincloth of one of the dead yellow men. Indrajit had held the Wixit close to his chest with one hand while all six warriors had passed through the chamber on their way down, making certain Conker was still and was still breathing.

Only a trickle of light came up from the shaft in the floor; the Udayans had taken the light with them.

"Up the ladder, quickly now," Fix said. He led the way.

"We bar the door once we're through," Tufo added, following.

"I have thought of an epithet," Indrajit announced.

"This," Fix said, "this is why I like being your partner. Tell us the epithet."

Indrajit cleared his throat, climbing the iron rungs out of total darkness toward the square of light where Fix and Tufo now waited, the squirming Samwit Conker clutched under one arm. "Yellow-skinned Udayans," he chanted, "blue-eyed and deadly."

There was a brief pause.

"It probably sounds better in Blaatshi," Fix said.

"Everything does," Indrajit said. "This epithet, in particular, is highly alliterative."

"Perfect," Fix said.

Indrajit handed the Wixit to his partner and climbed out of the chute, then they barred the door.

* * * * *

D.J. Butler Bio

D.J. (Dave) Butler has been a lawyer, a consultant, an editor, and a corporate trainer. His novels include *Witchy Eye*, *Witchy Winter*, and *Witchy Kingdom* from Baen Books, as well as the forthcoming modern fantasy novel, *The Cunning Man*. He also writes for children: the steampunk fantasy adventure tales *The Kidnap Plot*, *The Giant's Seat*, and *The Library Machine* are published by Knopf. Other novels include *City of the Saints* from WordFire Press.

Dave also organizes writing retreats and anarcho-libertarian writers' events and travels the country with the Bard's Tower to sell books. He plays guitar and banjo whenever he can and likes to hang out in Utah with his children.

# # # # #

The Hill to Die On by
J.P. Chandler

Vreeza stopped.

His legs burned from climbing the hill and sweat stung his eyes. Dust filled his nose and coated his skin. The weight of his armor and pack pulled at him. He glanced back and noted he was only a third of the way up the slope. The ground was even, but the soil, dry, granular, and mixed with grass that had been pounded to chaff, shifted until his weight settled, forcing him to make every step careful and deliberate.

The column of refugees passed him, crossing the face of the hill to make the climb half as steep and twice as long. They trudged along about ten abreast. The head of the line was over the crest of the hill. Some moved in groups for comfort, but many moved alone, barely watching the ground before their feet. The clouds of dust could not hide the smell of sweat and worse.

He walked several paces away from the passing throng and turned around. The slope stretched for miles to the north and south, remarkably straight and regular as if engineered by the hand of a god. To the west, a similar hill faced them across two hundred paces of mostly flat ground, rising with a more gradual incline. The sunken middle of the flat ground probably filled with water in winter, but it lay dry this late in summer. A thick carpet of heavy grass covered the ground, peppered with shrubs and white-barked trees, except for a thick stand of trees just south of him, straddling the dry stream bed. He imagined it appeared much prettier in spring when the grass would be green.

Vreeza dropped his spear and watched it bounce in the dirt. He removed his pack, shield, and helmet and laid them upslope of where he stood. He unbelted his short sword, and it joined the rest. He sat down facing west, drew his knees up slightly to brace his weight, and leaned against his pile of gear, using his stiff cuirass for support.

"Taking a break?"

Vreeza looked up to find a young man behind the raspy voice. Tall and broad-shouldered, his skin appeared barely adequate to cover his bony frame. He held a wooden shield in one hand and a battered spear in the other. A thick leather apron, split at the legs, the kind a blacksmith might wear, served as his only armor. He looked at Vreeza from under a mass of dark curls.

"This seems a nice place to die," Vreeza replied.

The boy looked around for several seconds. The throng of refugees moved in eerie silence, their shuffling feet the only noise of their passing. He shrugged and removed his pack, then took a seat on Vreeza's left.

"It is a lovely valley," the young man agreed. He leaned his head back and sighed in relief.

They sat in silence.

Another man stopped nearby. His gray stubble showed him to be close to Vreeza's age, and he wore his pack over thick shoulders with surprising ease. He looked around briefly with a scowl before taking a seat on the other side of Vreeza.

"How long, do you think, until the horde gets here?" the blacksmith asked.

"Tonight. Maybe tomorrow. No later," the man to Vreeza's right said.

Vreeza noticed heads turning toward them as their voices carried across the silent hillside. Several paces down the hill, a man stepped out of line and looked at them before heading their direction. Vreeza marked him as a soldier by the weapons he carried.

"How far will they chase us?" the young man asked. "I thought they would have stopped before now."

"The Mage King is never satisfied," a new voice offered, as another man took a seat behind them. "He will not stop."

The group fell silent, and they watched the other refugees flow by. A few more men peeled off from the column and joined them.

"Hard to imagine," somebody said, "we should be preparing for our harvest festival soon. Maybe next year."

"I'll be a grandfather before the end of the summer," another said.

"My family owned a wine shop…"

Vreeza listened to them with half his attention. They told of their homes, their local traditions, their future plans. Some longed for what was lost, others looked to a future without the Black Horde or the Mage King. There would be no festivals in the village where Vreeza was born, no children or grandchildren awaited him.

"This is a good spear," the blacksmith said. He examined it closely with his eyes and hands. "The shaft is strong, but the head is little more than scrap."

"Keep it," Vreeza grunted. "I won't need it anymore."

"I've never seen this type of wood before."

"The Ahiri called it wood of the heart," Vreeza answered.

"Ahiri Heartwood?" another man said from behind the smith. A hush fell among the men nearby.

Over his shoulder, Vreeza nodded to a balding man stretching his thin neck to see past the smith. His eyes sparkled with intellectual avarice. Vreeza knew the type: a scholar—mostly useless and best kept from underfoot.

"I've heard stories about heartwood," another man said.

"Yes," enthused the scholar. "Ahiri Heartwood is rumored to be magical. Weapons made of it are supposed to reflect the strength of the heart of the wielder and grow stronger with each new owner."

A murmur rippled through the gathering.

"I don't know about stories," Vreeza said with a chuckle. "I know it'll leave a good knot on your head." Some of the other men chuckled with him.

"I can replace the blade," the young man said, lost in his concentration. "I'm a blacksmith. I brought extras in case mine broke. I have one left."

Vreeza looked at him skeptically and shrugged.

The smith opened his pack and dug down to the bottom. With an effort to wiggle something past all the supplies, he pulled out a bundle wrapped in thick leather. From it, he pulled a spearhead half a pace long. Vreeza gaped at the shiny steel, sleek and refined in its smooth lines and precise symmetry.

Laying the spearhead aside, he continued to reveal a head for a battle axe. A perfectly uniform curved blade formed one side while the other boasted a thick spike with a slight arc. The men around them leaned forward for a closer look, making noises of appreciation.

"This is my masterpiece," the blacksmith said, smiling proudly. He handed it to the man on his left, who looked it over in appreciation before passing it on. "The guild approved my advancement when they saw it. I was planning to make something delicate, but we learned the horde was approaching. A weapon seemed more appropriate."

He pulled out a second pack and unrolled it to reveal a collection of tools. The smith detached the old spearhead and began shaping the haft to fit the socket of the new blade with practiced certainty.

Remarks of appreciation followed the axe head as it was passed through the group. When it made its way around, the man to Vreeza's right nudged his shoulder and handed it to him.

"This is some of the finest steel I've ever seen," Vreeza said, genuinely impressed. Setting the socket for the haft on two fingers, the blade and spike balanced each other exactly.

"I come from Tenara, fine steel is our specialty," the smith said without slowing his work.

"Tenara does make fine steel," someone said.

"You'll be a great master," another said.

"It took longer than I hoped to get it right." The smith tested the fit of the spearhead as he spoke. "I couldn't decide on the haft I wanted and then the horde attacked before I could mount it. That was last summer."

"Some of that heartwood would make a nice handle," the skinny scholar said brightly. Grunts of agreement passed through the group.

Holding the axe head stirred a sharp memory in Vreeza. He twisted around and pulled his pack in front of him. After some rummaging, he extracted a section of wood similar to the shaft of the spear but only the length from his elbow to the tip of his longest finger, one end sheared off cleanly. He handed it to the smith along with the axe head.

"This'll be perfect," the young smith breathed reverently.

"It's only a scrap," Vreeza said with a shrug, "a memory of the last stupid act of sacrifice."

"You fought with the Ahiri?" the scholar asked.

Returning the man's gaze, Vreeza noticed others watching, waiting for his answer.

"I fought with them," he said quietly, reluctantly. He watched the other hilltop where refugees continued to arrive.

The men around him fell quiet. Only the smith's tools scraping on wood and the incessant shuffling of feet in the dirt disturbed the hot afternoon.

"I thought the Ahiri were destroyed years ago," the scholar said.

"To the last," Vreeza confirmed. He continued as if speaking to himself. "Their skin was so dark, I feared they were creatures of the Mage King when we first met them. They believed battle was a game and death just the beginning of a new life. They relished the challenge of facing the horde. It took the jaws of an erymanth to snap that spear."

"An erymanth!" someone said. "You fought one of the great boars?"

"Did you kill it?" another voice added.

"An Ahiri killed it," Vreeza answered. "He shoved the spear down the monster's throat, but the damage was done. The boar broke our lines. None of the Ahiri escaped in the retreat."

"Always the beasts," a quiet voice said.

"Where does he even find them all?" another asked.

"How does he control them?" yet another said.

"I heard he summoned a dragon when he destroyed the city of Layphellen."

"That he did," Vreeza whispered.

Watching the endless train of refugees cresting the hill to the west, Vreeza noticed the sun was descending toward the horizon.

The group around him discussed the monsters. The Mage King always started with monsters. For the fear. Beasts of magic and legend, some powerful enough to defeat an army alone. Then his mages attacked with foul spells that would kill or blind or disarm. Finally, if any defenders were still standing, the black-armored soldiers and cavalry would finish the job.

"And you." The blacksmith nudged Vreeza, ending his reverie. "What do you think about the monsters? You must have faced many of them." The smith tested the fitting of the spearhead to the shaft, smiling at the result.

"The first monster I remember was the amarok," Vreeza said quietly. The voices around him hushed. "Like a wolf, but taller than any horse and wider than a bear, it had poisonous claws and fangs that dripped with acid. It came in the night and started pulling people from their homes. I was just short of seventeen. We swarmed the beast, but it killed half the village. I put a knife in its eye. Then came the black mist, killing any it touched and then the hooves of the cavalry. The few of us left ran to the next town. The town surrendered instead of fighting, so I ran to the next town. And the next.

"That was twenty-five years ago," Vreeza murmured.

He fell silent. Not far from the gathering, dirty, tired faces watched him intently as refugees continued past, plodding forward, bent under the weight of bundles and packs. Their clothes or the color of their skin or, sometimes, the shape of a nose marked them as coming from a dozen lands. Peasants and princes were indistinguishable from tradesmen and merchants. Only the soldiers were easy to identify, carrying little more than armor and weapons.

He wished them speed with faint hope. He knew what waited.

"How many wars have you fought?" a deep, sonorous voice asked from behind him.

"Just one," Vreeza said.

"You've been fighting the Mage King that long?" the blacksmith asked, his eyes wide and hands frozen over his work.

"I've lost to the Mage King that long," Vreeza replied. "He wasn't called the Mage King then," he continued, as if speaking to himself. Those near strained to hear. "We called him the Black Mage. When he defeated my homeland, he called himself king. I ran away with those who survived. At every town and fortress, we lent our strength, but it was never enough. We sent for aid, but most only recognized the danger when it was fast upon them, usually when we arrived at their gates begging for entry. His ranks grew as he forced the defeated to join him. I have always wondered if I would eventually wear that black armor. Maybe I'll find out this time."

The setting sun silhouetted a group of figures cresting the peak of the western hill. Guarded by a squad of cavalry, several men bore a litter, while one followed behind holding a standard. With the sun behind it, Vreeza could not identify the squad. Nobody else followed. Forming a symbolic rear guard, they moved at a measured, stately pace.

Vreeza shook his head in awe at the sight. These men had waited behind the slowest and weakest of the refugees to bring up their master and maintain their dignity. Even with death following, they had chosen to give courage to others rather than lead the retreat.

By the time the group of soldiers reached the bottom of the hill, a light mist began to form along the path of the occasional creek. The mist was growing rapidly into a fog, which appeared to glow from within in the silvery light of all three moons rising close together.

Vreeza stood and faced the rear guard as the soldiers approached, still maintaining their careful pace. He straightened his posture and saluted. The men around him stood and followed his example. From his limited vantage, he could see several different salutes, each person following the tradition of his home.

The lead cavalry officer barked a command, bringing the squad to a halt. The litter bearers and standard bearer also stopped. At another command, the cavalry saluted together. At a third command, the squad continued. The lead officer caught Vreeza's eye and nodded.

Vreeza sat and watched the other hill. How much longer? How far back were the Black Horde and the Mage King?

* * *

"You know where we are, don't you?" The excited voice of the little scholar over his left shoulder woke Vreeza. He had intended to stay awake, but his soldier's instincts had taken over.

"Does it matter?" somebody asked.

"It might," the scholar said.

The moons above were brighter than Vreeza had ever seen, and they were almost lined up across the sky, following the same line as the valley. Low fog covered the floor of the valley but only reached a short way up the slope. Despite the light, the facing hill stood cloaked in shadow, and Vreeza could feel malevolence emanating from across the wall of mist. The horde had arrived.

He had seen the trick before, but it felt obvious and less intimidating under the light of all three moons.

"I don't think any of us come from this place," another voice said.

"Me neither, but I know this place," the scholar said reverently. "This is the Valley of Athalas. According to legend, the God of War defeated Medmirickelianar right here."

"A god with a name that long deserved to be defeated," Vreeza quipped. Several people chuckled in response.

"He was cast down to become the God of Death."

"Your Athalas has a good eye for terrain," Vreeza noted.

"Well, she's not mine. Athalas is a local deity. There's a shrine to her at the top of the hill," the scholar said, also smiling. "But the stories have traveled."

"What gods do you believe in?" the smith asked Vreeza with a nudge of his elbow.

"All of them," Vreeza answered, "and none. The only thing I have ever asked of the gods is a quick death. None have obliged."

"Maybe we can call upon the gods," the scholar exhorted. "This is a special place, historic. The link to the gods must be strong here."

Contempt clouded Vreeza's scowl when he turned to meet the scholar's sincere eyes.

"What did I say?" the scholar asked.

"Don't you think that's been tried? Don't you think these men around you, those who believe in gods, have already prayed for victory? Don't you think the people of all the kingdoms destroyed or conquered by the Mage King or the Black Mage or whatever he prefers to call himself, all prayed to their gods for victory?"

Vreeza didn't hold back his growing anger as he continued, "They prayed. I watched them. They prayed, they made sacrifices, they did everything they thought their gods wanted. And still they died.

"I don't want anything to do with any god that waits to hear me pray while ignoring the prayers of others. I've been fighting the horde my entire life. If the gods wanted to stop the Mage King, they had many chances. If the gods cared, the Ahiri would stand beside us. If they cared, they would never have waited this long to stop such horrors." Vreeza spat in the dirt.

"We can still hope," the scholar countered, breathing heavily.

"No, my friend," Vreeza stated. "If the gods exist, and if they care, they're not listening to the likes of you and me. They're listening to him and his horde."

"What do gods care about the lives of mortals?" the man with the deep voice asked from behind Vreeza.

"Gods allowing the deaths of mortals can prove little about the gods," the quiet man to Vreeza's right concluded. "I think most religions teach that we mortals will achieve our greatest existence after death. If there's any truth there, then death itself is not evil. That would make your Ahiri friends right. From the view of a god, death is just another trial—or maybe the end of them."

"Then the Black Horde is doing the work of the gods," Vreeza concluded.

The hill fell silent.

"This is a terrible way to prepare for battle," someone said. "Preparing for battle should involve lots of drink."

"And women."

"You sound like a dwarf."

"Well, the dwarves knew the proper way to prepare for battle."

A chuckle passed among the group.

* * *

"You can't do that; it's suicide. I thought Dwarves condemned suicide," snapped Vreeza.

"We do, but we also love a noble sacrifice," Rothgar countered. "You'll need to write a song about us."

"I don't want to write a song about you. I want to fight next to you like we have for months. And I don't write songs."

"It was your idea, lad."

"I was drunk!"

"It's still a good idea."

"Digging yourselves into holes so you can pop up behind them just to attack the archers and engineers is not a good idea. It's suicide," Vreeza repeated. "Even if you succeed, you'll never get back to the army. There aren't enough of you to manage a retreat if the horde turns on you."

"Stop, Vreeza," Rothgar said firmly. He placed his powerful hand on the soldier's upper arm, forcing Vreeza to meet his ancient brown eyes. "It's decided. I know the risks. It's worth taking. Replacing archers and engineers can take years, and those daft mages will never see it coming. This isn't the kind of fight you hope to live through. You just hope the people you love live through it for you."

* * *

Vreeza blinked in the bright light of the three moons at a nudge from the smith. He had drifted to sleep again. He wiped dust from his eye, ignoring the moisture with it.

"Something's happening," the smith said, leaning toward Vreeza. "It looks like the horde doesn't plan to wait for morning."

"I thought it was morning," Vreeza said.

"It's barely midnight," someone answered.

Looking up, Vreeza confirmed the moons had all lined up across the exact center of the sky, closer than normal, looking directly at the valley floor.

Vreeza shook his head to dispel the reverie and the last wisps of his memories of the dwarves and their sacrifice. He had only slept a couple of hours but felt refreshed.

Across the valley, the Mage King's magic no longer concealed the Black Horde. The soldiers in black armor covered the hill from foot to crown, lined up in strict ranks and blocks. Heavy cavalry on matching black horses waited at the top of the hill. Behind the black-clad army, another army waited. Smaller and less uniform in its equipment, but still formidable, it would serve as a reserve and clean up the mess after the slaughter. Its mere presence proscribed hope.

"They look like they're preparing for battle," Vreeza remarked. "What's the point? There's nothing here to attack."

"Look around," the smith said with a smirk.

Vreeza stood, and his mouth fell open in shock.

To either side of him, men sat in rows along the slope as far as he could see. Their ranks, sloppy but discernable, climbed all the way to the crest of their hill, which stood even higher than the hill occupied by the horde. In their midst stood banners from a dozen or more nations and hundreds of others. Men of all ages had joined, many too old or too young to face battle. Roughly a third of those in the ranks were women. Armed with anything that could be used as a weapon, they watched the horde grimly.

"What are they doing?" Vreeza asked. "They should keep running. They'll be killed."

"They decided they were finished running," the smith said, "just like you did."

"I stopped to surrender, to let them kill me if they want." Vreeza's shoulders felt heavy. *What had he done? Why didn't they run?*

"It's time," the quiet man said, standing. He pointed to the fog now obscuring the valley floor with his spear before setting about tightening his armor and hefting his weapon and shield.

The moons seemed to hold their place above the valley. A gentle breeze at Vreeza's back tickled his hair.

"I don't believe I have another battle in me," Vreeza told the smith. His shoulders drooped deeper.

"Nonsense," the scholar said, rising as well. "This is your chance to challenge the gods and see if they truly are on the side of the Black Horde. Stand against them. Let them smell your contempt."

Vreeza smirked at imagining himself making a vulgar gesture toward the heavens.

The smith held out Vreeza's spear to him as well as the newly finished axe.

"Those are yours," Vreeza said.

"You should have good weapons for your last stand," the smith countered. "My spear is still good, and I've never fought with an axe."

"My last battle."

"Well, you are right in front," the man with the deep voice quipped. "You'll have a short one."

Vreeza smiled, and a bright chuckle passed among the men around him.

"You won't be far behind," Vreeza said, grinning.

"Truth!" the man said, and laughter rolled through the nearby ranks.

"One more?" The smith held out the weapons again.

Vreeza took the spear with its new blade. He straightened his shoulders and planted the butt of the spear firmly in the dirt, feeling the thump through his boots. Taking the salute as a signal, the men around him stood as one and began preparing their weapons and armor.

Vreeza took the axe and slid the handle through his belt at the small of his back. He lifted his short sword out of the dirt and handed it to the smith, then replaced his helmet. Around him, voices grew nervous as every soldier helped his neighbors check their armor. They exchanged greetings, jibes, and a few oaths of brotherhood.

Across the valley, the horde stirred. Something moved in the fog. Vreeza's lip curled in a sneer.

"Be merry, brothers," he said over his shoulder loud enough for his voice to carry for several rows. "There's no point to dying sad."

He knelt on one knee, as he had so many times before, and planted his rectangular shield firmly in front of him, holding his spear upright. He turned his head to meet the eyes of the scholar. "This night we are soldiers, all. The gods of death and war demand our blood. They are not worthy. But, if there is a god of soldiers, let our spears be our oath and our shields be our prayer."

A chorus of rough grunts responded. The quiet man to his right set his shield so the edge braced Vreeza's. They did not meet up as well as Vreeza would have liked, but it would serve. On his other side, the blacksmith did likewise. All along the front line, soldiers prepared to form a shield wall.

He watched the fog intently. The Mage King would attack first with a monster to break their lines and sow chaos, as he always did. A shadow darkened a portion of the mist, growing steadily until the snout of a great wolf poked through. Another amarok. It stalked out of the mist and began to climb the hill, its head swaying back and forth, searching the lines for a likely section to target.

Moonlight sparkled off silver strands amidst the wiry fur, shifting as the beast moved. Its massive head swayed to and fro. Moonlight glinted off the beast's left eye. This was the very same beast who had slaughtered his friends and family. Looking closer, he saw the muzzle was grey, and its joints protruded sharply. The creature was still powerful, but much reduced by age. It no longer held quite the awe he remembered. Fair enough. Vreeza was no longer young and strong, either.

An arrow stabbed the ground next to the beast's feet. At least the refugees had archers. It charged off, aiming toward a different section of the frontline. Arrows struck the ground behind the wolf, driving it faster.

"I'm here!" Vreeza cried, standing from the wall. "Come get me you sack of bones!"

Vreeza stepped back into the wall in a smooth motion. He expected his brothers would be angry at the display, but they grunted their approval as the beast turned quickly to angle its charge toward them. He poked his head above his shield to see.

"Come on, then!" Vreeza yelled. His voice echoed through the valley. "Finish it!"

The amarok skidded to a stop in the sandy dirt thirty yards from the line, its one good eye wide and red. Acid dripped from its jagged fangs to smolder in the dirt as it growled its hatred at the old soldier.

"Ah! You remember me. Come on and let me send you to heel for the gods."

The beast shook as it braced itself to charge.

A whisper through the air ended with a quiet thunk as an arrow struck its ribs. The amarok howled in pain and started its charge.

But it had paused too long. Dozens of arrows slammed home. All the archers in range had seen the first shot and joined in. Many of the arrows bounced off the evil hide or snapped on impact. Most did not, though.

The beast fell silent and slumped to the ground. The valley waited silent as death. *Was it really dead or was this a trick of the Mage King?*

Vreeza stepped out of the wall once more and approached the carcass, his shield and spear held ready. The breeze carried away the stench. The amarok lay quite dead, nothing but carrion. Blood oozed into the soil and down the slope.

Careful to avoid the acid pooling by the maw, Vreeza leaned over and pulled his knife from the creature's eye. He struggled for a few seconds before it came free. The deer antler handle had broken off, revealing most of the tang. He knew the men of the line watched him closely, so he wiped the blade against the beast's fur with exaggerated motions. He then turned to face the refugees and held the knife high with a broad grin.

The hillside erupted in cheers. Vreeza slogged back to his place in the shield wall.

"Think you can fix it?" Vreeza asked the smith.

"Maybe," the smith replied, "but I don't think I'd want to."

Whispers traveled through the ranks formed by the refugees, people hushing each other. As the hill quieted, Vreeza could hear voices, quiet in the distance. There, from beyond the mist, he heard chanting. He knelt again behind his shield.

"The mages are conjuring an attack with their magic," he said. The men around him agreed and spread the news. "I hate these. They're always the worst part."

The mist cloaking the bottom of the valley began to darken in a spot almost exactly opposite Vreeza. The darkness spread slowly across the valley floor, then grew even darker.

"I've seen this before, too," Vreeza said, stunned. "This can't be real; they can't really mean to try this here. The mist will kill everything it touches."

"Well, I hope it's quick," the scholar said behind him, affecting a brave tone. "Or should we run?"

"Are you as crazy as they are?" Vreeza looked at the man and shook his head. "The breeze is going the wrong way."

Murmurs of understanding passed among the ranks.

"I hadn't noticed," the scholar admitted.

"Neither did they, it seems," Vreeza replied. "This should be interesting." He set his shield to the side and sat to watch.

The chanting grew louder and angrier, until the mages screamed a crescendo into the night. The mist had become almost pure black, swallowing the light of the moons wherever they touched. At the last command from the mages, the blackened fog rose from the ground, ghostly and unnatural. When the fog reached the height of two men from the valley floor, a shouted order echoed across the valley.

Vreeza shook his head. The fog resembled a long bolt of black cloth floating in the air. It settled and appeared to relax when the last command sounded. No longer held in place by their magic, the breeze took control. The deadly mist drifted away from the refugees and toward the Black Horde.

Panicked screams rang out. Mages yelled incantations or fled the approaching abomination. Whips cracked to keep the black armored soldiers in place. They fell where they stood.

It didn't last long. The mist simply emptied itself of the black that had infected it and then disappeared. Vreeza watched with relief and horror as thousands among his lifelong enemy died. The Mage King had accidentally killed close to half his soldiers. They still outnumbered the refugees. However, Vreeza took great pleasure from the wail and cries of distress from the other hill.

More than an hour passed, and the moons still appeared disinclined to move on.

The men of the lines watched while the horde reorganized. Vreeza resisted sleep this time; the moons were just too bright. Finally, horns sounded, and the horde moved forward. Drummers set the pace. At least, this time, the Mage King's strategy had failed. He would need to win this battle without his tricks.

Cavalry took up the first rank, hundreds strong, and led out at a stately walk. They would wait until much closer for their charge, especially climbing the hill. The refugees tightened their ranks and prepared their shield wall.

When the riders approached within two hundred paces, the archers among the refugees attacked. They did not have the numbers to overwhelm the charge, so they scattered their shots all along the front ranks. Vreeza smiled. Despite the lack of numbers, the arrows slowed the advance. Stricken horses did not simply disappear, they became obstacles to those behind, causing them to lose their footing and crash down the slope, as well. Vreeza could hear the anger and frustration in their shouts and screams, even if he could not see the fear hidden behind their helmets.

This was the strangest battle Vreeza had ever seen. The Mage King was suffering a lifetime worth of mistakes and mishaps in a single battle.

The horns blew the charge when the cavalry came within fifty paces of Vreeza's ranks. The wall tightened, and the men braced behind their shields. A panicked scream drew Vreeza's attention, so he peeked through a gap between shields. Horses and riders continued to drop from arrows, creating chaos. The cavalry had failed to account for the body of the amarok in front of him. Two horses charged toward the carcass side by side, with no room to go around. One horse tried to stop but crashed into the beast and broke its own neck. The other tried to jump the obstacle. It landed awkwardly on the corpse. Bones snapped. Both man and horse wailed in agony.

Seconds later, the first rider stood up, screeching. He had landed on the amarok's head, which had been eaten away by the creature's own acid. The acid now coated much of the cavalier's head and shoulder, dissolving his armor and his flesh.

The charge never reached Vreeza's section of the wall and failed against the defense. Their mounts had struggled up the hill and around their dying fellows until they lacked the strength to break through or try to jump over the shield wall. The charge devolved into an absurd scramble, with the horde killing more of its own than the refugees did. Men and women in the shield wall perished as well, but only at great cost to the enemy.

The defenders had no time to celebrate before the infantry arrived. Now this, this is what Vreeza knew best.

The horde lines hit. The shield wall braced. Men screamed and died. Spears and axes sought flesh. Again and again, the call came to push, and the wall pushed. His spear became an extension of his own arm, the new blade punching through armor like paper.

The horde soldiers fought uphill on poor footing. The weight of their armor, normally an asset, became a dangerous burden. The loose dirt slid out from under them. A good push frequently knocked several down the hill several paces. Then blood turned the soil to mud, robbing them of strength against the wall.

The fighting paused as the field before Vreeza held none of the enemy.

"Breathe!" he yelled. The shield wall collapsed as the men relaxed and sat where they were. Vreeza remained standing and looked down the line to both sides. He could see wounded getting pulled from the lines.

But the line had held.

The hillside below the refugee army held a city's worth of dead men and horses. Red tinged the dark mud now painting the slopes. Vreeza had no idea how long they had fought.

Near the bottom of the hill, officers of the horde worked to re-form the remaining men to prepare another attack.

Vreeza took a careful look around him. The faces who had started the battle with him looked back. Even the little scholar sat in the dirt, panting like a dog in summer.

"I wonder if this Athalas will welcome these soldiers to her rest," Vreeza mused.

"I don't know," the scholar said, "and I don't care. They fought bravely. Stupid but brave—

"Often the same thing," another man interrupted.

"But I hate them, nonetheless," the scholar said soberly under the laughter. "The gods of death can have them for their dogs."

Vreeza only smirked in response. The scholar had a spine, after all.

"How long, do you think?" the quiet man asked.

"We have a little time," Vreeza said after a moment. "Their generals need to decide whether to clear the battlefield before trying again. I think—"

A blast of thunder cracked over their heads to drown his voice. It took several seconds to pass and forced some to grab their ears in pain.

A lone figure on a horse, crossing the ravine, was the only movement in the valley. The figure flicked the reins, guiding the horse up the hill. It climbed with unnatural ease. It took only a few seconds for Vreeza to realize the horse came straight toward him.

Vreeza adjusted the grip on his shield and on the haft of his spear.

A hundred paces away, the Mage King pointed the spear he carried at Vreeza. "YOU!" The voice came as thunder, inhuman and powered by magic beyond Vreeza's understanding.

Vreeza looked around to be sure he wasn't pointing to someone else.

"IT. IS. ALWAYS. YOU!" He stabbed the spear toward Vreeza with each word, and the voice grew louder, driving everyone around him to the ground as if pushed by an invisible force. "ALWAYS, YOU. EVERY LAND I CONQUER, EVERY CITY I DESTROY, YOU ARE THERE AND OPPOSE ME. YOU BLINDED MY WOLF AND FINALLY KILLED IT. OF COURSE, YOU ARE HERE WHEN MY ARMY BREAKS ON THIS CURSED HILL."

The Mage King stopped his horse down the hill from Vreeza near the body of the amarok. The face inside the helmet had light-colored eyebrows with finely angled features. Dark clear eyes bore into the soldier.

Vreeza's mind froze as he stared at the mage in person for the first time.

Him? Opposed the Mage King? Vreeza had fought in the wars started by the mage, but he could hardly credit his constant defeats as defiance. Yet, the Mage King was not wrong.

"And I always will," Vreeza spat. "Kill me here, and I will haunt you beyond your death. I swear by any gods listening I will never yield!"

"AAAAAH!" The inarticulate scream broke against Vreeza like a blast of wind. Despite its power, Vreeza noticed it was surprisingly light. "THERE WILL BE NO HELL FOR YOU. I WILL DESTROY YOU UTTERLY." He cast his spear.

Vreeza batted away the spear with the dark wooden haft of his own. The Mage King flew from his horse and attacked Vreeza with a large, two-handed sword that appeared to be made of pure magic. He moved as if not tethered to the natural world, as fast as thought, avoiding the dead and other obstacles without care. The black color of the blade reminded Vreeza of the deadly mist the Mage King conjured.

Vreeza hunkered behind his shield as the first blow landed, driving him to one knee. Blow after blow hammered the metal, impossibly fast. There was no finesse or art to the attack, only fury and power.

But Vreeza had not survived so long solely by chance. He counted the rhythm of the strikes, not listening to whatever the king muttered with each impact. Between strokes, Vreeza shifted and changed the angle of his shield. The blade scraped along the metal and into the dirt. Vreeza attacked low with the spear, stabbing the king in the ankle joint. The slope put the ankle at the very end of his reach, so Vreeza stepped in and to the side to close. The wail of pain made the old soldier wince.

The king's counter missed as Vreeza stepped back to where he started. Vreeza now moved around, keeping the king downslope. Vreeza blocked and dodged swing after swing.

Yet, despite the injury, the Mage King grew stronger with every strike, while Vreeza, already tired from the battle before, grew close to exhaustion.

The Mage King attacked with renewed fury. Vreeza dodged. The king countered with a side swing. Vreeza caught the attack with his shield. The power of the strike drove the shield against him and off his feet into a spin, sending him several paces through the air. He lost the spear and landed hard with his face in the dirt. He could hardly breathe.

The Mage King stood over him, as if he had covered the distance in a single step. He rolled Vreeza over with his foot, pinning his right arm under and behind him. Then the Mage King stepped on the old soldier's breastplate with his armored foot. He batted away Vreeza's shield as if he were a child. The Mage King raised the black sword over his head.

The hill felt still. He could no longer hear his new brothers fighting the pain of whatever magic the Mage King had attacked them with. He could no longer feel the breeze or smell the horrors of the battle. Vreeza met the eyes of his enemy, prepared to finally have an end to it.

His fingers felt the head of the battle axe still secured behind him.

The Mage King stepped off him and braced for a final blow.

Vreeza rolled downslope, pulling the axe from his belt, and rose. He grabbed a shield from the ground while still moving. Not his, but good enough. Turning uphill to face the shocked king, the axe felt strong in his hand.

The Mage King leapt and landed in front of Vreeza, his strike in motion. Vreeza blocked the magic blade and hacked at his enemy's injured ankle. Even the slight graze caused the king to cry out in pain.

Vreeza charged the king, shield first, knocking him over, using the slope to corner his target. His axe bit deep into the king's hip and the Mage King's blood now mingled with the blood of his army.

A word from the king sent a burst of power at Vreeza, and he sailed through the air once more. He landed hard on his back, and the air fled his chest. His shield was gone but he still gripped the axe. The moons winked out, and he saw nothing. *Would there be gods to greet him?*

Vreeza opened his eyes at a grunt of pain. The Mage King took a last tortured step to stand over him. His helmet was gone. Blond hair fluttered in the wind.

A rush of motion and clang of metal knocked the Mage King sideways. Two armored men stood over Vreeza facing the mage, swords readied. Vreeza recognized the armor from the squad of soldiers who had escorted the last of the refugees. More men rushed in to form a ring around Vreeza. These stood only chest high. Dwarves.

"You finally stayed still long enough for us to catch you," Rothgar said, holding out a hand to Vreeza. "Your damn legs are too long."

Vreeza looked in shock at the craggy, bearded face of the friend he thought dead weeks before.

The men who had fought near him during the battle joined the circle. Shields locked in place.

Another wordless cry broke the air around them as the Mage King raged again.

"DIE! TODAY YOU DIE! AND ANYONE WHO STANDS WITH YOU! EVERY! ONE!" The ground shook at the sound.

Taking Rothgar's hand, Vreeza stood stiffly. Someone held out Vreeza's spear and shield to him. He slid the axe back through his belt before taking them.

"Let me through," Vreeza said quietly.

The men hesitated, then parted and let him pass between. They cast fearful looks at him—fear *for* him. He stopped just in front of the two swordsmen, facing the Mage King.

"I will make you a deal," Vreeza said. "If killing me will save them, I will die, and die happily. I am a soldier. My life protects others. Take it. But if you refuse to spare them, we will continue to fight you. We will fight you beyond this life if it's needed."

"Unacceptable." The Mage King raised his sword again and began uttering words Vreeza could not follow. The great blade throbbed with surging power. The men closed ranks around Vreeza and readied their weapons. Power continued to build in the mage's sword. "You overestimate the value of your success here."

The Mage King stretched his hand toward Vreeza and pushed it forward as he spoke a strange word. A wall of power rolled forward to press against the gathered soldiers. They braced themselves and leaned into the force. Vreeza kneeled and braced behind his shield. The Mage King sneered and swung his sword like a fan, behind a shout of rage. The pressure burst across the soldiers and threw back all the men around the old soldier like leaves on the wind.

The power dissipated and Vreeza stood and readied his spear. He quickly moved to place himself upslope of his enemy.

"Give up," the Mage King grunted as he pounded Vreeza's shield.

"Never." The next blow bruised Vreeza's arm and shoulder.

With a wild backswing, the black sword caught the edge of the shield, forced it aside, and exposed Vreeza. Only a desperate block with the sturdy spear deflected the next attack.

The eyes of the Mage King burned hotter than before.

Vreeza screamed in rage and slammed his shield into the Mage King, pushing him backward down the hill. The enemy stopped himself after two long steps. Before Vreeza could recover, the Mage King lifted his sword over his head with both hands and threw it. He spoke a word of power. The sword struck Vreeza's shield point first, knocking him back against the slope. Something snapped. Pain pierced Vreeza's arm and burst over it. The shield cracked and scattered across the bloody mud in pieces.

The black sword flew back to its master's waiting hand.

Vreeza changed his grip on the spear and stood, holding his useless arm against him, pain screeching through his side. He reached back, then stepped into a long-practiced throw. Through tears, he saw the spear slice into the Mage King's black armor between his arm and chest.

The Mage King pulled out the spear and tossed it aside. Vreeza could see blood, but his enemy appeared unhindered. Vreeza pulled the axe from his belt, breathing hard as the Mage King approached.

Vreeza squeezed the axe handle, feeling its strength. But his knees folded, and he sat in the mud.

"First you. Then the rest." The Mage King sounded tired.

"I hope the gods receive them well," Vreeza replied. "I'll be waiting for you."

The Mage King loomed over him and raised his sword. He winced as the motion stretched his new wound.

"You end here!"

Lightning struck the ground at the Mage King's feet, hurting Vreeza's eyes.

"STOP!"

The voice came from everywhere and nowhere, even more powerful than the Mage King's. Vreeza could feel it rise from the ground, up through his chest. Fear sparked in the eyes of the Mage King, who struggled to move.

A figure stepped from behind the Mage King. The woman radiated beauty and peace, a vision of impossible perfection. "Your evil war is at an end, Medmirickelianar," she said, her voice rapturous music. "When I cast you out, I told you never to return. You have offended me and killed in my sacred place. You shall be cast down again. And you shall be cast down again and again until you learn your lesson."

"Athalas," the scholar whispered, suddenly standing next to Vreeza. The woman turned and nodded at the scholar.

"Now," the woman continued speaking to the Mage King, "you will start at the beginning, once more."

Athalas reached one hand to the other's head and another toward the king's hip, embracing him. When Athalas turned around, she held an infant. The Mage King was gone.

"Vreeza," Athalas turned her glorious blue eyes to the old soldier. "You have outlasted Medmirickelianar. He was the god of magic and art before being cast down and later banished entirely." Smiling, she gestured up at the waiting moons. "We have been watching."

Vreeza looked up. Athalas waved her hand in front of his eyes, and the moons became…something else. They looked like people, yet held many different forms at once. He looked to those coming to stand around him but nobody else appeared impressed.

"They can't see it," Athalas explained. "Medmirickelianar's transformation leaves empty a place among the gods. We invite you to take his place. Would you like to become the new god of magic and art?" Her tone was patience itself.

"Why? I am grateful you saved us. But why me? Why not the scholar? Or the smith? Or any of these others?"

"They are all worthy of a measure of praise," Athalas responded, "some more than others. You are different. You fought and you fought, no matter the strength of the enemy, always at the front. No matter how many times you lost, you still fought. No matter how many friends died, you fought. No matter how many kings surrendered, you fought. Here, you chose to stand once more with no hope of victory. You called for the help of the gods but not for yourself. At the end, you even offered your life for those you chose to protect. This ends your journey. You have won the favor of this god of war."

Vreeza looked around him, then at the axe he carried. *He never desired to be a god but turning from such favor might offend them. Still...*

"No," he answered, straightening his shoulders, "I know little of art and nothing of magic. I'm a soldier. My place is with them. If I were to be a god, I would be a god for soldiers and see my brothers again."

Athalas smiled, and tears flowed down her cheeks.

"That would make you my little brother," she said. "So be it."

* * * * *

J.P. Chandler Bio

J.P. Chandler was born and raised in California, where he now resides with his wife of many years. He uses writing in the genres of Science Fiction and Fantasy as his excuse for pursuing interests in history, science, and culture, among many others. He first started writing fiction when he was fourteen.

# # # # #

Magnum Opus by Rob Howell

Nevenka knocked on my door, sending her cruel emotions seeping through its polished oak. My magic had never seen anyone like her. She might very well have been the most beautiful of my whores but for eyes that held nothing. Edward had compared her to a shark once, which was as accurate as anything I'd ever heard before. Still, she'd earned me thousands of silver denarii over the years.

"What is it?" I asked.

She cracked open the door. "A messenger is here to see you."

"Indeed? Should I allow him to deliver the message?"

"He's from Davorin." She licked her lips. "I might find it enjoyable. And, wearing that dress, I believe you'll find it enjoyable, too."

I bared my teeth. "Then by all means, send him up."

Nevenka was right. I looked positively delicious in my blue silk dress. Modern fashions called for high necks, which I appreciated these days.

I poured myself a glass of rakija, apricot at the moment, and reclined on an Old Imperial chaise. The antique might not have been as comfortable as some, but I hadn't fought this hard not to indulge my whimsies.

I felt a series of emotional tendrils approaching. They were all the ones I'd come to expect and exploit: lust, greed, arrogance. I bade him enter. He was of no importance, but I'd felt his tendrils before. He had visited the Bronze Rose enough that I recognized his perversions.

A valued customer.

"What could possibly bring you to Tresinova's Treasures?" I asked him, languidly sipping at my rakija. "More importantly, can you afford the price?"

He took in my reclined body, my dress showing off exactly the curves I intended. I wallowed in his tendrils of lust.

"Davorin Gropa wishes the pleasure of your company at the next meeting of the Bronze Rose," he finally croaked.

"He does, does he?"

"He also instructed me to give you this, as a token of his affection." The man held out a small box.

Inside was a necklace of sapphires linked with gold. It matched the dress I wore perfectly, so I put it on immediately. "Well, Davorin certainly knows how to get a girl's attention. Please pass on to him that he has captured my heart, at least for the evening in question."

The man hesitated, hoping he could relieve some of that lust.

I leaned forward provocatively. "You have seen what Davorin paid. Have you the same?"

The man pursed his lips and shook his head.

"I thought not. I'm sure I have someone you can afford downstairs. Or you can save what little you have for the Bronze Rose. Either way, I suggest you return to Davorin before I take too much notice of you. Were that to happen, I might find the prospect of flaying you most appealing."

His lust twisted into fear, which I then strengthened and slammed back into him. I do, after all, have perversions of my own.

For a moment, he stood stock still, staring with wide eyes, then he nodded hurriedly and left.

I wonder why Davorin sent that one. Not up to his usual standards, and that means he had a reason.

* * *

"Why did you send that creature?" I asked Davorin.

We stood with our backs to the wall, wearing masks, as did all the clients of the Bronze Rose. My people had chosen an older mansion overlooking Lake Achrida for tonight's festivities. Outside, the shimmer of recent snow glistened in the moonlight. Inside, the paneled walls of oiled Sabinian cedar gleamed red in the soft candlelight.

Davorin took his eyes away from the evening's offerings. "For several reasons, of course. He was handy, for one."

"I'm sure another was so I would send him away with his tail between his legs."

"He has been thinking too much of himself of late, something the Enchelei can no longer afford since our zupan became nothing more than your possession."

"Which you have truly enjoyed."

"I hadn't realized just how bored I was." Davorin sipped from his rakija. He'd laced it with whichever powder from Amaranth suited his fancy at the moment. "Pal's treachery has been delightful, though I have lost some of my fortune."

"You still have enough to provide me with this lovely gift." I fingered the necklace at my throat.

"It matches your eyes so well. Besides, the greatest whore in the Empire deserves no less."

I smiled in agreement. "And now that you have me here, for reasons that, given your predilections, surely have nothing to do with my normal wares, I am curious as to why."

Davorin turned his eyes back to the center of the room. They glinted in the flickering light with greed and lust. "Are they not truly awful? It is no wonder I was bored."

"Yes, though I have some fondness for them since they pay me for the privilege of being appalling."

"I sometimes wonder about it all."

"You, Davorin? Can any here match what you've given me at these little gatherings?"

"I certainly hope not. If so, I'll have to spend more."

I lifted his necklace to catch some of the flickering candlelight. "I won't mind."

"I have, of late, had reason to wonder about it all. Not that I intend to change anything, of course. I am who I am and completely lack the ability to be ashamed of it. Yet, I am not without an ability to understand philosophy."

"Another result stemming from Edward discovering Pal's treachery?"

"Actually, yes. Just as he has not been far from your own thoughts of late."

"It is hard to forget someone who saved your life."

"That he exposed that creature surely matters, for if there was any in Achrida more awful than those here, it might have been him, but we both know Edward means more than that to you."

"Oh, Davorin, you can't imagine I have fallen for a barbarian from the Seven Kingdoms. Even if I *could* love, I wouldn't be a part of such a story as cheap as that."

"No cheaper than the production of *Bellerophon* these people will line up to see on Helsniht." He chuckled. "We are not whole people, but unlike your Nevenka or—" he waved about, "—most of *these* people; you and I know we aren't."

The tendrils of lust and greed twining about the floor, for the first time in my life, repulsed me, if only for a moment. "Why do you say this now?"

"Because Emperor Nikephoros himself has noticed Edward. Not surprising, really. Edward brought one of the Empire's greatest nobles to his knees and then defeated one of the emperor's own plots."

"It was quite enjoyable to watch Edward's tendrils when he sent the emperor's spy away. Hers too. They could have truly loved each other."

"I'm sure." Davorin's eyes turned hard. "But neither of us has as much time to wallow in our pleasures as we once had."

"What concerns you? It's not as if Andreas will do anything. Even Nevenka cannot make the governor potent." I giggled. "And the Lady knows she's tried."

"You know the emperor sees threats under every curtain, and he apparently thinks Edward is after his throne."

"Edward?" My tendrils of astonishment curled among the lust of the participants. "Sure, outsiders have taken the Imperial throne before, but…Edward?"

"The point isn't whether the Sevener is thinking about it, it's whether the emperor believes he is. Nikephoros has a certain cunning and, if examined in one way, Edward is truly a threat to him."

"Ridiculous."

"Nikephoros made Andreas the governor of this province because it's wealthy and in an important place. We've always been divided, though. The feud between the Enchelei and the Dassaretae goes back to before the Empire existed."

"Every Achridan knows that. Stop wasting my time."

"Then look at what Edward has achieved in a matter of months. He's gained strong allies from both major families, some of Achrida's clergy, and in the Imperial bureaucracy of the whole province. Then consider you and Gibroz and the underworld of the city."

My astonishment faded. "Gibroz owes him, as do I."

"And, as an outsider, he can even gain support there, which all know is significant. Should Edward try to unite this city, he might very well succeed, and Nikephoros is cunning enough to see that."

"Edward would never think of it, though. Astonishing to even contemplate the thought."

"Nikephoros is cunning, as I said, but not wise. Striking at Edward gains him nothing but trouble, yet is he not doing the same sort of thing with the Empire's neighbors?"

I nodded. "At much greater risk."

"So, yes, our *cunning* emperor does many foolish things, and my sources suggest he has sent two women, powerful kurioi both, to Achrida. They are to make sure Edward *never* poses a threat and to do so in a way that shows Nikephoros made it happen. That suggests to me, given the time of year, his plan involves Helsniht celebrations. The winter solstice. The day of death. The perfect day for the emperor to pass judgment, don't you think?"

"He does like his spectacles." I wrapped my tendrils of rage around me, using their power to keep my outward calm. "Do you happen to know what kind of magic these ladies can do?"

"We can exclude, I think, Lore Magic. That requires patience which he does not have. Land Magic would likely be too messy for there to be enough evidence to show the emperor's involvement."

"So, Life, Line, or Love."

"I believe that's what I said, my dear."

"Why do you tell me this?"

He sipped from his rakija again, closing his eyes to savor whatever sensations his additional drugs gave him. "Because I can only do this—" he waved at the crowd, "—all of this, if I know more than anyone else. It is the same for you, of course, but nothing that's happened of late has changed me."

"No?"

"Pal's downfall has changed my circumstances, but it hasn't changed *me*. I still know who I am, but I wonder about you. The emperor has presented me with an opportunity I cannot miss. I'm telling you, my dear, so you may serve as Edward's ally, should you choose."

"Why?"

"It should be obvious, my dear." He took another sip. "I've enjoyed watching you climb over bodies, rung after rung, all the way to the top of a kral. Gibroz, like most kraljevics, is terribly boring, but you never are, even for me."

"So?"

"So now that you know, you'll have to be there to watch whatever happens. You can't not."

"Get to the point, Davorin," I growled.

"If you let Edward get killed, then the Enchelei are avenged. More importantly to me, a number of ventures I think are too risky with him around become viable."

He finished his rakija and turned his empty eyes to mine. "But if you *save* Edward, I get to enjoy watching him continue shaking this city like a dog with a bone, not to mention tweaking our dear emperor's nose. Best of all, either way, I'll learn something about you, and I'm sure that'll serve me in good stead at some point in the future."

I had my hand on my poniard.

Davorin looked at me for a long moment, giving me a chance to strike.

When I didn't kill him, he turned to the mass of debauchery. "I do believe it's time to begin my evening's festivities." He left, leaving only tendrils of mirth at my frustration.

* * *

I slept poorly and only felt better once I accepted that Davorin was right. I might not help Edward, but I had to be there when it happened.

I put on one of my disguises. The whitesmith, in particular, was always a favorite choice.

It was the only thing I liked. The cold day's rain turned to slush. Fatigue picked at me. Worst of all, I hated that Davorin knew me well enough to involve me.

I lounged against a wall in the Square of Legends, drinking cheap rakija and thinking.

Two women would have no problem getting at Edward in the first place. They'd ask for his help and become another of his projects.

I could warn him. I was, after all, dressed for a visit to the Frank Faerie where he lived. I could get some of Ragnar's excellent ale and then just walk away. I snorted at the absurdity.

Besides, if I did, Edward might be more cautious, but also more likely to help than before. Worse, if he was too alert, too cautious, they might just kill him straightaway, and I needed time to discover who they were.

Of course, it wasn't out of the question that he might kill those kurioi, though he'd have problems facing two at once. However, that would just mean the emperor would send others to do the job.

If I'm going to help, I'm going to make sure it matters. How do I deal with these women and make sure the emperor never tries again?

The cheap rakija burned my throat. Unfortunately, it gave me no better idea than to make sure everyone saw the emperor's *failure* instead of his success. And that meant I had to figure out what they planned and get into position to make my decision at that point. Which Davorin had known all along.

I really need to kill him someday.

About midday, Edward came down Medusa's Way from the Frank Faerie.

Normally, the constant underlying guilt in his tendrils got annoying, especially since I was there when he realized he hadn't actually betrayed his king and his father. It was by far the most tedious thing about him.

But emotions are slippery things, which is why I have so much fun with them.

In this case, his guilt allowed me to trail him from a distance. My skills at disguising myself had kept me alive, given me treasure after treasure, and hastened my climb to kraljevic, but those skills had never worked against him.

Damn you, Davorin! He's the only one who's ever really looked me in the eyes.

I followed him up the Trade Road, which was busier than normal as those who lived along the road decorated for Helsniht. I routinely kept my senses open for any great emotions near me, especially ones that spiked. I sensed nothing unusual, though some recognized Edward. When he reached Heartsquare, he went into the Imperial Building, presumably to visit with Kapric and Zvono.

His business often required their help, and that suggested I was right. These kurioi had become his project.

I decided to go visit Emilija. She spent her days at the Frank Faerie and might have heard some details.

Of all my whores, she was probably the most conscientious. She was exactly where she should have been, dressed in something entirely unprovocative.

Older than most in our profession, Emilija had always made her way less with looks and more by competence and discretion. This let her ply our trade in districts that would have shunned Nevenka, no matter how lovely and delicious that shark might appear.

I approached her and soon reached the expected contract. I let her lead me up into her plain hostel room. Once inside, I dropped the act. "It's so lovely to see you, Emilija."

Her eyes widened. She took a step back in shock, but after a moment, straightened.

"Aren't you happy to see me?" I asked.

"No. Are you here to kill me? I pay my share and follow Dubravko's instructions, so I can't think of a reason. Of course, I'm not so stupid as to think you need one."

"You're too smart. Knowing me as well as you do would be just as good a reason as any."

Emilija's tendrils of fear turned to resignation. "Very well. Get it over with. Truth be told, I'm tired. So very tired."

"Maybe a client will grant you that, but when have you ever known a pimp to give up a whore so easily?"

She glared back, now with tendrils of exquisite hate. "I've no time for your puzzles, Katarina. By all the gods, even the Readers don't have that much time."

I laughed. "I have a job for you."

"I lay on my back and tell these craftsmen covered in sweat and grime they're wonderful. Oh, they're not as bad as the merchants. My clients are dirty, not disgusting, but still, is that not enough?"

"I need to know more about Edward."

"I'm not spying on him for you anymore! Might as well slaughter me now."

I caressed her cheek and wrapped her tendrils of rage about me like a smooth, soft stole. "Ah, but you will."

She shook her head.

I took all that fresh juicy collection of anger, hate, and fear, with just a hint of love for Edward, and ripped it away.

She staggered at the sudden lack, putting hands to head in agony. I refined all but the love into a sharp-pointed stiletto of terror and thrust it back into her mind. She collapsed, whimpering and crying. I stood above her for a long moment, digging the stiletto around.

And then I used that hint of love for Edward to heal the wounds I had just made.

Slowly, she sat up.

"You know what I can do, Emilija." I shrugged. "You said it yourself, I don't have to have a reason. I never have before."

"You can make me, but I won't do it by my choice."

"Do you doubt I can force you?"

"No."

"Then listen to what I need. Edward visited Kapric and Zvono today, and that suggests to me he has some new project. I wish to know what that project is."

"Why do you care?"

"Because I believe this project is aimed at destroying him."

Tendrils of surprise and suspicion shot from her. "Why? You've never cared about anyone besides yourself before."

"That's prying, and one shouldn't do that to a lady."

"We're whores, bitch," snapped Emilija. "And you want me to do you a favor. I'll ask what I want, even if you kill me."

"If only I had more like you, Emilija, we'd rule this city and maybe the Empire." I laughed. "I'm not going to tell you, but I'll swear on Edward's honor I won't slaughter him when he's vulnerable."

"On Edward's honor?"

"It's not like *I* have any."

She narrowed her eyes. "You promise not to betray him, but you didn't promise to help him."

"That would be going too far, don't you think?"

"Yes." Emilija sighed. "I've not heard anything anyway."

"What about last night? Any chance he was visited by a couple of people?"

She pondered for a moment. "You know, now that you mention it, someone did meet with him yesterday afternoon."

"And?"

"I don't know any details since I was here working, just that Karah and Ragnar teased him at lunch today about some ladies who had nice clothes and jewelry. Makeup, too. Karah thought they were some of yours."

"Not any that I've sent. I prefer to visit him myself."

"I know, but I wasn't really paying attention. You know how it is with Ragnar though. Can't really not listen to anything he's saying."

"Too loud and never shuts up." I sniffed. "But, to be fair, I only despise him because he seems to be enjoying himself."

Emilija snorted.

"Did they say anything about the women's clothes other than they were 'nice?' Or anything about the makeup?"

"Not that I heard. Truly, that's all I know." She trailed off. "Though…"

"What?"

"The Feroun are the company assigned to gate duty right now."

"And you spend a great deal of time taking care of that company."

She nodded. "Last night, one of them was especially needful, given that he'd noticed two women during his shift at Southgate."

"Which means they had to be especially attractive and probably well dressed."

"*Very* well dressed, he said. He also noticed they weren't traveling. No packs, no horses, nothing like that, and besides, who starts traveling at dusk?" She grimaced. "I wouldn't have cared, but he wouldn't stop talking about them."

I almost felt some empathy. "It's not like we expect our clients to care about us."

"Be nice if they didn't rub our noses in it, though."

"Even I understand that. Anyway, that means these two were just going to the southern villas."

"Nowhere else they could have gone." Her tendrils showed no deception, and besides, she wouldn't have a reason at this point.

"Thank you, Emilija. One last thing. If Dubravko asks, tell him you think Karah was serious about them propositioning Edward. I think that might be very convenient for me."

She stared at me with narrowed eyes, then nodded. "I understand."

When I reached the door, I turned back to her. "There will come a time when even you won't be able to make a profit on your back. Assuming I'm still alive, I'll make sure you don't end up in a gutter."

"More than being a whore already is, you mean," she snarled.

I wanted to snarl back, but in the end, I just shrugged and left.

* * *

I needed to change before visiting anyone I knew in the southern villas, and that meant going back to Tresinova's. Plus, I was a kraljevic. No sense controlling half the crime in Achrida without using it. Anyone acting like whores gave me an excuse.

So when I got back I summoned Dubravko. "I spoke with Emilija today. She heard that two women might have offered their services around the Frank Faerie late afternoon yesterday, and we can't have that."

"Indeed not. Did she hear anything else?"

"Only that they were well-dressed, wore nice jewelry, and had good makeup."

"I will spread the word, my kraljevic. We'll find them."

"Good," I said just a touch too vehemently.

He raised his eyebrows. "They seem to have irritated you."

"Truth to tell, I have an itch. They aren't just trying to nibble at my business; they're aiming at a fairly high-class market, if Emilija's report about the nice clothes and jewelry is accurate."

"That's true, and Emilija is usually truthful. I'll also send a message to Ruzica."

"No need. I think I'll go see her about a new dress." I fingered the workman's clothing of my disguise with an impish look. "I just don't have anything to wear these days."

"Can't have my kraljevic look anything other than beautiful." He smiled and went to the door.

"Also, tell Nevenka to come up."

He bowed and left. As I was pouring some persimmon rakija, Nevenka arrived.

"How can I help, my lady?"

"I heard a hint the governor is planning to annoy me."

She bared her teeth. "I hoped Davorin would suggest something like that. It's been almost a month since I saw Andreas, and I have so much fun playing with him when it's been that long."

"Good. Why don't you go offer him some companionship and find out everything he knows? Especially what he's heard from the emperor. Let's make sure Nikephoros isn't planning something stupid, especially since Helsniht is close."

After she left, I made my preparations to go visit the southern villas. I wrote several short notes and sealed them with a hint of perfume. I wrote another without perfume. I made sure I had a pouch with exactly the right sort of coins. Then I changed into a moderate dress. Not something an important lady would wear, but something fit for an important lady's servant. I also packed a bag with some things I thought I might want later.

I headed first to the villa owned by Bardas, strategos of the provincial legion. He had loyal, alert, trained guards, so I made no attempt to hide my approach. They asked my business, and I told them I bore him a message. They offered to take it, but I said I'd been told to give it to him directly. I showed them the message, and let its hint of perfume waft to them.

A predictable dance, with the predictable result. They admitted me inside to wait until he could see me. I chafed at the delay, but I'd expected it.

Eventually, a guard summoned me back to the patio overlooking Lake Achrida, where Bardas often worked. He had to use smooth pieces of granite to keep the constant breeze off the lake from blowing documents around, but he put up with the inconvenience for the view.

I proffered the note to him. He opened it, then stared at me with eyes narrowed.

After a moment, he directed the guards to leave us. They gauged my threat to their strategos for a moment, then accepted the command.

He held the note up. "You think I owe someone something?"

"You're speaking to me alone, aren't you?" I shifted the way I held my jaw, changed my posture, and grinned.

"I should have guessed." He pressed his lips together. "What do you want, Katarina?"

"I believe we both owe Edward a debt of gratitude, don't you think? I have some inkling about how you felt about the first of Athmose's victims here in Achrida, and I'm still alive, despite that creature's best efforts to strangle me."

"Which is a pity."

"So I've been told."

"Let's say I do feel some debt to Edward; why isn't he here to claim it?"

"I doubt he's aware your emperor has sent assassins. Oh, Nikephoros would never call them that, of course, but I have it on good authority, he's sent two kurioi to deal with Edward. Probably in some public and very messy way."

He tapped his desk and considered what I'd said. And why I'd said it. "That'd be the way he'd do it, alright. Of course, if you're right, you're asking for my help against my sworn emperor."

"If you insist, I'll just leave you be." I paused. "However, let me point out that Edward has gained a certain reputation in Achrida among the most important people in the city. In other words—"

"In other words, if I don't help you, I'll do what my emperor wants, but if I do help, I'll do what my emperor needs."

"You have the soul of a poet, strategos."

"What help did you want?"

"One of the Feroun at the gate noticed the two women I believe the emperor sent go south to one of the villas." I explained my reasoning.

"They're not here."

"I never thought they were. You are not the sort of tool the emperor would use for this task. However, you or your guards might have seen them."

"That's all you want to know? Where they're staying?"

"For now."

He gauged risk and reward. "What if you find them? Will you come back asking for help?"

"Who can know the future?" I replied primly. "I mean, other than the clikurioi, and we all know that's not my magic."

He picked up one of his smooth granite stones and tossed it back and forth. "I believe it's time to give some of my guards a day off tomorrow," he said when he stopped. "Have you a suggestion of someone who might give fair work for fair coin?"

"Emilija is favored by the Feroun, so she knows how to take proper care of soldiers." I described her normal location.

"Very well."

I left Bardas to deliver the other messages I'd prepared. These said nothing important, but neither were the people who received them. However, they might have actually hosted the women, so visiting them let me use my magic to hunt. Unfortunately, I sensed no surprising emotions, just the usual sense they hid something, as everyone in Achrida did, as well as normal anticipation for Helsniht.

I found a secluded spot and changed my disguise to become a harried tradeswoman. A wealthy woman's maidservant would be out of place at the Golden Sea, an inn in the southern part of Achrida. One of five men I wanted to see would be in its taproom, and besides, I needed dinner.

Their food wasn't much, but Spiridon shoveled it in. I went to his table, acting like I was trying to be secretive, which of course failed spectacularly. But then, that was the sort of client these five usually dealt with.

He waved me to a seat and shoved another hunk of mutton into his mouth.

"I've a problem," I whispered. I handed him the note without perfume. "I must speak with Sebastijan."

Spiridon nodded, took it, and ate more mutton. "Wait upstairs."

The grease he added to the parchment wouldn't matter, though. The interesting question would be what Sebastijan would do. It was a fun consideration that spiced the bland meal I ate while I waited.

Meeting him was my kind of risk. He knew me pretty well, and he despised me in delightful ways. However, he knew what he was doing, had a crew he trusted, and he stayed bought. He was also a good friend to Edward, which might be useful later.

My disguise worked perfectly. I didn't let any of my smug pride show as I told him, "I believe two women have been stealing from me and others like Ruzica."

"What evidence do you have?" he asked.

"I saw them," I protested. "Is that not enough?"

He chewed his lip. My excuse was flimsier than he liked, but I inserted a small touch of outrage into his tendrils. "What do you want me to do about it?"

"Nothing! I mean, nothing like that. I just…"

"Just what?"

I hesitated for just the right amount of time. "I just want to know who they are so we can spread the word."

"Just their names?"

I nodded. "I think they're outsiders. I'd not seen them before, goodman."

"Just their names?"

I nodded. "I have silver." I hunted through the bronze in the pouch I'd prepared until I came up with two silver denarii.

"Very well. I'll let you know," he said.

"Before Helsniht, if you can."

"Everything's always before Helsniht," he growled. "But I can see that, if they're taking from the seamstresses, they'd probably want it before the celebrations. What do you want me to do after I've found out their names?"

"Can you tell Ruzica? We all talk to her regularly, after all."

He nodded, and I could see some of his concerns about me disappear. He might not know me, but everyone knew her.

Ruzica's shop was back toward the north, and I waited until she had no other customers before going in.

Like Edward, my disguises never worked with her. She had a reason, though. She turned her piercing, milky-white, unseeing eyes to me as I entered. "You're too late if you want me to make you something for Helsniht, Katarina."

"I actually have my outfit chosen, but I could use something new for Styrtendeniht."

"I have a fresh bolt of cotton that's been dyed with elder. It's a deep green that should suit you well."

"Sounds delightful."

"Since you're in one of your disguises, though, that tells me you came here for something else."

"How can you always tell?"

"I have ears, my dear. You walk differently depending upon the shoes you wear. And you smell different. Let me guess, a tradeswoman?"

"You're amazing." I chuckled. "And you're right, I do have something else." I told her Sebastijan would come with a message for me. Then I explained why. The whole reason, including Edward, since she had her own reasons to help him.

"My uncle told me you might be along for some reason. Said you had to make a choice."

I sighed. "I should have guessed Davorin would do that. It's just the kind of thing he'd do to play with me."

Ruzica chuckled. "Don't worry about him. Anyway, I can tell you those two ladies haven't come to visit me. Truth to tell, I couldn't have helped them anyway. Miljana Milomir decided that, this year, the costumes for *Bellerophon* just had to be replaced."

"Miljana? That pinchfist? She routinely tries to underpay my employees. She never spends anything more than she can."

"To be fair, you know the Amphitheater doesn't make all that much money, even with those special plays like *Bellerophon* or *The Courting of Aegiala*. However, she suggested one of her patrons had made a donation, and while she's cheap, she does care about putting on a good show."

"True." I pursed my lips in thought. "Does she still live in that villa to the south?"

"Be serious, lass. Where could she live that would allow her to preen as much as she wants without spending money other than her family's estate?"

I nodded.

"Quit nodding at me. That's annoying."

I nodded again, this time adding a chuckle.

Ruzica threw up her hands in mock anger. "Sometimes I think only the blind can see. Get out of my shop."

She had given me something to think about, but I couldn't focus on it immediately. This was my night to check through the kral's books.

I'd never caught Dubravko making a mistake, but it never hurt to keep us both on our toes. I thought it especially important this time. Whatever choice I made might prompt one of my subordinates to think this was finally the time. Breaking from my routine might give them thoughts, and I didn't want to have to deal with the question.

Still, I couldn't concentrate on the numbers. I'd rarely found anything but a simple mistake, and my heart wasn't in it. I kept thinking about Miljana and *Bellerophon*.

The people who attended that play would be exactly the ones Nikephoros would want to understand the extent of his power. There would be no better spectacle than killing Edward there.

It now seemed almost too perfect for his purposes, but how would he do it? Miljana would never allow something to interrupt one of her precious performances.

Unless, of course, the two kurioi hadn't told her.

* * *

I never liked waiting, but there wasn't much else to do until information flowed back to me.

Dubravko reported first. Unfortunately, while my whores dutifully provided all they could, none of it helped. Business was always brisk before a holiday, but it had been an interesting year in Achrida and people were eager to begin their Helsniht celebrations early. I suppose I couldn't blame my lads and lasses for getting me money instead of information.

Still, I was in a foul mood. It would be hours before anyone told me anything else, so I decided to enjoy myself.

People expect crime lords to be volatile. I had also taught everyone in Achrida to expect, in particular, me to be volatile. Fortunately, a pickpocket had been harassing my whores near the Square of Legends. Dubravko had finally gotten confirmation Gibroz wouldn't care what happened to him, so I got to take my frustration out on him.

In the crowds that usually filled the Square of Legends, I had immense emotional power at my fingertips, and I used it ruthlessly. At the same time, ripping all that emotional power away from the witnesses to make an object lesson told everyone Love Magic was involved.

And who else could do this but Katarina the kraljevic?

The emperor would have approved. More importantly, it was useful to remind everyone just what I could do.

Especially depending upon my choice.

Nevertheless, I still hated waiting and everyone tried to avoid me. Even Nevenka didn't want to talk to me, but she was too smart to give me a real reason to kill her. Not reporting after finishing with the governor would be a reason.

"Get in here, Nevenka," I snapped when she knocked on my door. "Tell me of Andreas."

"Helsniht seemed to excite him. He was surprisingly active. Not enough, of course, but—"

"I care not for his potency," I snarled. "What does he know?"

Her eyebrows rose. "Very little, of course. But what he *thinks* is that he'll be able to claim even more control of Achrida from the zupans since Pal's downfall. He bragged that the emperor has sent him messages promising help taking down the other great nobles here."

"Did he actually receive such messages?"

"Perhaps. I do know he got some specific instructions from the emperor."

"Such as?"

"Raise tolls on the lake trade after Helsniht. Same for farms in the whole province. Also, Andreas is to assign people coming from Basilopolis to various local cohorts."

"He can't be serious!"

"Andreas? I assure you that's what he believes. He pranced about, preening he would be one of the Empire's greatest nobles."

"What an idiot."

"If he weren't an idiot, the emperor wouldn't have sent him here."

"I meant the emperor," I snarled.

She chuckled. "Him too. Well, you can pay proper respects to the emperor if you like."

"He's not coming here, is he?"

"Oh no, but apparently he has something special planned for Helsniht."

"What?"

"Andreas was coy on that part. As coy as he can be at least. He wants me to be on his arm that night, though."

"Of course. Anything different from previous years?"

"Not that he said. He wants me there early to make him feel good. Then we'll have the banquet where I'll get to be a logothetes ghenikou once more."

"What a useless title that is," I spat.

"Ah, but I'm more of a lady than most of the extended Imperial family, don't you think?"

"Some know you work for me."

"And which noble family hasn't a courtesan here and there?" She smirked. "In any case, after the banquet, we go to the production of *Bellerophon* and then the dance. Same as always."

"Will the special thing happen during the performance?"

"I got the impression it would be at the dance. At least, he felt it would be memorable." She snorted. "Told me to polish up my skills. What a waste. That cretin couldn't be graceful with all the gods helping him."

* * *

A good night's sleep would have improved my mood. I didn't get it. The Lady squabbled all night in my dreams with Aita, with Hermes riling them both up.

Nothing makes a bad situation worse than knowing the gods are playing with you.

I changed back into my tradeswoman outfit and left Tresinova's early in the morning. Well, early for me.

Anyway, I headed first to Ruzica's.

"If you're going to be a kuja, you can just leave now, Katarina," she snapped the moment I walked in.

"Wha…"

"As if I can't tell you're in a foul mood with the way you're stomping about. Not to mention I heard what you did in the Square of Legends."

"People need to know not to mess with my whores."

"Here's a note from Sebastijan. Take it and get out, at least until you're ready to act like I expect here. I hope you choose to save Edward, but, no matter what, I won't let you stand in *my* shop wondering who all you're going to destroy because you can't figure out what to do."

Tendrils of rage shot from me. I almost twisted them into a club to hammer at her. Nothing she could have done to stop me. She couldn't fight. Had no magic.

But she was right.

I nodded and turned.

"And by the gods, stop nodding at me!"

I chuckled, despite myself. I'd never seen any fear in Ruzica's tendrils, at least not for me. Suddenly my mood improved. Whatever I chose, I'd still be me, whatever Davorin might think. And, if I had to fight to defend myself and my position, well, I'd done it before. I leaned back in. "Thanks, Ruzica."

I went around the corner and looked at Sebastijan's note. It said the two women had been seen in the area of Samiel's Castle but he hadn't discovered their names yet.

Near the castle. Why there?

I had no immediate answer, and it would be about time for Emilija to get to her normal spot. I scurried through the streets like any other tradeswoman. It took far longer than normal, for the streets were packed. All the farmers and their families in the province had come into the big city to celebrate.

Even so, I got to Emilija before her business could pick up.

"Good. Let's get this over with," she snapped when I approached her. "I suppose I owe you thanks. A busy day taking care of soldiers is better than most."

"I know," I said with a smile. "I had that thought when I suggested it to Bardas."

"Here's what I'm told to tell you. None of them have seen the two women. The pair didn't pass Bardas's guardpost going south, so you can eliminate over half of the villas. None of his guards or servants heard anything about anyone other than family visiting any of the other villas. The only exception is Miljana's, which always has a number of actresses in fine dress going here and there this time of year."

I nodded. "That makes sense."

"You know what you need now? Going to leave me alone?"

"I think so. Only one thing troubles me."

She rolled her eyes. "And what is that?"

No reason not to ask her, and who knows…

"I'm not surprised that Miljana's villa is their best guess, because I think whatever happens involves the production of *Bellerophon* at the Amphitheater. However, I have a report they were seen near Samiel's Castle, and I've no idea why they'd be there."

She chuckled. Tendrils of amusement shot from her. She peered at me, then her chuckles turned to laughter. She put a hand on a wall to hold herself up while she stared at my confusion.

"What is it, Emilija?" I snarled.

"Where do all the actors live?" she finally sputtered.

"Oh." I could only join her in laughter. "They live in the Castle District, which, now that you mention it, includes both the castle and the amphitheater."

"Exactly."

"And the report I got came from someone who had no reason to think of the amphitheater."

"The castle's a far bigger landmark." She finally got control of herself. "I know, I know. If I tell anyone you missed something that obvious, you'll kill me in an even worse way than that pickpocket."

"I'll have to, of course."

"Sure. But I'll always know. If you want to kill me for that, well, it'll be worth it."

"I'll think about it." I chuckled. "But don't worry. I have too much to do right now to add you to the list."

A farmer came down the street, and Emilija glanced at me. "I think I have a client."

"Then get to work."

"You too."

I knew where they'd strike now. Couldn't be anything but the *Bellerophon* performance. Now I had to figure out how to arrange things best for me.

I'd gain nothing by alerting Dubravko. Not enough, at least, to outweigh him making preparations he might not otherwise make.

Nevenka would be at the show, along with a number of others in my employ. There'd also be courtesans whose position gave them some insulation against my power, and each of them would see if I did anything. That would make them harder to control in the future.

Bardas would also be there. The emperor's strategos in Dassaretum Province has to attend such functions, after all, and he'd have at least some guards there. If I needed an ally, he would do just fine.

I ticked down the list from zupan to thug. I realized there was only one other person on that list who mattered, and I'd bet all I had that Davorin already knew.

And if I had any doubt, the message that awaited me at Tresinova's eliminated it. His invitation even suggested I wear the blue dress and sapphires.

I'm really going to have to do something about him.

* * *

"You look delightful, my dear," he said as I came down the stairs into the main room of Tresinova's. I'd been a bit surprised Davorin would come here publicly, but it wasn't like anyone in this city doubted his corruption.

"You bring that out in a lady. Besides, I had to match your own finery."

He wore a blue tunic to match my dress, and if I hadn't worn my sapphires, he might have outshone me. Embroidered with gold thread and accented with pearls, his tunic was worth more than the entire neighborhood around Tresinova's. Of course, he had enough guards to protect him, and even the Dassaretae in the area were smart enough to know not to mug one of the Enchelei's leaders.

"Shall we, my dear?" He held out a hand to help me up into his carriage.

With the streets as full as they were, it took some time to get to the amphitheater. Davorin's guards helped clear the way, though, so we reached it well before dusk, when the play started.

"Perhaps you'd like to mingle," he said.

"I would. How can I pass up an opportunity to spend time among such lovely folk?"

"I do love to see someone so skilled in their craft at work."

As I mingled, I hunted for Edward's tendrils. I couldn't find his guilt, which bothered me. If he was anywhere in the amphitheater, I should have sensed it, though someone with my skills could have easily suppressed it.

It had served me well to learn as much as I could about the other types of magic, even if I couldn't use them. Who knows what warning sign might save me, after all? I searched up and down for any of those signs, but found nothing.

I tried to go backstage, fluttering about like some dainty. For most shows, this worked fine, but Miljana's doubling of the stage guard and undoubtedly draconian instructions and threats thwarted me. I could have forced my way in with magic, but probably not without making a scene.

The time had not yet come for that.

About the only thing I accomplished was to pass by Bardas. I didn't tell him to be alert, but I hadn't needed to. He noticed my presence, raised his eyebrows, and leaned over to one of his guards without my saying anything.

Always nice to have smart allies, even if only an ally just this once.

I saw Davorin watching me, eyes sparkling.

And I don't mind an ally this time.

Just before the show, he came up and offered his arm. "Shall we, my dear? You know where my box is, of course. Right up front. Best place to see everything, don't you know?"

"I know," I said behind gritted teeth.

He led us in a winding path that ensured all could see us make our entrance. "Did you think I'd pass up this chance?" he murmured to me. "Those who don't know you will wonder at such a beautiful woman at my side. Those who do know you will wonder even more."

"I get paid for every favor, Davorin," I whispered back.

"Have I ever quibbled at your price?" he asked as we sat down.

"No."

"I thought not. Else you wouldn't be here." He made a small wave to several people and began social chit-chat with many of our neighbors.

Fortunately, all of his neighbors knew me. They knew exactly what I could do, which meant they avoided talking to me after I dismissed them. That allowed me to think about the timing. *Bellerophon* was an ancient play, dating back almost to the War of the Giants. It's about a hero standing up to the gods, but at the end, them driving him to death.

How obvious could the emperor get? I sighed as I looked around at the people there. *But then, these wouldn't understand anything more subtle.*

So I knew when. And I could guess what. They would force Edward to come out on stage when the gods would slay the hero.

I wondered if the actors knew. Given Miljana's temper, I guessed if any did, it would only be one or two. Unfortunately, that's all it would take to make sure the emperor's name came up. If the actor playing Bellerophon were, say, offered a chance at a favored position in Basilopolis, he would certainly jump at it.

Now all I needed to know was where they were and just how they controlled Edward.

I could have controlled him with emotions of course, especially with the power of this crowd. I sorted through the immense number of tendrils, looking for any hint someone used them to do that. I didn't see anything, but that could mean they hadn't tapped into them yet, or they were being subtle.

Line Magic could probably influence Edward, but I doubted it could control him. Edward's mentor had trained him well, and Line Magic was the weakest of all magics. It might be used in conjunction with something else, though, and I kept an eye out for any odd symbols.

I had no way to sense Life Magic, though, and it could very well control any person, especially if the zokurios could touch their target. Life and Love, especially at close proximity, would be extremely effective.

It was all so obvious now.

Davorin leaned in with a smirk as if he'd gone through every step with me. "Life and Love, don't you think? At the part where Bellerophon is killed, with the actor wielding a real sword just this once."

"When did you know?"

"Know?" He smirked. "I don't *know* yet. But what else would our dear emperor do?"

"So before you even talked to me."

His smirk widened. "More fun to watch you go through the motions, my dear."

The amphitheater's gekurios lit its lightstones precisely when the sun set past the western mountains, and the play began.

"Two acts to figure out what you're going to do," he whispered.

I ignored him because, well, I had two acts to figure out what I was going to do.

At both intermissions, he gave me an opportunity to tell him, but he appreciated it even more that I hadn't decided. His tendrils of amusement and cruelty filled me with rage that I gathered into me.

The third act progressed. The gods began their relentless assault upon Bellerophon's arrogance.

I still could not feel any hint of Edward.

Then Davorin said, "Over there."

Edward and the two kurioi stood in the far back. He did not move at all. Not a muscle. I hunted for Edward's guilt, but they had suppressed it. I saw no tendrils coming from him at all and few from the kurioi. Simply the confident expectation of craftsmen.

"Not much time now," murmured Davorin.

Bellerophon danced about, waving his sword and countering the gods' arguments. The crowd joined in, as all here knew the words of both gods and man that led to Bellerophon's death on the winter solstice each year.

Aita's condemnation of Bellerophon's heresy was a particular favorite.

It was exactly the time I would have begun the process, and the trio moved forward. Edward did not move with his normal balance.

Fight them Edward! I urged.

"He's very strong, I must say. Maybe he'll defeat them without your help." He chuckled. "Before you have to decide."

"Shut up, Davorin."

He laughed and joined in, reciting Bellerophon's lines as he stood up to Zeus.

Zeus and the other struck back, and in the same steps actors had used for as long as anyone here remembered, Bellerophon dodged strike after strike.

Amidst this, the trio had almost reached the front of the stage.

"Or maybe you'll have to decide after all," gloated Davorin.

The time for Bellerophon's final retort came, but the actor raised his sword to the heavens in a dramatic pose that was supposed to come much later. The other actors looked shocked, and the crowd stumbled as they had already begun reciting Bellerophon's lines.

"Well?" Davorin asked.

Edward stumbled out to the front of the stage next to Bellerophon, and the crowd muttered in wonder and anger. He looked out to the audience, and even controlled by those kurioi, he could see everything.

His eyes locked with mine.

A hint of sadness appeared in those blue eyes from a far barbaric land when he thought I was there to mock him.

Maybe I can help him fight. He's the only one who's ever, really and truly, looked into my eyes.

In a place with this many people enjoying a play, power was not a problem, so I skimmed through the tendrils, taking just enough so no one would know what I'd done. I shaped them into courage and sent them in as quickly as I could.

He stiffened and reached for his sword.

Yes!

He started to turn, steel gleaming from the lightstones on the stage.

But before he could strike, one of the kurioi stepped up and touched him. He staggered and slid his blade back into the sheath. The woman then glanced out to the audience curiously, wondering how he might have been able to manage even that small rebellion.

She didn't see me, of course, but she knew something had happened.

"Looks like you'll still have to make a choice," murmured Davorin with a sly smile. "Too bad, I thought you might have succeeded with whatever you did. But now you know you have to reveal yourself or watch him die."

Bellerophon launched into a new speech, one of betrayal and death, the same sort that the gods had just heaped upon him. Only this one described how all should respect and love the emperor, thereby proving that Edward had earned his execution. It was a truly excellent oration that kept the audience and actors spellbound. He swirled about with his sword, clearly reaching the conclusion.

Edward continued to stare at me.

The only one. I thought again.

"And what will you do now, Katarina?" asked Davorin. "You can't put it off any longer." He laughed.

Stagehands had finally overcome their surprise and had started to run to the interloper, but they wouldn't get there in time.

The magic I needed to do would make me obvious, as Davorin knew.

Edward's eyes held me. Those eyes.

The only eyes that had ever seen me. Seen Katarina.

"Too late, I think." Davorin sighed. "Ah—"

I hissed at him and stood. I swept the emotion of the crowd into a vast club, and I hammered it down at the kurios controlling Edward's emotions. The vast power of that club sent her staggering backward, blasting away her mind and magic. That strike would keep her for a long while, for I had infused that club with all the cruelty a lifetime of murder and hate could create.

The disappearance of that emotional control gave Edward just enough freedom to draw his sword and deflect Bellerophon's strike.

The actor's mouth dropped open. He only had enough skill with blades to act a part, and Edward was a trained warrior who had earned a reputation in Achrida. The Sevener raised his blade to strike.

The actor yelled, "The emperor made me do it!" Then Bellerophon fled in a most un-heroic manner.

The crowd roared in confusion and amazement. Many turned to watch me.

"Excellent!" cheered Davorin.

Edward started to turn to the kurioi, but the one who remained standing touched him, and he dropped his sword. Then, struggling, he pulled something out of a pouch.

She's still using Life Magic.

I realized Edward held a vial in his hand, and it surely held some poison. He unstoppered the vial and started to raise it to his mouth.

I grabbed the crowd's emotion again and, this time, filled Edward with happiness and joy. The two most difficult emotions for me to work with, but the ones that would give him the most chance to fight killing himself.

Edward stopped moving his hand to his mouth. He stood there looking at it, muscles tensed as her magic and his will battled.

Then the other kurios put her hand on his shoulder. I saw something change in his mind, something I had to fight directly.

I took the fresh astonishment from the crowd and stalked forward, driving my magic against what she'd done to his mind. Still, his hand crept closer to his mouth.

I pulled even more from the crowd. Edward's hand dropped down a couple of feet, but he couldn't drop it. He started lifting it again.

But it gave me time to switch my focus to the zokurios, whose mind held only frustration.

I reached the stage and took each step deliberately, now hammering the audience's tendrils at the kurios, trying to turn her frustration into uncontrolled rage.

Davorin's cheers followed me.

I had to help Edward fight too, so I couldn't send all of my power at this kurios. And what I could send wasn't enough.

Instead of succumbing to rage, she struck back, cracking my forearm bone with a wave of her wand.

It broke my concentration for a moment. Edward's hand shot toward his mouth.

I filled his mind again with joy and happiness, and he stopped, poison nearly to his lips.

Where are those stagehands!

But everyone had stopped moving except for me and the emperor's agent. Surprise and wonder had overcome all, except of course Davorin, who cheered, oohed, and ahhed enthusiastically.

I stepped closer. Edward's hand dropped.

Anger filled the zokurios for the first time.

I had a moment to strike with all the power I could muster. I took all of the crowd's surprise and wonder, switched it to a crescendo of rage towering to Olympus itself, and hammered it back into her.

The rage overcame conscious thought, and she stepped forward to smash me with her magic. The crack as both of my legs broke echoed around the amphitheater, and I fell to the ground.

But she no longer touched Edward, and she had sent all her reserves at me. In my agony, I watched Edward's eyes fill with hope.

He picked up his sword and, swifter than Hermes, swept it through her neck.

Blood splashed across the astounded gods, and her head bounced past me.

In the sudden silence, Davorin stood in his box clapping. "Bravo! Bravo, I say! Truly a magnum opus!"

* * * * *

Rob Howell Bio

Rob Howell is the best-selling creator of the Shijuren fantasy setting and an author in the Four Horsemen Universe. He writes primarily high fantasy, space opera, military science fiction, and alternate history, usually with mystery mixed into it all.

He is a reformed medieval academic, a former IT professional, and a retired soda jerk.

His parents discovered quickly books were the only way to keep Rob quiet. Without books, it's unlikely all three would have survived.

You can find him online at www.robhowell.org, on Amazon at https://www.amazon.com/-/e/B00X95LBB0, and on his blog at www.robhowell.org/blog.

# # # # #

Cranky Bitch by Glen Cook

The lightning was like nothing we'd ever seen. Continuous. Ripping the night, setting gravid-bellied clouds aflame. And yet, despite the bellicose squabble of sound and light, those clouds would not give up more than a scatter of tears.

Elmo, the Lieutenant, Darling, and I haunted the quarterdeck, slack-jawed, hardly able to exchange a word amidst the incessant crash of thunder. Darling clung to my left arm, shivering, frightened. Deeply frightened. That child who fears almost nothing.

I tried to tell the Lieutenant that something unnatural must be happening. Some twist of sorcery must be tainting the weather—elsewise it would not have this impact on our beautiful only child.

Sorcery will not germinate or prosper in Darling's proximity, but she had no trouble catching its growing stench and taste. "It feels like dead things talking," she signed.

She shuddered and squeezed my arm hard as Elmo bellowed and the Lieutenant threw up a hand to indicate something I could hardly have overlooked had I been blind. Spiderwebs of lightning slithered across the slopes where Chimney sprawled, tiny, fine threads that came and went in a blink, but so intense they etched themselves on the inside of your eyes.

They crawled? It looked like they were searching. But…their crawl lacked any pattern. It appeared random but determined…though the whole show lasted just more than a minute. Then every twisting thread swarmed to one point, seething like a great ball of writhing worms. Then that imploded in a blinding flare that faded as slowly as did the afterimage inside my eyes.

The riot overhead would not stop. And now, those pudgy clouds did surrender their moisture. Some came down in chunks.

We fled belowdecks, into the vast master cabin, where the light was so weak as to seem almost pallid.

* * *

Head tilted back, awed, Elmo said, "Listen to that!"

He meant the hammer of hail on the *Bitch*'s decks, not the vigorous thunder, voice muted by a heavy oaken barrier.

I grunted, distracted by Darling. Her fear had fled, but she had not yet reclaimed her usual aplomb and sparkle.

Cranky Bitch's timbers moaned.

The Lieutenant grumbled, "And now we get the wind and waves? Otto!"

One of the soldiers infesting the cabin barked, "Sir?" He folded his hand, tossed in his cards, and pocketed his winnings to the accompaniment of complaining from others at the table.

"Pass the word. All fires out. Not even a candle until this is over."

Despite their wedding to water, wooden ships burn with frightful enthusiasm.

Our leader wasn't done. "Volunteer the rest of these malingerers and go look for leaks."

Otto was a good man, but among his companions were several masters of the art of producing superficially plausible excuses for malingery. But it was Otto who made a case. "How do we look for leaks without no lights? Sir. You having all the lights put out. Sir."

"Don't confuse me with facts. Grab One-Eye or Goblin or Silent, whichever is closest to sober, and have him conjure a witch light."

Elmo said, "Them three is all taking liberty."

"At the same time?" The good Lieutenant thereupon plumbed his vast talent store of expletives. Nobody was so bold as to remind him that not one of our petty wizards even marginally conceded that any rule ever applied to them particularly. Especially One-Eye and Goblin. Those two were scofflawing before any of the rest of us began breathing. "Really? Silent too?"

Silent does have moments where he is responsible, and it's not at all often that you find him outside touching range of Darling.

"Yes, sir. Him, too."

Some more rouzbassle and frickin' frackin' from our boss.

Said I, "They'd probably all still be too drunk to do any good anyhow." I patted Darling atop her stringy-haired head.

"Yeah. No doubt. How come this crap's gotta rain down on me?"

Some stray god, ambling past, noted his complaint.

Out of sight, seeing as how we were belowdecks in almost complete darkness, a monster wave hurdled the harbor's breakwaters and galloped our way.

It tried to flip us and to spin us end for end, but our luck was in. By the time it reached *Cranky Bitch*, it was no longer robust enough to manage that. However, it did make the *Bitch* drag her anchor. We felt the grind across the rocky harbor bottom. The *Bitch* shook like a soggy dog.

Some turned scared. The *Bitch* was as solid a tub as ever was built, but she was not proof against the ire of an aroused nature. No human construct is.

Timbers groaned. The waters outside muttered threats against the hull, while a redoubled barrage of hail hammered a drum solo on the weather decks. And then, sword-slice sudden, silence struck.

Somebody said, "Shit! Here comes the hammer."

Fifteen seconds of nothing happened. The Lieutenant said, "Show Boy, go take a look."

Show Boy got his name because he talked a great game till it came time to play. The Lieutenant followed his suggestion with a look red-edged with promise. Show Boy wouldn't be dancing through the violets come fair weather, he didn't do this now.

One of Show Boy's squadies flipped a hand, volunteering. He scuttled topside. Back in seconds, he reported, "The worst is over, sir. Still some lightning and thunder headed south, but the clouds up top is breaking up. Already, you can see some moon is going on behind them."

The remaining sky lumps were showing silver edges when we returned to the quarterdeck.

* * *

The first boats back, bringing guys who spent the night ashore, all brought cargoes of faces stunned by the damage to the *Bitch*. She had taken a lightning strike. Two fathoms of mainmast top were gone. The tag-end looked like a fat bundle of singed wheat straw. There was no sign of the missing top.

Repairs proceeded at no great speed. Like many of my Company brothers, most of the Juniperen crew were hung over. Those who made it back at all. We did not have spares to replace everything that was broken.

* * *

So there we were, the Black Company's Juniper survivors, having not much luck low-profiling it, anchored out in Chimney's harbor. Those people yonder knew who we were.

Try getting One-Eye and Goblin to be discreet.

Them knowing was why we had to anchor out, going ashore only in small boatloads. Chimney's folk hoped to minimize the damage.

The Black Company? More like the Black Platoon these days, masterful evaders of the wrath of the Lady and her Taken. A sorry lot stuck aboard a sorry ship, us unemployed, and the ship in desperate need of repair.

And too many of us being who they were: the sort who figure low profile means not blowing up more than a half dozen tenements at a time.

Speaking of: Goblin and One-Eye sprawled like wet carpets in the bottom of the first boat back, so blasted they had to be slung aboard with the smaller cargo hoist. The Lieutenant, with Darling on his hip, was there to greet them with cold water baths, owning less mercy than a starving snake.

Darling's nose wrinkled. They needed bathing. One or more had puked on himself. I could smell it from yards away.

Goblin moaned something like, "I didn't have nuttin' to do wit' it. It was a nat'rul 'saster."

Elmo dragged the little turd to the rail, pointed him at the harbor, whapped his back. A couple gallons of divine nectar came back up.

Somebody in the next boat, just warping in, narrowly missed it and expressed hearty indignation.

Alas, Goblin was in better shape than One-Eye. It looked like it might take a couple shovels to scrape him off the deck.

Holding Goblin up by the scruff, Elmo opined, "Not gonna get no news outta these two, Lieutenant."

The Lieutenant said, "Anything to recommend, Croaker?"

"Keelhauling therapy? Or, because they're runts, you could just throw them back." But then my natural empathy took over. "I don't have a medicine that'll cure stupid. I did, I'd be too rich to hang around with these dicks. Chain them up till they get straight. But lay down some sailcloth where you stash them. Pieces you can throw away later."

"You are a prince of compassion, Croaker."

"Ain't I just?"

Goblin kept speechifying in fluent Drunkenese, something about devils exploding out of light. The Lieutenant told Elmo to put the pair away. Darling gave me the stink-eye. That child refuses to see anything but the good in everybody and is perfectly willing to give One-Eye types two hundred thousand second chances. Someday, she'll be sorry.

I shrugged, signifying my lack of remorse. The kid sort of hopped, scowled, rubbed her eyes with one hand, and scowled some more, head cocked as though listening to some whisper that only she could hear.

Our ever-efficient Sergeant Elmo had the two wizards' least-wasted boatmates haul them away, gentle being no consideration.

The Lieutenant grumbled, "I need to find us some work. We can't fix this scow with wishful thinking."

Somebody, possibly the Company physician, said, "Maybe I'll hunt around for a genie in a bottle next time I hit the beach."

The Lieutenant sneered. "That's helpful."

Darling stared my way, I feared meaning to deliver another dose of "Don't be a shit!" but, instead, seemed flustered and in need of reassurance.

* * *

Candy brought us a pair of newbies, boy-girl twins, thirteen or fourteen, so identical I couldn't confirm the gender diversity till I did physicals later. Their hair and eyes were brown to almost black, shiny, and their skin was olive, as though they hailed from farther south and east. They clustered, eyes downcast, uncomfortable.

Candy said, "Now they see reality nose to nose, maybe they aren't so sure the Company is where they want to be. Starving in an alley might not be so bad after all."

Candy is the Company number two, a low-key guy who gets stuff done without much showoff. As is usual with us, his background is mysterious, but his shadowed wellspring had gifted him with social skills superior to those of his compatriots. In most cases, he can solve a problem without applying hammer strokes to an obdurate skull. As in, "*Mister* Barker. If you pursue that ambition even one more step, you will find yourself walking to the beach with stones in your pockets."

Trooper Barker had been eying the kids like they were fresh-out-of-the-oven steaming meat pies.

Darling stepped into the space between Candy, the twins, and Barker. She stared the latter in the eye. And in two blinks, he went red. "Yes, sir. I understand you completely, sir!"

Darling is deaf, dumb, young, and female, but no one in this mob disappoints her deliberately.

Candy told me, "Give these two the once-over. Get rid of their livestock; see if they're in good health otherwise." He turned to the twins. "Croaker is our physician. Do what he tells you. He's harmless."

Thank you so much. Sir.

Darling joined us in the hutch of a cabin that served as *Cranky Bitch*'s sickbay.

I asked, "Do you have names?" The kids were, reluctantly, shedding their rags, encouraged by Darling. I hoped they understood me. We hadn't been in Chimney long enough for me to get much of a grasp on the local dialect.

The boy said, "Traveler."

I knew he was male by now. The girl, surprisingly, was less shy about getting naked. And she was, however young, already seriously ripened. The boy, though, was, by a whisker, the prettier of the two.

Whyever Candy swept up those two, he might have wakened a bushel of snakes. Few of my brethren are known for their self-restraint.

"And you?" I asked the girl.

"Traveler's sister," the boy said.

"Dumbass," the girl said. "I'm Lacksluck. He's Luckless."

"Really? Interesting." I signed the names for Darling, who, no doubt, had them already, having read their lips. "Have I seen you before? In the street somewhere, maybe? You seem familiar."

The boy looked alarmed, but the girl said, "That's not likely. We only came to Chimney last night."

They looked like they had known hard times. Both showed signs of malnutrition. Both hosted vast tribes of parasites. And the girl...

"What happened here?" I asked.

An ugly wound adorned her left side between her bottom rib and her hip. It leaked. It might be infected. It could turn deadly if not treated.

"I fell."

"What? Really?" I ground my teeth audibly.

Luckless the Traveler said, "Literally true. While the storm was roaring. She slipped and fell onto a broken pitcher."

That made no sense. Poverty was so all-pervasive in Chimney, any broken glass would have been snagged instantly for its miniscule resale value.

I glanced at Darling, bearing witness to my correct behavior. She nodded. She sensed truth. But, even so, she had mixed feelings.

* * *

I told Candy, "I cleaned the wound. Put in nine stitches. She'll be sore for a while. I did what I could about their lice and fleas, too."

"Good. Thanks." He seemed almost dreamy.

"They should be good, we feed them up. What's their story?" More, what was his? It was not like him to bring home strays.

He shrugged. "They remind me of somebody. Can't get at who, though. But somebody I cared about."

And so it went. Those two had a secret power. It stirred the ghosts of empathetic memory. It made our worst hardcases want to look out for them and, more importantly, not to abuse them.

Pragmatic me, I saw no value to them being under foot. But they quick showed me. They showed us all. They went to work in the galley, where they turned out to be the finest cooks the Company had known in decades.

* * *

We had brought us some ill-gotten out of Juniper but that was going fast. It might not be enough to heal *Cranky Bitch* completely. Consulting no one beforehand, the Lieutenant went looking for somebody who could both use and afford our special services. And those of the *Bitch*.

The tub was *Cranky Bitch* because she was so damned difficult sometimes, and as a nose-thumb toward our latest employer, the Lady of Charm.

I came up with the name. Me. Croaker. Physician and Annalist of the Black Company. The guys liked the name. It stuck.

The Lady was not likely to be amused.

The Lieutenant was back in time for a fine Traveler twins' lunch. "We have a job offer."

"Just like that?" Finger snap.

My cynicism must have leaked.

Candy said, "Maybe we better dust off our backdoor chastity belts. That seems a bit too convenient."

Goblin grumbled, "What's the story, eh?"

"Somebody from the Seamen's Guild caught me climbing up onto the pier. Took me to see somebody who said he's the General Secretary of the Guild. That guy practically dragged me off to the Seat of the Houses of Istven."

Blank looks from some who had gathered. One-Eye, whom I had thought was napping, cracked a lid and offered a nasal, "Hunh?"

I explained, "That would be the council of merchant traders."

"That I know. Bunch of sea-going crooks. We want to get mixed up with people like that?"

Candy opined, "Some of us *are* people like that."

One-Eye gave him the finger.

I asked, "What's the deal?"

"They'll give up a shitload of cash if we help with some pirates."

The pirates of the Pocatose, that would be, the Pocatose being an archipelago south and west of Chimney. The natives had grown bold lately. Their predations were all the chat in the waterfront dives.

The Lieutenant continued, "It's so bad that one in four ships that try don't make it through the Gap. The Guild and the Houses want us to do convoy work."

I heard no enthusiasm for the job. Darling's fingers twined and twisted in her lap. She offered no opinion but was not comfortable, clearly.

The Traveler twins brought refreshments. Nobody paid them any mind. They were just there, already, like everyone else. Except— One-Eye checked out Lacksluck so blatantly that Darling rose and stepped his way.

Even that hopelessly self-absorbed little antique so honored our mascot that he spun signs meaning, approximately, "I'll be good! I promise." A promise worth only the value of the wind upon which it was written.

Goblin asked, "They're really that eager? They don't know us."

"They've heard of us. League ships visit every port from Juniper to the Jewel Cities of the Sea of Torments. Stories persist."

And grow. The Jewel Cities have been absorbed by the Lady's empire. The Black Company helped make that happen.

I wondered, "You asking us if we want the contract?"

"Nope. The deal is done. Just letting you know you need to get ready."

Crap. I considered Silent, our third wizard, seated beside Darling. He offered no opinion.

Looked like I was the only swinging dick who had one. "You made a contract without consulting us? The payoff better be pretty damned sweet. And what if the crew won't buy in?"

The men who actually sailed *Cranky Bitch* were seamen from Juniper, orphaned by politics and their association with us.

No way could the Company manage the *Bitch* without them.

"Good point, Croaker." The Lieutenant went to his 'reasoning with slow children' voice. "I'll consult Master Sylus." Sylus being the man in charge of the crew. "But he'll see things our way. His people can't go home, and they can't go independent down here. Not even as pirates. They need sanctioned work, same as we do."

After too much palaver we all bowed to the inevitable.

Candy and the Lieutenant would work the public formalities. Professional rats Goblin and One-Eye would check it all out from the snake's belly side.

* * *

The Guild and Houses were, truly, balls in a vise desperate. Desperate enough to hire us without fingers obviously crossed.

Still, I wouldn't bend over without checking behind me first.

* * *

Eight days fled. The Houses found us a place at a pier. Local craftsmen swarmed the *Bitch*, dawn to dusk. Our sneaky boss kept us working after the locals went home. He wanted *Cranky Bitch* ready for anything: spiteful gods, demons, pirates, backstabbing friends, or just plain stupid sea-thieves.

The sailors from Juniper did not smile much, but they did not whine, either.

* * *

I was on the quarterdeck with Candy. He was playing Officer of the Deck, trying to learn the duties of a ship's officer. I was watching our first convoy take shape. Twelve ships total, big and not so big, destined for most every port south of Chimney. We would see them through the Gap and then some.

I observed, "They're all so fat compared to the *Bitch*."

He spouted something dull about cargoes and running seas that I reckon he made up on the spot, talking kind of distracted as he watched Lacksluck and Luckless serve lemon water to the shipwrights.

"Hey, I know I asked, but now you've had time to think, what made you take those two in?"

He had trouble shifting attention. "Thinking don't help. I don't know. I mean, yeah, they were pathetic but, so what? The world is crawling with pathetic. And we're doing our part with Darling. It just seemed right at the time."

Darling could be justified. She was a magical null. Sorcery would not happen around her.

"Speaking of, Darling is scared of them."

"You exaggerate, surely."

I did. "Some. But they do creep her out. Which she won't explain."

"Maybe she's scared she won't be our only princess anymore."

Petty, but maybe. Didn't sound like Darling, but we are all petty when no one is looking.

* * *

Three of the twelve ships chickened out. They decided to wait and see. *Cranky Bitch* stood out well to starboard, to be in the way if the Pocatose came. Or when. Cynical me, I figured the pirates had spies in Chimney. They would want to know which ships would be the richest prizes and if their prey had come up with some scheme to cripple their enterprise.

I reckoned they knew about us. But they would not know the whole story.

Our employers would not know the whole story.

That story was ages old.

The Guild and the Houses meant to use us up. Their kind always think that way.

We would do some using of our own.

The nine ships were fat with valuable cargo. The Houses of Istven did not want the pirates able to resist. They expected us to take a horde of buccaneers along as we went down fighting. Situation ideal, value added. A gang of dangerous professional killers would be eliminated while crippling the pirates.

My friend Elmo summed it up: "Same old song, one more verse."

* * *

The pirates came in a swarm of smaller craft, at least two score vessels, each with fewer than twenty men aboard. Massed artillery fires backed by the crap that One-Eye, Goblin, and Silent threw out—spells that compelled the pirate vessels to give up their pegs and nails—did for the majority. Five vessels got past us. We turned in behind them.

Many Pocatose women became widows because their men could not swim all the way home.

No Houses ship was lost. Casualties aboard the merchantmen were few. Not one corsair boarded the *Bitch*. Our lone casualty was Lacksluck. She suffered a cut to her right bicep from a ricocheting arrow.

"Seven stitches this time," I told her. "You stay with us for long you'll end up with seams like a ragdoll."

She responded with a pained smile. "What's my name, Doc?"

"Eh? Oh. Sure. Got you. Only, the way I see it, you've got more than your share of luck. It's just all bad."

She looked around at the *Bitch*'s sickbay. Her twin was not to be seen. Remarkable. The boy seldom was out of her sight. "You've got that right." Pause. Then, "We could end up being a curse on you and your ship."

"No good deed goes unpunished." I began fitting her with a sling. She flashed a ghost of a smile. "I'll make this real tight. You don't want it moving around. Where is your brother? I need to tell him how to deal with this."

Now a ghost of worry. "Don't know. The idiot went up in the rigging so he could get a good view of the action."

On cue, old soldiers Otto and Hagop arrived with a stretcher occupied by the missing brother, dripping saltwater.

"Master Sylus threw on hard left rudder to bring the bow chasers onto a pinnace that got past us. This idiot slipped off the maintop yard. He bounced off the main yard and ended up in the drink. They just fished him out."

"Not totally out of luck, then."

Hagop: "No shit! Nobody else on the gods' green earth would've made the effort."

Otto: "Not true. How you been eating since Dumbass came aboard?"

"Good point. We're spoilt now. Wring him out, Croaker. Only two hours till first mess shift."

Traveler's sister giggled despite her discomfort.

* * *

*C*ranky *Bitch* left the convoy off the Strait of Vermust, the long passage to the Sea of Torments. We would be wise to avoid those waters, plus, piracy was no problem inside the Lady's empire. She permitted no crimes but her own.

We put in at Kadith, there to await formation of a convoy headed north.

Really? Would the pirates be stupid enough to make the same mistake twice?

Seemed unlikely but I am fully cognizant that the most common element in all creation is Stupid.

* * *

Back to the evening of the day of the fight. Darling caught me as I was closing sickbay. Silent was with her, no surprise. Both looked troubled but not sure why.

Darling signed, "Silent saw something during the fight." She signed slower and more carefully than usual. She wanted to make sure I understood.

Silent, too, made sure of his signs. "Right after the ship heeled in the turn that dumped Luckless, I saw something, north by northwest, in the sky."

Chills trudged up my spine.

"Maybe a fish eagle. But…if it was farther away…"

We risk little by being paranoid. "You tell Candy and the Lieutenant?"

Two shaken heads. One hand-tilted sign from Darling.

The bosses were more likely to listen to me. Even decent guys sometimes equate handicapped with mentally deficient.

"I'll let them know."

* * *

Fourteen merchantmen joined the convoy headed for Chimney and ports north. *Cranky Bitch* stationed herself to port.

You can't fix stupid.

Would-be pirates came out. We made more widows and orphans. This time, Traveler's sister made Traveler stay below. She would not let him test his luck again. Even so, the boy sprained an ankle, falling when the *Bitch* made a hard turn.

We returned to Chimney thoroughly pleased with ourselves. Our employers were just as pleased. They showed that pleasure by handing over buckets of coin—followed immediately by a suggestion that we take on another fraught passage.

* * *

So there I was, no demands on my time, luxuriating in a bout of premium shuteye. There were no limbs to trim, no wounds to stitch, no pitch to smear. Nothing to do but snore.

A hot icepick buried itself in my right shoulder, ricocheted off the blade. The pain was seriously awful. I started to get up...

That brought me face to face with the most beautiful woman ever to have entered my life. Yes. Her. The Lady.

I produced a last-gasp-before-drowning rattle. I was lost, the victim of awe, a slave to ancient adoration...while in the crushing grasp of unbounded terror.

She had found us. Me. Croaker. Annalist. Her prisoner, once upon another time.

Me. Croaker. Her criminal accomplice in murder, once upon another time, caught in her attention again.

Those remaining specters of recollection included almost nothing happy. Trying to reclaim specifics was like trying to follow a passion play performed by foreigners at a distance behind a light fog. But always, there was that will-'o-the-wisp suspicion that there had been an emotional entanglement, once upon another time.

I could not master that fragment of myself addicted to the belief that we had been lovers, once upon another time.

The encounter lasted just seconds, remained soundless, and fled so soon that by morning I was not at all sure it hadn't been a slice of a dream. Had she been there? Had she been trying to communicate? None of the icepick pain remained. Could I just be tempting emotional self-abuse?

Crap. I am a grown man working on becoming an old man. No way should I swallow the crazy and sink into some mad obsession, however tasty the featured splittail. However, and yet, obsessed I was, and likely ever would be.

She blew me a kiss before she faded, never having spoken.

* * *

I arrived at morning mess to find everyone brewing up rumors about the flying carpet seen in the distance during our late scuffle. I tried tracing the story to its source, with no luck. Half the guys couldn't remember where they heard it first.

"Like some of our sketchier gods, the story seems to have given birth to itself," I told the Lieutenant. "But we should take it serious, anyway. They do know where we are." I revealed my nighttime encounter.

"That wasn't a dream? Not just wishful thinking?"

"Not even a nightmare. Just her letting me know that we haven't gotten away."

"So. All right. On your way to sickbay tell Goblin, One-Eye, and Candy that I have need of their expertise."

Annalist dismissed. Always the default when there is something the boss doesn't want written down.

Behold a miracle season! One-Eye, Goblin, and Candy were all aboard, and two out of three were sober. And the drunk was not a wizard.

* * *

After our accomplishments at sea, I figured the surviving pirates would reconsider the joys of farming and fishing as ways to eke out a living. No marginal, subsistence economy could sustain so sorry a loss of manpower and go on treading the same deadly trail.

However...our employers succumbed to the siren call of mission creep. While our next convoy was assembling, some genius inside the Houses suffered a stroke of wicked brilliance. *Cranky Bitch* and the Black Company could take the game to the Pocatose.

In sickbay to have her side examined one more time, Lacksluck suddenly blurted, "Don't do it!"

"Eh?

"Don't go after those people in the islands."

"Eh?" again.

"I know you think I'm just a kid, but...don't go there. You'll die if you go there."

"Eh?" yet again. What was that about? She was right, first shot. She was just a kid. But maybe a kid with precognitive powers.

"Just don't do it. Don't go." Then she got herself out of sickbay.

Traveler and Traveler's sister turned invisible for two days. Disgruntled sailors and soldiers declared old Snoggle's stand-alone cookery an affront to poisoners everywhere. How soon we become entitled.

Found and confirmed, in their absence, was the Lieutenant's sure knack for recognizing a game almost as soon as some skel began to knit it.

Cranky Bitch would not purge the Pocatose. *Cranky Bitch* would undertake no mission not already contracted. The idyll at Chimney was but a step. The *Bitch* would be around only long enough to prep herself for a longer haul. Not that anyone had a clue where she might go.

It would be a long run with the Lady out there nursing a cannibal grudge.

Never bluntly stated was the bare-naked fact that those who wanted to manipulate the Company were no nearer immortal than were the pirates they wanted decimated.

No way anyone paying attention could misconstrue the unstated message. Don't poke the bear. You poke the bear, he'll take your stick and make you eat it from the backward end.

No one possessed by an overestimation of their own worth is pleased to find themselves fallen into such a situation—especially having brought it on by trying to puff themselves fatter.

* * *

But something happened. Traveler and sis resurfaced. Then an insanity storm blew in. Somehow, suddenly, the mission creep made total sense to the Lieutenant. It became his obsession, on a scale grander than that proposed by our employers.

He declaimed, "What the Empire did about piracy around the Sea of Torments will be our model." Piracy had been a plague in those parts fifty years ago. The Empire's prescription had been the traditional cure for plague. Fire.

Any coastal hamlet where even a fishing smack had gone a-roving was identified. Imperial task forces visited. Imperial marines exterminated down to the last rat, mouse, and cockroach, then set what was left aflame. The marines never took so much as a corroded copper as booty.

Ten years into the program, a galleon overloaded with virgins wearing nothing but gold skivvies could make a circuit of the Sea without suffering so much as a catcall.

I exaggerate, but not far much.

The Lieutenant actually made us a presentation, the gist of which was, there could be no more trouble with the pirates of the Pocatose if there were no more people in the archipelago. And whoever handled that could sweep up all the loot the pirates had accumulated over the decades.

As if they were seated on dragons' hoards instead of using their ill-gotten to stave off starvation.

* * *

The night before we began our second convoy, Candy, Elmo, Darling and Silent caught me leaning on the midships rail, drinking in the light of an almost full moon while, yet again, brooding about my nighttime visitor. No matter how often we disappointed her, she never seemed to blame me personally.

"What's up?"

"Smelling danger," Candy said. An old Company slogan.

Elmo, the leading sergeant surviving and generally spokesman for the enlisted, was blunt. "Something's gone wrong with the Lieutenant."

Darling held up two fingers. She meant, "That's twice."

"Yes?"

"How come? We already decided there's nothing in it for us, going after the pirates at home."

Being on the periphery, I tended not to be familiar with leadership's rationale. However, I was uncomfortable with the Lieutenant's rabid relapse.

Darling signed, "The Luck twins must have something to do with it."

Silent agreed, with reservations.

That fit the timing but made no sense to me. "Why would a couple of foundlings even care about the Pocatose?" I addressed that to Candy, who had gifted us with those gastronomic devils. "And what kind of leverage could they have on him? Threaten to reduce his ration of apple tarts?"

And why always bring the weird stuff to me?

I guess, if you promote yourself as the smartest guy in the gang, someday some fool will actually believe you.

Candy said, "I can't get him to talk. Maybe you can con him into thinking you have to get it down in the Annals."

"I'll take a shot. Maybe about the time we deliver this lot to the Strait of Vermust."

The moonlight was fiercely bright. That meant moonshadows everywhere, densely dark. Shadows make me edgy. Have for years. I'm not sure why, but down deep in my core, I suffer from a conviction that shadows have eyes.

* * *

Headed south, we spotted just two Pocatose vessels, lookouts who watched briefly, then scooted. I hoped those people had learned, but feared not. I was in a seriously pessimistic place, sure that we had gone too far already in defense of the Houses. We might have distorted the Pocatose worldview to the point where those people abandoned raiding for outright warfare. With the *Bitch* on the heart of the target.

* * *

In the brightness of high noon each day, I went for a roam, for a private chat with our lookouts. Whether Company or crew, they were supposed to watch the sky as well as the sea.

Some of us had begun to suffer the down-deep suspicion that our progress was being monitored by unfriendly eyes.

The reports were inconclusive. Sometimes things were maybe visible way out yonder, but that could maybe just be a lonely seabird planing the air not so far away.

They would want it to look like that.

Nobody discussed it except in whispers, but the old hands understood. Something was afoot. And something was being done about it, quietly.

* * *

A day short of the Strait. We had made good headway thanks to marvelous weather and winds. Traveler's sister turned up for sick call, my only patient for the morning. She said her side wound was troubling her again.

"Looks like it's doing what it should, kiddo. So?"

"So. Well... Something's gotten strange. Nobody won't hardly talk to us anymore except about the menu. And everywhere we go, there is Darling watching."

"Why would that be?"

"That's what I want to know."

"How about because everybody figures you for evil intentions? You and you brother keep tripping the alarm strings."

She eyed me with open mouth. She turned, saw Darling staked out in the sickbay entrance. Darling. The girl round whom no sorcery can take shape.

"You-all might not be as slick as you think, baby girl."

This happened less than two hours after my conversation with the Lieutenant about his freshened urge to scourge the Pocatose. Darling had been there for that. The Lieutenant had come off like a little boy lost.

Lacksluck sighed. "So it goes. I'm sorry, Dad. It's sad. Too bad. Just more sour luck." She did project sad and sorry. Then she perked up. "Well, then, back to the galley. Bacon and beans next up." Off she went, sliding past Darling. Darling lifted an eyebrow my way before following.

* * *

A key element of our recent success was artillery installed anywhere that it would not cripple efforts to work the ship. Candy managed the engines. He was our siege specialist and artillery expert. His designs had served us well.

Never explained, work on those engines continued. I noted that a wizard or two always joined the armorers.

Candy was more adept at detail prep than was the Lieutenant.

The Traveler twins were curious about everything but resigned to getting no answers to questions about anything but the ship's mess. Deserved or not, they stood silently accused of, maybe, having had something to do with the Lieutenant's bizarre gyrations.

* * *

We hit stormy weather. That was almost a relief. The blow was neither big nor dangerous nor made much difference to our longer tale but made a break from the relentless fair weather we had suffered for over a week. Our northbound convoy of nineteen emerged from the excitement in the wee hours as we approached the south end of the Gap.

Elmo wakened me. I bounced up, frightened, but lost my dream before I could grasp why. Elmo carried a safety lantern. It put out just enough light to show him with his finger to his lips.

Something was up.

I didn't ask. He tried to sign a message. He was not skilled at that. "Luckless is up on the mainmast, so high he is at the edge of Darling's null." He added the sign for Silent, meaning there was a watcher, then said, "We will need a physician."

I dragged some trousers on, headed topside, reached the main deck in enough pre-dawn light to see the boy, ghastly of aspect, staring down at Hagop and his sniper's crossbow. Hagop comes unencumbered by much excess of scruple.

A surgeon might be needed, indeed.

Hagop did not miss. The boy could not dodge without letting go, meaning a fall into the drink after ricocheting off several yards on his way. This time, no one would fish him out. Let him walk home, he wanted to be this way.

The boy yelped, sagged, but did hang on.

The Lieutenant consulted Master Sylus. "Can you have a couple topmen bring him down? We'll have questions. Extra lookouts might be in order, too. Silent, want to skip up there and see what he was doing?"

Silent refused.

I said, "Silent doesn't do high places."

"Right." The Lieutenant turned to Goblin, too late. One-Eye had scrambled into the rigging and swarmed up like he was twelve instead of older than the sea itself.

Amazing! That little shit had spent my whole Company life pissing and moaning about how he hated ships, and this time aboard the *Bitch* was no exception. But because Goblin might do something...

One-Eye reached the boy first. He knocked the kid out with a flick of his right forefinger. Scritch-scratch! He came back down with something crimson wrapped around his left wrist. He hit the deck, unwrapped the red, a two-yard long pennant he handed to Darling. "That was set to unfurl later, I figure to mark the *Bitch*." He squinted—a sight on his weathered, ugly old face—and glared around. "Where's the girl?"

That stirred up a plague of consternation because, as everyone said, she was right here with us just a minute ago.

Otto said, "She ducked into that shadow." He indicated the shadowed side of the deckhouse abaft the mainmast, where mooring cable, spare line, and topside tools were stored. That shadow wasn't much as shadows go, but it had to be the best hiding place ever, because no trace of Traveler's sister remained.

Show wrapped, One-Eye reverted to form. High drama ensued. He was going to die of the sea wobblies before lunch.

Sailors brought Luckless down. He was only vaguely aware. He mumbled in a language I did not recognize till I brooded some. It was TelleKurre, an olden tongue, the milk tongue of the foremost of our enemies, she of the Tower at Charm. Me figuring that out meant nothing. I could read the language, some, but did not understand three words of it spoken.

We moved the boy to sickbay.

Excitement surged back and forth through the *Bitch* while I worked. Part was the search for the sister, part Master Sylus and the Lieutenant preparing for a serious shitstorm.

* * *

Traveler remained only partially aware because of the painkillers given him before I extracted Hagop's bolt. A sailor came to report, "They've looked everywhere. There's no sign of the girl."

Surprised? Not me. I asked for Darling, but here she came like she had read my mind. I said, "Will you sit with him so he doesn't disappear, too?"

She nodded, signed, "But the other did vanish while I was just twenty feet away."

I did notice. Might she be losing her mysterious talent? I did not ask. She was plagued by self-doubt already.

The sailor asked, "It safe to leave her alone with him?"

"He's hurt. And this gal is tougher than you think. Don't mess with her."

Darling could handle most men her age. She had traveled with a stone killer for years. He had taught her to deal.

* * *

Elmo danced my way when I emerged onto the main deck. "Looks like we got some weather coming in."

The sky did remain overcast, the trailing skirts of the night's blow. But that was not what Elmo meant.

I pushed the sides of my face in and squinted hard and then could just barely make out three airborne dots dancing against that

difficult background like flies in a mating flit. Ever the master ob-
server, I observed, "That isn't good."

The general mood agreed, though every man jack was set to do a
little something should a shitstorm sweep on in. Master Sylus began
easing the *Bitch* away from the convoy. The merchantmen would
suffer less spillover if we were farther away.

Candy and the wizards continued crooning to a select group of
ballistae.

* * *

The Lieutenant joined me at the port rail. "Looks like we
didn't get the fight spanked out of them yet." Small craft
were headed our way, in no rush. Must have been fifty
boats, few as large as those we had seen before. "So how does this
make sense? From their point of view? They have to know that it
can't end well."

"They have no choice. Or this is the least painful choice." I indicated the bobbing dots. "Maybe they've never had a choice."

"Figures." He surveyed the ship. Candy and the wizards were
done playing with the ballistae. "Almost feel sorry for those people.
Almost."

Yes. This would not be a day long celebrated in the Pocatose.
"Eyes to the sky, boss. Eyes to the sky."

He grunted. "Go teach your granny to suck eggs."

* * *

Reluctantly, the pirates came on. Goblin and One-Eye
did what they do. Boats came apart. Drownings began.
One-Eye worked from the mainmast crow's nest, daring the universe to do something about him. One-Eye, the guy who

has to be drugged and lugged aboard unconscious to get him onto anything headed out to sea.

I muttered, "That idiot is way too cocky. He's going to get handed his ass on a platter." He had to have helped himself to a double dose of artificial courage beforehand.

One mote left the sky dance. It came closer, possibly meaning to arrive as the pirate attack peaked.

O me of little faith!

One-Eye was, indeed, asking for it.

A flying carpet, of the small personal size given the least favored Taken, came on about a thousand feet high. It paused. Its rider considered the *Bitch*. Then it tilted and plunged.

The Lieutenant bellowed, "Time! Shift!"

Eight ballistae lifted their noses to an impossibly high angle. One-Eye did something in the crow's nest. Goblin and Silent did something on the main deck. Eight engines discharged.

A fat black something left the decelerating carpet.

Only three missiles missed. Their targeting was what the three wizards had been about. One shattered the black thing. That generated an oily fireball, falling toward the *Bitch*. Goblin and One-Eye squealed. The Lieutenant thundered something foul.

Most of the fire hung up, then, the Taken and his carpet still coming. With multiple shafts through him, he could no longer concentrate on maneuvering.

He impacted the deck a dozen feet away. I jumped in to help fight the fire. The carpet rider still had one shaft through his belly and another through his left hip. More had passed all the way through, falling among the boat people. Of those, most survivors were in flight, the more courageous plucking swimmers from the water as they went.

The Lieutenant passed the word: Do not fire on vessels with their sterns toward us.

The Taken's face was a mask of startled agony.

Sailors waded in with boathooks and whatnot and soon had the remains over the side. The Taken went under, surfaced, still burning in spots. Elmo and I watched the carcass fall behind. He asked, "Which one was that?" Being favored of the Lady, I ought to know such things.

"You got me. I never heard of one with only one hand. A new one, maybe. She always finds more when she loses some." We had done for one called the Limper not so long ago.

Elmo grumped, "Well, them high angle shooters was our last trick. And there's still them over yonder." Meaning the remaining distant bobbing motes—only now they were not dancing. Now they were going away.

The region's foremost prognosticator, stricken by massive precognition, the Company Annalist himself, prophesied, "We'll see them again."

The Lieutenant called, "Elmo! Otto! Catch me some of those swimmers! Two or three healthy enough to talk."

Muttering unflattering reflections on the Lieutenant's ancestry, Otto and Elmo gathered crewmen and put a whaleboat over the side.

* * *

The pirates' story was one big basket of sorrow. Three Taken had arrived in the islands the same morning Candy went unnaturally merciful with Traveler and his twin. The Taken quickly established a new order. They were in charge, now. The Pocatose would become a desert archipelago if something ugly did not happen to *Cranky Bitch* and all who sailed within her.

Somebody was lugging a serious grudge. That did not sound like the Lady. She was all business and often playful in her vengeance. Three pirates from three villages offered similar stories. In a benevolent gesture, in appreciation of their cooperation, the Lieutenant had them put aboard a small boat, encouraged to rejoin their brethren.

* * *

We met in the master cabin. The Lieutenant said, "We've used up our best trick. Those other two won't come in overconfident."

Candy said, "It looks like they've backed off till they get reinforcements. You can bet your sweet ass they'll be more careful now."

For sure, double. The Taken we dispatched was our second such kill since we went on the run. We delivered the coup-de-gras to an old nemesis, the Limper, less than two months ago.

The Lady would be disgruntled. It wasn't good for business having people defy her and make it stick. Other folks might get notions.

That was not a truth inaccessible to even the most naive Company brother. Our recent success just assured us a deeper grave.

Discussion became lively. Some wanted to turn *Cranky Bitch* and scurry south as fast as we could scuttle. Others observed that we had equipment and animals back in Chimney, too valuable to abandon— *and* we had wheelbarrows full of money coming for having masterminded another massively profitable trip.

Money hunger won. We had to collect.

But then?

Some wanted to set the *Bitch* galloping. To where? Don't worry about the mules, just load the wagon, same as when we headed for Chimney. Only...

"At least then we knew where we were headed!" Goblin protested.

A faction of guys like One-Eye, haters of ships and life at sea—One-Eye's main reason for refusing to bathe likely is that he might get seasick—insisted that we head east, overland. Just inland from the coast lay the western verge of a vast wilderness, country known almost entirely through rumor and legend. The Company should have no trouble getting lost out there. The Lady would forget us. She would have other fires to stomp out.

I heard somebody whistling past the graveyard at midnight.

Yammer continued. No decisions got made. Otto reported that some of the *Bitch*'s crew were not happy because they were scared that we would abandon them to the Taken. Candy suggested, "If they think the Company might run off, tell them to sell the scow and join up."

Right. That would be an easy sell—to maybe three sailors, total. Those guys were human. All they wanted was to go home. More than three might conjure the notion of selling us out in exchange for that.

* * *

Another confab, with the *Bitch* easing into the Chimney roads. Silent, often unnoticed by those not watching for him, reported having overheard crewmen wondering, in whispers, how they could get in touch with our enemies. Maybe they could work a deal.

Hope does spring eternal.

Deal they might, but the agreement likely would be worth less than the wind upon which it was written, good only until the Lady had dealt with the Company.

The Lieutenant said, "How about we bring that Traveler kid up here? We still haven't put him through his paces."

As yet there was no sign of Traveler's missing sister.

Otto and Hagop went to fetch.

Otto came back. "He wasn't there. Darling was asleep. Hagop is trying to wake her up."

Crap. Crap redoubled and squared.

Another search. This one turned up a whole big bushel of nothing, too. Not a sign, not a clue.

"You had to fix him up."

Yeah. Make it my fault the kid was healthy enough to get away. I told the Lieutenant, "Stop the ship. Right here, right now."

"Yes?"

"I'm thinking some thoughts in my head." I heard somebody say that one time and tucked it away for a special occasion. "Did those kids mark us so the Taken can find us wherever we run? We need to find out before we do anything. And it occurs to the natural-born paranoid side of me that the masters of the Houses, and the Seamen's Guild, don't need us anymore. They could sell us out to save themselves a shipload of money."

The Lieutenant reflected for about seven seconds. "Goblin, Silent, One-Eye, time to go to work."

The Company had endured that sort of treachery so often that we assumed immediately that it was about to happen again.

* * *

*C*ranky *Bitch* eased into her berth, nudged by tugs whose oarsmen looked like men being marched to the gallows. If they glanced up at the *Bitch*, they had to look into the angry teeth of ballistae and the cold eyes of archers dressed for a righteous squabble. Armed Company brothers and sailors faced the pier, too, pretending to be an honor guard on parade rather than men ready to shed unfriendly blood.

We suspected this would be where our employers, should they indulge in treachery, would bring the hammer down. This might be the point where they would figure us to be least prepared for a stab in the back.

One-Eye, though, being naturally slimier than the usual skel, argued that their more sensible approach would be to pick us off one at a time after we started getting rowdy in the waterfront stews. My counter was that that would work only until the rest of us noticed guys had begun to disappear.

* * *

You cannot cure stupid. Arrogance, either.

Mooring lines were doubled up. The gang plank went out. Before it got made fast, a Houses mob invited itself aboard, a dozen bravoes and six senior officials. They greeted Candy and the Lieutenant. "Good-day, sirs. You will now disarm your men and…"

That stopped there. The Lieutenant interrupted. "Over the side with them." And before the locals could grasp their situation, most of them had been hustled across the *Bitch* and chucked into the harbor. The few who tried fighting went into the water and failed to resurface right away because of all the holes in them.

Sailors with poles manned the rail and pushed away anyone who tried to cling to the side of the ship.

After a pause to assure himself that he had made his point, the Lieutenant let the native spear carriers climb out and drip their ways home. Those boys had the word. I reckoned we would not see them again.

Their bosses were not allowed out, although our guys did stop pushing them away. After a few drowned, the Lieutenant figured that even the stupidest understood. He had three hauled aboard. They sat dribbling on the deck. The sailors who would have to mop up grumbled and began lobbying for recommittal to the deep.

Ever mindful of his duties as a host, the Lieutenant let the locals pull themselves together before he asked, "Have we made ourselves understood?"

One chubby old fart managed a nod.

"That's good. Uhm. Oh, yes. That's good." Then, "What the hell were you thinking? You hired us because you knew who we are. Hell. Never mind. No matter how fathomless your store of stupidity, you must have gotten the message."

He waited until all three nodded.

"Excellent, then. Now, as to our compensation." He talked for a while and a while because he wanted most of that delivered in kind instead of coin. And he wanted his shopping list very clearly understood.

Our mob had talked and talked, but that was all we had accomplished, so he made a decision himself.

The Company would head into the wilderness instead of trying to outsprint its destiny at sea.

In time, he would explain making his choice in the conviction that the Traveler twins had marked the ship some way that we would not notice, but that they could sniff out at will.

I expect he had that right.

* * *

Local shenanigans subsided dramatically. Clearly, those who messed with us were doomed to lose their messing fingers. We got to enjoy several nights on the town before we took our show on the road yet one more time.

* * *

Heavy weather. It was seriously drunk out. Elmo and I were having one hell of a time finding a high-class hook shop lauded by the *Bitch*'s sailors. Neither of us was much as a navigator, and I had not thought to bring a sextant.

I said, "Gotta catch my breath for a minute." I settled on the rim of a neighborhood fountain. "We got to find a better way to make a living."

Elmo settled beside me. "I heard that, brother. So, now, take a gander over yonder." The poet pointed.

I looked.

Luckless and Lacksluck, side by side, leaned against a building, considering us. The boy still wore his bandages. Me being me, I tried to get my feet under me so I could go get that dressing changed. Elmo sat me down.

Traveler's sister blew us a kiss, sent us a smile, then she and he stepped into deeper darkness, never to be seen again.

* * * * *

Glen Cook Bio

Glen Cook is the perpetrator of several story collections and more than 50 fantasy and SF novels. He is best known for his Black Company series, which has been continuously in print, in more than a dozen languages, for more than 30 years. Sometimes credited with being the godfather of the Grimdark sub-genre, he has been both Guest of Honor and Special Guest at The World Fantasy Convention. His most recent books are *Port of Shadows* for Tor and *The Best of Glen Cook* from Nightshade.

Glen was born in New York City in 1944, grew up in Northern California, served as Walt Disney's gopher at the 1960 Winter Olympics, joined the Navy after high school, then went to work for General Motors after discharge. Most of his earlier novels were written on the assembly line. In 1969 and 1970, he attended the Clarion Writers' Workshop, and it was there that he met his wife of 50 years, Carol Ann Fritz. He (and she) have three sons. The eldest, Christain, commands 2nd Battalion, 7th Cavalry (in the footsteps of G. A. Custer & G. S. Patton.) Second son, Michael, is an architect specializing in airport renovations. Third son, Justin, is just wrapping up his doctorate in music. Glen has a whole herd of grandchildren, almost all of them female. He hopes to live long enough to finish the thirty-some novels still racketing around inside his head.

# # # # #

The Dregs by
Larry Correia

The trapper came down his mountain to sell his furs and stock up on supplies for the winter. It wasn't really his mountain. It was the Conglomerate's mountain. Except the Lords of the Conglomerate were hundreds of miles away, safe back in the civilized lands. The new King had granted the entire range to that particular guild to administer, only the trapper had never seen a Kingsman or an Agent in this godforsaken territory. They probably wouldn't last a single winter.

This would be the trapper's fifth winter here, so for all intents and purposes it was *his* mountain. His castle was a log cabin he'd built himself. His subjects were a few pack animals and Krug. He'd cut his own kingdom from the wilderness. And he ruled it. Alone. Just how he liked it.

The closest settlement was named Montrose. The trapper hated going there. There were too many people in a town, and as a general rule, he hated people. Not all people—he'd known a few over his long life who were worth a damn—just none of those were here. In fact, everyone he'd ever liked was probably dead, but it hadn't been a very long list to begin with.

The people of Montrose didn't care for him much either. The children were especially frightened of the grey-bearded giant who wore a bear's head for a hat. All the settlers told stories about the scary hermit who lived way up on the north slope. *Surely a man like that is hiding from something.* The rumors were many and varied, that he was a deserter, a wanted criminal, a madman…but the trapper welcomed those stories, because the more people distrusted or feared him, the less likely they were to waste his time with their vapid attempts at meaningless conversation.

They might not like him, but they still wanted to buy his goods. A few times a year, his train of mules would go down the mountain carrying the finest pelts and hides, then they'd return loaded with all the useful supplies he couldn't easily fabricate himself. If he made more profit than he could carry home in the form of supplies, he'd spend the remainder at the brothel. At least the whores understood him well enough to not waste his time with talk.

Many of the animals he hunted upon his mountain were capable of hunting him back, so he had to remain alert the entire trip. A donkey was an easy lunch for a leap cat. Weighed down with heavy packs and roped to six other donkeys made it an even easier target. So the trapper kept an eye on Krug, because the slab hound had a keen nose for danger. Old Krug was about as sullen and unplayful as his master, not the sort of hound to run off distracted by squirrels, so if Krug alerted to something, it was time to get ready for a fight.

On the last ridge before Montrose, Krug let out a whine. It was an unsettling noise, coming from a two-hundred-pound beast that was usually fearless. Slab hounds had been bred for combat and were very even tempered, but something had upset him.

The trapper stopped, looked around, and listened. It took him a moment to put his finger on what was wrong, but the forest was too quiet. Montrose was a frontier mining town, a place of constant industry. There was always the perpetual racket of hammers banging and wheels turning. Now there was only the chill wind rustling the leaves. The sky was grey and ready to rain, but there was no smoke in the air. It was fall, and cold enough that a great many hearth fires should have been burning.

Curious.

He had been walking with the lead rope in one hand and his spear in the other. The spear had been chosen not just for protection, but because it also doubled as a cane. Two winters ago, he had slipped on a narrow path and plummeted over the edge, twenty feet, to the boulders below. The leg had healed remarkably well, considering he'd set the compound fracture himself, but it had left him with a limp, and the old injury had been aggravated by the day's march. His grip subtly shifted, from walking stick to weapon.

"What is it, Krug?"

But the slab hound had no wisdom for him, just a small growl, indicating nervous energy and general unease.

With that ominous warning, the trapper led his pack train over the final ridge. It began to rain. Heavy, ponderous drops.

The town came into view through the trees. The last time he had been here, he'd guessed that maybe two hundred people lived in Montrose, with a never-ending stream of settlers passing through. Today he saw no one. It appeared that several more houses and outbuildings had been erected over the last few months, and the small valley Montrose was situated in was rapidly filling up. Most of the buildings were simple wooden structures. The whole town only had eight streets, laid out in a rough grid pattern. Only the central main street had buildings with more than one floor.

"Krug." That got the slab hound's attention. He made a clicking noise with his tongue.

The monstrous dog understood the command and immediately ran off into the brush to hide and wait. He would only come out when the trapper whistled for him. Krug had a fearsome look to him, so he didn't want any of the soft townsfolk to mistake his slab hound for a wild beast, panic, and start launching arrows.

He entered the valley from the rarely used northern road, but by this point, the locals normally would have seen him coming. Dogs should have barked. Children would have run off to warn their parents that the wild man had come down from his peak. But there was nothing.

Montrose seemed eerily empty. There was no traffic in the muddy streets. The boardwalks were devoid of life. There were no whores on the brothel's balcony, advertising their wares. He told himself it must be because of the rain, and everyone had gone indoors. Yet as he passed one of the town's two taverns, it was the first time he'd not heard noise coming from inside the place.

The trapper reached his destination. The general mercantile was owned and operated by the Conglomerate. Their banner—red and black with a golden griffon—hung over the door. He let his donkeys drink from the nearby trough and then tied them to the hitching post. Normally, he would be worried about some casual thief making off with some of his pelts while he went inside, but that didn't appear like it would be a danger today.

A small bell rang when he opened the door. There was nobody behind the counter and no other customers. Annoyed, the trapper called out, "I've come to trade." He walked along the aisles, noting that many of the goods he needed were in stock. Flour, tools, medicines, oil, and salt—both the eating kind and the kind used to ward off ghosts. "Hello?"

He went to the counter and looked on the other side to see if the shopkeeper was napping, but there was nobody. The drawer where they kept the coins was open and empty. There was a sign that said only Conglomerate staff were allowed beyond this point. He ignored it and went into the storeroom. There were more goods inside, though the weapon racks were empty. That was odd. The Conglomerate always had some of their cheap, mass produced swords to sell to desperate colonists. But all the tools useful for bloodshed were gone, except for a bunch of arrows that had been spilled on the ground. It annoyed the trapper that someone would leave perfectly good arrows on the floor to be stepped on.

The thought did cross his mind that he should just steal what he needed. The Conglomerate wouldn't miss it, and the shopkeeper deserved to get flogged for abandoning his post, but he despised thieves even more than he despised everyone else, so he would not become one. So he left the goods alone and walked out the back door.

He checked the stables next door. The stalls were empty. All the tack and harnesses were gone. Exiting through the front, he returned to the main street. His donkeys were still there and undisturbed. He crossed the street to the smithy. The fire in the forge had died down to just warm coals. There was a wagon inside with a broken axle, and he realized it was the only wagon he'd seen the entire time he'd been here. Everything else that could roll away, had.

Not the sort given to irrational worry, the trapper returned to his animals anyway, but this time it was to retrieve his spear.

The next street had several small farmhouses along it, but it didn't look like anyone was home in those either. The sporadic rain had turned into a constant drizzle, yet valuable iron tools had been left outside to rust. He noticed that the chicken coops were empty. Gates had been left open on corrals, and the livestock inside were gone. He squatted down and checked the sign. The tracks showed the cows and pigs had been herded through town. Their shit hadn't even had time to dry.

He went to the nearest farmhouse and knocked. He did this a few times, loudly, because entering someone's home uninvited in this territory meant you were a bandit deserving a good stabbing. When nobody answered he opened the door and went in to check. Their breakfast was still on the table, half eaten. Chairs had been knocked over in their rush to escape. Pulling off a glove, he touched the stove, and found that there was some small residual bit of warmth. It had been used this morning. Random bits of clothing were scattered around the chests, as if the essentials had been gathered in a great hurry.

The trapper's search continued. Two more homes were found to be in a similar state of disarray. It appeared the people of Montrose had fled, but from what, he had no idea. The trapper had been so cut off from the affairs of man that he'd heard of no looming threats. The kingdom had been a peaceful place since the people had revolted and overthrown their former tyrant king. Montrose was not close to any border, and there was nothing in this mountain range worth invading over anyway. If not war, perhaps it was a plague? Or a witches' curse?

When he got back to the main street, he got his first sign of human life, which came in the form of music. Terrible, awkward music. Someone was playing a piano. Badly. Immediately, he knew right where the noise was coming from. There had been a great deal of local excitement during his last visit to Montrose because a piano had just been delivered to one of the local taverns. To these poor settlers, a piano was a magnificent instrument, only enjoyed by the high and mighty in their great walled cities, and rarely by the lower classes, so that had been a big treat.

The tavern was one of the larger structures in town, not too far from the general mercantile. It was close enough to where he had left them tied that the terrible uncoordinated banging of keys was clearly annoying his donkeys. The animals appreciated silence as much as he did. Using the butt of his spear, he pushed open one of the swinging doors and entered the tavern.

There was a lone man inside, sitting on a stool in front of the small, obviously poorly crafted, upright piano. Even though it was a terrible example of its kind, the piano was probably still the single most valuable item in Montrose, but it must have been too big and heavy to take during their hurried evacuation. The pianist obviously had no idea what he was doing, but he was doing it with great enthusiasm, obviously trying to imitate the movements of someone who actually knew how to play. There were several bottles atop the piano, and an empty one beneath his feet.

The trapper thumped the butt of his spear hard against the planks to get the piano player's attention. The noise was so sharp, it cut through the drunken cacophony. It was apparently sufficient to scare the man enough that he leapt up in surprise.

The terrible pianist blurted out, "Please don't kill me!"

As an imposing man, clad entirely in thick black furs that made him look even bigger, with a bear's jaw atop his head and a necklace of savage leaper claws around his neck, he was used to people having an adverse reaction to seeing him, but this was more histrionic than usual. "I didn't intend to."

"I know I'm not supposed to play with the music machine, but nobody was around, so I couldn't resist. Sorry, I thought you was Kinnock, the owner of this place." The man was probably around the trapper's age, every bit as unkempt in grooming, but far filthier. He was wiry and thin to the point of gaunt. His clothing looked like it might have once been the red uniform of a Conglomerate guardsman, but it was torn and stained now, barely more than rags. The trapper could smell him from here, like he'd drowned himself in liquor.

"Hey, you're that scary mountain man fellow they all talk about."

"And I know who you are as well," the trapper muttered. He had seen the locals tossing this man out of their establishments, usually headfirst into the muddy streets, on more than one occasion. He'd known this sorry sort before. Too stubborn to die, too annoying to live. They would sober up long enough to scrounge, beg, or steal a few more coins, which they would use to buy enough drink to send them back into oblivion. A cycle that would repeat until they passed out in the wrong place and froze to death, were eaten by beasts, or accidentally run over by a wagon. Considering the sorry state of the man the last time the trapper had passed through Montrose, it was a little surprising he was still alive. "You're the town drunk."

"I've got a name."

"I don't care." The trapper looked around. The tavern appeared to have been vacated as rapidly as the rest of the town. "Where is everyone?"

"I don't know. I woke up a little while ago, and they were all gone. I kinda slept through whatever happened, I guess."

"I bet you were passed out in a hog wallow."

"How'd you know where I woke up?"

"The smell." He turned and headed for the door.

"Hey, wait up, Trapper." The drunk hurried after him. Then he stopped, went back, and scooped up the bottles he'd previously looted to take with him. Treasure safely in hand, he followed. "Where are we going?"

"*I* am going away from here. Whatever curse is upon this place, it's none of my concern." He walked down the boardwalk, back toward the general mercantile. Regardless of what threat had caused the evacuation, there was no reason to wait around for it to arrive. He'd come here to trade, and there was no one to trade with. So, he would find what he needed to survive the winter, leave a note saying what inventory he had taken, return to his mountain, then square it up with the shopkeeper in spring.

Then he heard something. It was faint and muffled, but it sounded like someone was shouting. It was coming from down the street, from a small building that was also flying the red and black flag. The trapper pointed with his spear. "What is that place there?"

Even though it was cloudy, the drunkard had to shade his bleary eyes from the light. "Oh, that's the guard station. There're only two guardsmen assigned to Montrose. It's just some bunks, a little armory, and a jail cell for the troublemakers inside."

"You know it well."

"I used to work there."

So those rags *had* once been a proper uniform after all. The trapper started toward the guard station. "I assumed you'd spent nights in that cell."

"Oh yeah, I used to do that a lot. But they kinda gave up and just leave me where I fall now." He took a swig from one of the bottles. "Buncha ingrates. After everything I did for this town."

Sure enough, the shouting was coming from inside. A man was calling for help, though he sounded indignant rather than desperate.

The trapper tried the door, but it was the first one he'd found locked. "Do you still have keys, Drunkard?"

"They confiscated my sword. You really think they'd let me keep the keys? That door's pretty stout. We'll need to find a hammer or an axe or—"

The trapper kicked the door in.

The former guardsman winced at the sharp noise. "Wow. You really are a big fella. I thought they was exaggerating when they said the mountain man was half ogre."

"Hello?" the trapper called out as he entered.

"Back here."

The jail cell was constructed of iron bars, with no furnishings other than a cot and a bucket. A large iron padlock secured the gate. There was a single occupant locked inside. He was a young man, perhaps twenty, with a hooked nose and dark countenance indicating western blood. Surprisingly enough, he was wearing the black cloak that marked him as a member of the Occultist's Guild, as nefarious and suspect a group as could be found in the kingdom. They were a shifty lot who straddled the gap between the old gods and the modern sainted path. The Guild was allowed to exist because their auguries and rites were sometimes useful to the kingdom, but their kind were never liked. Between the cloak and the nose, the man brought to mind a vulture.

"It's about damned time. Wait. You're not the town guard."

"Used to be."

The trapper shushed the drunkard. "Where did everyone go?"

"Let me out before their scouts come back. Then we can talk." He shook the heavy gate. "I've been yelling myself hoarse since I heard that infernal cacophony."

"I was playing the piano," the drunk declared with pride, as if it was his greatest achievement.

"I thought it was someone murdering cats with a hammer. The keys are in that desk, hurry."

The trapper went to the desk and began pulling open drawers.

"Hold on, Trapper. I remember this fellow now. He's a killer. He murdered farmer Griggs after Griggs caught him vandalizing the church and grave robbing. They were supposed to hang him today."

"Is that so?" He stopped searching, because it didn't seem wise to set a murderer free.

"That was a misunderstanding. It was self-defense," said the murderer.

"No it weren't. I heard you stabbed old Griggs ten times," protested the drunk.

"I had no choice. He interrupted a very important work, which I have to finish, or we are all doomed. You must listen to me. You can't leave me here. The guards ran off with everyone else and abandoned me."

"Well, you're scheduled for the gallows this afternoon, so you'd think you'd be thankful for the delay." The drunkard laughed.

"Far better to hang than it is to face what's coming unarmed and trapped. Please, I beg you, let me free. If you won't, at least leave me a knife so I can cut my wrists rather than fall into their malignant hands."

"Enough of this foolishness," the trapper snapped. "What scared everyone away?"

Then his donkeys began to scream.

"Too late." The killer retreated to the far corner of his cell. "They've returned."

The trapper ran outside.

Some of his animals were already dead. It was hard to tell how many because there was blood everywhere. The others had torn free of the hitching post in their panic and were running away.

Then the thing that had done the slaughter rose from the red mess and scuttled his way.

Wherever it wasn't painted with blood, its skin was stark white. It moved on six legs, and for a horrible moment, he thought it was some kind of great insect, about as big as a white tail deer, only as it drew rapidly closer, he realized each of its legs was shaped and jointed like a human arm, and each one ended in a *hand*.

And then it was upon him, and there was no more time for thought.

The trapper reacted instinctually, thrusting his spear at the creature's body. It stopped suddenly and leapt to the side, rearing upright. Two hands still planted in the mud, the other four reaching for him. He could see its chest now, muscled, manlike, but its bottom half was bulbous, like a gourd made of stretched skin. It had a head, the top of which looked like a bald man's, but that ended beneath the two piercing eyes, for below those was no jaw, but rather mandibles that clacked menacingly.

It grabbed at his weapon. The trapper pulled back, retreating down the boardwalk, keeping the blade between his body and the terror. It followed, swatting at the spear, trying to knock it aside so it could rip into his guts. The hands looked nearly human, but the fingers were too long, and they ended in points, still red with the blood of his loyal team.

The sight of that blood filled him with rage. Those animals had been his loyal subjects. They had demanded nothing but water from his stream, grass to graze, and the occasional carrot from his garden as a treat.

He stabbed for its face. It leapt to the left, and several of its hands stuck to the guard station's wall. It came at him, sideways, clawing. That movement had been unexpected, but a man who hunted leap cats was not easily taken by surprise.

Spears can do more than stab, as he educated the beast by smashing it across the mandibles with the haft. He'd carved it himself from the incredibly dense wood of an axe-breaker tree, so it was harder than bone. The powerful blow stunned the creature, knocking it from the wall. Spinning the spear back around, he drove the point into its chest.

The monster screeched but continued to fight. There was a steel catch after the long, sharp blade, designed to keep bears and boars from crawling up the shaft. He drove the blade in until the catch hit ribs, then he began to lever it back and forth, slicing through organs. Purple blood sprayed from the wound. He was far heavier than it was, and even with its many limbs clamping onto the walls and boardwalk, he shoved the spider thing back to the edge. Then, with one brutal twist, he wrenched the blade out and flung the creature out into the street. It flipped and landed on its back.

The hideous thing twisted and flailed, clawing at the mud and blowing frothy purple bubbles from its broken face. It was clear he had struck a mortal blow.

"By the saints!" The drunkard had stumbled to the door and was staring at the creature in shock. He rubbed his eyes, because this was probably not the first time he'd seen monsters in the streets, only this one wasn't a hallucination. "What manner of evil is this?"

"It's something from the old gods," the trapper muttered, even though he knew such things were no longer supposed to exist. They were stories, told around campfires to make the city folk afraid of the dark, or to scare naughty children into behaving. *Heed your elders, respect your king, or the old gods will carry you to the dark below.*

The monster stopped thrashing and lay still, the rain washing the blood off the sick white carcass.

"The scouts work in pairs!" the killer shouted from his cell. "There's got to be a second—"

The trapper didn't hear the rest of that warning because another monster swung itself down from the guard station's roof, knocking him off balance and sending him back into the wall. The impact knocked the air from his lungs, and he fell to the planks. The monster dangled from the overhang with two hands, as two more reached for the town drunk. Despite his sorry condition, he was faster than expected and managed to escape back inside the guard station. He shoved the damaged door closed, just as the creature swung itself onto the boardwalk and began clawing at the door in a frenzy.

Trying to catch his breath, the trapper began crawling away. The monster saw him and let out a hiss. It pursued. He aimed his spear and thrust, but without precious air, the attack was too weak, and the monster caught the shaft with two of its hands. It tore the spear from his grasp. The weapon landed further down the boardwalk with a clatter. Then the monster came at him.

It was odd. After all he had been through, being killed by a myth was an unexpected way to die.

Except that wasn't the death the gods had in store for the trapper, because the drunkard flung open the door, a broadsword in hand. He charged with a roar and slashed at the monster's back. Purple droplets flew. The monster turned and swung, but the drunkard stumbled out of the way. Then something odd happened. It was either long-forgotten training coming back or the luck of the inebriated, because his reflexive response cleaved that long white arm down to the bone.

That should have crippled it, but the monster was able to contort itself in some surprising directions. One of its bottom hands suddenly shot out, grabbed the drunk by his ankle, and yanked. The poor man hit the planks hard, then rolled off to drop two feet into the street with a splash.

The monster's head swiveled toward where the drunk had fallen. It assessed that threat and must have decided the drunk could wait. It would finish off the trapper first. The mandibles swung back toward him. Its eyes were in the shape of a man's, but the color of coal, solid through. One arm was crippled, but it had five more it could attack with. The trapper pulled the hunting knife from the sheath on his belt, but there was no way he could hold this thing off without breath or reach.

Then Krug attacked.

The slab hound came seemingly out of nowhere, colliding with the monster and sending it into the wall. Krug's kind were trained to go for the neck, and he did as he'd been taught. The hound's heavy weight settled on the thing's back, pinning it. Krug bit deep. The monster reached for the slab hound with the few arms that were free, but its claws scratched ineffectively at the leathery bands of armored hide that had earned the slab hound breed its name. In return, Krug savaged the thing. Blood squirted. Vertebra crunched. It flopped onto its belly, clearly dead, but Krug was not done. The hound was furious that this awful thing had threatened his human. And Krug would not be satisfied until he tore the monster's head off.

When the thing's head was only hanging by a few strands of muscle, Krug looked at the trapper to see if he was alright. His grey muzzle was dripping purple.

"I'm fine." He hadn't even needed to whistle. "Good boy."

The drunk had struggled back onto the boardwalk. He looked at the bloody, massive slab hound and then at the dead monster, then he shook his shaggy head in disbelief. When he saw that one of his stolen bottles had been shattered, and its precious contents were seeping into the floor, he sighed.

"I can't see from in here," the killer shouted. "What's going on? Are you alive? Are they dead?"

"Aye. They're very much dead, and we're mostly alive," the drunk said. Then he held up the sword in his hand and studied it. "I'm glad they still had my blade on the wall. It's been a while since I've swung one of these."

"I'm glad you didn't forget how," the trapper said as he got to his feet.

"Well, I used to be rather good with a sword, believe it or not."

It felt like he would have a mighty bruise on his chest, but the trapper was otherwise fine. After retrieving his spear, he went back inside and headed straight for the cell. "Speak quickly, Murderer. I'm in no mood for games. I'll have the honest truth from you, or I'll leave you in there. Are there more of these things?"

"Many. And they're coming here. Those two were just scouts for their raiding party. From what the guards said before they ran off, the spawn slaughtered a mining camp yesterday, and they were heading for Montrose next."

"How do you know about these creatures?"

The young man let out a bitter laugh. "My guild saw the signs last year. Their return was written in the stars and in the shapes of the flocks of birds. We tried to warn the kingdom about what was coming, but nobody wanted to listen to the likes of us. The king dismissed our warnings as superstitious rantings. Say what you will about the old king, he may have been a ruthless bastard, but at least he was smart enough to heed our guild when we warned him of dangers. These current fools are too proud to listen, but they'll have no choice now. Only it may be too late. This territory will be the first, but there will be more. Many more. The invasion has just begun."

That was too grim to be anything but the truth. The trapper went to the desk, found the ring of keys, then tossed it through the iron bars. The surprised prisoner barely managed to catch it. "Don't make me regret this decision."

Outside, Krug was grooming himself and licking the blood from his paws. The drunkard was cleaning his sword on the Conglomerate flag while watching the street nervously. "What do we do now, Trapper?"

"I'm going to find my surviving donkeys and go home."

"Wait," the murderer shouted as he searched for the right key. "You can't leave. This town needs your aid."

The trapper snorted. "No one wants my help."

"I do!"

"You do not deserve my help." He whistled for Krug, and the slab hound obediently followed. "What do you intend to do, Drunkard?"

"I'll probably go back to the tavern, drink myself stupid, and play that piano some more until more beasties come to eat me."

"A fine plan. Good luck."

"Both of you must listen. The evacuation won't be fast enough. All those settlers will never make it back to the kingdom in time. These things are far faster than heavy wagons and herded cows.

They'll be chased down and slaughtered in the open. We're their only hope."

The trapper paused in the street and looked around for his donkeys and their valuable cargo. They were nowhere to be seen. He paused, frustrated. "What hope is he babbling about?"

"I've got no idea," said the drunkard.

"There's a ritual." There was a loud click as the murderer got the cell unlocked and then a creak as the heavy door swung open. He hurried outside, gingerly stepping over the puddles of purple blood. "That's what I was trying to do at the church. If I can perform it before the spawn become too strong, the wrath of Saint Angus will drive them from these lands for at least a season. That will spare the settlers; they'll be able to warn the kingdom that my guild was right, and it'll buy the army time to prepare for the invasion."

"Go do it then."

"The ritual takes time. When the spawn sense the ritual being performed, they'll attack. I'll need help to hold them off until it's complete. It's the only thing that will save the people of Montrose."

"The same people who couldn't be bothered to look for me before they fled? Worst part is, I don't know if they forgot about me or they remembered I was alive but just didn't care." The drunk let out a melancholy sigh as he stared at his old sword. There was a lot of rust on the blade. "I fought for them before. Hard, like you wouldn't believe. Now, they throw me out with the trash and dump their chamber pots on my head while I try to sleep. Why should I fight for them again when they've got no gratitude for all the things I did before?"

"Because it's the honorable thing to do!"

The trapper and the drunk shared an incredulous glance, then they both laughed.

"Please, good sirs, I'm begging for your aid." He was rather earnest, for a grave robbing murderer from a band of lunatic cultists. "Our actions could save thousands of lives."

"Or do nothing but cost us ours." The trapper knew he should have kept walking. These were not his people. He had no people anymore. He had a slab hound, some missing donkeys, and a cabin upon his mountain. That was his kingdom now. That was where he belonged. Not here, among the short-sighted and fickle mob, with their simplistic slogans and petty games.

Except he didn't walk away. He stood there in the rain, like a fool.

He looked to the drunk, who was staring back at him with tired, bloodshot eyes. The trapper saw the man in a different light for the first time. Regardless of whatever he was now, he'd been a soldier once. And instinct suggested, probably a good one. An understanding passed between the two of them then. Even outcasts could retain a sense of duty.

No words were spoken. They simply nodded at each other.

"Very well, Murderer," said the trapper. "What must we do?"

"Thank you! Oh, thank the saints. I could tell you two were honorable men."

The drunk got up and clapped the young man on the back. "We'll help you, but if you assault my ears with any further words about honor, I swear I'll run you through."

Krug bumped against the trapper's leg, nudging him to continue back toward their mountain. He scratched behind loyal Krug's ear, because the slab hound was clearly the smartest one here.

* * *

They gathered supplies and prepared for the ritual.

The church was a small building erected by the Order of Saint Gilbert to see to the spiritual needs of the settlers. Luckily, the Gilbertain monks insisted on using stone for their walls instead of wood, which would make the place slightly more defensible. The monks had added a small belltower, but no church bell had been delivered to out of the way Montrose yet. In the meantime, it would make for a good archer's nest. His hunting bow had been on one of the donkeys that had been killed, so at least he'd not had to go off searching for it.

They lacked the time to prepare any elaborate traps, but his years on the mountain had made him very efficient at laying snares that could catch and entangle a limb, and there were spools of wire and rope at the general mercantile. A snare probably wouldn't stop a creature with six hands for long, but they were fast, so slowing them even a bit would make them easier to hit.

While the trapper had gathered every arrow in Montrose, the drunk had gathered every bottle and the best food. If they were to have a siege, it would be a comfortable one. The murderer had gathered skulls.

The Occultists Guild were truly an odd lot.

Two of the heads stacked on the altar were from the spawn scouts they had killed. The third had come from the recently dug up grave of the town's former Gilbertain Canon. The ritual required the bones of a holy man in order to draw the attention of Angus, the saint of war. Saint Gilbert's realm was explorers and pioneers, so hopefully a Gilbertain's skull would suffice. When the trapper had asked the murderer about this doctrinal point, the young man had assured him that it would be close enough. Probably.

Their few windows had been boarded up. The door had been barricaded with stacked up pews. Snares had been set. It was time to begin.

They had already been over this, but it seemed to help the murderer to say the words over again, as if reassuring himself that this wasn't impossible. "When I begin the chant, the spawn will know, and they'll do their best to stop me. It could take a while. If they interrupt the chant, I must start over."

"If it comes to that, I doubt you'll have the opportunity," the trapper said.

"I know. That's why you must hold off the spawn, or all is lost."

The drunk just shook his head. "You know, lad, this would've been a lot easier if we had fifty able bodied men defending this place rather than a has been, an old hermit, and an armored dog."

"I tried to warn them, but nobody would listen. Dig up one dead priest, and everyone loses their damned minds." The murderer cracked his knuckles. "All right. Here we go."

The trapper had never bothered paying much attention to religious pageantry, even when he'd been surrounded by the stuff, so he wasn't about to start now. So as the murderer began chanting and burning incense over the skulls, the trapper went up the ladder to the bell tower.

From up here, he had a good view of most of Montrose. The town looked dead and grey in the rain. There was no sign of the spawn raiders yet, but he strung his bow anyway. Below, he could hear the monotonous chant in the old tongue.

After a few minutes, the drunkard climbed up the ladder and joined him in the tower. It was impressive that he'd managed the long climb with a bottle in one hand. "That repetitive gibberish talk is making my head hurt."

"It's the old tongue. It'll do that."

"You know what he's saying?"

"A little." The murderer was beseeching the war saint for protection, so that Angus' furious retribution would rain down upon the heads of the enemies of mankind. The trapper hoped it would work. He doubted it would, and their deaths would be painful and pointless.

"Nice view of a lousy place." The drunk pulled the cork with his teeth and then spit it over the edge of the tower. The cork bounced down the shingles and out of view. He took a drink, then said, "Don't worry. I'll just have enough to stave off the shakes. I figure, if we live through the hour, then I'll celebrate proper."

The trapper just grunted in agreement.

The drunk leaned on the rail and looked over Montrose. "It's a miserable hole of a town, filled with miserable people. Hardly seems worth saving."

"Indeed." The sentiment mirrored his feelings about the kingdom as a whole.

"Then why'd you stick around?"

The trapper shrugged.

"Same here, friend. Same here." He took another bitter swig. "You wouldn't know it by looking at me now, but I was in the Wolves Regiment once. The best of the best. Then the revolution came."

The trapper remembered it well. "Bad times."

"Not what most folks nowadays would say about our glorious ruler unseating a despot. Unless they were on the side that lost, that is." The drunk gave him a knowing look. "Mere soldiers who fought for the wrong side, such as myself, ended up with petty jobs, doing things like working as guards for merchant guilds. But our plotters and nobles hung from the gallows... though I suppose some of them might have escaped and gone to hide in the forest or something."

Perceptive. "And here I took you for a clown."

"They've got sad clowns too. Those are the ones with the frowns and tears painted on. Mine were real enough."

"So that's what makes an elite swordsman crawl into a bottle?"

"You make war on your countrymen long enough, you've got to do something to keep the nightmares away. How about you?"

"I did nothing wrong. I sleep fine."

"I bet you do. You strike me as a man unburdened by conscience." The drunk pointed. "Movement."

There was a flash of white near the guard station. Then there was another behind the stables. Then several more in rapid succession as the raiding party swept through Montrose. There had to be dozens of the things. They were all headed toward the church, drawn by the magic in the murderer's chant.

There were arrows staged everywhere. He picked one from the nearest pile and nocked it to the bowstring. "Thank you, Drunkard."

"For what?"

"This was the most conversation I've had in years."

The monsters rushed the church. There seemed to be no tactics, no plan, just a wave of monstrous bodies crashing toward them. In one fluid movement, he drew the powerful bow, aimed, and let fly. He was accurate enough he routinely hit running rabbits with this bow to get his dinner, but it generated enough force to reach a fat grizzly's heart. The broadhead pierced clean through the chest of the first monster and out its back. It crashed, momentum carrying it forward through the mud.

He let fly another and another. Two more creatures went down, screeching. His next missed, as the spawn realized they were being attacked and began to move erratically. They could change direction so quickly, it made leading them virtually impossible.

Then they blundered into his snares.

One of the runners was jerked to a halt as it dropped its hand into a wire loop. The harder it pulled, the tighter the wire became. It's struggling came to a sudden end as he planted an arrow into its brain.

"To the south, Trapper!"

He turned to see that some of the monsters were coming from that street as well, and they were nearly to the church. He killed one that had tripped on a taut rope. Then he hurried and took aim at another—missed—and then a third—killed.

"East! East!"

The first of those was already so close to the church that he could no longer get an angle on it because of the pitch of the roof.

Except then he was presented with new targets as the creatures began to climb. A mere ten feet below, spindly white fingers appeared over the edge of the shingles. He aimed, and the instant the head rose into view, he drove a broadhead through its eye and out the back of its skull. It fell but was immediately replaced by two more.

"West!"

The muscles of his back and arms were burning. The hunting bow had a mighty pull to it, and it had been years since he'd worked it this hard. There were so many targets now that the drunkard no longer needed to call out warnings. All the trapper had to do was keep turning in a circle, picking up arrows from the pile and launching them downward. Bodies were piling up around the church. Others were dying on the shingles. Rain was washing purple blood down the gutters.

There was a terrible banging below them. The spawn were trying to force the door. "I've got to go!" The drunk took one last pull from the bottle and then hurled it at a climbing monster. It shattered against its head, and the thing tumbled to its doom. "What a waste," he said as he started down the ladder.

"I'll be along shortly," the trapper said as he killed another. What he had thought had been a very large quantity of arrows was already drastically depleted, but he would keep going as long as he could. Except every time he turned, the monsters were a little bit closer. They covered the roof now and had begun scrambling up the bell tower.

Lightning crashed across the sky, revealing even more of the creatures in the distance. The drunkard spoke of having nightmares. This was a living one.

Arms aching, fingers bleeding, he launched his last arrow into a monster's heart and then lurched for the ladder. He dropped the bow and let it fall down the shaft. Hopefully, it wouldn't be damaged on impact, but it was too long to maneuver, and he had no time to spare. Already, white hands were grabbing hold of the bell tower's railing. He hurried and slammed the trap door closed above him, then shoved an iron spike through the latch. It would not hold them for long, but, hopefully, it wouldn't need to, because he'd prepared another trap for this eventuality.

Ten rungs down he'd nailed a basket of oil-soaked rags to the wall. He stopped there long enough to light the matches he'd taken from the general mercantile. The rags caught immediately. They flared up so violently, they singed his beard before he got out of the way.

Above, the monsters tore at the hatch, yanking it violently until the nails popped, and the boards came apart. They started down, only to blunder headlong into the rising smoke. As the trapper continued downward, he could only hope the fire would be sufficient to block that entrance for a while. And that the rain would be enough to keep the entire roof from catching fire, because it would be rather unfortunate to hold off an army of monsters only to be killed by a fiery falling beam.

Though he was in a rush, it was a mistake to drop the last few rungs of the ladder to the hard floor, because that caused the pain in his bad leg to flare. Inside the chapel, white hands were poking through the boards of every window, trying to tear their way inside. The drunkard was running back and forth between them, desperately stabbing his sword between the gaps in the boards. Every time he did so, a monster shrieked on the other side. But there were more openings than they had defenders. Krug began to bark a warning as one of their nailed-on boards was pried off the wall.

The murderer was still at the altar, dutifully performing his chant. Yet as he did so, he was watching the windows in growing horror. There was no way they could keep all the monsters from reaching him.

"You're beseeching Angus himself. Surely, the war saint would love for you to fight and pray at the same time," the trapper said as he picked up a woodsman's axe from their pile of collected weapons and tossed it toward the altar. "Just try not to get too winded to chant."

The murderer picked up the axe and gave the trapper a determined nod, even as he continued his ritual.

The bow hadn't been cracked by the fall, which was good, because it was more efficient for him to stand in the middle of the chapel to fire in every needed direction than it was to run back and forth from window to window. He took up an armful of quivers and dropped them on the floor at his feet. Each time one of their boards was knocked off, he launched an arrow through the gap, into monstrous flesh. At this range, with the bodies so densely packed, he couldn't hardly miss. Unfortunately, he would run out of arrows and strength long before the old gods ran out of spawn.

The pile of pews they'd stacked against the door was shaking. There had to be a great number of monsters hurling themselves against the other side. Splinters flew as they clawed the door to pieces. It wouldn't last much longer.

"Pray faster!" the drunkard shouted as he headed for the door.

As the trapper kept piercing anything that tried to squeeze through a window, the door slowly came apart. Monsters surged through the gaps, trying to clamber through the pile of pews.

Only to be met by a very determined swordsman. "I'll hold them. Kill anything that slips past me."

The Wolves Regiment had been the finest in the kingdom. Though he had clearly lost much of his might in the ensuing years, the town drunk still retained some of their legendary skill. Within seconds, there was a growing pile of arms beneath the pews, and a veritable flood of purple blood.

Except it takes health to wield a sword, and the drunk had spent years ruining his. After the furious flurry of blows, he was gasping for air. A few swings later, and the sword was moving a lot slower than before. Grey faced, the drunk was forced to retreat. Within seconds, their piled barricade came crashing down.

"That didn't last long."

"I'm old, alright!"

"I'm fifty-two this winter," the trapper said calmly as he took aim and felled a monster climbing over the pews.

"I'm only forty." He panted. "I think."

And to think, he'd first assumed they were the same age. It was a truly sorry circumstance which aged a man faster than living off the land atop a mountain in the wilderness.

The monsters were pouring through the door and windows now. They had no choice but to fall back to the narrow alcove that contained the church's altar and one very worried murderer who was still keeping up his chanting. The trapper dropped his bow, grabbed his spear from where it had been leaning against the wall, and limped for the back.

A monster leapt at him, but Krug intercepted it in mid-air. The two bodies crashed to the floor, rolling, but Krug popped right back up with a mouthful of monster throat and chased after them.

They reached the alcove and then turned to face the growing horde that was filling the church. The fire he'd started on the ladder must have died off, because monsters were crawling down the ladder from the bell tower and then spilling out, to hang upside down from the ceiling beams.

"How much longer?" the drunk shouted. Except of course, the murderer couldn't answer them, because he was still busy chanting.

There was a massive clap of thunder. It shook the entire church. The monsters paused, as dozens of mandibles turned upward at once. The trapper could only hope that was a sign that their efforts had drawn Saint Angus' attention. And perhaps it had, because a few seconds after that distraction, the horde of monsters attacked with renewed frenzy.

The alcove was only about eight feet wide. The trapper and the drunk stood shoulder to shoulder, sword and spear raised, Krug right behind them, fangs bared and growling.

Only the monsters weren't coming at them this time, they were going *through* them. The spawn were desperately heading for the murderer to try and stop the ritual. The men went about slashing and stabbing as the monsters tried to rush past. Krug bit and savaged anything that got to him—a well-trained slab hound was a primal force of nature.

Despite not being the direct target, there was no way to stand before a crashing wave of claws without getting cut. The trapper winced as his cheek was sliced open. Then his bicep. Then his leg. And two across his abdomen.

Monsters made it past the wall of steel and teeth, scurrying over the altar, knocking the mummified skull of the old priest off to roll across the floor. But rather than stand there helpless, the murderous occultist hacked them out of the air with the woodcutter's axe. He embedded the blade in a monster's shoulder, drove it into the altar, wrenched it out in a spray of blood, and then added a new head to his collection.

All the while, he never broke his cadence.

Krug yelped in pain as a claw sank past his leathery hide. The drunk screamed as one of his eyes was gouged out. The murderer was thrown to the floor and cut deep, but he just kept on chanting, even as the trapper pulled the creature off of him and slammed it against the altar until its brains came out.

How long this blood-soaked massacre went on, the trapper couldn't tell. His mind had gone blank. There was only animal savagery. Batting monsters to the ground with the haft and then driving the blade deep into their guts, yanking it out, and then doing it over and over again.

The murderer finished his prayer.

All the monsters froze and then slowly lifted their heads to look upward.

This time, the clap of thunder tore the roof of the church right off.

The trapper had seen hurricanes before. This was no hurricane. This was the vengeance of the gods.

The wind flung the humans down, but it picked up the spawn and hurled their bodies hard enough to splatter them against the stone walls. Monsters disappeared shrieking into the sky.

The trapper looked out the door as the whirlwind passed the church to rip through the streets of Montrose, throwing creatures through the wooden facades or hurling their bodies hundreds of yards into the forest.

The whirlwind died off. All of the monsters were dead or gone.

The spawn had been rebuked for now. The old gods had been reminded of their place. The rain began to fall inside the church. It might have even been hard enough to wash the blood away.

* * *

It took several days for his many cuts to heal enough that he felt he could make his way back up the mountain without popping his stitches. His surviving donkeys had wandered back into town looking for feed, so he had gathered them up. He had left his pelts at the general mercantile and loaded the supplies he'd need to survive the winter. Of course, he had left a note detailing exactly what inventory he had taken, because even though he had helped save their town and its inhabitants' lives, that was no excuse for dishonesty. He had, however, not included the arrows he had shot into various monsters. The Conglomerate would just have to consider those a donation. Frankly, it was the only thing the useless bastards had done to help.

Montrose was still deserted. Its people were probably just barely reaching the kingdom, so it would be at least a week before reinforcements arrived here. Hopefully, the army would act before the spawn returned in greater numbers. Regardless, that was no longer his problem. He had his own kingdom to tend.

The trapper thought about leaving without saying a word, as was his usual custom, but that seemed wrong this time. So he sought out the others to say goodbye.

They were at the tavern. He could tell because of the infernal noise being created by the continued attempts at playing that piano. If Saint Angus truly cared about these lands, his mighty whirlwind would have tossed that thing into the sea to spare all their ears.

Two of the four current residents of Montrose were inside. Krug did not care about farewells. Krug was taking a nap.

The town drunk was in worse physical shape than before, having received several deep lacerations, and he was still adjusting to the loss of an eye, but surprisingly, he was far less drunk than customary. The trapper had found that, if you gave a man a bit of purpose, he was far less likely to destroy himself. The old sword had been cleaned and sharpened, and the drunk had claimed one of the spare uniforms from the guard station as his new clothes.

Meanwhile, their murderer was as vulturous in appearance as before, only he'd passed the time documenting the effects of the ritual, doing autopsies on dead spawn, and writing copious notes about the whole affair to be passed back to his strange guild. To him, this had been a grand vindication of his life's work.

Men such as these could not ask for much more.

Thankfully, the drunkard quit playing the piano when he saw the trapper enter. "Ah, look who has decided to join us."

"Not for long. It's time for me to leave."

"But you can't. You're one of the few who've seen these things. The kingdom needs you," said their remarkably civic-minded murderer. "They'll be back. Troops will arrive, but they'll need guides to help them root out the beasts."

"That's exactly why he has to leave, lad. Trapper here knows that some of those troops are sure to have served in the east during the revolution, and they're bound to recognize a dead man."

"I don't understand."

The drunk gave the trapper a knowing smirk. "It took me a while to put it together, with that massive beard and dressing like a bear now. Plus they burned all the paintings and melted all the coins that bore the dread tyrant's image."

The murderer was very confused, because his mind was more adept at processing the supernatural than the political. "What?"

"The tyrant king is no more. Everyone knows he was killed during the revolution," said the trapper. "It's better that way." Then he gestured at the piano. "May I?"

The drunkard slid off the bench. "Sure. But I'll warn you, the damned thing's near impossible to decipher."

The trapper sat on the bench, shook out his massive, scarred hands, and then gently set his fingers upon the keys. It took a moment for the memories to return, but some things are never really forgotten, just pushed to the back. He began to play. It was as rusty as the drunk's sword had been, but the skill was still there. The instrument was battered and out of tune, but he played his favorite part of Marcin's Concert Number Four, the Woe of Saint Gertrude. It was passable to his ear. His old teachers would've been disgusted, but they'd been dead for decades, so their opinions were irrelevant.

He finished and stood. The other two men were staring at him in shock.

"That was the most beautiful thing I've ever heard."

The murderer was just as stunned, surely not expecting such artistry on the frontier. "That was astounding."

"That piece is about how what was is not what it is now, and what it is today is not what it is destined to be in the future," the trapper explained. He looked toward the town drunk. "Do you understand?"

"I think I do," answered the town guardsman.

"Good." The trapper began walking away.

The occultist was still baffled. "How did you know how to play like that? Do they have a lot of pianos in the forest?"

"No. But there are several in the royal palace. Farewell...Your Majesty."

Outside, the trapper whistled for Krug, who immediately came running to join his master. It was time to return to their mountain.

* * * * *

Larry Correia Bio

Larry Correia is the New York Times bestselling and award-winning author of the Monster Hunter International urban fantasy series, the Saga of the Forgotten Warrior epic fantasy series, the Grimnoir Chronicles alternate history trilogy, the Dead Six thrillers (with Mike Kupari), the sci-fi adventure *Gun Runner* (with John D. Brown), and more. He's also collaborated with bestsellers John Ringo and Sarah Hoyt on novels set in his Monster Hunter International universe, has edited two anthologies, and has published two collections of short fiction. A former accountant, gun dealer, and firearms instructor, Larry lives high atop Yard Moose Mountain, Utah, with the lovely Mrs. Correia and their fearsome Krasnovian Waffle Hound.

# # # # #

About the Editors

A Webster Award winner and three-time Dragon Award finalist, Chris Kennedy is a Science Fiction/Fantasy/Young Adult author, speaker, and small-press publisher who has written over 25 books and published more than 100 others. Chris' stories include the "Occupied Seattle" military fiction duology, "The Theogony" and "Codex Regius" science fiction trilogies, stories in the "Four Horsemen," "Fallen World," and "In Revolution Born" universes and the "War for Dominance" fantasy trilogy. Get his free book, "Shattered Crucible," at his website, https://chriskennedypublishing.com.

Called "fantastic" and "a great speaker," he has coached hundreds of beginning authors and budding novelists on how to self-publish their stories at a variety of conferences, conventions and writing guild presentations. He is the author of the award-winning #1 bestseller, "Self-Publishing for Profit: How to Get Your Book Out of Your Head and Into the Stores," as well as the leadership training book, "Leadership from the Darkside."

Chris lives in Virginia Beach, Virginia, with his wife, and is the holder of a doctorate in educational leadership and master's degrees in both business and public administration. Follow Chris on Facebook at https://www.facebook.com/ckpublishing/.

Rob Howell is the best-selling creator of the Shijuren fantasy setting and an author in the Four Horsemen Universe. He writes primarily high fantasy, space opera, military science fiction, and alternate history, usually with mystery mixed into it all.

He is a reformed medieval academic, a former IT professional, and a retired soda jerk.

His parents discovered quickly books were the only way to keep Rob quiet. Without books, it's unlikely all three would have survived.

You can find him online at: www.robhowell.org, on Amazon at https://www.amazon.com/-/e/B00X95LBB0, and his blog at www.robhowell.org/blog.

* * * * *

The following is an
Excerpt from Book One of The Balance of Kerr:

Burnt

_____

Kevin Steverson &
Tyler Ackerman

Available Now from New Mythology Press

eBook and Paperback

Excerpt from "Burnt:"

Tog shrugged. "I like chicken," he said as he pulled out his dagger. Standing nearly seven feet tall and weighing nearly three hundred and twenty pounds, a dagger for him was a short sword to most men. He cut a piece off. He didn't bother blowing on it and poked it into his mouth. There was instant regret on his face. He began breathing through his teeth with the piece of meat between them, the sharpness of his incisors giving away that he was half Orc, if his size didn't already reveal it. He grabbed his mug and drained it.

Kryder shook his head, cut another piece for himself, and blew on it. Before he took a bite, he said, "If I had a copper for every time I've seen you do that, I could exchange them for a piece of gold. I'm talking about a whole coin and not a quarter piece."

Tog wiped his mouth with the back of his hand, ignoring the remark, and said, "So when are we going to be contacted? Besides the cost of mugs, this place isn't cheap. It's not like we have coin to spare. We should think about an inn more in line with our coin purses."

"I don't know," Kryder answered. "The old man said someone would contact us here. If we go across town, whoever it is may not find us."

"Well I…" Tog started to say when he was interrupted by a loud voice two tables away.

"Look here, halfbreed," a man dressed similarly to them, in leather armor covered with a travel cloak and a sword on his hip, said loudly. One side of his face had a scar stretching from eyebrow to lips. He was speaking to them. "I don't eat with such as your kind."

The three men sitting with him laughed. One wearing a half-helmet with leather flaps hanging on each side added his own loud insult, "Since the rape didn't kill his mother, surely bearing an Orc bastard did the deed." The group laughed even louder.

Kryder reached down to his side and drew another smaller, more ornate dagger with his free hand. He laid them both on the table. He stood, turned around, and looked at the four men. Tog, on his feet nearly as quickly, reached over his shoulder and grabbed the axe strapped to his back with one hand. It was dual-headed and meant for two hands when used by a normal-sized man. He placed it on the table beside his own large dagger. A hand's length of the worn leather-covered handle hung over the edge.

The four men realized the object of their harassment and his companion didn't intend to leave. They meant to fight. They scrambled to their feet, knocking over chairs. Several groups stood and moved away from the center of the room, while others left the tavern completely.

The owner's sons looked toward their father. He shook his head. Fights happened, even in his establishment in the better part of town. Usually he had his boys put a stop to it. This time, the insult thrown at the large patron was more than he could tolerate. He decided to let the man demand his apology, even if it meant he had to beat it out of the four. It was an easy decision.

* * * * *

Get "Burnt" now at:
https://www.amazon.com/dp/B0861FRWFH/.

Find out more about Kevin Steverson & Tyler Ackerman and "Burnt" at:
https://chriskennedypublishing.com/imprints-authors/kevin-steverson/burnt/

* * * *

The following is an

Excerpt from Book One of The Milesian Accords:

A Reluctant Druid

Jon R. Osborne

Available Now from Blood Moon Press

eBook, Audio, and Paperback

Excerpt from "A Reluctant Druid:"

"Don't crank on it; you'll strip it."

Liam paused from trying to loosen the stubborn bolt holding the oil filter housing on his Yamaha motorcycle, looking for the source of the unsolicited advice. The voice was gruff, with an accent and cadence that made Liam think of the Swedish Chef from the Muppets. The garage door was open for air circulation, and two figures were standing in the driveway, illuminated by the setting sun. As they approached and stepped into the shadows of the house, Liam could see they were Pixel and a short, stout man with a greying beard that would do ZZ Top proud. The breeze blowing into the garage carried a hint of flowers.

Liam experienced a moment of double vision as he looked at the pair. Pixel's eyes took on the violet glow he thought he'd seen before, while her companion lost six inches in height, until he was only as tall as Pixel. What the short man lacked in height, he made up for in physique; he was built like a fireplug. He was packed into blue jeans and a biker's leather jacket, and goggles were perched over the bandana covering his salt and pepper hair. Leather biker boots crunched the gravel as he walked toward the garage. Pixel followed him, having traded her workout clothes for black jeans and a pink t-shirt that left her midriff exposed. A pair of sunglasses dangled from the neckline of her t-shirt.

"He's seeing through the glamour," the short, bearded man grumbled to Pixel, his bushy eyebrows furrowing.

"Well duh. We're on his home turf, and this is his place of power" Pixel replied nonchalantly. "He was pushing back against my glamour yesterday, and I'm not adding two hands to my height."

Liam set down the socket wrench and ran through the mental inventory of items in the garage that were weapons or could be used as them. The back half of the garage was a workshop, which included the results of his dabbling with blacksmithing and sword-crafting, so the list was considerable. But the most suitable were also the farthest away.

"Can I help you?" Liam stood and brushed off his jeans; a crowbar was three steps away. Where had they come from? Liam hadn't heard a car or motorcycle outside, and the house was a mile and a half outside of town.

"Ja, you can." The stout man stopped at the threshold of the garage. His steel-grey eyes flicked from Liam to the workbench and back. He held his hands out, palms down. The hands were larger than his and weren't strangers to hard work and possibly violence. "And there's no need to be unhospitable; we come as friends. My name is Einar, and you've already met Pixel."

"Hi, Liam." Pixel was as bubbly as yesterday. While she didn't seem to be making the same connection as Einar regarding the workbench, her eyes darted about the cluttered garage and the dim workshop behind it. "Wow, you have a lot of junk."

"What's this about?" Liam sidled a half step toward the workbench, regretting he hadn't kept up on his martial arts. He had three brown belts, a year of kendo, and some miscellaneous weapons training scattered over two decades but not much experience in the way of real fighting. He could probably hold his own in a brawl as long as his opponent didn't have serious skills. He suspected Einar was more than a Friday night brawler in the local watering hole. "Is she your daughter?"

Einar turned to the purple-haired girl, his caterpillar-like eyebrows gathering. "What did you do?"

"What? I only asked him a few questions and checked him out," Pixel protested, her hands going to her hips as she squared off with

Einar. "It's not as if I tried to jump his bones right there in the store or something."

"Look mister, if you think something untoward happened between me and your daughter –" Liam began.

"She's not my pocking daughter, and I don't give a troll's ass if you diddled her," Einar interrupted, his accent thickening with his agitation. He took a deep breath, his barrel chest heaving. "Now, will you hear me out without you trying to brain me with that tire iron you've been eyeing?"

"You said diddle." Pixel giggled.

"Can you be serious for five minutes, you pocking faerie?" Einar glowered, his leather jacket creaking as he crossed his arms.

"Remember 'dwarf,' you're here as an 'advisor.'" Pixel included air quotes with the last word, her eyes turning magenta. "The Nine Realms are only involved out of politeness."

"Politeness! If you pocking Tuatha and Tylwyth Teg hadn't folded up when the Milesians came at you, maybe we wouldn't be here to begin with!" Spittle accompanied Einar's protest. "Tylwyth? More like Toothless!"

"Like your jarls didn't roll over and show their bellies when the Avramites showed up with their One God and their gold!" Pixel rose up on her toes. "Your people took their god and took their gold and then attacked our ancestral lands!"

"Guys!" Liam had stepped over to the workbench but hadn't picked up the crowbar. "Are you playing one of those live-action role playing games or something? Because if you are, I'm calling my garage out of bounds. Take your LARP somewhere else."

"We've come a long way to speak to you," Einar replied, looking away from Pixel. "I'm from Asgard."

"Asgard? You mean like Thor and Odin? What kind of game are you playing?" Liam hadn't moved from the workbench, but he'd mapped in his mind the steps he'd need to take to reach a stout pole which would serve as a staff while he back-pedaled to his workshop, where a half-dozen half-finished sword prototypes rested. From where he stood, though, he didn't feel as threatened. He knew a bit about gamers because there were a fair number of them among the pagan community, and he'd absorbed bits and pieces of it. Maybe someone had pointed Liam out to Pixel as research about druids for one of these games—an over-enthusiastic player who wanted to more convincingly roleplay one.

"Gods I hate those pocking things," Einar grumbled, rubbing his forehead while Pixel stifled another giggle. "Look, can we sit down and talk to you? This is much more serious than some pocking games you folk play with your costumes and your toy weapons."

"This isn't a game, and we aren't hippies with New Age books and a need for self-validation." Pixel added. Her eyes had faded to a lavender color. "Liam, we need your help."

* * * * *

Get "A Reluctant Druid" at
https://www.amazon.com/dp/B07716V2RN.

Find out more about Jon R. Osborne and "A Reluctant Druid" at:
https://chriskennedypublishing.com/imprints-authors/jon-r-osborne/

* * * * *

The following is an
Excerpt from Book One of The Watchers of Moniah:

The Watchers of Moniah

_____

Barbara V. Evers

Now Available from New Mythology Press

eBook, Paperback, and (soon) Audio Book

Excerpt from "The Watchers of Moniah:"

The queen focused on the gentle bubbling and ignored the stream of sweat trickling between her shoulder blades. "Send in the champions."

The assemblage shouted their approval as two foreigners walked forward to accept the accolades they deserved. The men's lighter coloring no longer startled Chiora unlike the day she and a squad of Watchers found them at the bottom of a muddy cliff. The man on the right, Micah, saved her life during the war with Maligon. Her gaze ran over his tall, lithe build in appreciation. Light hair, bleached white from the sun, glowed against his Monian-kissed suntan like bones on the prairie. Clear blue eyes gazed at her with startling familiarity, stuttering the pulse in her neck.

She drew another calming breath as his companion knelt before her. Unlike Micah, this man's fair skin had blistered and burned in the harsh sun of their land, a point that favored the reward she would grant him.

Micah maintained his focus on her and nodded in acknowledgement before kneeling. Chiora breathed deeper to suppress the shiver of excitement prompted by his forthright behavior.

"Our dear champions." Her low-pitched voice echoed throughout the huge open hall. She thanked the Creator that it came out strong and clear, with no hint of the emotions tumbling her soul. "Your journey from beyond the northern mountains came at a fortuitous time. Your courage in the face of our recent struggles brought peace to our lands. As reward, the kingdoms have decided to grant you titles and property." She turned to Micah's companion. "Donel, you will be known as Sir Donel and receive land as a vassal to Queen Roassa of Elwar."

A glimmer of a smile ghosted his face. She suspected his pleasure stemmed from admiration for Roassa rather than the title and cooler climate. Her sister queen shared this interest and had suggested his placement in Elwar rather than Moniah.

Whereas, Chiora could not stop thinking about the other man before her. Micah.

She stood and approached him, placing her hand on his shoulder in the formal greeting reserved for one of her subjects. "As for you, Micah—"

As her fingers settled on his rough, leather vest, the bond with Ju'latti surged into her mind in a flash of light. She gasped, closing her eyes. An image appeared. Micah stood by her side. Between them stood a young girl, her skin a blending of Chiora's amber-colored skin and Micah's pale complexion. The child's hair was twisted into a Watcher's braid the shades of a lion's mane. In the image, the girl walked away from her parents. With each step, they faded from view, first Chiora, and then Micah. The girl continued to walk forward, alone.

The landscape around the child changed, first the flat plains of Moniah, then the mountains and forests of Elwar. With each step, the girl matured. She halted at the top of a hill, now a young woman dressed in leathers, a quiver of arrows strung over her back, a sword at her side. The shadow of a man emerged from the forests and stood beside her. A divided path lay before them, one route blocked by a monstrous blazing fire, the other by a wall taller than the eye could see. The young woman raised her head, blue eyes blazing, and stepped forward, aiming for the point where the two paths merged together in a wall of conflagration. The man's shadow followed.

Chiora bent over, gasping for air, as the vision faded. Two Teachers of the Faith rushed to her side, their green robes swaying in their urgency to support their queen, but Chiora remained upright, her fingers digging into Micah's shoulder. He rose to steady her, a look of concern in his eyes. She gazed back at him, the warmth of his touch flooding her veins.

The Creator had not only sent her a champion to help defeat Maligon, he had sent her a partner. They would make a strong child together, an heir to Moniah's Seat of Authority. A child who would face insurmountable struggles.

* * * * *

Get "The Watchers of Moniah" now at: https://www.amazon.com/dp/B08QRJTHHC.

Find out more about Barbara V. Evers and "The Watchers of Moniah" at: https://chriskennedypublishing.com/

* * * *